Illusions Of Privacy

Murder, Identity Theft & The American Way

Seven Major

Illusions of Privacy
Murder, Identity Theft & the American Way

Seven Major

FIRST EDITION

ISBN: 978-0-692-73021-8
978-0-9977630-0-3 (Hardcover)
Ebook: 978-0-9977630-1-0

Library of Congress Control Number: 2016943377

Copyright © 2016 Seven Major
All rights reserved

No part of this book may be reproduced or transmitted
in any form or by any means without express written
permission of the publisher.

HARRIS COUNTY PUBLIC LIBRARY

Major
Major, Seven,
Illusions of privacy : murder,
identity theft & the American way
$14.95   ocn958464987

Illusions of Privacy

This novel is a work of fiction.

*When the lies become your truth,
then your truth will lie within.*

For Mom and Dad:
Forever in my heart, wherever you are.

And for Jerry, the bartender.
I couldn't have done it without you.

Contents

Preface — i

Who I Was

Chapter 1	Wednesday's Child	3
Chapter 2	Mother's Little Helper	11
Chapter 3	The Russo Way	19
Chapter 4	Mud Hole Haven	37
Chapter 5	Sweet Sixteen	53
Chapter 6	The Definition of Crime	67
Chapter 7	A Cowboy's Way	79
Chapter 8	Best Date Ever	87
Chapter 9	Good Times	103
Chapter 10	The World According to Cici	119
Chapter 11	Tough Love	131
Chapter 12	The Trouble I've Seen	147
Chapter 13	There's No Place like Home	165

Who I Am

Chapter 14	Thursday's Child	189
Chapter 15	Latour Court	203
Chapter 16	As Fast As You Can	217
Chapter 17	Hide-and-Seek	233
Chapter 18	Almost Heaven	249

Chapter 19	Scattered Sunshine	257
Chapter 20	Home Again, Home Again. Jiggedy Jig.	275
Chapter 21	Goat-Roping Russo Style	285
Chapter 22	Game On	301
Chapter 23	To Tell the Truth	315

Who I Want to Be

| Chapter 24 | Cut & Run | 337 |
| Chapter 25 | Epic Ending | 341 |

Preface

There was a time in my life when I believed we were all completely separate beings aimlessly floating through life, simply taking up space. There was no destiny; there were no concrete answers and only unlimited choices. I believed my actions only affected the people who were immediately present. That time has long passed; over the last several years, I've come to realize that nothing could be further from the truth. But, as I often say—who I was, who I am, and who I want to be are three different people.

For those that I have directly or indirectly caused pain, I ask that you accept my most sincere apologies. I'm truly sorry for who I was ... and some days for who I still am. I've lied about so many details that those lies became my truth. Maybe not so much in the beginning, but most definitely as time went on. The stories were simply more believable than the actual sequence of events. Even to me. The lies have become a big part of who I am.

Who I want to be is continuously evolving. Today, I'd like the sun to shine, to live my quiet life, enjoy those I love, worship God, and cause no pain. And, maybe in the course of doing all these things, I will find the time and energy to write.

For my children—if you believe nothing more, please know that my love for you has been and is very real. If you know nothing else, remember that while the names have changed, the players have remained the same. Your father and I are still your parents. We're still a family. It was all survival, self-preservation, and name changes before you were born and there was no time to think about things like family trees, genetics, or answering our children's questions one day. We thought we could leave the past behind us. We thought we could live the lie forever. We had come dangerously close to doing so, but we'd thought wrong.

For my extended family—there'll be no getting around the fact that you're going feel played. I really am sorry I'm not who I pretended to be. I had no right to step into your lives and assume the role of someone who died tragically before her time, but that's exactly what I did. Again, I didn't always get how my actions affected others. For what it's worth, I do get it now. I'm truly sorry you were not given the opportunity to grieve the loss of your sister/cousin/niece/daughter/friend/neighbor/pal. Your family is very different than mine or than mine *was*, different in a way I found charming and down-to-earth and interesting and loveable. You can hardly blame me for wanting to stay a part of all that. Please know that my words and our heartfelt conversations were authentic; there were no lies there. It's the person you thought I was that's a lie. *I* am still very much a reality—though I struggle with who that is and exactly *what* reality is. All of life isn't black and white. But I'll do my best to explain.

For my friends—many of you never knew any Brooke Hutchenson other than me; some have only known me as Brooke Bronson (my married name). For you guys, I just wasn't entirely honest about my past … or my family … exactly. Everything else was true. I was honest about Brooke Bronson's past! I spent relentless hours studying that crap. The ground work and history were tough; the new lies came more easily. With luck, this text might give me the opportunity to at least offer some explanation to all those I've successfully deceived.

I'm not a big believer in confessing the sins of others; however, in telling my story, there were times it was simply unavoidable. Oh well—when we're all dead and gone, only the facts will remain. This is my book of facts. You don't have to read it.

For those who mourned the loss of Cici Russo in 1984, I miss me too some days. For Giovanni, my brother and beloved friend, I still cry. I loved you from that first morning when I was taken from my home in New Jersey as a child and flown to your home in Washington, DC. Yours was truly the first warm and friendly face I can remember seeing.

Daddy Sal used to say, "Knowledge is a funny thing. You can't go back and *un*know something once it's known. Leave it alone Cici." And *still*, I want to know. So too, in the spirit of treating others how I would like to be treated, I offer this text. Just know there'll be no turning back; you won't have the option to *un*read the words or *un*know the truth. Sometimes walking away is the smartest thing you can do; it's your choice.

For Brooke Hutchenson—may you rest in peace knowing that the truth is now told. I was perfectly horrified at the idea of stepping into your life at first (I thought you were a bit of a nebbish), but I've come to really enjoy being you. You have friends on Facebook that remember you as far back as Annandale High School, junior high at Edgar Allen Poe, and even at Annandale Terrace Elementary School. You touched lives Brooke Hutchenson. I often turn to your sister and my best friend Bailey to make sure I'm replying to Facebook friend requests and such appropriately. I positively cringe whenever someone says "You've changed" or "I wouldn't recognize you." Bailey says it's the nose, but I think it's something going on with my lips. I really wish I could've kept that part of my face. I feel like I can still see the lines where my full lips once were. I'm told they're old age wrinkles and to get over it. *How I do wonder what I would've looked like aging—minus the plastic surgery more than twenty five years ago. I wonder too if you would've aged as I have.*

I've certainly blurred the line that once separated you and me, Brooke. At first, I just tried to think logically how you would respond, what you would think. And then one day, I became you and somehow picked up where you left off—calling your life and making your life my own.

No one cried. No one attended a funeral for you, Brooke. No one even knew you'd died. No one, that is—except those present the night of your most unfortunate demise. Fuckers—I hate them all. I hate what they did. Perhaps time will avenge your death. I hate what we did too. It was weird for me and my family. There was so much more going on that you wouldn't have been aware of as you were probably too busy focusing on your own close, rewarding, normal relationships in your normal life.

For us, it was quite different. 1984 was wrought with investigations and threats of huge fines and imprisonment for much of my family and their comrades. I had my own problems as all of hell was breaking loose around me. Taking the identity of a young woman who died tragically one evening was the very least of my concerns. It wasn't like you had any need for your identity anymore and I damned sure could use it. I was about to lose everything and everyone I ever cared about. I was headed for an emotional Siberia—the likes of which were devastating and unimaginable. I'm truly sorry.

For my beloved husband—it's been a crazy ride, but I'm glad I got to do it with you. No one will find it that hard to believe I was an evil bitch. Oh, but they will be shocked by your story. I know I was.

I've spent a lifetime playing by my own set of rules, trying to forget who I was and another lifetime learning how to lie about the rest. I've become quite proficient at it. Telling the truth—now there's a whole new challenge for me.

But where to start? I've been told there's no place like the beginning.

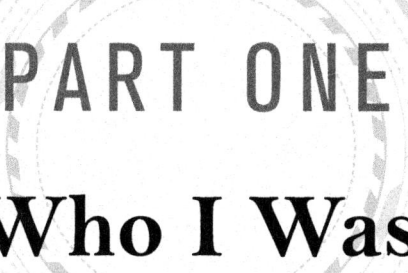

PART ONE

Who I Was

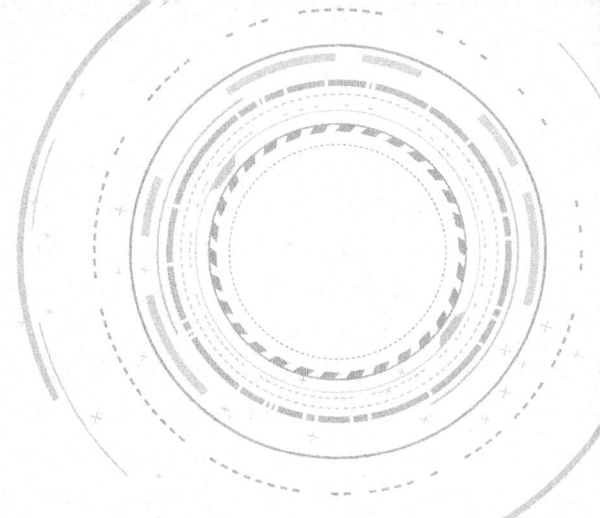

CHAPTER ONE
Wednesday's Child

I was born Camilla Colleen McPherson (seven pounds, eight ounces) in the middle of a New Jersey snow storm on March 7, 1962 to proud parents, Finn and Clare McPherson. It was Ash Wednesday during what some called "The Great Storm of '62." And by "great" they meant great devastation, great pain, great loss, great number of fatalities, great destruction—a great, big, ugly, life-altering, evil kind of "great". So "great" was this storm, entire communities, power companies, EMS, and hospitals were overwhelmed. It was during this storm, my mother went into labor.

John F. Kennedy was our president and had set the goal of putting a man on the moon before the end of the decade. He would be assassinated before my second birthday. Gas was twenty-eight cents per gallon. The average rent for the average family was $110 per month and minimum wage was on the rise at $1.15. That same year witnessed the introduction of the smiley face and ongoing parades of yellow, smiling circles were popping up *everywhere*. My mom was ahead of the curve, wearing miniskirts and tall leather boots, while Dad opted for paisley shirts and velvet pants. They were totally groovy—at least in my estimation.

The Beach Boys were fresh on the scene and kids in California put wheels on wooden planks to "keep surfing" on land when weather conditions wouldn't allow it on water. The Beatles were to record "Love Me Do" that same year in England and our country's greatest fears were the Russians and the missiles they had set up in Cuba—only 90 miles off the coast of Florida. Nuclear war had become a definite possibility and the entire world seemed to be on a path to self-destruction. Music began to take on tones of protest and disenchantment with artists such as Bob Dylan leading the way.

The Beverly Hillbillies was to air for the first time and the world would be introduced to James Bond in *Dr. No*. Silver screen favorites included John Wayne, Doris Day, Rock Hudson, Elizabeth Taylor and Elvis. Johnny Carson was young. Robert Redford was just beginning his screen career. Joan Cusack, Demi Moore, and Jodie Foster would be born that same year, and Marilyn Monroe would be found dead later that summer.

Meanwhile, the first Walmart was opening in Arkansas and the first Kmart was opening in Michigan. Albert Sabin developed an oral polio vaccine and the University of Mississippi saw riots following the attempt of a black student to enroll. Ninety percent of all U.S. households owned a television set (that worked with an antenna and electricity and required nothing more.) In time, America would be folk music and flower power and civil rights and crazy riots. But before that, there was me ... *Wednesday's child*.

As I've said, I've spent a lifetime pushing those memories to the back corner of my brain—to the point where I'd convinced myself they were no longer real, but merely fragments of memories of a disturbing dream—the kind of dream that replays itself over and over again in one's sleep and whose reason cannot be found in waking life. But those first five years of my life were real—they're more than just torn snapshots of memories distorted by time. My life was full of love and promise, sunny days and belly-cramping laughter. Looking back, it feels like a dream ...

I can remember walking in between my parents, holding both their hands and tugging, pulling, and swinging as if they were my own personal jungle gym on our way to the neighborhood playground—a magical playground complete with a tower sporting its own sliding board exit. And I, the tower princess, sharing with the local townspeople its ample space, steep ladder, and slick escape. I was completely convinced of my royalty. The other children were the commoners I graced with my daily presence—except when Holly was there. Holly was no commoner. She was my best friend and, on those days, we co-princessed the playground tower. My parents remained my most loyal subjects.

Our townhouse had two upstairs bedrooms. My room was decorated in pink and my parents had bought me a canopy bed for my fifth birthday—completely fitting for the little princess I was. I had dolls and stuffed animals and a charm bracelet with a treasure chest charm my dad bought me at the beach and an artist's palette charm my mom bought when we went shopping in Savannah the previous year. Even as a child, I knew that bracelet would one day be filled with nothing but precious mementos from fabulous experiences. It was easily my most prized possession.

Sometimes conversation from the television seemed to be piped directly into my small, upstairs room. I hated loud, angry voices and developed a coping technique that involved my head under a pillow while I focused on thoughts of playing playground princess.

Sometimes I'd let the loud voices from the TV represent angry commoners gathered around my tower. Then I'd use my magic princess powers to resolve their every problem. Everyone pretty much loved me for it. And when one or two obnoxious boy commoners refused to abide by palace rules, I'd simply banish them (in my mind) from the entire kingdom/playground. If only ignoring people away worked as well in adulthood … well then, I probably wouldn't be reliving this all now.

One of my most vivid memories is of a blizzard in February 1967. It was just before my fifth birthday. I can remember pondering the meaning of life according to a child's brain while sitting in a house with no electricity, staring out at a storm that effectively whited-out nearly all of my vision, yielding only occasionally to reveal a fleeting glimpse of a tree or a lump where our car used to be. It was mesmerizing. I felt like the storm was whiting out my thoughts and making everything go blank. I heard my mom say something about my birthday next month and I wondered if the snow would stop by then. I knew it was possible to be snowed in on one's birthday, but I also remember thinking that God wouldn't do that on someone's fifth birthday. *Five years old* for crying out loud! Even as a youngster, I knew this was a big one. The snow continued to blow huge sheets of icy frost, making the world seem whiter and whiter and whiter. Five would be a good year for me.

I felt like I was ready and, as I stared at the sideways blowing snow, I knew that same wind would be carrying me off to school in the fall. My mom would be packing my lunch—watching me get on the school bus with all the other kids whose moms packed their lunches. Holly would be there too. We'd laugh and joke and try to dance like our parents (which was pretty far out.) That's what Holly and I did sometimes because we were very mature for our age and had no problem mimicking the adults in our lives. I knew with all my heart and soul I'd grow up to be just like my mom, Clare McPherson and that one day I'd meet and marry my own Finn.

"Hey Princess!" My dad had startled me out of my day dream one day. "You've been entirely too quiet!" Before I could respond, he had scooped me up and tossed me on the overstuffed/overworn piece of furniture we called our couch. He tickled me and I laughed till I cried. I tickled back and screamed for help. Mom came in and wrestled me out of Dad's reach. Then Dad grabbed us both and the tickle match began all over again, ending in painfully contagious, belly-cramping laughter tapering off to sheer, happy exhaustion. My parents were my heroes.

Finn McPherson was tall and broad-shouldered. His muscular build was softened by wispy strawberry blond hair, sparkling, baby blue eyes, and a slightly crooked-tooth smile. He was strong and kind and loving. My mom and I were everything to him. I know he worked in a factory, but I can't remember a single conversation about his job. He walked in the door, smelling of machine oil—coveralls half off, exposing his white t-shirt pulled snugly across rock hard abs and tucked neatly into blue jeans. It became all about us and how *our* day had been from the moment he crossed the threshold. Dad was handsome; there's no doubt about that. But it was his warm, gentle touch and how I felt so safe when he held me that I remember most. Safe—I've spent a lifetime trying to get that feeling back.

Clare McPherson was of medium build with narrow shoulders, slim waist and hips, and next to no butt whatsoever. Her skin was pale and perfectly ivory except for a few freckles spattered randomly across the bridge of her sloped and somewhat upturned nose. Her lips were full and pink and perpetually glossy.

I remember my mother's hair, long, wavy, and blonde—nearly reaching her waist. Her eyes were sea foam green, outlined and darted with teal. Her hair is what would've caught your attention at first, warranting a second look. Her smile would've drawn you in closer. But it was her eyes you could've gotten lost in forever. I suspect that's what happened to my dad.

My hair was a crazy mass of dark copper curls hanging over hazel eyes, my mother's nose and her pouty lips—kissed by sunshine. Mom said the sun loved redheads for their beauty and would kiss them with freckles, but over time the sun becomes jealous of their radiant beauty and burns them deeply. We sought shade whenever we felt the sun's jealous rage coming on.

I was probably a pretty average "cute" kid, but my parents raised me as if the entire world revolved around my very existence. It'd be a big-time bummer when that world ended.

Before Mom was a blonde, she had been a redhead. And before that, I saw pictures of Mom with short, straight black hair. I didn't even recognize her.

"Mom! Who is this with Daddy?"

Laughing, "That's me, sweetheart."

I laughed back "Oh." She picked up the pictures, we had a snack, and I never saw the photos again. But she did have black, red, and blonde hair at different points in time. She was a free spirit, an artist, and an activist who would not be held down by the man. Unless that man was her husband, Finn, then she made an exception. Clare McPherson loved her husband. When he walked in the room, her world stopped revolving and she sparkled.

The summer of 1967 went by in a blur of all-day stays at the public pool, late afternoons playing princess, planning for school days ahead with Holly, back-to-school shopping, and quiet evenings with my parents catching lightening bugs and dreaming big dreams from the front steps of our modest townhouse. Sometimes we'd watch "I Dream of Jeanie" or "Bewitched" or "The Monkees" who I adored. Saturday mornings meant cartoons with "Tom & Jerry". Color TVs were coming down in price and everybody but everybody was buying one. Peace rallies protesting the Vietnam War were becoming commonplace and Lyndon B. Johnson was president. It was called the "summer of love" and many were smoking pot and feeling groovy.

Men were growing their hair longer and colors were getting brighter in my world as the psychedelic era grabbed Mom and all of her friends. Their skirts went from minis to maxis—hemlines were shifting dramatically, adding to the rainbow of ever-changing fashion trends.

I slept well in those early years. Or, at least I can't remember tossing and turning or waking up exhausted and completely spent before the day had even started. I don't remember having dread or insecurity or anything so horrific a good night's sleep wouldn't cure—which I felt was pretty much a given *every* night. I don't think I really experienced true insomnia till I was completely on my own and off the "mother's little helpers" Mick Jagger had warned us about in 1966. I had no way of knowing how soon that addiction would have begun.

I knew our little family was different. I noticed the obvious absence of aunts and uncles, cousins, and grandparents. I knew it didn't matter and I liked my world exactly as it was.

What I didn't know is that my whole family was essentially born on March 7, 1962 at 3:00 a.m. I think that storm was God's way of creating a diversion and giving my parents a new lease on life. Perhaps, in all the mass hysteria of a hospital overflowing with casualties because of acts of God, no one noticed the un-dotted i's, uncrossed t's, or unchecked IDs of Finn and Clare McPherson. No one noticed that, prior to that very moment, they didn't appear to have existed at all. They'd almost gotten away with it. I wish their lie could've gone on longer. But alas, as all good stories go—there's a beginning, middle, and an end.

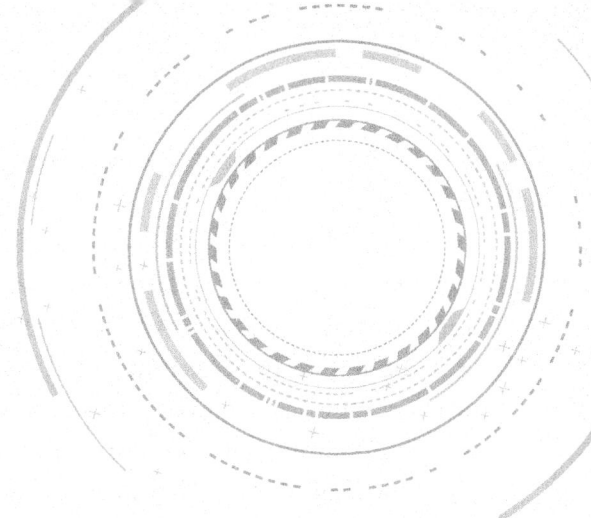

CHAPTER TWO
Mother's Little Helper

My name was Camilla Colleen. I was five and could barely sleep for thinking of starting school in a few short weeks. My parents were the most awesome people I knew. I loved everything about them—their warmth, their attitudes, their voices, their words, their affection, their looks. I loved the square angle of my dad's jaw and the way his muscular arms felt when he held me. I loved my mom's ivory complexion, long wavy hair, and the way she always smelled of exotic spices.

And then there was me—curly copper hair, freckled face, hazel eyes, my mother's sloped and slightly upturned nose and pouty lips, my father's... gosh, was there anything about me that was like my father? Maybe my coloring—a little. People commented that I was the perfect combination of the two, but I'm not certain what they saw. It's hard for me to see either of them in me anymore. Most days it's hard for me to remember Camilla Colleen McPherson or her parents at all. I had the name and parents for just over five years. I had the face up until the fall of 1984.

Later, when I went to college and studied some psychology and sociology, I had a class where we examined recessive and dominant traits, some of which were one's coloring. I had zero idea about grandparents and ended up guessing my mom was a brunette based on her eyebrows and lashes being dark brown. It's so weird the things that end up making a difference in your life. She truly may have been a natural redhead or maybe a strawberry blonde who kept her brows and lashes dark. *Missed opportunities and unanswered questions.*

What I do remember is that I was Finn and Clare's only child and my memories were always of the three of us together—having breakfast, playing at the park, going to the beach (where my mother went out of her mind trying to keep herself and her fair-skinned child from being sunburnt, bedtime stories, late night snacks, trips to the theatre—we were all always together. I had no reason to believe things would have ever been any different.

It was August 8, 1967. We'd just gotten back from an amazing two weeks on Lake Hopatcong (located in northwest New Jersey) two days earlier. Dad was due back at work and Mom and I were enjoying the last days of summer.

We'd been shopping for school supplies, had stopped and had lunch in an outdoor café on a perfect summer's day and spent much of our afternoon lounging around the house. I had enjoyed Lake Hopatcong—canoeing, swimming, hiking, exploring, roasting hotdogs and marshmallows, and hanging out with the coolest parents in the world. But, I was glad to be home and in my own bed and was enjoying the surreal and yet-oh-so-familiar sensation of "home" one experiences after a long time away from their ordinary, everyday life.

Dad came home, just like any other night. We had dinner and watched TV. I took a bath and went to bed. My ultra-normal routine was back in full swing. Sounds from the TV set below found their way through the duct work like hard-wired speakers. A loud bang and one high pitched scream later—and my head was under the pillow and headed for the princess tower of my dreams. I floated somewhere between reality, fantasy, and sleep.

The commoners were unusually agitated this particular evening. They were talking over each other and I found it difficult to follow. Every time I focused in on one face and one voice, another would interrupt and then another and another. Before I knew it, all hell had broken loose. I was beginning to doubt my princess powers and spoke a quiet prayer for God to send help.

Before long, the commoners became still and an angel dressed in a dark suit climbed the ladder to the tower to assist me. He was a very large man. Had it not been for the fact that he was there to help me, I think I might have been intimidated by his size alone. But, despite his large build, chiseled jaw, dark hair, and hard-angled features, his smile was that of an angel. When he looked at me, there was so much joy that a drop of it spilled out of his eye and ran down his cheek. He must've been happy to have made it in time to rescue me from the chaos.

The angel scooped me up in his arms and then, gently and lovingly, said "I'm here to take you home."

I wrapped my arms around his neck and rested my head on his shoulder. We glided down the sliding board, the crowd parted, and I fell asleep in the arms of my angel and remained there for days, hours, maybe just minutes. I have no idea.

The limo hit a pothole and I awoke to loving, rich chocolate eyes—the color of a Hershey bar melting on a warm day. I stared at my angel (who's center was no doubt made of the sweetest chocolate), confused and unsure if I was dreaming. "Where am I?"

"We're taking you home Cici." The voice came from a woman sitting opposite me and my angel. She smiled as she spoke the words and stared at me in happy disbelief.

C.C. Who is C.C.? Are they calling me by my initials?

But she wasn't saying "C.C."; she was saying "Cici."

"Where am I?" I whined. "Who are you? I want my mom and dad!" The last words were choked out with tears that turned to sobbing that turned to snot-bubbling, incoherent bawling.

The woman then took a small pill bottle from her bag. She broke one of the blue pills in half and then quartered the second half. Pressing the small, pie-shaped quarter pill into my mouth and holding her index finger there for just a moment, she said, "Shhhh. It'll be alright." She lifted a glass of water to my lips and I swallowed my first grown-up pill ever in the back seat of that limo.

The angel leaned closer, keeping his arm around my shoulders and looking deeply into my eyes. "I'm Sal Russo. I'm your father, Cici. And this is Mama Luciana." He motioned to the lady across from us. "We're here to take you home, princess."

I was a princess. That explained everything. I thought Dad called me that as a nickname, but perhaps I was *real* royalty and had been lost at sea, only to be found by the McPherson pirates—who, after finding me, gave up their lives of pirating to raise a princess. My five-year-old brain swung wide with possibilities. I missed my pirate parents already. I relaxed deeply into my Valium-induced delusions of grandeur and hoped Finn and Clare McPherson were okay.

I vaguely remember walking to the plane—holding both Mama Luciana's and Daddy Sal's hands. Not swinging between them so much as stumbling terribly and trying to keep up. Daddy Sal picked me up; I remember thinking the inside of the plane was bigger than the whole first floor of our pirates' townhouse.

A tall, skinny, young man stood up, smiled, and introduced himself as "Mikey". He looked fuzzy to me. Other men in dark suits occupied seats in both the front and the back—leaving the spacious middle section for the three of us. I heard the engines start, settled into a big, cozy seat and, before I knew it, Valium took over and I was out like a light.

I awoke in the most amazing pink princess room in the entire world—complete with canopy bed (much bigger than the one in my pirate home), beautiful dolls, sheer pink curtains, and a white shag rug. Before I could take it all in, I was greeted by big, dark brown eyes and a mop of black hair.

"She's awake! She's awake! Cici's awake!" I guessed the boy to be about my age, maybe a year older. He was olive-complexioned, with a beautiful dimpled smile and liquid brown eyes that seemed to sparkle. He began to jump up and down on my bed. My head felt foggy and my mouth felt furry. Later, I discovered this sensation was called a "Valium hangover."

"My name is Giovanni and you're my sister Cici and we've been looking for you for a long time and Mama said Daddy would find you and he did ..." The boy panted as he continued to jump and talk. "But it took longer than we thought it would, but we don't care because you're finally home and Cici is awake! Everybody! Cici is awake!"

Giovanni was the epitome of "too much sunshine." He woke up like that every day—bouncing off the walls and happy to be alive. I loved him instantly, but wished he'd stop jumping, or talking, or both.

"Gio, take it down a notch." A seven year old boy entered and extended his hand toward me. "I'm Emilio." I shook his hand.

"You probably haven't noticed your closet yet." He swung open double doors that led to a dressing room full of dresses and shoes and bags and accessories. My mouth dropped open.

Emilio was round faced and pleasantly plump. He reminded me of a teddy bear. His hair was medium brown and his eyes a milky brown—he looked almost like a washed out, heavier version of Giovanni with that same dazzlingly perfect smile sitting below his black-rimmed glasses.

"Dad and I built this." He put his hands on his hips and admired the handiwork, nodding his head. "There's a ton of room for more shoes and stuff. Mama says girls have more shoes, but I can't see anyone filling up all these cubbies with nothing but shoes. You can use them for anything you like." He looked at the completed project, keeping his hands on his hips, and then back to me very seriously. "I've been working on this most of my adult life. I hope you like it." I smiled at his very serious demeanor. My pirate mom would've called him an "old soul".

Giovanni continued jumping. "Cici is home now! Cici is home now! I got a sis-ter!"

My head was fighting a bulldozing wave of Valium fog and, despite all the commotion, my eyelids were growing heavy again and began to flutter. Mick Jagger might have been singing about "mother's little helper," but I was living it—or perhaps more accurately, sleeping through it. The last image I saw before passing back out again was of a third boy—older with dark, wavy hair, bushy eye brows over-shadowing hazel eyes and wide lips. I'd later learn this was my oldest brother Antonio.

"Shut up Gio. You must be boring her to death because nobody could sleep through *your* mouth."

- - - -

I awoke to bright sunlight beaming directly on my face and squinted hard against it. For the second time that day I thought, *too much sunshine.*

I staggered from my room and started down the enormous, winding staircase ahead of me. I was sure I was in a castle. I'd never seen anything like it before, outside of maybe watching a Disney special on TV.

I heard voices from below and could make out Sal and Mama Luciana and the three boys appearing to be having lunch in the grand dining room. As I rounded the corner, all conversation stopped and I was greeted by wide eyes and gaping mouths. The marble floors suddenly felt cold beneath my bare feet.

Sal sat at one end—wearing a black suit, white shirt, and patterned, red tie. Mama Luciana was at the opposite end of the table dressed in a pale yellow sundress. The boys wore polo shirts, shorts, and sneakers. I didn't even notice what I was wearing. Mama Luciana picked me up quickly—me and my faded purple, tie-died cotton nightgown from my old pirate life.

"Cici, we don't come downstairs in our pajamas." She quickly trotted up the stairs with me in tow. It seemed the rules would be different in Washington, DC.

Luciana picked out a pink, cotton sundress, white sneakers, and pink socks with white lace. She brushed my frazzled curly copper hair and it pulled it into tight pig tails—securing them both with pink bows. She then directed me to the bathroom and had me wash my face and brush my teeth. Before long, I was "ready to go back downstairs."

I thought of my pirate parents and wearing pajamas to breakfast and sometimes staying in them till late when the weather was too crappy to go out. I started crying, then sobbing, and then— you guessed it, snot-bubbling bawling my eyes out. Luciana did her best to console me but, when all else failed, she turned to what she knew and understood best—pharmaceuticals.

Luciana pushed one-fourth of a blue, 10mg Valium in my mouth, and like in the limo, she held her index finger at my lips for just a moment shushing me. She filled a Dixie cup with water and I swallowed my second grown up pill ever. *Mother's Little Helper.*

This ritual of compassion was repeated often during those first several weeks with the Russo's. I imagine Mama thought I was too weak to deal with all the change sober. I imagine I was too.

What I didn't know was that her 'acts of love' would lead to a lifetime rollercoaster ride of addiction, mixed with moments of unbearable sobriety.

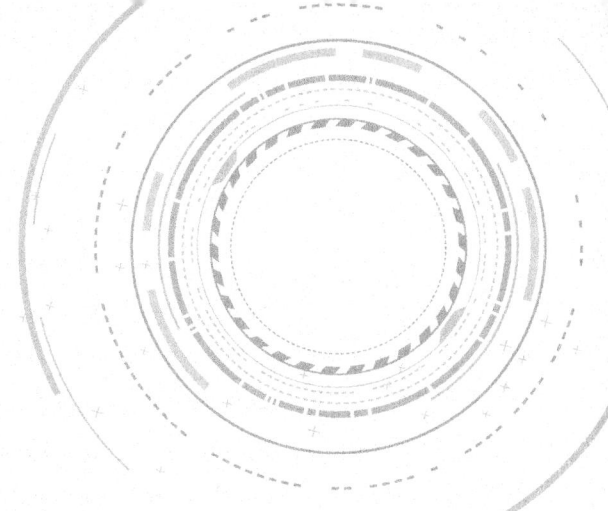

CHAPTER THREE
The Russo Way

Much of those early days were survived in a Valium haze with one day melting into the next and the next. Gratefully, I was able to discern simple commands—stay, sit, speak, eat, run, play, get dressed, brush your teeth, and don't forget your jacket. For the most part, I was able to carry out these commands as well. I was basically fine with someone else writing, directing, and producing my every move. But I was five and all that was bound to change.

I learned tears were a sign of weakness and unpleasant emotion should be held in. I learned to cry in the shower or late at night alone in my bed with my head under my pillow—sometimes I'd find myself back at my princess tower. I'd see Holly looking for me. I'd wave and jump up and down, but she never saw me. Some mornings, I woke up and intentionally showed up for breakfast with tears in my eyes, just so Mama Luciana would numb my pain and I wouldn't have to think about any of it, at least on that particular day. Other times, I'd hide the pain, so Mama wouldn't medicate me and I could go about my day *not* being a total stupid head.

Daddy Sal kept regular business hours in his office. Our home was at the far left end of a row of townhouses; Sal's office occupied the other end unit on the right, with three other families occupying the middle three houses—two elderly couples (apparently friends) and one middle-aged guy who lived alone and traveled a lot. I dreamed of the day that someone with kids might move in.

I didn't get to go to public school. The Russo's were above all that mess. They hired a private teacher to educate us from Sal's library. It was the only time we were allowed in there. I think part of my child's mind believed I'd be riding the same bus and going to the same school as Holly. It was a huge disappointment to discover that wouldn't be the case. I missed Holly and our friendship terribly. But every minute of every day seemed to be consumed with school and homework and hair appointments and shopping and changing outfits every time my mood changed; there was little time left for much of anything else. Heaven forbid anyone sit still.

School sucked the worst for me. I had been the very center of my pirate parents' life. They praised me for my ability to laugh, sing (badly), set the table, kick a ball, or color a picture. Now suddenly, I was in a class with three boys—older and more educated than me. The idea of competition was completely foreign before then.

My first day of home school with Mrs. Kathleen Hodges (and no Holly) was beyond humbling and disappointing. Mrs. Hodges was kind and attentive. She was tall and slender, with high cheek bones, strawberry blonde hair twisted up in a bun, a tiny waist, and a butt as wide as a yard stick. I considered her to be a good teacher though I had no one to compare her to.

Mrs. Hodges opened with prayer followed by the Pledge of Allegiance. I stared blankly and Gio quickly grabbed my right hand and put it over my heart. He anxiously motioned as he pledged for me to jump in. Antonio (my oldest brother) said I was a communist because I didn't know the words. If only Mrs. Hodges could've broken into a round of Hokey-Pokey—I believe I could've shined a little earlier in the game. Instead, she opted for the "alphabet song." Giovanni sang loud and proud. Emilio seemed to give every letter serious thought. And Antonio belted out the tune with all the enthusiasm one might expect from a lecture on safe dental practices.

But it was Antonio's exaggerated eye-rolling and mock wonderment at my lack of education that really took its toll on me. He went out of his way to appear bored and jumped on every opportunity to let the rest of us know that he was smarter and that I was a perfect retard.

Sadly, Antonio was right. There was no getting around the fact that I was five years old, knew all the words to Kumbaya, and could hokey-pokey with the best of them, but had absolutely no knowledge of this alphabet song or Pledge of Allegiance that seemed to be held in such high regard. I didn't even know what a "communist" was. Oh, but I would find out. Maybe one day when my head wasn't stuck in a Valium haze.

Gio helped me to memorize the pledge—we said it over and over and over again, emphasizing different words and phrases with each new round. We even sang and danced to it. Gio was so animated; he made everything fun.

When we weren't in school, Daddy Sal often held meetings or was on the phone in his library during business hours. We'd hear laughing or loud voices, or the low murmur of a whisper. There were always people coming and going—gardeners and housekeepers and decorators, men in dark suits, and women in designer clothes. I always thought my parents had a boatload of friends and were excessively busy people.

Out of all the people who worked for Daddy, we loved Mikey the best. Mike Kramer had been there that first night on the plane and he seemed to be forever close by—entering the room or coming around the corner the second he was needed. Sometimes when Gio and I were working on a project that required memorization (which, for us, meant singing and dancing), Mikey would join us—dancing some kind of crazy Mick Jagger-on-Quaaludes dance as he did so. He always made us laugh—his tall, lanky frame, silly faces, and exaggerated moves often had us in stitches. I had no clue what his actual job was, but house jester was my guess.

Mama had a friend named Cecelia, who came over at least a couple times a week for lunch. She was petite with an olive complexion, bleached blonde hair, and a French accent. Mama had begun adopting some of Cecelia's phrases and pronunciations, although her attempt at a French accent was a little embarrassing.

The Russo's ate nearly every meal together as a family. Daddy Sal enjoyed a regular ritual of coffee while reading through his dozen or so newspapers, followed by bacon and eggs and orange juice for breakfast. He seemed to focus mostly on the business section and the classified ads while we kids fought for the funny pages and the promised prizes hidden within our cereal boxes. We'd discuss our plans for the day before going our separate ways. And God help you if you didn't have *any* plans—Mama Luciana had a long list of things that needed to be done if you had no idea how you wanted to spend your time outside of school hours.

Lunch was always served at noon. Sharp. During the week, Mrs. Hodges had us wash our hands and be seated at the table by 11:57 a.m. Mama was sitting and waiting for her husband by 11:58 a.m. Daddy joined us anywhere between 12:00 and maybe

12:15 or so. The moment Sal Russo sat down, Maria (or whoever was Luciana's cook de jour) would instantly appear, serving the man of the house first, followed by Mama, and then each of us kids in order of descending age—generally Antonio and Emilio at the same time and Giovanni and I last. So, at least Gio shared the humbling position with me. We ate and conversed for exactly thirty minutes.

Conversation centered on whatever we were studying in home school or current events or how the meal was.

"Antonio," Sal began over lunch one day, "what have you learned this morning in school?"

"We learned that Cici is an idiot. She doesn't even know the states."

Sal slapped the table sharply giving Antonio a contemptuous, threatening stare. "Do not make me ask a second time!"

"Yes sir," Antonio corrected himself. "We reviewed the fifty states and their capitals."

Sal nodded and turned his glance toward Emilio, who had nothing to add because the truth was that's all we had done. Poor old Mrs. Hodges struggled to get me caught up and, unfortunately, it slowed everyone else's progress down.

Emilio looked like a deer caught the headlights and reluctantly stammered, "Cici colored a map."

Antonio snickered under his breath and tried to cover it up by taking a big drink of water.

Sal ignored him and turned his attention to Gio, who was busy shoveling spaghetti into his face.

Gio looked up smiling, with pasta hanging from his mouth. "Lunch is my favorite part."

Sal chuckled and Luciana chimed in with a forced laugh. Gio was always her favorite and I think it pleased her to see Sal take notice of her baby boy and to see Sal's anger dissipate.

Sal looked up from his meal to consider me for a moment. "Your hair looks very nice pulled back, Cici. Perhaps you can wear it down for dinner tonight." Daddy Sal rarely questioned me about learning. No doubt for fear of having his and his oldest son's worst suspicions confirmed: that I was, in fact, an idiot.

If there was something wrong, you simply didn't talk about it in our family. Repression became my best friend. I hit "expert" level years ago. I hate to bad-mouth repression at all; it got me through some tough times and worked really well—until it didn't.

In the beginning, I had tried to ask questions about my pirate parents and got greeted with so much Valium and "what's important is that we found you and you're home" lines, my head would spin. I gave up asking. Sometimes Gio and I would play make believe and I'd be the princess being rescued by a handsome prince—leaving the pirates weeping, but headed for a better life. It was just make believe—at least, the "better life" part. That one I can never know for certain.

I overheard one of Sal and Luciana's many fights late one night when I was probably nine or ten. It was a loud, angry, glass-breaking fight—one likely everyone in the house heard.

"I'm sick to death of your pretty, fair-skinned whores masquerading through my house as maids!" The sound of breaking glass echoed and we all guessed Luciana would be getting the new lamps she wanted for the master bedroom after all. She liked breaking stuff she'd long-since grown tired of but that Sal didn't want to replace, because if it ain't broke, right?

"Luciana, you know we only keep a maid on staff to assist you with all the domestic affairs," Sal offered.

"Yours or mine, Sal? Whose affairs are we really talking about? Maybe you'll get another one of your whores pregnant!"

A loud thud cut Luciana's rant short. Perhaps it was Sal's fist hitting a wall or a piece of furniture. He never once laid a hand on his wife that I'm aware of.

Silence followed. Was it the calm before the storm? Sal breathing in deeply before he exploded? Or did one simply walk away from the other? I waited on the edge of my bed, shaking. I was a child, but I understood the overall implication of my daddy cheating with another woman. The next voice I heard was calm and controlled.

"Luciana, what's in the past is in the past," Sal spoke pleadingly. "Perhaps you're failing to see the bigger picture. If I remember correctly, you wanted another child—a female child. The idea of putting your beautiful body through a fourth pregnancy wasn't an option for you; you wanted to adopt. Instead, Clare acted as a surrogate and gave us something much better than an adopted child. She gave us a child of my own loins. So much better than a stranger's child. Wouldn't you agree?"

It was the first and only time I heard my mother's name spoken in that house. "Clare." I whispered her name and filed the information away with all the other things of which I was never to speak.

Dinners became more and more formal over the years and, by the time I was eleven or twelve, required a change of attire from our play clothes. Manners were strictly enforced and any deviance from acceptable dinner etiquette wasn't tolerated and was often met with immediate disciplinary force.

One should never question Sal Russo. Ever. Emilio learned that lesson one evening over dinner. He was probably fourteen years old. Sal always started the boys driving when they were young and Emilio had only recently begun his driving lessons, but was already cocky about it. I wasn't even allowed through the kitchen door that led down to the garage, much less behind the wheel. Someone was always pushing or pulling me away if I so much as tried to steal a peek. It was just a stupid garage. I didn't get what the big deal was. I guessed it was a "no girls allowed" thing, which I thought was total bullshit.

On this particular evening, Emilio was bragging about hanging out in the garage and being the next great Russo driver. Maria served salad and garlic bread and pasta. Sal broke a piece of garlic bread and took a moment to enjoy the aroma. He looked up at Emilio.

"After dinner tonight, bring the Cadillac around."

Emilio took a bite out of a piece of bread. "I thought you wanted the Mercedes."

We all froze. Every person at that table knew the only acceptable response would've been "yes sir."

Sal stood up quickly and, in two giant steps, was jerking Emilio up out of his chair with one hand and slapping him hard across the face with the other—leaving the large red mark of Sal Russo's anger on his cheek.

"How dare *you* question *me* at my own table? You dare disrespect me in my own home?" Daddy Sal was fuming. He pushed Emilio backwards. "Get your ass to the garage. Clean up the Cadillac and have it out front in fifteen minutes."

Emilio hung his head as he left the room. Mama continued to eat her pasta. "The sauce is delicious Maria. Did you use the Roma tomatoes I bought at the market?"

Daddy Sal motioned to Maria and then to Emilio's untouched pasta. "Clean this up. He could use a few less calories."

"But of course," Luciana agreed in her most nonchalant, bad French accent. She nodded to Maria who was already busy clearing Emilio's dinner and place setting from the table.

We all got Sal-slapped at least once, but Emilio definitely got more than his share. He was funny and witty and couldn't pass up the opportunity to share his sense of humor or point of view at the most inopportune times—such as dinner time. Plus, he was heavy and a little awkward and I think he tried to compensate with his wit and personality.

Daddy turned to me without missing a beat, "What did you learn in school today Cici?"

Crap! I felt my heart sink as my mind went completely blank. Gio came to my rescue. "We learned about Christopher Columbus."

Just the reminder I needed. "And after school," I chimed in, "Gio and I made up a song to help us remember the story. Mikey helped us study and even taught us a couple new moves."

Gio jumped up and started dancing and I jumped in. Daddy and Mama both smiled brightly as Antonio rolled his eyes and focused on his pasta. We sang our version of history and then Mikey came around the corner and sang the last part with us—showing off his choreography to the now hysterical audience of two.

Mama and Daddy applauded and Mikey excused himself, pushing his glasses back up the slope of his nose. "Now that the entertainment portion of the evening has been taken care of, I'll let you good people finish enjoying your meal."

Emilio could've taken lessons from Mikey's timing. He was perfect—leaving his audience wanting more and knowing instinctively when to joke and more importantly when *not* to joke. Emilio's instincts weren't quite so developed.

Through the laughter and accolades, the pasta and clinking of silverware, I swear I could hear Emilio's muffled sobs from below. No one ever got up to check on him and, when fifteen or twenty minutes had passed, Daddy grabbed his briefcase and headed for the Cadillac that was awaiting him out front.

As a family, we had really good times and super crappy times and damned little in between. The poker parties were big fun—Daddy would be in a good mood and the rest of us were along for the ride. If Daddy was angry with you, it pretty much just sucked for you. But if he was generally distracted or angry at no one in particular, it sucked for everyone. Poker was the one game that got Sal Russo's mind off his worries.

I don't remember exactly when the guys' poker parties started—I couldn't have been more than thirteen. Daddy occasionally had business trips to Las Vegas and had decided to teach the *boys* how to play poker. Sal Russo was a killer poker player—tough to read, impossible to deceive. It was those same qualities that made him a force to be reckoned with and a terrifying parent.

It wasn't considered "lady-like" to play poker, but I was allowed to hang out, fill drinks, fetch snacks, and play waitress. It actually wasn't so bad that I was treated differently from the boys—the expectations of them were much more demanding. Sal was harder on them—at least in the beginning.

As no one took me seriously, I was able to walk around the table and look at everyone's cards and watch their expressions and mannerisms.

Emilio pretty much laughed or joked no matter what his cards were, so I looked for more clues. Before too long, I noted a tendency for him to tilt his cards inward when he thought he was holding something worthwhile—almost as if to protect them.

Antonio tried to mimic Daddy's style—showing no emotion whatsoever. He tried, but he failed. If he was happy, you could see one corner of his mouth begin to smile ever so slightly for a second. And if he wasn't happy, that same corner of his mouth went south for a second. I had nothing better to do than watch. I'm not sure anyone else even noticed.

As for Giovanni, he simply loved the game. Happy if he won; happy if someone else was raking the pot. He was still an easy read—eyes lighting up with promising cards; a sigh and more serious face with lesser cards. But, it really didn't matter either way. When Gio was winning, there was no stopping him. As he got older, he'd say "When you're good, the cards just come to you," eyes sparkling and smile radiating as he spoke. Giovanni Russo was pure awesome in my eyes.

Eventually the party grew to include a friend or two of Sal's or Antonio's. I think Emilio or Gio's friends would've been considered too young—or maybe none of their friends played poker. I don't remember.

Joey Marconi was one of Antonio's pals. Joey was hot. He had undeniable charm, piercing blue eyes, a dead-sexy voice and a smile that made hearts around the world melt. He wore wire-framed glasses, blue jeans, and cotton dress shirts with snow white sneakers. He was fit and of medium height with broad shoulders and the beginning of what looked like a hairy chest. His wispy light brown hair was often peeking out from under a ball cap—making his polished good looks somehow friendlier and more approachable. I liked him instantly. One day, Sal smacked him in the back of the head for wearing a hat in the house. I worried Joey Marconi wouldn't return after that. I worried unnecessarily.

The only thing I remember being super creepy about Joey back then was his infatuation with death. He'd wanted to be a funeral director since he was seven. Daddy Sal laughed and nicknamed him Joey "The Torch" Marconi. In years to come, Joseph Marconi would more than earn the title. As for me and Gio, we would purposely mess up Joey's name and ask Antonio if Joey "Macaroni" would be at the weekly poker game that week. It totally pissed Antonio off, which totally entertained us.

One Friday night, Joey brought his younger sister Tess with him. She was slightly older than me (less than a year), with untamed strawberry blonde hair, bold freckles, and crazy energy. She was a wild one.

ILLUSIONS OF PRIVACY

I thought it would be so much fun to have another girl playing waitress with me, but Tess had other ideas. I showed her my room and she closed the door and showed me a deck of cards. We used vanilla wafers for chips and I got to put my knowledge of the game into practice. But with Tess, one never knew what was really going on in her head. She made up games and changed rules to suit the hand she was dealt, which was ridiculous because we had a whole box of vanilla wafers. But that was Tess—always going for the big score.

Over the years, Tess and I became close friends—mostly because Antonio and Joey were friends and it was Joey's job to watch his little sister, which he failed at miserably. It was easier to head over to our house and leave Tess in my company for a few hours than take any personal interest in his sister. Tess was a leader. She didn't need no stinkin' big brother telling her what to do anyway. Tess Marconi was a woman of the world who knew it all and enjoyed sharing her knowledge. She taught me how to smoke cigarettes and how to smoke pot, what alcohol was all about and that, while the buzz was similar, how a hangover was quite different from Valium. As we got older, she'd end up teaching me how to snort cocaine and boot heroin. I learned a lot from Tess.

Joey was too busy being Antonio's bitch to notice. He laughed too loud at Antonio's stupid jokes, and would lean in and listen to his every word, touching Antonio's arm or leg as he did so. And Antonio would whisper secrets to Joey and laugh rudely as Emilio or Gio or I walked by. Evidently, they were both members of the Mutual Asshole Admiration Society. Still, I liked Joey Marconi and sometimes daydreamed about being his girlfriend—because I was a naïve child loaded on pharmaceuticals and completely uneducated and inexperienced in the ways of the evil, freaking world. Plus, being home schooled, there wasn't an exorbitant amount of other options—I could crush on Bill Bixby all day long, but real life was slim pickings.

Aside from being an arrogant ass, Joey was a straight arrow even as a teenager—drinking an occasional beer and rarely opting for a second. He and Antonio were the best of friends, with Joey joining us for dinner nearly every night of the week. At family parties, Joey kept close watch on Antonio—who did *often* opt for a second, third, fourth, and fifth beer.

Our family parties were freaking huge—it was not uncommon to have guest lists including up to two and three hundred people. On these occasions, property lines were ignored between townhouses, neighbors were invited, tents erected, and people were everywhere. I thought my parents were queen and king of the neighborhood.

Uncle Guido and Aunt Bunny never missed an event, bringing their angry-looking son, Dante (along with his twelve-word vocabulary), with them. Guido would do absolutely *anything* for Sal without question. We were to show him respect for this reason. He was short and fat with greasy hair and smelled of garlic and onions. Sal used to say that Guido was "short and squatty; all butt and no body." We all thought that was hugely funny.

Aunt Bunny was a loud Italian woman with brightly dyed red hair and a mouth big enough to swallow a whole chicken. Her body was proof that she'd done exactly that on more than one occasion, along with whole pizzas, pot roasts, and chocolate cream cakes.

Dante was tall and skinny; he wore nothing but black, tight-fitted clothing (which made him look skinnier) and spoke in two-word sentences. More often than not, he answered with sneers and exaggerated sighs. I wasn't sure if he was retarded or just had a bad attitude. One look at his parents and I considered the latter to be more likely.

At one party, I found myself alone in the kitchen—the door to the lower level garage ajar. I heard distant voices and was aching to know who was in the garage during a party. Maybe it was Antonio or Emilio talking cars with one of their friends? Or a mechanic getting in some overtime? A girl and a boy sneaking off to make out?

I quietly pulled the door open, took one step down the encased stairwell and closed the door behind me. I tip-toed down the steps. The voices sounded like they were far away or on the other side of a door. As quietly as I could, adrenaline racking every fiber of my being, I peered around the corner.

My mouth dropped open as I looked across the huge area—10 or 12 vehicles parked in two rows, a work bench, car parts, tools, a hydraulic lift, several metal chairs, tool chests, and what looked to be a door to an office on the far end. Our garage had to be the full length of all five townhouses together! I wondered if our neighbors knew we parked these cars below their living rooms. Or maybe some of these cars were theirs. I only recognized the Mercedes and the Cadillac. I looked around the room. There was a ramp that led up to a garage door on the backside, but no sign of any other entrances or exits. Years would pass before I'd even be able to imagine the horrendous shit that took place or horrific crimes that were covered up in that secret basement.

I wanted to investigate further, but the voices got louder and the office door opened. I hauled butt back up the stairs and through the kitchen without waiting to see who was down there, past the dining room and front entrance and zipping through the back French doors off the deck where I disappeared into a crowd of family and friends, and strangers.

I grabbed a shrimp off one waiter's tray and swallowed it hard with a glass of champagne off another tray wandering by.

One more glass of champagne and I gained the courage to turn around and look back at the doors I had just rushed through.

I saw Daddy talking with two men in dark suits—business associates, no doubt. Daddy Sal smiled at me and I smiled and waved back. Slowly and casually I made my way back across the yard.

"Hi, Daddy!" I kissed my father's cheek. "This party is wonderful!"

Sal Russo laughed. "And this angel, Vladimir, is my beautiful daughter Cici."

"Cici, this is Mr. Petrov," Daddy put special emphasis on the "v". Vladimir extended his hand.

Vladimir Petrov was six five and two-hundred and fifty pounds of solid muscle. He was clean-shaven with a square jaw and hands the size of frying pans. Despite his sculpted features and brilliant smile, the man's size gave him a menacing edge. I was pretty sure he could've snapped me in two without flexing a muscle.

Vladimir took my hand in his, brushed his lips across my knuckles and kissed the back of my hand. "It's a pleasure to meet you Miss Russo," he spoke with a slow, deep Russian accent.

"My pleasure," I squeaked out before reclaiming my hand and excusing myself. I'd been so busy snooping and hiding, I'd neglected my champagne-filled bladder terribly. My brothers would say their "back teeth were floating."

I rounded the corner and, as I opened the powder room door on the main level, I felt a hand grabbing my shoulder and yanking me back around. Instinctively, I gasped and jumped back.

"Cici, Mr. Petrov is a special guest. Make sure his glass is never empty." Daddy smiled and walked back to the party going on outside.

Geez, mind if I empty my bladder before filling his glass?

"Anything for you Daddy!" I shouted. I hated being extra nice to people who made me extra uncomfortable.

The '70s in the Russo household became an ongoing ride of highs and lows—huge parties and private family vacations, big fights and loving conversations, mercy and forgiveness, Sal-slapping and name-calling, sobriety and addiction, devotion and abandonment. We were a family of hot and cold; never lukewarm.

Meanwhile, more people were traveling and fashion began to take on an ethnic trend with macramé bikinis from Greece and crocheted shawls from Spain, clothes from India and Africa, big puffy sleeves, bell bottom jeans, interesting patterns, Tibetan and Chinese jackets of quilted silk, and long, softly-pleated skirts. Fashion-wise, color was still king, but he'd taken textured patterns as his queen, knighting ethnic diversity and sexy lines in the process. The '70s had a lot to say about fashion. Sometimes, it seemed as if all the designers were yelling to be heard over loud colors and bold designs.

For the Russo kids, Saturday mornings meant cartoons from 6am till noon. It was the single best TV day of the week. It was worth staggering out of bed early, brushing my teeth, and throwing on a pair of shorts and a t-shirt, before collapsing in front of the TV for six glorious hours, while housekeepers vacuumed and dusted around us.

I owe my knowledge of the Constitution to Schoolhouse Rock, although I do think Gio and I came up with the idea of singing to memorize historical facts first; they just had animation and a TV station, while we were live action. It was the '70s. Cartoons trumped reality every time. Times have certainly changed.

Roller skates, pinball machines, and pogo sticks were popping up everywhere—every small town had a rink and an arcade and a group of kids that would live there if they could.

Waterbeds hit the scene in a big way, but Mama was worried they would break and one of us would surely drown. *But of course.*

We watched The Waltons, Starsky and Hutch, The Dukes of Hazard, and The Brady Bunch. Bewitched, Happy Days, Monty Python's Flying Circus, and Charlie's Angels were favorites as well.

From rock-n-roll a new wave of music was born—progressive rock. Genesis, Yes, and Pink Floyd topped the charts. Some of the old school rock bands jumped on board with huge continued success—bands like The Rolling Stones, AC/DC, Led Zeppelin, and Aerosmith.

We rocked out to Queen, fell in love to ABBA, and never wanted to stop dancing to David Bowie.

There was an oil crisis, an end to the war in Vietnam, the birth of women's rights, an increased interest in electronics (from calculators to televisions to primitive video games), the scandal of Watergate, affordable microwaves, computers for hobbyists (no one else really cared), and beanbag chairs for everyone.

The '70s taught us the word "inflation"—in 1970 a new house cost $23,400; in 1979, that same house was up to $58,500. Gas was thirty six cents per gallon in 1970; in 1979 it was eighty six cents. The average income in 1970 was just over $9,000; by 1979, it had nearly doubled to $17,500, (unlike the cost of gas, which had way more than doubled, it was a trend that would, unfortunately, continue.)

We waited in gas lines, played board games, had Barbies, and were home in time for dinner every night; a dinner free from cell phones and texting and television and computers. Yep, we had to actually *talk* to each other. In my family, learning a foreign language in two days would've been less demanding with fewer rules.

But pay back was coming—puberty was hot on my trail. And soon enough, my parents would regret the day they "rescued" me. I'd call that par.

Meanwhile my knight in shining armor might as well have been a million miles away. Decades would pass before I'd recognize him.

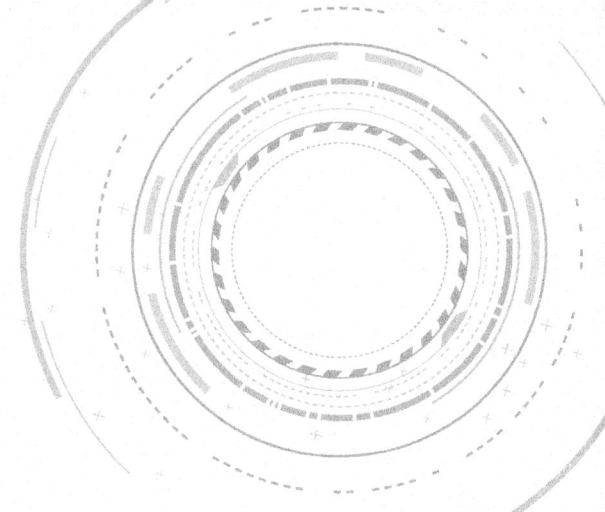

CHAPTER FOUR
Mud Hole Haven

There were big parties and there were quiet nights in with just the family—curtains drawn and not an employee or staff member in sight. We'd watch TV till late and eat popcorn, which broke two rules: staying up late *and* eating in front of the television. Breaking rules was fun.

Sometimes the whole family would camp out together in the living room, leaving the TV on till it turned to "no transmission" snow. Emilio's friend used to say that Emilio was "so funny they should put him on TV at 3 o'clock in the morning." The joke being that not only was it an unpopular time to watch TV but, more importantly, that even if you wanted to, you couldn't; no one transmitted television beyond 3am. Ever. And if I remember correctly it was much earlier during the week—like going to broadcast snow by 11 p.m.

Some nights we'd have pizza delivered. Growing up in the big city, I took a lot of things like that for granted. I thought everyone had pizza delivery. Twenty years later, I'd find myself living in a place that, to this very day, still doesn't have pizza delivery.

Growing up in Washington, DC, we had delivery *everything*. In the mid '70s, Zachary Stoner created "Stoner Z Ice Cream Delivery"—delivering retail pints of ice cream to select neighborhoods during limited evening hours, at crazy, inflated prices. The name came from his old Army days when friends had nicknamed him "Stoner Z."

Zachary Stoner worked as a mechanic after serving overseas and was looking for ways to supplement his income. Beaten up from a long day at the garage, Zachary collapsed on his couch one night and wished he had some ice cream in the freezer to go with his evening ritual of TV, which included *getting up* to change the channel (he was living large with *five* channels to choose from). Too tired to move, he thought "I'd pay twice retail for a pint of ice cream delivered to my door right now." From that one, small, seemingly insignificant, terribly lazy thought "Stoner Z Ice Cream Delivery" was born.

Eventually the name morphed into "Stonerz Ice Cream Delivery." During an interview on public access television, Zachary Stoner announced to the audience, "Two words: Stonerz Ice Cream." He went on to explain that while the original company name was based on an old nickname and there was a space separating "Stoner" and "Z," folks were pronouncing it "Stonerz" and "well then I suppose the people have spoken."

Zachary Stoner didn't realize he'd said anything wrong; yet, he never lived down the "two words." Local stations began to air the five second clip over and over again, "Two words: Stonerz Ice Cream." It became our way of asking for ice cream with one of us saying, "I just have two words" and the rest of us chiming in with "Stonerz Ice Cream!"

Zachary Stoner could've hung his head and beaten himself up over the faux pas; instead, he embraced it, making "icecream" one word and adding a tagline to the company name, "All Day, Every Day from 7pm-midnight." As business grew, drivers became more creative with their attire—looking like flower children or Cheech and Chong or rock stars. Some played music and danced their way to the customers' doorsteps. Some would throw a cup of water in a cooler of dry ice just before they opened the door to achieve the effect of smoke rolling out of the back of the vehicle. Others added flashing green lights and personalized auto graphics. It was a special treat to order from Stonerz. Customers loved it— Stonerz became synonymous with icecream and super popular with pot heads; tips for the entertainment became standard; and rumors of an illegal drug operation surfaced. Kids quickly began referring to smoking weed as "getting stoned" —which was often followed by getting pizza and of course, getting Stonerz Icecream. By the late 70's, the single word spelling of "icecream" had become an accepted alternate spelling and business was soaring, but Zachary Stoner was constantly under fire by local authorities for every trumped up charge they could remotely justify.

Zachary Stoner had nothing to hide; he was a decent man and by no means a drug dealer. He could've no more stopped teenagers from talking about "getting stoned" than he could've stopped his own generation from saying "groovy" or "far out." What authorities didn't like was that he'd capitalized on the stoner generation, made it acceptable terminology, and he'd done it really well.

The truth was, Zachary Stoner had never so much as seen a marijuana cigarette, much less have smoked or sold one—though the same could probably *not* have been said of all his drivers. After several failed attempts by local authorities to catch the company peddling pot, police eventually gave up and backed off in search of bigger fish to fry.

Several years later, the police officer who led the investigation against Stonerz Icecream retired to Florida and purchased his own franchise. He drove a bright green golf cart, proudly displaying the Stonerz logo with a flashing green light on top. On weekends, he even threw on his long wig and hippy clothes and it's been reported he did a little dancing as well. I wish I lived in his neighborhood. I'd be willing to pay seven dollars for a pint of ice cream to see that show—maybe ten with a tip.

Tess and I got stoned and turned to Stonerz on more than one occasion. We'd laugh about the stupidest stuff, blow milk out of our noses, and were unable to stop snickering until tears streaked our cheeks and our sides ached. I'd never shared that kind of laughter with my parents or Antonio or even the very entertaining Emilio. Gio and I laughed often, but if it weren't for Tess, those early teenage years may have been completely void of blissfully uncontrollable *girly* laughter.

Tess told me all about public school—she was a sophomore at Annandale High School in what she called "Action-dale, Virginia." She seemed so bored with it all, but I was fascinated—all the people, names, teachers, lockers, and the three smoking pits out back. I ached for the high-school experience; I got the Russo way instead.

Once Tess had her license, she was off and running. I would've been running with her more often had I not been raised at the Russo Maximum Security Penitentiary with minimal yard privileges. Holy cow, it was amazing I was ever able to sneak out back and burn a joint with Tess on the rare occasions she had nothing better to do.

I welcomed Joey "The Torch" Marconi's somewhat-less -than-eloquent flirting. It didn't matter that he lacked sincerity and was essentially just practicing lines on me; I was bored out of my mind and it didn't hurt for me to practice a little on him either. Sometimes, I'd daydream about Joey asking me out and Sal actually allowing me to go without Mikey, my personal babysitter. I wasn't sure which was more unlikely. But, I did kind of have a thing for Joey. Kind of.

I had to absolutely beg for driving lessons. All the boys started driving when their feet could barely reach the pedals. I wanted to drive too. I'd be sixteen in a less than a year and had never been behind the wheel one freaking time. Truly, it was ridiculous. And, in a family that put such a premium on that skill, I felt cheated and pissed off. But, how to approach the subject yet another time without being disrespectful? Timing would be everything.

Antonio started growing his hair out and allowed a beard and mustache to take up residence where his face had once been. Our family was all about appearances—everything had to be nice and neat and organized. It was odd that Daddy never said anything. It occurred to me that, perhaps, Sal Russo was allowing his eldest son some personal freedom. But, when Antonio started packing on the pounds and Daddy continued to encourage second helpings, I was confused. He'd always been so hard on Emilio for being chubby. I couldn't figure out why he'd want Antonio to be overweight, especially when he'd been spending so much time beefing up at the gym.

I supposed it could just be Antonio acting out because my big, rockin', sweet sixteen party was right around the corner and *boys* don't have sweet sixteen parties—too bad, so sad! I was sure Daddy was probably letting him do it to make some kind of point. At least Antonio was keeping up weekly manicures and scrubbing his fingertips with pineapple juice or lemon juice every night. The Russo men were completely meticulous about their appearance—especially their hands. With the constant fruit acid peels and exfoliating, it was a wonder they had any fingerprints at all. I really didn't understand that was actually the point.

Mama began planning my sweet sixteen party from the moment I arrived in DC at the ripe old age of five and the last year of planning was here—it was crunch time for Luciana Russo and *everything* would be perfect. She sat down to breakfast like every other day with her long list of important things to do. She was freaking out because *someone* needed to pick up dry cleaning and Daddy and all the boys were running in opposite directions. Show time.

Mama Luciana would go crazy making arrangements and drove all the rest of us crazy in the process. There were a couple different parties she was wound so tight for, that she lined us all up and doled out the Valium. I think the Valium would've been better saved for her. It was probably wrong to take advantage of her current state of frenzy, but I really, really wanted to learn to drive. Driving would mean freedom and road trips—sweet, reckless abandon. The end justified the means. I was adopting family business attitudes without even knowing what the family business was.

I turned on my sad and somewhat distraught look and gazed up at Mama. *Big sigh.*

"Cici, whatever is wrong with you? You look as if you've lost your best friend."

Another big sigh. "I just wish I could help you, Mama. You've worked so hard to make my party beautiful and I can't even drive to the dry cleaners for you." *Small sniffle.* "I wish I could drive so I could be a useful member of this family!" *Big sobs.*

I ran to the end of the table and threw my arms around her neck. Antonio rolled his eyes. Emilio continued to read the back of his cereal box. "When will I ever be able to drive Mama? No one has time to teach me! And I really want to help you with my party!"

Gio smiled—seeing right through me. Before Mama could reply, Daddy stood up and applauded. "That was very good Cici. You're a fine actress. Antonio, teach your sister to drive." He sat back down, "Let me know when *you* think she's ready."

Antonio's mouthed dropped open, "Wh ... " A million questions circled his brain, but he repressed the urge and opted for "Yes sir" instead. Smart kid.

I smiled brightly and ran to my father. "Thank you Daddy, you're the best dad in the whole world!"

Daddy Sal hugged me back. I think he was proud. For Sal Russo, manipulation was a skill, a technique—not remotely a problem or a personality disorder. Heaven forbid. Sure, he saw through my little act, but he also saw potential.

At first, driving lessons with Antonio consisted of him driving and talking, while insisting that I take notes. I remember fighting nausea as I did so, but refusing to complain. I was riding with my big brother and he was taking an interest in me. In return, I'd be the best student I could and after every lesson I'd say, "Thank you Antonio. I appreciate what you're doing." As Antonio got shaggier and heavier, he seemed less scary and more approachable.

He'd usually shrug it off or messed up my hair and told me I was going to owe him big time. But, on one occasion, his eyes met mine and he said, "We all do what we can for our family, Cici. Besides, this is good for me too—it's an opportunity for me to show Sal I have leadership skills, while being able to take orders and exceed expectations."

Antonio put his hands on my shoulders. "So don't screw this up kid. The Russo's are kick-ass drivers. If you suck, we'll have to give you up for adoption." He laughed at his own comment, and then smiled and nodded approvingly at me. It was the first time Antonio had ever spoken to me as if I mattered.

Driving just kept getting better and better—drifting, hydroplaning, screaming, laughing, shaking, sailing up ramps, flying through the air, landing hard, and bouncing to a stop. Antonio was the single best driver ever. He told me that Gio was all math and physics and Emilio was pure instinct, but that the best drivers had to be both.

We spent endless hours in mud holes and abandoned quarries and the back roads of Virginia's Shenandoah Valley. Places with crazy curves and places made for ramps and mudslides and awesome escape route scenarios. We had big fun. Antonio taught me how to get away and how to blend in when getting away wasn't an option. He taught me how to calculate the odds between out-running and out-maneuvering various vehicles. Antonio had a brilliant mind and he reminded Daddy Sal of himself as a young man and future business leader.

Antonio taught us all to drive. Grandpa Sam taught him. I can remember Grandpa Sam bringing us candy cigarettes and bubblegum cigars when I was quite young. I never got to know him very well. He was shot and killed in his own home. Mama and Daddy didn't like to talk about it much.

During the summer of my fifteenth year, all four of us would often go out together (my three brothers and I)—spending hours getting somewhere, to spending hours driving, to spending the end of the day driving back home. Those days, when it was just us kids out driving, remain some of most treasured memories of adolescence.

We had a garage full of cars—Mama's Jag, Daddy's Mercedes and Cadillac, a Gremlin, a Jeep, a non-descript white Chevy van, an old Ford pick-up, muscle cars that remained under drop cloths, along with the occasional "just visiting" automobile.

Both Mama and Daddy were super picky about their vehicles. So, for fun, we chose the vehicles they would most likely say yes to and were less likely to scrutinize for every small defect or minor change in general appearance when we got back.

For curve-hugging speed, we took our 1972 AMC Gremlin Voyager—easily the most deceptive and underestimated getaway car I ever drove, complete with a 304-cubic inch V-8 and a custom nitrous oxide boost. Ours had the ever classic Grem bin in the back as well—a favorite amongst gun runners and drug dealers alike. The speed, the low cost, and the fact that more than 600,000 Gremlins were built with its one body style over the years, made it a fast, expendable, and difficult-to-eye-witness-accurately vehicle. The only thing that would've made it any better would've been the following year's Levi Jeans edition—in two-tone denim blue with logos on the seats and front fender. Sal hated denim. He hated everything trendy and considered denim to be particularly undignified. Our Gremlin was brown and tan and matched a lot of the mud we slung driving it. It was a badass little car—ugly as sin, but badass nonetheless. It wasn't necessarily dignified either, but it served many other purposes for Sal Russo.

The old 4WD Jeep was another favorite choice—a 1974 Jeep Wagoneer generously equipped with a 401-cubic inch, four-barrel V-8, independent front suspension, and heavy duty springs. In her day, she was the new sheriff in town with a bulldozer body and a horn that screamed "CHARGE!" I learned to shift gears driving that urban cowboy's dream machine. I still drive an old Jeep today.

One of my all-time favorite memories of my brothers and I was when we were out driving through the Shenandoah Valley on a breezy October Saturday. We left the house early. Gio and I drove the Gremlin out, playing leapfrog westbound on I-66 with Antonio and Emilio in the Jeep. Daddy Sal would tell us that "One day, I-66 will go straight through into Washington, DC."

We all longed for a shorter trip to the valley, but years would pass before that dream would become reality.

Antonio and Emilio jumped in front of us and signaled to take the next exit. We got off the interstate, turned, and stopped at an old apple house in Front Royal, Virginia. The whole place smelled of cider and cinnamon. I used the bathroom and came back to find all three brothers playing with souvenirs and laughing at each other. What goof-heads. I remember being surprised that the staff was so tolerable. Maybe I thought laughing was against the rules, because the boys weren't doing anything wrong. They weren't stealing or vandalizing or moving merchandise around; they were shopping and laughing. If Daddy had been there, we would've quickly and quietly used the bathroom and exited the store immediately, while Daddy would make some small gratuitous purchase.

We played and shopped and left with two bottles of the best apple cider ever, a dozen freshly-baked cinnamon donuts, five scenic postcards, some homemade bread, a bag of apples, and a chunk of cheese from the refrigerator section. Emilio wanted a raccoon tail fur hat, but we talked him down on that one. Fashion wasn't Emilio's strong suit.

We switched vehicles and drivers—me driving the Jeep with Gio now riding shotgun and Emilio driving the Gremlin with Antonio in the bitch's seat. At one point, they dropped back behind us a good ways. Glancing in the rearview, I thought I saw smoke trailing out the passenger window. I started to say something to Gio, but then it was gone and I assumed it was my imagination.

Antonio was equipped with a map and a compass and we found some awesome back roads through apple orchards and past old farm houses. Then, we arrived at an abandoned rock quarry. It was huge. Antonio jumped out of the Gremlin. "I knew we'd find it!" He'd heard tales of this great mud hole and was anxious to start playing.

The Gremlin couldn't handle the rough terrain, so we parked it and piled into the Jeep Wagoneer—taking turns driving and exploring the newfound territory. We were out there for hours before we remembered the apple house snacks and stopped on the high edge of the quarry for lunch.

Emilio grabbed a blanket from the "emergency" duffle bag we kept in the back. We broke out the homemade bread and cheese and apple cider. The four of us sat and laughed and talked about cars and Daddy and Mama and how our family was crazy in general. Mama would've died had she seen us sharing cider straight from the bottle.

Then, Emilio reached in his front shirt pocket, pulled out a joint, and held it up. Holy crap, I knew I was busted. Where the hell had I left a joint just lying around? Maybe Tess had dropped one in the house somewhere. Was all of this some kind of screwed up intervention? I felt a horrible sinking feeling in my chest and was dreading the impending lecture and admonishment.

I wondered if they'd tell Daddy Sal and Mama Luciana. Oh shit. I was definitely going to get Sal-slapped over this. Daddy hated pot, pot heads, and pot dealers. I don't think he liked the word "pot" in general. It didn't matter Mama was the biggest pill-popper to grace the planet or that they both drank nightly. To them, pot was the greatest evil of all time, which was positively ridiculous. Unlike alcohol, tobacco, and narcotics—marijuana is not physically addictive. Further, it's easily one of the most predictable substances, allergic reaction is rare, and it's nearly impossible to overdose on—not to mention that it is a naturally grown herb and no one ever stays ripped long enough to even have a hangover. Plus, weed has medicinal properties unlike alcohol and tobacco. The argument was already forming in my brain. The argument that would, no doubt, be Sal-slapped short.

"What the hell Emilio?" Antonio looked at him hard. "In front of the kid? All our asses will grass." His hair was long and shabby; his mouth barely visible under beard and mustache, his belly seemed to be getting rounder every day. Wow. Was my oldest brother a pot-smoking hippie? The thought had never before crossed my mind.

Gio grabbed the joint from Emilio, "Screw that. Let's torch this baby up!" Reaching into his jeans pocket for a lighter, Gio bumped me with his shoulder. "The kid's not going to say anything." He smiled that amazing smile—dimples accentuated, eyes sparkling, and no one even thought to stop him. Best of all, I hadn't been busted.

It was always good to have Gio on my side. Sometimes, it seemed as though he got thrown in with me as we were split into two groups—"the older kids" and "the younger kids". Maybe the two groups existed before me and he was happy to have someone share the spot and take over as "baby of the family." I don't know. But I think I loved him the first time I saw him smile; I think he'd loved me way before that.

I stared blankly without speaking as Giovanni Russo lit the joint and passed it to Antonio, who passed it to Emilio, who passed it to me. I inhaled deeply (just as Tess had taught me) and handed the joint back to Gio—looking up to see all eyes on me. Smirks crossed their faces and we all cracked up realizing at once, that I had busted myself.

We smoked and talked and opened up the second bottle of cider. Antonio stood up and walked to the edge of the high quarry wall. He put his hands on his ever-widening hips—taking in the scenery of our new playground. He turned around and started to say something, but was interrupted by Emilio.

"Hey Jeremiah Johnson! You reckon you can skin a bear?"

Gio spewed a mouthful of cider, making me choke on my smoke. Emilio's mountain man accent was as funny as the Robert Redford film reference. Antonio started to scorn, but couldn't help snickering himself watching us roll back on the ground, holding our sides, trying to stop laughing and coughing, but being completely over-thrown by contagious, painfully joyous oblivion.

We divvied up the cinnamon donuts and Gio and I drove the Gremlin back to DC—well, Gio drove and I passed out. The last thing I remember him saying as he chuckled was "lightweight."

I awoke to the sound of Antonio's voice, "Gio, drop the kid off out front and meet us around back. We need to get some of this mud off before we park 'em in the garage."

The garage—a "no girls allowed" playground. A playground I was convinced was full of magic and mystery. I got it half right anyway. If only they'd recognize my potential. I was too tired to argue though.

I sleepily got out of the car and, with a groggy "Thanks, that was fun," went inside and got cleaned up for dinner.

Antonio, Emilio, Gio, and I bonded that day—we'd become an "us" versus "them" (*them* being the parents); a single team of siblings united with the help of an old rock quarry, a Jeep Wagoneer, and a big, fat joint.

We'd have many conversations debating who might win a race driving the Jeep up against the Gremlin on various terrains—especially once winter time would settle in and driving conditions were considered hazardous. All we could do was talk and plan and dream of spring. But I'd become part of "us" and just dreaming was fine by me.

I found the winter before my sixteenth birthday to be exceptionally long and boring. Both Antonio and Emilio had graduated from home school and were spending their days in the office with Sal, while Gio and I were left behind with Mrs. Hodges. Much as I hated to admit it, I was missing my oldest brothers. I knew it wouldn't be long before Gio joined them and I'd be alone with Mrs. Hodges. I wondered if I'd work with Daddy and the boys one day as well. It seemed unlikely, as the line between men's work and women's work was a solid brick wall.

Joey "The Torch" Marconi continued to hang around our house and at the office with the guys and was staying for dinner more and more often. I liked looking at him; he had a nice smile. Besides, the only other men in my life were my father, brothers, Mikey (who definitely kept a respectable distance) and Steve—the super-hot mailman with sexy green eyes, dark wavy hair, a friendly smile, and the prettiest legs I'd ever seen on a man. However, at the ripe old age of fifteen, it was hugely unlikely I'd have the opportunity to hook up with the mailman.

"Lovely to see you again Cici, is that a new dress? Your hair looks nice." It was sad Joey's compliments sounded like something smarmy Eddie Haskell from old reruns of "Leave It to Beaver" would say. Still, I crushed on Joey hard and enjoyed his gracious, albeit short and cheesy, interludes of attention. There was no getting around the fact that he simply liked Antonio better. Tess showed up less and less at the house and I guessed she had other friends who were actually allowed to go out and run the roads.

As the holidays passed and pure excruciating boredom set in, I was happy to have the distraction of my sweet sixteen party plans and endless shopping trips with Mama. I let her pick out colors and flowers and caterers; it seemed to bring her a lot of joy. We argued some over my dress, but I convinced her to buy me a fun, flirty, white halter dress designed by Halston. She reminded me that it'd be March and probably still chilly outside, but I couldn't care less—I got one glimpse of me spinning around in front of the mirror wearing it, silky material flowing as I did so and I *had* to have that dress. She bought it.

Then I *had* to have a pair of white and silver platform shoes with a clear Lucite platform. Yep, I got those too. Then I *had* to have Farrah Fawcett hair—and my nails done. It didn't matter that my party was almost two months away and I'd need my hair and nails done again before then, Mama was in shopping mode and I was along for the ride.

We hit the finest shops, large and small. Rarely (if ever) did we leave a store without buying *something*. We were treated like royalty and Luciana Russo could spend money like it was going out of style. Ten milligrams of Valium may have been cheaper, but nothing beat a good old-fashioned shopping-induced euphoria (which is not to say we didn't take Valium to come down a little from our designer-labeled high when we got back home.)

I do miss the stuff—the designer clothes, shoes that cost more than every car I've owned as an adult, the comfort, the security, the private jet, Mama's Jag, Daddy's Mercedes, the Gremlin, the Jeep, the weird way my family showed love, the money. It does hurt that it all rather went on without me. I had no idea anyone lived any differently. Oh, but reality would be harsh.

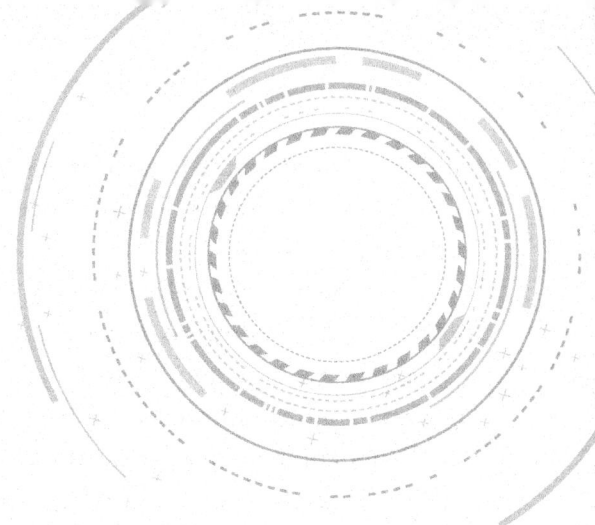

CHAPTER FIVE
Sweet Sixteen

One night over dinner, Daddy announced, "My little girl will be sixteen years old next week. Antonio, is she ready for her driver's exam?"

"Yes sir. She handles the Gremlin like a pro and she's gotten the Jeep over some tough terrain without getting stuck or rolling it—which is more than Emilio can say." Antonio smiled. "Cici has completed all of her training with these two vehicles and has done so with such skill, it's my belief she could handle either end of a run utilizing any one of our vehicles." Antonio spoke with pride and confidence.

I blushed and couldn't help but smile. I'd never heard my older brother say such nice things about me. I was proud. Antonio, Emilio and Gio were smiling as well—proud of their little sister. It felt really good. That lasted about five seconds.

I looked to my father—expecting him to be beaming with pride. The realization of Antonio's words brought Daddy Sal's hand down hard on the table. Glasses and silverware rattled. We all froze. His face was red and his eyes went to steel. "Antonio. In the library—now."

What the hell, right? Emilio, Gio, and I exchanged confused looks. Mama stared down at her plate—not saying a word.

Sal slammed the door behind them, but we could still make out every angrily bellowed word from his mouth.

"What the hell were you thinking?" We heard Sal's hand slap the back of Antonio's head. (A slap to the face is a higher pitch; this was more like the sound of thumping a cantaloupe—hard.)

"I give you the simple task of preparing your sister for her driver's license exam and you do this? She's fifteen years old—a child. Emilio!" The windows rattled. Passersby grabbed their children and scurried off. I sat paralyzed.

Emilio jumped up and joined the men in the library. Hushed growling noises replaced actual words. Another melon thump, then nothing. I strained but could hear naught. Mama continued to stare at her plate. I felt anxious and wondered if anyone would notice a missing bread stick. Maria entered with a tray of salads, looked around the table and retreated quickly.

The door to the library swung open. "Giovanni, join us." Sal's voice was even and without emotion. Gio looked at me, raised his brows, and shrugged before leaving the table. Silence blanketed the room and became suffocating. My heart pounded; the air was hot and thick. I tried to breathe deeply, but could only take in small wisps of air. I began to shake all over and felt certain that my demise was inevitable, though I had no idea why.

The door to the library opened. The four Russo men walked out and sat back down at the dining room table. "Maria!" Sal beckoned.

Maria appeared, instantly serving salads. Bread was broken and salads were picked at; not a word was spoken. Halfway through the main course, Sal cleared his throat.

"Well Luciana, I regret to inform you that a misunderstanding has occurred. Rather than prepare Cici for her driver's license exam, Antonio has taught the child to drive using the Grandpa Sam method."

Luciana pressed her lips together nodding—careful not to speak.

Sal continued, "Cici, while all your brothers seem to agree in regard to your recently acquired driving skills, you will forget what you've learned. Emilio will go over parallel parking and complete stops with you; Giovanni will be prepping you for the written exam. And you young lady, will go back to being a *young lady*. No more uncharted driving trips."

In that instant, my world collapsed. I'd finally forged a relationship with my brothers based on those "uncharted trips"; that would be no more. Driving was the one thing that connected us and it was only during our adventures that I felt like a peer and not the little sister. I choked back my tears and answered the only way anyone ever answers Sal Russo and lives to tell about it, "Yes sir." Our big, fun, back-roads driving adventures were over. I was just a stupid girl again.

I received my driver's license the following Tuesday on my actual birthday. My party was all set up for Saturday. I was allowed to drive to the beauty shop to get my hair and nails done that morning. Sweet freedom! Well, *almost* sweet freedom—Mikey rode shotgun and stayed outside of the shop keeping an eye on me. It was Saturday, March 11, 1978. Four days after my actual birthday. Funny the dates we remember.

My sixteenth birthday party was fabulous. There were bands and dancing and tons of people and even more presents—like really nice, expensive presents. Mama Luciana was fashion forward and trendy in every way except when it came to jewelry; her attitudes were those of her mother and of her mother's mother: "Diamonds go with everything." So, on my sweet sixteenth, I was gifted with bracelets and necklaces and earrings and everything sparkly in celebration of me joining the "I want jewelry for every occasion" club—a membership expected of all Russo women on their sixteenth birthday. But the best gift of all was given to me by my father—nonchalantly.

The house, much like my head, was all abuzz. Everyone was lit and I was dizzy from drugs and alcohol and an overdose of excitement. I was swirling through the back doors and laughing and feeling like the true princess I was that day when Daddy stopped me. "Cici! Happy birthday, my beautiful daughter." He hugged me warmly and pulled slightly away to smile into my face. "So tell me, Cici, have you had a happy birthday so far?"

"Oh Daddy, it's been the best ever. Thank you." I threw my arms around his neck and kissed his cheek as he bent over, before twirling around to head upstairs and roll a joint for later.

"Cici," Daddy was reaching into his pocket as I turned back around, "I almost forgot this gift."

I heard the soft jingle of metal on metal and caught the glint of silver like an eye-magnet. Daddy was smiling as he held up a large ring with two glorious GM keys dangling freely from it.

I screamed a blood-curdling scream, ran to him, grabbed the keys, jumped up and down and screamed some more. "Oh my god, thank you Daddy!" Then, I hesitated for a moment, my heart ready to beat out of my chest. "Where is it?"

Daddy laughed his big rumbling laugh and nodded towards the front door. "Make it last."

I ran out the front door. I don't remember my feet actually touching the steps; I staggered back a bit. The car took my breath away and I stared in disbelief at the incredible vehicle that was evidently mine. My mouth dropped open and my hands covered my heart.

Daddy bought me a brand new 1978 silver Corvette. Tears flooded my eyes and, when I turned around, guests were coming from inside and around back to see what all the commotion was about. Daddy didn't need to make a big show of his gift; I'd done that for him. He showed his love with gifts and his joy in doing so was reflected in a single tear tracing his face. Before I could even take the Corvette for a spin around the block, I was whisked away back to the outdoor party arena to celebrate with more champagne and more indulgent food and dancing and whirling and swirling.

Mama Luciana got up on stage and dedicated "You Are so Beautiful" to me. The cake was chocolate, the bar was open, and the band was loud. And most of this I know because I've seen the old footage. My memory gets fuzzy, but there are some things one cannot forget. No matter how hard one tries.

Mama was singing when Uncle Guido picked me up and started swinging me around the dance floor, singing along with Mama. "YOU ARE SO BEAUTIFUL TO MEEEEE!!" Everyone was laughing. I looked at his big fat greasy face and his yellow teeth and I took in his too-much-beer and cigar breath and I puked all over him.

I couldn't blame Uncle Guido entirely; I had been drinking too much for a sixteen year old. Anyway, Daddy Sal came to my rescue, smacking Guido in the back of the head, "You idiot!"

Daddy scooped me up in his arms (puke still lingering in my hair) with all the drama and flair of a good father, dropping everything to care for his sixteen year old daughter. Sal Russo enjoyed a good show, but that's all it was. After stepping inside away from the crowd, he set me down at the bottom of the stairs.

"Run along and get cleaned up. Your mother will be up to check on you shortly."

Sal cleaned himself up and put on a fresh shirt, fixing himself a drink before stepping back out. "Cici's fine. She's just had a busy day and is now resting. Please. Everyone, carry on." He made the announcement as if anyone there cared; still, he looked like a hero doing it.

The music started back up and the noise of insignificant chatter rose to party level. I took a shower and brushed my teeth. I threw on a t-shirt and a pair of underwear and crawled into bed thinking of the silver Corvette I'd be driving as soon as I sobered up. The party would go on and be considered a huge success despite the guest of honor's absence.

I don't think I'd been asleep long, before I heard the commotion downstairs. Evidently, Emilio had accidently walked in on Joey Marconi using the bathroom.

"Dude? You sit down to pee?" Emilio was laughing his ass off. Gio joined in. I staggered to the banister and caught Joey's glance. He was saying something about it being a "combo deal" and Emilio was arguing that Joey was already starting to stand up before he opened the door and that the proof was in the toilet. Guys are so freaking gross. I went back to my room and lay down.

Later, I'd put together bits and pieces of that night via snippets of overheard conversations. Evidently, Joey went back outside and told Antonio (who was preoccupied with a cute blonde) that his stupid little brothers cut his bathroom action off short and asked if it was okay to use the kids' bathroom upstairs so as not to be interrupted again. Antonio sighed.

"Do whatever the fuck you want dude. I don't care."

And so, Joey did just that. He crept into my room as I was passed out—spent from a day of Valium, champagne, singing, dancing, and excitement.

I've spent too much time over the years trying to piece the story together in my mind and make sense of it all.

When I came to, Joey Marconi was on top of me finishing up his thirty-second performance. I cried out "Get off of me!" but he was already jumping up and getting dressed. He opened the door and quickly left without a word. I felt disgusting and used and uncertain of what had happened.

I got up and showered again. Then, somehow my little girl's mind rationalized that Joey and I were boyfriend/girlfriend. Why of course, that was it. I decided we'd have to talk soon.

As the days came and went, it became clear that Joey wasn't coming around anymore, so I called him. Why not? It was completely outdated for a girl to sit around and wait on a man.

As it turns out, Joey was outdated too. He politely turned me down for coffee and informed me that he preferred to be the one doing the asking out. But, he sure didn't *ask* for sex. What a dick. It would be sometime later, in the early '80s, that I'd read an article in *Ms. Magazine* titled "Date Rape." Only then would I know what Joey "The Torch" Marconi really was—a rapist. Screw "age of consent." I was unconscious and unable to consent, refuse, or even struggle.

I'd never heard the term "date rape" prior to that article; it referred to "acquaintance rape" as well. I thought rape was something that happened in dark alleys by evil strangers to unsuspecting women. Date rape—well, that was kind terminology for what that common dog motherfucker did to me. I was raped of my virginity during my sweet sixteen party by a cowardly sissy-britches who peed sitting down. The chip on my shoulder felt like a boulder.

Summertime slinked in and I found myself sneaking off to the beach in Ocean City for the day or the movie theatre in the evening or to the mall to shop and get my nails done; Mikey always tagged along—either riding shotgun or following me in another vehicle. I loved Mikey dearly, but it was embarrassing to have a constant chaperone at my age.

The boys were busy running the family business with Daddy Sal and I kept busy figuring out ways to kill time or meet Tess somewhere on the outskirts of the city to smoke a joint. I never said anything to anyone about Joey. I accepted it for what it was—something fucked up that happened to me when I was a kid. I had a lot of things that went under that heading. It helped to compartmentalize.

Mid-summer boredom lazily staggered into fall boredom and into another year or so of the same. I began to become way curious about my father's and brothers' daily activities. So, I listened and I learned. The more I appeared to be absorbed by TV or uninterested in conversation, the more they talked with me in the room. Though, Tess had recently introduced me to snorting cocaine and my listening skills were probably foggy at best.

I heard "pizza connection" mentioned on several occasions and wondered if they were considering going into the restaurant business. I learned that it's way better to be "this guy" than "that guy." *This guy is good. This guy saved my ass. This guy knows what he's doing.* That guy, on the other hand, *that guy had it coming. That guy didn't know what hit him. That guy swims with the fishes.* I always felt sorry for "that guy," though I secretly hoped Joey Marconi would one day be that guy. *But this guy—oh, he'll be just fine.* He always is.

It didn't take long to figure out that the time to *really* listen was when one of the boys dropped their voice to a whisper. I'd sit on the couch scribbling in a notebook with headphones on, tapping my foot. If anyone looked, the cassette tape was rolling. If anyone had ever listened, they would've heard the quiet buzz of a blank tape playing.

I'd still get bored with them talking in broken sentences and playing the pronoun game. Then, one night I awoke to voices in the library—happy, laughing, celebratory voices. I opened my bedroom door a crack for a better listen. I could make out Daddy's voice and Emilio and ... yep, that was Gio and Antonio. Fuck. Definitely heard Joey Macaroni. And then, I heard an unfamiliar voice—a female voice. A female in the library with the men? And it definitely wasn't Mama. It was the middle of the night. What the fuck?

I wasn't allowed to drive with the boys. I couldn't work with them. All the rules were different for me *because* of being a girl. And now some strange girl was down there laughing and hanging out with *the men* in the library? Oh hell no. This was total bullshit to me.

I crept out into the hallway and crouched behind the staircase wall. The girl was just stepping out of the library into the foyer with Sal and the four salivating young men close behind.

Her name was Bailey and I hated her instantly. She was probably about my age—which had to have been around eighteen or nineteen at the time. She was cute enough in a Joan Jet-eat-your-fucking-blackhearts-out kind of way. To be honest, I really didn't pay that much attention to her slim five-foot, five-inch, one-hundred and five pound frame, shiny mahogany hair cut into long choppy layers, heavily lined almond-shaped green eyes, perfect little body, big boobs, round butt—completely obvious in the Levis she no doubt had to lay down on the bed to zip up that morning; right before she stole her t-shirt from the toddlers department at the Harley Davidson store. I don't think she could've fit much more than a baby comb in her back pocket or a drop of perfume in her shirt. Her black leather handbag looked like a knock-off, but it was hard to tell as she slung her black leather jacket over the same shoulder. Her boots had an expensive appearance (from a distance), but weren't a designer I recognized and I would've loved a closer look. She had a sexy kind of confidence going on but, other than that, she was just okay.

All the Russo men wore Armani—tonight they all opted for slightly different suits, all in black. Daddy had already taken his jacket and neck tie off and stood in the foyer with his sleeves rolled up and shirt unbuttoned—smiling like he'd just won the lottery. It was gross.

Antonio's black tie hung loosened around his neck and lay perfectly over his unbuttoned red silk shirt. He stood with his legs at shoulder width and hands in pants pockets—pushing his jacket out of the way for a better look. He'd gained a lot of weight, but hadn't lost a pound of arrogance. Emilio's tie was still intact and jacket even buttoned—he was doing his black on black on black look back then, but he did it well. Gio was all charm and sparkles and well, I'll say it—kind of trampy.

The first problem was that he wore his suit in a way that made women blush—my guess is that his pants were spray-painted on by Armani himself earlier that day. Next were his unbuttoned-to-his-bellybutton white, silk shirt and the way he let his jacket swing widely open. Could he be any sluttier? Oh, and we simply must talk about how he stood in the door, leaning on one forearm poised so that his fist was aligned with his square jaw—bare feet casually crossed. Dressed to sell.

When any one of them spoke, all I could here was "blah blah blah *drool drool* blah blah blah." I found it all to be a little embarrassing. Men can be the biggest whores ever.

And then there was Joey "The Torch" Marconi—blue jeans, baby blue dress shirt, white sneakers. I'd considered him to be so handsome but, at that moment, he appeared small and insignificant in the company of Sal Russo and his sons.

Sal shook Bailey's hand and thanked her again.

Bailey smiled. "My pleasure. I'd never turn my back on rhinestone cowboys, on the wrong side of town no less."

They all stood and watched her walk out the door. They all waited and listened for her to start her bike and ride off into the night. They were a group of perfect drooling idiots.

The story I pieced together over the next several weeks of eavesdropping was fairly impressive—for a girl who looked like an Irish version of Joan Jett and kicked ass like a man.

Bailey Hutchenson happened into a garage somewhere off Columbia Pike in Arlington, Virginia that night where she found the "three rhinestone cowboys standing on plastic and about to meet their maker." I never understood why the hell they were there to begin with.

The man with the "high end automatic" had his "big ass" weapon pointed at the Russo boys. Bailey went around the back and snuck up on the asshole's right—"smashing his head like a ripe melon" with a pipe wrench she'd grabbed from *that guy's* tool box. Oh, the great laughs that would be shared over Bailey taking out a man using his own tool. Gosh, who says my family doesn't know how to have a good time?

She then used the plastic to discard of the "garbage" and had him "almost rolled up and in the trunk" before the boys knew what happened.

Evidently, Bailey saved their lives that night. For that, I am eternally grateful. And, as it turns out, Sal Russo was most grateful as well.

She's still a murderer. You can't call it self-defense, and I don't think the "rhinestone cowboy" defense has been used in our court system effectively as of yet. In my family, that just wasn't a concern.

Nancy-boy, Joey Macaroni, started showing up at the house and for dinner on a more regular basis again. I fantasized about

Bailey smashing his head in like a melon too. He wanted to be the guy who asked a girl out on a date, but had no problem having sex with a passed out sixteen year old without asking at all. People have been killed for less. Speaking of which …

Bailey. Bailey. Bailey. One night over dinner I thought I would puke if I heard the name one more time. Sal, Antonio, Joey, Emilio, Gio—they all sucked. Joey must've noticed my expression of nauseating jealousy.

"You look lovely tonight Cici." Condescending asshole.

"Really? You look like the same piece of shit you've always looked like Mr. Marconi."

Sal slapped his hand down hard—rattling dinnerware and everyone there. Lips sealed shut around the table—all but mine.

"And I simply must say what a common dog motherfucker I think you are."

"Cici! Enough!" Sal was pissed. He started to get up.

"No, Daddy. Allow me." I slapped myself across the face—pre-dinner cocaine dulling the sting. "Shall I go to my room or the garage now?"

I went to my bedroom and slammed the door. I ached to scope out the garage in greater depth, but was certain now wasn't the time to push the issue—fucking he-man women haters club.

I must've sulked and paced for a good half hour—half ready for battle and the other half dreading it. Sal's knock rattled my door and my nerves simultaneously, the stuttering vibration of my voice concealing nothing.

"Yes?"

The door swung open and Sal stood for a moment before stepping in and closing it behind him.

"Cici, sit down."

We both sat on the edge of the bed—me shaking; Sal looking down thoughtfully prior to commencing. He rubbed his fist across his lower lip and breathed in deeply. Again, he looked at me and then through me.

"I know more than you can understand Cici. I have reasons for my choices and actions that are beyond your grasp." His eyes remained locked with mine. "I *know* things," he said.

"You must learn to bide your time and never let your enemy know what you're thinking or what you're *feeling*. Your anger with Joey's understandable. I share this anger, but have plans for Joey. He brings an aspect to our business that was formerly lacking. When I'm done with him, he'll be no more. But until then, let's keep it civil. Capisce?"

"Yes sir," I replied without understanding. Did Sal know *all* about Joey? Did he know what he'd done to me? And if so, how? I'd told no one.

Daddy Sal stood up, taking both my hands in his and helping me to stand. "I love you Cici. Try not to fuck this up." He squeezed my hands and kissed each cheek. Then, smiling, he turned and left. I didn't even know what I wasn't supposed to fuck up—his love, Joey's role in the family business, simply the moment? Regardless, Sal smiled and I felt better.

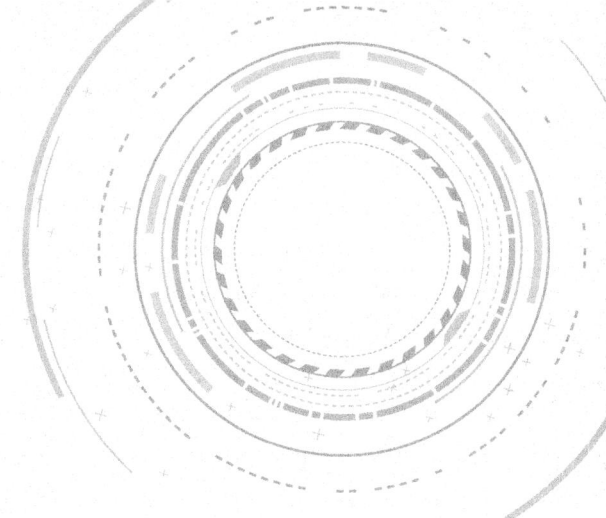

CHAPTER SIX
The Definition of Crime

The early '80s are a bit of a blur. I did a lot of cocaine back then and even had a very short affair with heroin—which I never really liked, but did with Tess out of sheer boredom. Sex and drugs and rock-n-roll—our idols glamorized promiscuous sex and drug use while we rocked out to their tunes, thinking them to be so brilliant and free and deeply spiritual and connected to real life. It's no wonder our parents' generation thought we, the baby-boomers, were leading us all straight to hell.

Hairstyles mimicked insane times and over the course of the decade, I had every length, cut, and color under the rainbow. It was fun, but I did it mostly for shock value. Seeing my parents' jaws drop open and turn pale from spikey orange hair or a rat's nest of blue brought me a certain amount of satisfaction in my late teens-early 20s.

Technology was changing as well—we were the first on our block to have hands-free car phones in every vehicle. Sal didn't mind shoveling out $800 a unit and the $300 to $500 per month phone bills that were to follow. But, when cable TV became available, he refused to pay for the right to watch his own damned television set. I went to friends' houses to see MTV and watch Showtime and HBO. MTV was *all* music videos; no commercials, bullshit interviews, boring chatter. It was easily the coolest thing ever.

Inflation was a word that continued its commonality throughout the 80's with a new home running just under $69,000 in 1980 and up to $120,000+ by 1989—making buying a new home a greater challenge as the average income only rose from $19,000 to $27,000 in the same period. Yet, the price of gas went down a few pennies—going from $1.25 per gallon in 1980 to $1.12 per gallon in 1989.

Women in the '70s burned their bras seeking equality in the workplace. Men had no desire whatsoever to take on more responsibility around the house in the '70s, '80s, '90s, or even now. So, women traded being full-time homemakers for being full-time businesswomen *and* full-time homemakers at the same time. By the '80s, two incomes became necessary to make the American Dream of homeownership a reality.

Today, women still don't make the same money their male counterparts do and our quality of life seems to be on the decline while technology is on a constant rise in pursuit of an easier way of living. *Maybe* bra-burning wasn't the answer. Bummer. It would've been cool had it worked. I remain grateful to the trail-blazing women that came before me nonetheless.

John Lennon was killed outside of his New York apartment at the beginning of the decade and, before it was over, Bart Simpson would make his debut on the Tracey Ullman Show, Michael Jackson would release the Thriller album, and we'd all go through some big hair, clothes with padded shoulders, and white stilettos. Then, when ZZ Top's "Sharp Dressed Man" video came out, we all *ran out* and bought lace-trimmed ankle socks to wear with our ever-growing wardrobe of stilettos. MTV was setting the pace for fashion.

Huey Lewis kept the heart of rock-n-roll beating while everyone was Kung Fu fighting over the shortage of Cabbage Patch Dolls in Trivial Pursuit of Teenage Mutant Ninja Turtles that were dressed for success because girls just wanted to have fun so they'd wake suddenly and be in love. Or something like that—I came into adulthood at the beginning of the decade and saw the same decade end as someone else entirely. Between all the drinking and drugs and family crap—I probably missed a lot.

Still, life lessons were being learned. I learned "organized crime" wasn't always so organized. It's about money, control, and power; it's about information and who has it. It's many things, but hardly organized. It can be more of a goat-roping than one might think.

Though there is almost a hierarchy of sorts—at least according to Sal Russo. Drug runners are pretty much bottom of the totem pole, with marijuana and hashish distributors at the very bottom of that stack—guessing one might theorize this to be because of lower profit margins and lack of physically addictive qualities versus higher profit margins and greater addiction possibilities of the powdered stuff. I don't know for sure—maybe because pot heads are less edgy and demanding than coke addicts. What I do know is that Sal had little use for a laid back/take life as it comes weed burner. But, as for edgy and demanding, those were qualities he could put to work and I think that scored a couple points for the coke heads in Sal's mind, though they were still very much below him.

Next on the heap are the gun runners—with those handling smaller weapons and fewer of them on the bottom, and those arming both sides of a war dominating.

Making up the apex of this mess are the collectors of information and sellers of secrets: the spies. Be it corporate, private, political, military, governmental, or purely personal—espionage is king and damned near necessary for drug and gun operations to run smoothly.

Daddy Sal was a middle-of-road gun runner who had the mind, money, and absolute desire to be king of all spies, owner of all information. He had a plan to dominate and control. God be with anyone who stood in the way of Sal Russo and his plan.

That's how Sal viewed all the "alphabet agencies"—the CIA, the FBI, the NSA; politics and bureaucrats—simply in his way. They were a competitive force with unlimited resources and an unfair advantage. But Sal Russo loved a good challenge and he'd take them all on before it was over. Well, not him personally—Sal Russo never got his own hands dirty.

That's why he had sons, I suppose. Girls had different value. The boys could always do the heavy lifting. The boys would learn a whole different skill set than I ever would.

One evening, Sal invited Mikey to join us for dinner in the formal dining room. Mikey was always fun and since I had turned eighteen, Mikey and I had become drinking buddies—he was going to be there no matter what, to keep a close watch on me; might as well have some fun while babysitting the boss's kid.

I could come in as late as I wanted when I was out with Daddy's trusted employee, so long as Mikey was checking in with Daddy on a regular basis. When I was with Mikey, I was safe—safe and freaking satisfied. That man had skills and talent beyond my wildest imagination— at least, at the time in my life. I was less likely to pick up a stranger when I was sleeping with Mikey. What would the point be? It was not likely that I'd be glowing afterwards like I most certainly did with Mikey. He was the reason I became so attracted to older men. He was really good to me, and really good in bed. I liked the combination immediately.

When Sal invited him to join us for dinner, I was pretty sure that was all about to end. I was eighteen years old. I attended classes at Georgetown University just so the 'rents could have me well educated *and* home every night. Gio got to go to Harvard Law. Freedom appeared to be nowhere in sight for me and I was about to lose my designated driver and most reliable lay. I was bumming before bread was broken.

"Mikey, I hate to ask you to work late," Sal looked at me with a sly grin and raised eyebrow, "but my friend has given me two tickets to see some guy named Root Boy Slim tonight." Sal laughed, "I have no time for this silliness, but don't wish to offend my friend. I was hoping you might take Cici. She's always looking for a way out." Daddy Sal smiled at me again.

"Sure thing Sal—I'd be honored to escort Miss Cici to the concert."

Sal handed Mikey a plain, white envelope. Daddy always solved problems with plain, white envelopes—whether with cash, instructions, or tickets to a concert.

I couldn't believe it. Sal obviously had no clue who Root Boy Slim and the Sex Change Band were. Root Boy who sang songs like "Boogie Till You Puke," the ever-classic "Dare to be Fat" and who could forget "Quarter Movies on My Mind?" Good stuff.

I loved hard rock and the people at the DC clubs back in the day—the harder, the better. But, when I got home, all I listened to was Electric Light Orchestra—ELO spoke to my soul. I was married to Jeff Lynne and had his children in a magical, alternate universe I like to call "my dreams."

But heading out clubbing that night with Mikey, I was in "Boogie Till You Puke" mode. I wore tight-fitting, straight-legged Armani acid wash jeans with a super sheer, low cut, white Versace blouse, white stilettos—Gucci, a white snakeskin clutch with gold accents, big gold hoop earrings, and really big pink and blonde hair with spiky platinum blonde and neon pink hair pieces. Mikey wore Levi's and some obscure band t-shirt—he *owned* that look with his high-top Converse sneakers.

DC's Cellar Door was packed. People were everywhere; there was no hope of finding even standing room on the main floor. Mikey grabbed my hand and led me up the stairs, through the crowd to the 2nd floor wrap-around balcony. What a crowd—everyone was pretty much jacked up on something and smoke of every kind filled the air.

Mikey scored a gram of cocaine and we snorted lines from my two-inch pinky nail and drank too many beers. We danced all night and laughed at ourselves and other people. We smoked random joints that were passed our way and had random conversation with random people. I adored hanging out with Mikey.

The band was insane—Root Boy pretended to snort from a huge pile of white powder on a serving tray and then faked a heart attack. He jumped up and grabbed the guitar player, turning and holding him upside down. The guy never missed a note and kept on playing. They were a party band and a big show. *Root Boy, you'll always be remembered.*

Mikey and I had fabulous-stoned-out-of-our-minds sex in the back seat of Sal's Mercedes. It rocked—both the sex and the car. I loved that man *and* his better than standard-white-boy-issue. Life was strange. If Mikey hadn't worked for Sal, I would've never met him. But, because I was Sal's daughter, he could never really date me. I was young and I thought that one day things would change. I just had no idea how much.

Mikey pulled up in front of the townhouse and escorted me to the front door. He used his key to unlock the door and pushed it open. "Good night Miss Cici. I had a wonderful time."

"Me too. Good night Michael."

I stepped inside, smiled, and closed the door. That man made my heart melt. I staggered up the stairs and fell flat on my face across my bed, sleeping on top of the covers crosswise. I dreamt of being married to Mikey and dancing with our children to ELO music.

I woke suddenly and looked around my room. No Mikey. No dancing children—which was a good thing because my head was killing me and I don't think I could've handled having kids. I felt dehydrated and made my way down to the kitchen and opened the fridge. A pitcher of ice cold water—perfect. I found a glass, filled it, and drank it down—barely swallowing, before filling a second and sitting down at the table. The smell of chlorine was overwhelming. Mama liked things smelling clean, but this was ridiculous. I put my head down and had nearly drifted back off to sleep when the kitchen door to the garage burst open.

Antonio had already grabbed two beers out of the fridge and was turning around before noticing me. He wore boxer shorts and a wife-beater with the smell of chlorine all over him like an overworked pool boy. His hair was cut short; his face shaved. He looked more like the old Antonio, except he was still fat.

"Hey Tony! Grab me one too. You guys got any chips?" Joey Marconi stopped short at the top of the steps. "Hey man, what's going on?"

Antonio looked at me and shook his head. I'm sure I was quite the sight—smeared lipstick, mascara under my eyes, rat's nest hair, bedraggled clothes.

"Nothing man. Chips are in the pantry. Cici, go the fuck to bed. You look like shit."

"Fuck you, Antonio," I muttered before zigzagging back upstairs and peacefully passing out.

I woke up thinking about Joey and Antonio in the kitchen the night before. It must've been close to daylight. My guess was that they were out a lot later than me and probably trashed one of the vehicles or puked or something and had to clean it up before Sal found out. Dumb asses. The thought of chlorine having blood-removal and evidence-destroying properties never crossed my mind.

I'm not sure what it is about kids liking to get their siblings in trouble, but I was no exception. As I said, the only wrongdoing I thought they were guilty of was breaking curfew and puking in one of the vehicles.

"So, Antonio—what were you and Joey doing up so late last night? Catching up on some laundry or just destroying the evidence?" I asked casually over dinner, alluding to the overwhelming scent of chlorine I'd experienced. I just wanted to see him squirm and knew both Mama and Daddy's ears would perk up.

Antonio gave me a dirty look and started to say something before Sal jumped in. "Cici, find something more pleasant to discuss over dinner. How was your concert?" Antonio smirked.

"It was big fun Daddy. Thank you so much for the tickets," I answered, smirking back at Antonio and somewhat disappointed neither Daddy or Mama took the bait.

Sadly, the exchange left me more curious than before. Why would Daddy Sal cover for Antonio? Why don't the boys have to answer for their actions? I swear they could get away with murder.

If I could go back in time, I wouldn't be so nosey; I'd mind my own business and not worry so much about others. I've learned the hard way that just because you *can* hear someone, doesn't mean you have the right to eavesdrop. I go out of my way trying not to overhear anything anymore. I ignore grocery store conversation and other people in general. If my neighbors are out back socializing, I turn on some tunes so as not to even accidentally hear something. And honestly—it's not that hard. I have a low tolerance for boredom and find conversations that I'm not a part of to be grossly unentertaining. But, that's not who I *was*. Back in the day, everyone else's life seemed more interesting than mine.

I was nosey and I simply had to know what was going on in our family home. The secrecy was excruciating. So, when Mikey and I went to the mall, I picked up a tape recorder—saying my Walkman burned through too many batteries and I wanted a backup for music. It came with a separate microphone and extra-long cord—perfect for my uses.

The definition of crime is: desire, ability, and opportunity. I was just waiting for the right time—I had everything else covered. I was more of a Russo than even my parents had imagined.

Vladimir Petrov arrived one evening as he often did—escorted by three other men. Two that came in with him and one that stayed outside by his car. While I found Vladimir to be big and scary, I also found myself to be intrigued. Perhaps it was his accent that gave him an air of mystery or his imposing size, shifty eyes, and loathsome smile; regardless, he was an enigma and I wanted to know more. I wish I could go back and *un*know what I know now.

Daddy and Vladimir and one of Vladimir's two inside guys stepped into the library—leaving the second inside guy posted outside the library doors. There'd be no way for me to slide the microphone under the door and hide the tape recorder in the closet as I'd planned.

I was just about to give up when I heard voices trailing up to my window. I peeked out and saw no one on the back deck. They must have opened the French doors from the library. I cracked my window and could hear Sal and Vladimir more clearly. Slowly, I lowered the microphone out of my window and down the side of the house until the cord was as far as it could reach, sitting the recorder on the window sill. I made sure the volume was all the way down and pressed record; the tape was rolling.

I'd have to find a way to get out of the house alone tomorrow, where I could listen to my findings without the chance of getting caught. I imagined I'd do it after Advanced Anatomy at G.U. in the morning and before I hooked up with friends to study Recreational Pharmacology in the afternoon.

Voices got slightly louder and I took another peek outside—the men had stepped out for a cigar. Awesome—this should be really loud and clear. I resisted the urge to turn the volume up to eavesdrop. Instead, I laid back in my canopy bed in the dark—the sound of tape running through a recorder with muffled voices below and me imagining listening to the tape the next day through headphones alone in a quiet, little park just off campus, finally learning what all the secrecy was about, or at least some of it. I felt a sense of relief knowing I might finally get some answers.

"WHAT THE FUCK IS THIS?" Vladimir's angry voice echoed through the walls. My trusty tape recorder slammed against the window frame and struggled before falling and being claimed by large Russian hands below—its power cord now hanging lonely from the outlet.

Angry muffled words traveled the floor below me, coming closer; hefty steps made haste up the staircase. My door swung open hard—the knob embedding itself in the drywall. I lay frozen—lungs only breathing in, pressure sitting fat on my chest—unable to move, yet unable to stop shaking.

He grabbed my arm, "Cici Russo, you've gone too far this time." Daddy dragged me down the stairs and into the dining room, where he kicked a chair away from the table, sat down, threw me over his lap and proceeded to beat my ass. I was almost twenty-one years old and nearing college graduation and still he spanked me like an insolent child.

Sal growled Italian with every slap. I was grateful I had refused to learn the language in my youth. I cried and begged him to stop; when I squirmed, he wedged my arms beneath me and clutched a handful of my hair—I could hear strands breaking and felt certain he'd be taking some of my scalp with him. He beat me with a vengeance.

Though my ass and thighs throbbed and I could feel my skin tightening with every rising welt, Sal didn't stop till he had completely exhausted himself. Bruised and battered, I stumbled backwards, tears streaking my face. I pushed my hair back and straightened my night gown. "I *hate* you!"

Sal didn't blink. "To tell you the truth, Cici, I'm not that thrilled with *you* right now either."

I turned feeling hurt and attacked and humiliated and ashamed, but knowing the worst was over. I nearly threw up when I saw Vladimir Petrov in the doorway, his three heavily-armed henchmen behind him—all watching and smiling.

Fucking freaks.

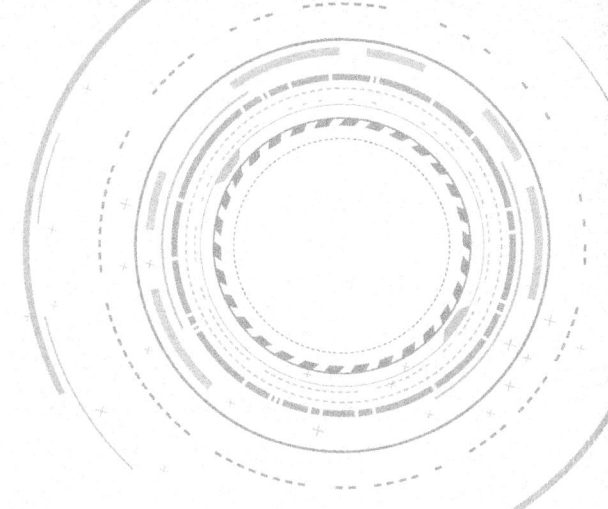

CHAPTER SEVEN
A Cowboy's Way

I blew past the Russians and marched up the stairs into my room—slamming the door behind me. I collapsed and cried until I had no tears left—only dry, raspy sobs, and a stopped-up nose. I got bored, feeling sorry for myself and then I got angry. I locked my door, rolled up a joint, exhaled smoke out of the window and vowed to do everything in my power to get the hell away from my fucked up family as soon as was humanly possible.

I gave up *almost* all of my pill-popping ways (sleep aids were still a pretty regular companion) and I tried to work on my problem-solving skills. Booting up hard drugs with Tess to fight boredom quickly became a part of my past. I took a break from clubbing as well and focused on finishing up my degree and applying to medical schools on the West Coast in the fall. Because I wasn't clubbing, I wasn't drinking so much either or picking up strangers—although I did still fire up a joint or take a roll in the hay with Mikey every now and again.

Giovanni was off to law school and had the glorious experience of avoiding family shit altogether. He came home every so often to visit and often Bailey Hutchenson would show up for dinner on these occasions. So, even when Gio was there, I had to share him with *her*. I supposed that had I killed a man in cold blood to protect the Russo boys, I'd be treated like a member of the family too. Both Antonio and Emilio speculated about a potential marriage. Seriously? Bailey wasn't Catholic or Italian. I just didn't see that happening. It was like they didn't know Luciana Russo at all.

Antonio became the son Sal Russo had groomed him to be—a younger version of Sal himself. Antonio lost his extra weight almost as fast as he'd gained it. He was, once again, a tall, fit, clean-cut, well-dressed businessman. When I think of Antonio now, it's the hippy in sloppy clothes, 4-wheeling and smoking weed that I miss. I thought it must've just been a magical phase he was going through. Years would pass before it would occur to me the many reasons one might wish to change their looks drastically—*other* than vanity reasons, that is.

Emilio became the carpenter in the family. He did some of the most creative and amazing drywall work ever in the history of drywall. So mesmerizing was his work, no one ever wondered what was behind it.

Emilio and I ended up spending more time together than we had in the past; he turned out to be a really nice guy. Sal would barely talk to me and Mama Luciana talked too much about things that didn't matter. Antonio gave up on polite English entirely and spoke primarily "asshole" and "smart ass" with an occasional blurt of "Italian thug." Emilio and I connected. We were twenty-one and twenty-three, still living at home and sneaking off to take bong hits in "the woods"—a narrow strip of trees and a beaten down path behind our house.

Nearly all of our generation moved out the millisecond they turned eighteen. Not us. We were Russo's. We'd move out when and where we were told to. "Sal's plan," remember? There was really very damned little any of it had to do with what any of us thought, felt, or dreamed about. There was no room for thoughts, feelings, and dreams in Sal's world—unless they were his, of course; only those had value.

Joey "The Torch" Marconi continued to work with Sal and Antonio, and spent much of his downtime with a local six-foot-tall, red-headed prostitute named Cinnamon who wore size 13 shoes and colorful scarves to cover her Adam's apple. Daddy smacked him hard on the back of his head when he asked if she could have Thanksgiving dinner with us one year.

I attended classes much more regularly at the university and often had lunch alone settling on one of the many park benches edging the walking trails that ran parallel with George Washington Memorial Parkway. Despite the cars and random joggers, it was a quiet place to retreat away from the world and into my thoughts.

I'd stare out over the Potomac and find myself thinking more and more of the McPhersons. Whatever became of them? Were they still alive? Did they ever look for me? Had they moved on with their lives and completely given up on seeing me again? I could have brothers and sisters out there that I've never met; maybe a few cousins even.

I had Clare McPherson's nose and pouty lips—at least in my memory of her when I was a child. I wanted to know what else I had and where it came from. It pissed me off that there was some fucked up rule that said I couldn't know the truth. I was finishing up a nursing degree and applying to med school. Damn, could I not just know for the simple sake of genetics and the pure science of it all? I wasn't asking for opinions or excuses, just facts about me and my biology.

Back in the day, we were charged for each and every directory assistance call. And, with each call, the operator could only give you two telephone numbers at a time. Too many 411 calls on the phone bill would've raised too many red flags. So, I searched New Jersey sporadically for listings under Finn and/or Clare McPherson. I made a few calls and never remotely found anyone close to what their ages and race should've been (I guessed those would be two things pretty tough to change). I checked random phone books and tried The Census Bureau and The Department of Vital Statistics—nothing from anyone, anywhere.

I even searched the faces of passersby—rationalizing that, over time and hundreds of analyzed features, it wouldn't be that much of a stretch that just *one* of those times I'd spot my pirate parents once again. I'd imagined what they would look like having aged—I tried to add gray hair and draw wrinkles on the pictures in my mind.

I lacked gratitude for what I had and focused on all that I'd missed in life. I gave no consideration to the fact that I lived in a beautiful home with people that, despite their issues, wanted to protect and care for me. I had an entire dressing room full of expensive clothes and designer bags and outrageous shoes. My nails were always polished; my hair was always fun and trendy. I drove a silver Corvette complete with antenna, phone, and free gas, repair and maintenance, was getting a pricey education, and wanted for no medical or dental care. Looking back, I think I could've had a little more gratitude and a little less attitude. But, I didn't.

I was ready for a break from school and welcomed Tess's call out of the blue one day after final exams. I agreed to go out with her the next night. We smoked weed and drank malt duck and wound up at Tracks—a gay bar on the rough side of town with two huge dance floors, multiple attractions, and outside activities. We danced for hours and then drove to the Denny's in Fairfax,

VA for breakfast. We ate bacon and eggs with toast, drank a couple cups of coffee and thought it was the single best meal ever. There's no better nightcap than Denny's on a drinkin' night.

Stepping outside in the parking lot that night in the wee hours of the morning, Tess spotted a group of people hanging out by what must've been an employee smoking area—ashtrays and ash covering a weather-beaten picnic table. "Let's go see what they're doing!" She was off and scooting across the lot before I could respond.

From a distance, it looked like a cowboy, a hooker and an astronaut. Up close—not that different, except the astronaut was just a waiter with David Bowie hair and make-up, silver boots, and accessories. The lanky waiter snuffed out his cigarette and reluctantly headed back to the land of unimpressive food, cheap people, and one dollar tips before introductions would be necessary.

The cowboy started the ball rolling. "Hi, I'm Dickie Bradford." He was cute with shaggy brown hair, blue eyes, and wire-framed glasses peeking out from under his worn cowboy hat. His mustache was scraggly and his hands looked rough—like a working man's hands. His stocky, muscular frame was clad in Levi jeans, a denim shirt, brown leather fringed vest, and old, scuffed cowboy boots. I guessed him to be five or seven years older than me.

The tall, skinny hooker put her arms around his neck. "But those of us who know him best call him *Big* Dickie." She kissed his cheek, cackled, and proceeded to apply more bright red lipstick. "I'm Topanga."

She had an olive complexion with badly-bleached blonde hair and wore a white vinyl mini skirt with a bright orange sequined tube top, red, yellow, and orange hoop earrings, and orange stilettos at the end of her skinny bird legs.

I smiled and said, "Hi."

"This is my friend Cici," Tess linked her arm with mine. "And I'm Tess."

Cowboy Dickie Bradford took my free hand. "It's a pleasure to meet you." He shook my hand and smiled—locking his eyes with mine just a couple seconds too long.

"So," I awkwardly pulled away, "what are y'all up to tonight?" *Y'all? Did I really just say "y'all?" One step out of the big city and into Northern Virginia and suddenly I think I'm in the Deep South. Luciana's horrible French accent would've been more palatable.*

"Big Dickie and I were just getting ready to smoke this joint," Topanga held up a Cheech-n-Chong sized joint to her massive red lips and leaned to Dickie for a light. I'd been drinking and smoking quite a bit that night and couldn't get over how much she looked like a cartoon character. I kind of wanted her to bump her head to see if multi-colored stars or blue birds would circle her blonde, frizzy brain.

We all laughed while we smoked that joint the size of my forearm. Topanga played the same cassette tape over and over again on her boom box—flipping from side A to B and back again. There are probably three times in my entire life that I felt like I really smoked too much pot. To this day, I can't remember what tape we were listening to that night.

I could tell Big Dickie was totally into me. I told him "I'll be on the West Coast before you can ring my phone," when he asked for my number, although *the thought* of bringing him home for dinner was entertaining. Imagine all the Russo's seated for dinner, dressed in Armani and having polite conversation, when Big Dickie walks up, kicks dirt off his boots and says, "I'm here for Cici." I imagined my parents going completely gray and aging in that instant.

Dickie seemed like a nice enough guy; my family would've chewed him up, spit him out, and named an appetizer after him before he could cross the threshold. Besides, I'd be off to California soon—Dr. Cici Russo. I loved the way it sounded and saw no reason to start something that would no doubt end the way long distance relationships so often do. Plus, I still had some pretty serious plans to marry ELO's Jeff Lynne one day. Still, I took the matchbook he handed me with his number on it. *Too bad. He probably would've been fun.*

I continued to spend time on campus even after finals were over. I liked a lot of the staff and the library was always open. It was a place to kill time. If the weather was nice, I'd head out to the Parkway—I'd keep finding new and different places to watch the Potomac from and dream of my life far, far away from my crazy family, where I would embrace "normal" life and live happily ever after. Dreaming was free after all.

I headed farther north up George Washington Memorial Parkway than I normally did one summer day and found a random park bench on the Maryland end of the great Potomac walking trail. I stared out over the dark water and fantasized about med school, my new apartment, my new life. I was in the middle of mentally decorating my new apartment when I heard someone say my name.

"Cici. Cici Russo? You're still here!" He was familiar, but I couldn't place where I knew him from. My head was in California and my heart wasn't up for grabs.

He smiled. "Dickie Bradford. I met you a couple weeks ago?"

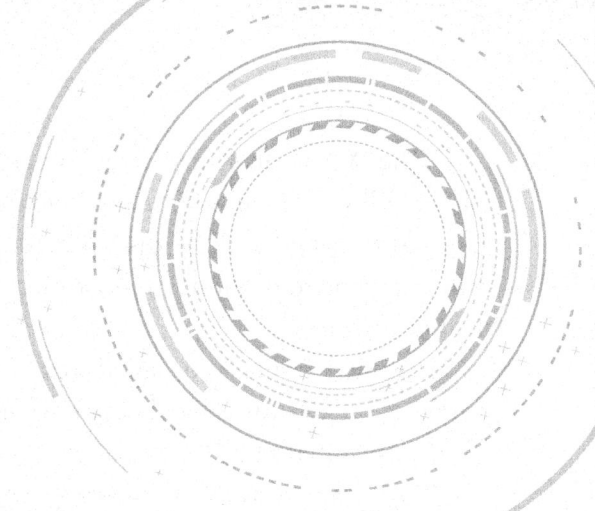

CHAPTER EIGHT
Best Date Ever

It was like that surreal feeling you get when you see your favorite hairdresser outside of their shop, like at Studio 50, and it takes your brain a couple seconds to compute. It was like that, except this wasn't Roxanne from the Clip Joint; this was a cute guy, sweat pants, t-shirt, ball cap, jogging up to me, covered in sweat, every muscle in his body completely pumped and totally hot.

"Oh, but of course. How are you?" *Oh but of course? Yep. I said it. What was it about this guy that rattled me?* Dickie was cleaner cut than I remembered and without the cowboy hat and cartoon hooker by his side, I almost didn't recognize him at all.

"I'm good. Hey, I never do this," he lied, "but do you want to have dinner later?" I hesitated. "There's a great seafood place I know in Alexandria. I can pick you up at 8."

I thought about it for a second. I hadn't been out on an actual dinner date in forever. What the hell. "Sure, but I'll meet you there. 8:30?"

"The Wharf on King Street," Dickie was starting to jog in place, "I'll see you at 8:30 *sharp*." He smiled and jogged away. I enjoyed the view until he disappeared down a wooded path. It was just going to be dinner. It wasn't like I was starting something I couldn't finish.

I headed home and called Tess. "Can you cover for me tonight?" Geez, it was like being a teenager all over again.

"Sure. What's up?"

"I have a date with that cowboy we met."

"No way."

"Yep and I want to have the flexibility to stay out all night if I feel like it. I'm telling Sal I'm going out to celebrate graduation with you and will probably spend the night at your house so I won't wake anyone up here if I'm out late. What do you think?" I asked hoping it sounded believable.

"Sal's never going to buy that you staying out all night has anything to do with you being *considerate about their sleep*. Skip that part and you'll probably be okay." I knew Tess would be the person to ask.

I thought about going with purple hair, but opted for strawberry blonde—maybe a shade or two lighter than my own copper-colored hair. I still wanted to look *fun*, so I did big, loose, tumbling curls—a carefree look that only took another two and a half hours to complete.

I wore clothes I'd bought on a shopping trip with Tess at Springfield Mall (my effort to appear more middle-class): a snug-fitting, cropped, emerald green, cotton/spandex camisole (that made my boobs look fabulous) with a black, loosely woven mesh, off-the-shoulder tank layered over it. The skintight black jeans were my one designer piece (Calvin Klein) and were adorned with multiple chains floating around my waist. I finished with black strappy sandals, too many bangles on both wrists and three-inch, and green metallic fishbone earrings.

Dickie was waiting for me in front of The Wharf. He wore stone-washed black jeans (we considered black jeans to be dress attire in the 80s), a pressed, white dress shirt, black leather vest, and black boots. Dickie kissed my cheek and opened the door for me. We drank wine and shared his lobster and my crab cakes—both were amazing. We split a piece of Key Lime pie and he told me about his family and growing up on the Eastern Shore of Maryland—it all sounded so normal and wholesome.

Dickie said he was a carpenter and worked on government contracts … blah, blah, blah … something about a Davis-Bacon act … more wine … blah, blah, blah … decent money … more wine … I don't know. I was completely lost in the way his eyes seemed to light up when he spoke to me. He was charming and funny and charismatic and his eyes never wandered from me *at all*. Oh, he definitely wanted me. I can have that effect sometimes.

We stepped out onto King Street after the rest of the wine and pie were gone and the bill was paid. I smiled at Dickie and wondered where I had parked my car. I definitely wasn't ready for the night to end, but I couldn't exactly invite him back to my place.

"It's a beautiful night. Want to go for a walk?" I hoped he hadn't been reading my mind the whole time. He was so cute and I was so buzzed, it sounded like a good idea. "Aww, c'mon," he pleaded, "Maybe I'll steal a kiss when we get down by the water."

I laughed and he grabbed my hand and off we walked hand-in-hand. I thought it was really sweet. I listened to him talk; he stepped up on the sitting edge of one of the raised gardens and offered me a hand up. I took his hand and we continued to hold hands and talk and play balance beam on the brick ledge—only stepping down to get around people who were actually *sitting* on the *sitting* edge; immediately jumping back up when we got around the less ambulatory.

We got down to the water, Dickie spun me around. "Let's go have a drink. I'll drive. I know just the place." We headed towards his car—a blue 1975 TR7 with a tan leather interior. It suited him.

We wound up at an Irish pub not too far from the restaurant, "Ireland's Own." Dickie seemed to know a lot of the people and a lot of Irish tunes; nearly everyone there was joining in singing the raunchy and borderline offensive lyrics. It was fun.

Afterwards we went back to Dickie's car—he opened the door and I got in without hesitation or question. He drove; I rode. It was comfortable and easy. I had no idea where we were going and couldn't have cared less.

We wound up in College Park, Maryland—not far from the University of Maryland. "One of my old watering holes is just around the corner. Indulge me one beer and one game of pool?"

"Sure, but I don't play pool. I don't mind watching and drinking though."

"Seriously? You don't play pool?"

"Nope. I don't play games I can't win."

"What about playing for fun?"

"Do you think it's fun to lose?"

"Depends on the stakes—but sure, I've had fun losing a game. It's just not very often that I do lose." Dickie smiled.

He pulled up to a pale green brick and stucco building; we entered on the right, which proved to be the bar side; the opposite side served as a liquor store.

All the pool tables were occupied except for the 2nd one to the end; the table at the end entertained a couple of big, biker-looking guys. I thought Dickie was headed for the empty table, but he kept going. He pulled a dollar out of his wallet and laid it on the table, "You boys up for some competition?" They stopped playing and stared angrily. "I just figured if I was going to lose a game of pool in front of my girlfriend, I might as well lose to the biggest bad asses here."

Holy crap, he's going to get us killed, I thought, but the two burly men laughed. Dickie ordered two beers and ushered me to the table against the wall, closest to the exit while Bruiser racked the balls and Bubba stood back to watch. (Yeah, I don't know their real names).

Dickie was really good and one game quickly turned into two then three games; he was taking turns kicking Bubba and Bruiser's asses and he was being a perfect, arrogant piss as he did it.

"Damn, I didn't even think *I* could make that shot." "When you're good the balls just roll your way." The men were more than obviously irritated and I was wishing Dickie would go grab himself a tall glass of shut the fuck up.

"Ha!" Dickie nailed the shot and won again. "Bubba, you up for another ass-whopping?"

Bruiser steeped in, "I'm going to kick your ass, you fucking weasel." He grabbed Dickie by the collar and slammed him up against the wall.

Dickie laughed. "Well, on the upside it shouldn't take you too long." It was a weird laugh, not nervous and not funny—just odd. I'll never forget it.

Bruiser hesitated and then started laughing so hard, he had to let go of Dickie; Bubba joined in. I smiled as best I could. "One more game," Bruiser announced. He turned to rack the balls. Dickie signaled the waitress for two more beers.

He careened over and smiled brightly. To anyone watching, it would've looked like a man flirting, but his words and tone were dead serious, "I'm going to get us out of here alive." Dickie kissed my cheek and leaned in closer, still smiling. "Sit tight for one minute and be ready to grab your gear and go when I tell you."

"Sure Big Dickie," I said sarcastically, smiling. "This is an *awesome* date." Then, he kissed me—his lips barely brushing mine. And for that split second, nothing else mattered.

Dickie went back to the table, cue stick in his left hand, the feel of his lips still lingering on mine—Bubba and Bruiser at one and two o'clock respectively. Dickie considered the table; it was his break. He reached around his back and pulled a Model 1911 .45 automatic pistol from his waistband. He shot Bubba then Bruiser square in the forehead, put his gun back, and then took his shot on the table with one hand—forcefully breaking the balls at the other end, "Hell yes!"

He seemed happy with his shot or *shots* as the case might be. Dickie nodded to me, I grabbed my bag and stood up; he stepped over Bruiser's body, put his cue stick back on the wall and was taking my hand and leading me out the back door while the entire place stood frozen. It all happened in like less than ten seconds.

Dickie opened the door to his TR7 and pushed me inside. I was numb; I couldn't speak or think or move or react. We drove in silence. I don't know what direction we went or how long we were driving. I just kept seeing Bubba and Bruiser's bodies on the floor with huge halos of blood encircling their heads.

"What just happened?" Shaking all over, I could barely whisper the question. Sirens screamed somewhere in the distance.

"I cleaned up a mess. Ever been to Florida?"

"Disney World when I was eight. Mess? Holy shit Dickie, it looked like you *made* a bigger mess than you cleaned up. You just murdered two men!" The words sounded foreign coming out of my mouth.

"I was just doing my job, Cici," Dickie said matter-of-factly.

"Oh, so you're a murderer for a living? That makes all the fucking difference."

Dickie explained that the rules are different for different people—if you kill someone intentionally, it's murder (which is what I thought I saw). If it's an accident, it's accidental death. In times of war, it's a casualty. But, if you're employed as a professional assassin by your government—well then, it's just called doing your job. All of life has different rules for different people. If you don't like your particular set of rules, change who you are.

Dickie Bradford wasn't who I thought he was. He wasn't a carpenter or a cowboy. I thought about meeting him in the parking lot outside of Denny's and how he was wearing a vest then too. I wondered if he had his .45 with him then. My mind wandered back to seeing him jogging on the parkway and how normal and healthy he'd appeared.

"Cici Russo. You said 'Cici Russo.'" It hit me suddenly.

"What are you talking about?" Dickie continued to drive like a bat out of hell.

"When you bumped into me the other day, you said 'Cici Russo.' I never told you my last name."

"Yeah, you did."

"No, I didn't. Tess and I never give out our real last names. If anything, we lie and say we're the Rockwell sisters. I never said 'Russo.' Oh my God—are you going to kill me too? Really, I'm off to California ... I'll be in medical school ... I won't even remember any of this I swear! I don't want to die," I sobbed. "Please. Just drop me off and I'll make my way home. Please, please don't kill me."

Dickie pulled over and parked next to a four-foot chain link fence. "I'm not going to kill you. I'm going to get us out of here till things cool off. Sorry if that episode back there freaked you out. Those two guys have been on my 'to do' list for months; they're fucking sociopaths. I had a clear shot and a quick exit opportunity. I'll explain everything later. Think you can climb a fence in those shoes?"

"Sure." I nodded, my head reeling and my heart pounding.

Dickie bounced out of the car and opened my door. He was on top of the fence and hopping over in two steps. I handed him my bag and was about halfway up when he grabbed me by the waist; I put my hands on his shoulders, stepped up on the top bar and jumped—his brawn both steadying and softening the impact. He'd definitely done this before.

We stomped our way over tall grass and through a wooded area—hand-in-hand, to a clearing where a very small plane awaited us on a very short runway. We boarded the plane and Dickie secured the hatch. "All set!" he yelled towards the cockpit.

So, Dickie Bradford was a CIA agent. He'd received a note with our dinner bill alerting him to the fact that his targets might be out and on the prowl that night. He'd walked me down by the water, where he never kissed me—trying to figure out a way to make the night last longer and, well, kill two birds with one stone so to speak. He knew he could either take me home and head out to Maryland alone, or he could have a beer and take me with him.

"Yay for me," I said flatly.

"I really didn't think it would bother you so much."

"Based on what?"

Dickie looked up from his note pad, "Who you are; who your dad is. What your family does for a living. Who their close business associates are." His eyes locked onto mine as he raised his right brow with the stare of a man calling my bluff.

"What the fuck is that supposed to mean?"

Dickie laughed, "You're Cici Russo: mafia princess and daughter to Sal Russo, himself. I think we should both stop pretending. We've got about an hour till we land. I need to debrief you and finish up this report."

"I need a drink."

"Soon enough princess; soon enough." Dickie kept writing as he spoke. "Tell me about your dad's business."

I was on a plane with a CIA assassin whose debriefing seemed to be a bit more of an interrogation. The truth was I knew damned little about Sal's business and his business associates. Dickie raised an eyebrow when I mentioned Uncle Guido and scribbled something down.

"What can you tell me about Vladimir Petrov?" Dickie inquired.

"He's an asshole." That was pretty much all I knew there. I didn't share with Dickie the humbling experience I'd had, which Vladimir had witnessed. Overall, Agent Bradford appeared disappointed that I wasn't involved with what he continually referred to as "the family business." I didn't care; I felt damned disappointed in him too.

I started to think about Sal Russo's reaction to all of this *if* he were ever to find out. The thought made my head hurt. I reclined my seat and closed my eyes. Dickie kept talking and asking questions. He said something about me being a confidential informant. My last words before fading into sleep were, "Piss off; I'm done with you." Sure, he could've taken me out in my sleep. I found the thought comforting; *then* I wouldn't have to worry so much about Sal.

I slept well until the plane landed. Dickie grabbed my hand and helped me up. I thought all the hand-holding crap was sweet at first, but it started to feel more like confinement rather than endearment. I tried to pull away; he held on tighter—like hand-cuffs without the trouble of a key and less obvious than shiny metal but constricting nonetheless.

A car was waiting off the tiny airstrip. Palm trees, warm breeze, people in socks with sandals—it looked like Florida to me. The driver handed Dickie a manila envelope and dropped us off at a car rental lot. Dickie walked past a ton of decent cars and stopped in front of a blue, four-door Camry. I'm looking over an ocean of Mustangs and SUVs and he's getting a key from the envelope for a Toyota. James Bond he was not. He opened the door. I looked at him with utter contempt and got in. Completely unaffected, he closed the door and got in on the driver's side.

We drove to a beachfront hotel; we had adjoining rooms. Dickie used one of the passkeys from the manila envelope to unlock the first room, "This is you." And he pushed me inside. He stepped in behind me, secured the latch, and pushed the desk in front of the door. He then went through the door to the adjoining room and plopped down on the bed.

I scoped out the room, found some great-smelling bath products, and decided to soak in a hot tub before going to bed. Big Dickie didn't look like he was going anywhere; I started running water and heard him on the phone—no doubt making some important *spy* plans. I didn't care; I was tired. I took my clothes off and slinked slowly into the hot water.

I opened my eyes dreamily and jumped, "What the fuck?!" Dickie was standing over me, shirtless with jeans still on, belt loosened. I wasn't up for anymore of his crap, "Just like a man to think every time a woman takes a bath it somehow translates into an invitation for sex. Not only no, but hell no." I relaxed back into the water, pretty satisfied with my preemptive blow-off.

"I just wanted to let you know I ordered pizza; it should be here in thirty minutes—hope you like mushrooms." He started to leave and then turned around smiling. "Dinner and a show—damn girl, you're just a barrel of fun." He walked off, laughing to himself and shaking his head. His mama knew what she was doing when she named him—what a total *dick*. If only he'd been half as funny as he thought he was, I may have been more entertained.

I guessed twenty minutes or so had already passed, so I grabbed a towel to dry off and drained the tub. Dickie's back was turned and he was on the phone again. I hated the idea of putting on the same clothes I'd been wearing for hours, so I jumped under the covers and threw the towel over a chair. The sheets felt really nice—800, maybe 1000 thread-count. I was impressed. Not bad for an assassin.

The pizza arrived and Dickie paid the kid, "Pizza's here!" He grabbed himself a slice and stretched back out on his bed.

"Do you mind bringing me a slice? I'm undressed."

"Sounds like a personal problem, princess."

I wadded up the sheet and wrapped it around me. "You suck." I got a piece of pizza and returned to my bed. "DICK!"

I ate the pizza and washed it down with a cup of tap water. I used the complimentary toothbrush and toothpaste and happily swallowed a sleeping pill with another swig of yummy Florida tap water. I turned off the lights and curled up to go to sleep.

"Good night John-boy!" Dickie called from the next room.

"I hate you," was all I could mumble before drifting pleasantly into a drug-induced slumber.

"Hey!" I woke to Dickie kicking my bed. "Are you going to sleep the day away? Get up—I got you some breakfast."

Coffee, eggs, toast, French toast, waffles, pancakes, bacon, sausage, sausage gravy and biscuits, cereal, orange juice, apple juice, and mixed fruit—the table was completely covered. "Holy shit, who eats this much breakfast?"

"You're welcome princess." Dickie poured a cup of coffee, "Cream? Sugar? Not that you're not sweet enough all on your own." He was wearing khaki shorts, sneakers, and a brightly colored tropical shirt. His hair was cut high and tight; his mustache gone.

"Cream." Dickie looked really different without his 'stache and I was just waking up and getting used to the new look.

"My pleasure." Dickie motioned to a couple bags on the dresser, as he handed me coffee. "Your clothes are washed and there's some other stuff there that's more Florida-friendly. I have errands to run. You'll be best off to stay around the hotel—there's a lounge, a weight room, and a swimming pool." He tossed a passkey on the bed beside me, "Anything you need, put it on the bill. I should be back before dinner."

I'll be long gone before dinnertime bitch, I thought as he left. I rifled through the bags and found shorts, tank tops, underwear, cheap sunglasses, two swimsuits, flip-flops, tanning lotion, make-up, body spray, deodorant, toothbrush, toothpaste, and a duffle bag to hold it all.

I laid out a pair of denim shorts, a white tank top, and the first pair of underwear I ever wore that came in a plastic bag of six. It was no secret how he got the right sizes—he did have my clothes from the night before to go through while I slept. He probably thought it would impress me, but all he'd done was given me everything I needed to get the hell out of Dodge. Dumb ass.

I showered and used the drugstore makeup. I got dressed and threw everything into the duffle bag. I glanced around the room and did a quick cash and ID check. My wallet was gone! I dumped my bag upside down on the bed—it was definitely gone. A single piece of hotel notepaper lay amongst my belongings. Scribbled in the worst doctor-like handwriting ever I read:

I'll make it up to you tonight. I promise. ~Dickie.

"Fuck," I collapsed on the bed, "All dressed up and no place to go." No ID, no cash, no credit cards; just a passkey. "I wonder how much damage I could do with this." I considered the power of the passkey. I suppose I could've called Sal, but I headed to the hotel gift shop instead. I had five pounds of salt water taffy, two huge arrangements of tropical flowers, six helium balloons, a big graphic mug that read "Clearwater, Fla.", and a three-foot stuffed green alligator sent and charged to Dickie's room.

I had stuffed grouper in a delightful white sauce for lunch with a bottle of the most expensive white wine I could find on the wine list. I was too full for dessert, so I asked the staff if they could leave two pieces of their chocolate mousse and another bottle of that fabulous wine in the fridge in Dickie's room. Gosh, such great service. They had no problem ringing up those charges on Dickie's bill. I tipped them accordingly, Mama Luciana's words to my father dancing playfully across my brain, "Don't be cheap. You know that's unattractive." She must've said it a hundred times. I adopted "Don't be cheap" as my personal motto.

By then, the bar was open—oh, how I enjoyed testing the limits of someone else's plastic. I never got turned down using one of Sal's cards, but Dickie was a government employee—surely, there'd be limits. My plan was to spend, spend, spend until I was stopped, stopped, stopped.

Jerry was the bartender and was hugely tolerant of my early-in-the-day tipsiness. I like that in a bartender. He was close to my age with sun-streaked brown hair, reflex blue eyes, and blue-tinted wire-framed glasses. He was medium height, fit and tan, and wore khaki shorts and a royal blue polo. I wondered if he was a surfer or a beatnik. He smiled and asked what he could get me. I felt comfortable with Jerry immediately and explained that my man had left me stranded for business and it was my goal to run up as big of a bill as was humanly possible before he got back. "Can you help me Jerry?" I smiled sweetly. Okay, I was pretty buzzed from lunch already.

"Hell hath no fury like a woman scorned." Jerry smiled back and looked at his inventory. "I have some thirty-year-old scotch … some Dom Perignon champagne … "

"Yes, champagne *definitely*," I interrupted. Jerry owned a small marketing company locally and was bartending part time, while his big dream was to be a writer. He was super entertaining—he did some way funny imitations using a corkscrew.

"Mark Spitz." Jerry held the cork screw flat and pulled the metal screw park back and forth, making the "arms" of the corkscrew swim. Then he held the corkscrew upright for some jumping jacks. "Jack Lalanne." And for the grand finale, Jerry spun the screw part around making the "head" spin. "Linda Blair." It was too funny, but you probably had to be there—or there and completely shit-faced as the case may be.

I'm sure I laughed too much and too loud, but it felt really good and I wasn't going to ever see any of these people again.

I thanked Jerry and tipped him fifty bucks for the one-hundred dollar bottle of wine, staggering across the lobby where I ran into Agent Dickhead. "Big Dickie!" I threw my arms around him. "I have been thinking about *you* all day." I said with a Southern accent, big smile, and raised eyebrows.

He was beyond-a-shadow-of-a-doubt some kind of pissed off. He grabbed my left arm and pushed me towards the elevator.

"Dude, that hurts—cut it out."

"Don't call me 'dude.'" The elevator opened. "Get in."

He was fuming as he shook a stack of what I guessed were room charges. "What the fuck Cici?"

"You said to get whatever I needed," I answered as innocently as I could, which looked like it pissed him off more.

He stopped the elevator between floors and gripped my arm tighter. "Evidently, you and I have a different definition of the word 'need', you spoiled rotten, ungrateful, manipulative, little bitch." He shook the papers in my face. "And this doesn't include your fucking bar tab with Phil Suckalooski! You think *your daddy* will cover this for you?" Dickie shook his head angrily. "The agency's going to have my ass for this. Grow the fuck up—all of life isn't a fucking free shopping spree. Some of us actually work for a living. It does seem you might've found a better way to spend your time." He looked away and muttered, "Bitch."

Maybe he was an idiot not see it coming or maybe he was falling in love and all those little red flags weren't visible as of yet. Either way, I didn't care. "Nope, I couldn't think of anything better than racking up charges and pissing you the fuck off you common, murdering, dog mother-fucker … " Dickie punched the wall beside my head before I could finish. It sounded pretty bad—bones breaking and all. Those commercial, metal elevator walls are damned sturdy.

Dickie's hand swelled up fast. "Looks like you fought the wall and the wall won," I jeered.

Dickie narrowed his eyes and restarted the elevator, "You know princess, everyone likes a little ass, but nobody likes a smart ass."

"Don't call me 'princess.'"

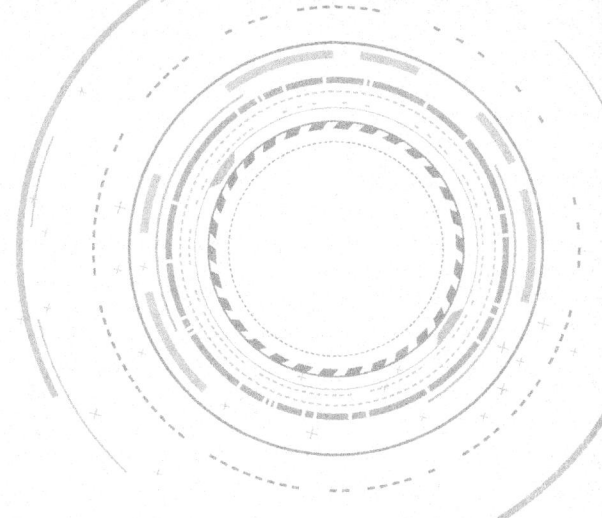

CHAPTER NINE
Good Times

Dickie opened his toolbox and pulled out some duct tape and plastic bags. He filled the bags with ice and taped them around his baseball mitt of a broken hand. It looked like it hurt way bad. I, on the other hand, wasn't feeling any pain whatsoever.

"Grab your gear."

"Where are we going?"

"It's irrelevant."

"It's relevant to me."

"Christ, do you just *need* to argue?" Dickie threw one bag over his shoulder and picked up the toolbox with his left hand.

"So, you're right-handed, eh? Looks like it's broken." I grabbed my duffle and the three-foot, stuffed green alligator.

"You're not taking that with us."

"I'm totally taking this. He's cute." I tilted my head and smiled at the stuffed animal.

Dickie laughed that odd laugh I'd heard just before he shot Bubba and Bruiser. "Fine." I threw the stuffed green beast back down on the bed. "It's not fucking worth *dying* over. Can I at least bring one of the flower arrangements then?"

Dickie sighed deeply and took one last look around the room, "Think you can grab the door?"

"Oh gosh that's right—your *hand* is full. Sure. It probably would've been better if you hadn't punched the wall, huh?" I opened the door for Agent Anger-Issues and remembered the bottle of wine in the refrigerator; I turned around, retrieved it and quickly shoved the bottle into my duffle. Dickie was already out the door and I just couldn't leave all the beautiful flowers behind—so, I wrapped my arm around one of the large ceramic vases and walked out with that as well.

I met up with Dickie at the elevator. "Can I please get my wallet back?"

"Nope," Dickie stepped to the side of the opened elevator doors. "After you."

"Damn dude, could you be any more of a jerk?" I stepped into the elevator.

"Don't call me 'dude,' *princess*."

"Seriously—if you're going for 'World's Biggest Asshole' save your breath; you already have my vote." He knew he had me between a rock and a hard place without my wallet. If I was going to call Daddy to the rescue, I would've already done it by now. What I would've really liked would've been another night or two in the hotel—time to collect my thoughts and figure out what I could possibly say to Daddy that would smooth things over until I returned. Without my wallet, I had little choice but to rely on Dickie's kindness—which seemed to be in short supply.

We rode in silence—North on I-275 and then East on I-4. Maybe Goofy and Mickey were on his *list* too; highway signs alerted us to the fact we were a mere sixty miles from Disney World. Dickie took one of the Plant City exits and stopped to gas up the car. Plant City, Florida: "Winter Strawberry Capital of the World." Everybody's got their thing; Plant City has strawberries. We went through a town in North Carolina one time that had a "Woolly Worm Festival." So, it could be way worse.

I got out and stretched. "I have to go to the bathroom." I grabbed my bag and headed inside the little convenience shop without waiting for a response. I took my time changing into khaki shorts and a black tank top. I touched up my make-up, poofed my hair, and headed back outside.

Dickie was leaned against the Camry, cradling his broken, duct-taped hand and waiting when I came out. "What? No shopping bags?"

"It's a convenience store, not Macy's. Never mind the fact that I don't have any fucking money. Dick."

Dickie sifted through a handful of change and managed to find a quarter and put the rest of the change back in his pocket with one hand, "Stay here." He walked over to the pay phone, dialed, and turned to face me. He talked low and showed no facial expression other than the scowl he'd worn since leaving the hotel. I got in the car and slammed the door. He had taken the keys with him, so I could neither roll down the windows nor turn on the A/C. What did I ever see in this guy? He turned away, lowered his head, and spoke into the booth. *Great ass.* I thought.

Dickie got back in the car and started the engine. "We're going to switch vehicles."

"Bummer. Hate to give up this *dream machine.*"

Dickie pulled up next to a closed car rental lot and tossed the keys in the ashtray. "Grab your shit."

I got my bag, duffle, and the huge flower arrangement and followed Dickie to a gray panel van. I froze. The back was unlocked; Dickie swung both doors open. Damn, this just didn't look like good news to me. I bit my lower lip.

"Do you need a special invitation?" Dickie nodded to the open doors.

There was a large, metal safe bolted in place; I put the flowers and duffle bag next to it and met him at the passenger side, where he held the door for me. "Thank you," I said without thinking.

"Wow, manners," Dickie closed the door and mumbled something as he walked around to the driver's side and got in.

"What is your problem?" I snapped at him.

"My problem," Dickie began, "Is you. I spent three months of my time on a lead and a few thousand of agency money—part of which was to pay off your pal Tess who, by the way, was more than willing to sell you out. Then, when I finally get at least one thing right, you freak the hell out and end up being the absolutely least valuable informant on the face of the planet. I had to *sell* the idea of getting close to fucking Vladimir Petrov via *you*. And then, to top it all off, the message from my supervisor was that he didn't know what kind of 'kinky shit' I thought the agency would be paying for and for me to understand the helium balloons, five pounds of taffy, and three-foot alligator would be coming out of my pay. Oh—and I was lucky my check wouldn't be docked for the whole fucking operation up to this point. And here I'm thinking, I'm in sunny Florida with a beautiful, exciting woman and maybe we could make the most of it and she turns out to be an ungrateful, spoiled brat. Other than that and a broken, throbbing hand, I have no problems." Dickie paused for a moment and caught his breath, "Do you like magic?"

"I dunno. Can you make all of this disappear?" My head was spinning ... three months ... I met him like three weeks ago ... Tess ... what the fuck ... and what did Dickie's boss think would be going on with a stuffed alligator? I had a million questions and no clue where to begin. Shit, I really needed to get home. My ass was sure to be grass.

Dickie pulled off the interstate and into the middle of nowhere. Before I knew it, we were in front of a magic shop in Auburndale, Florida. Directly across the street was an elementary school and within eyeshot—a gas station and what looked to be a long-standing restaurant. "Hoping some fairy dust and a magic wand will fix your hand?" I inquired.

Dickie just smiled and shook his head. He got out of the van and came around to my side and opened the door.

Dickie walked up to the entranceway, twisted the knob, and leaned in announcing our arrival. "Is there a doctor in the house?"

We were greeted by a man I guessed to be about the same age as Dickie. He was medium height and very tan with sinewy muscles, sandy blond hair, sapphire eyes, and a friendly smile. "Hey gator man! I don't know what kind of kinky shit you think the agency is paying for!" The man laughed and the two men hugged. Dickie shot me a quick grimace/one eyebrow raised look.

It would be awhile before he lived down my little shopping spree. The list of my room charges would circulate his office and endless speculation would be made to the various applications of said items. I think he encouraged and enjoyed it on some level. The best scenario I remember involved some Minnie-Mickey role-playing utilizing the helium to change our voices while initiating a rescue mission involving a rare fuzzy alligator. The wine was used to first knock out the villain and then for Mickey to romance Minnie. The five pounds of taffy were used to shut "Princess Minnie" up while Mickey used the chocolate mousse as body paint. All very legit CIA expenses.

"ARboc, this is Cici—she loves salt water taffy, over-priced wine, and stuffed paraphernalia." He was on a roll and just couldn't let it go. "She also enjoys long walks through shopping malls and dreams of what color her hair will be the next day."

I smiled to ARboc. "Hi. Is he always this charming?" Thinking, *Holy shit, is he always this much of a total dick?*

ARboc smiled, shook my hand and nodded. "Yep. Pretty much."

He invited us in and closed the door. I couldn't help lighting up—I love magic. I picked up a magician I met in a bowling alley one time and was thoroughly entertained by the magic but not so much the man.

"So, 'ARboc' sounds like a code name." No reply so I continued, "I want a code name too."

ARboc smiled. "You've already got one. Dickie's been calling you 'the mafia princess' for months. MP."

Dickie punched ARboc's arm. "What the fuck man?"

"What does it matter, Dick?" ARboc smiled at me. "She's in now." Which I thought meant like "inside the building." I was so naïve; nothing would be more obvious when reality came crashing in—as it most certainly would.

"How was your flight?" ARboc was asking me.

I looked at Dickie and then back to ARboc. "Completely uneventful—well, other than Dickie driving like a mad man, having to jump over a fence, run through tall weeds and race to the plane." My glance went back to Dickie. "Completely uneventful."

ARboc looked at Dickie and shook his head. "Why do you always do that when you know you can park right there by the plane? Then, the guy picking up the car has to trek through all that mess too. What is the point? Who was picking up?"

"Carl."

"Oh." ARboc thought about it. "I probably would've done the same thing." He laughed.

I listened and suspected that the fence-jumping was all part of Dickie's personal dog and pony show. Because there wasn't enough drama in my life already?

"Hey man, you got a stethoscope somewhere around this place?" I couldn't imagine why Dickie would want a stethoscope—not exactly the best diagnostic tool for a possible fracture. Idiot.

"Yep." ARboc laughed again. "Let me guess—you wrote the combination on your hand and now you can't read it?"

"It's been one hell of a trip. Can you help me out? I'd rather break my other hand than have to call the boss again."

"No problem." ARboc grabbed a stethoscope and followed Dickie out to the van; I followed ARboc. The two men jumped in the back of the van, while I sat on the bumper.

"Keep quiet," Dickie commanded with a stern glance.

"Fuck you," I silently mouthed back while flipping him off. I think I kind of wished he'd just shoot me. The thought of facing Sal was overwhelming. I knew I should at least call, but couldn't think of a decent lie and there was no way I was ready to tell the truth. I mean, not if I could somehow get away with it.

ARboc was already zeroing in on his task at hand, "It's all in the touch." He held the stethoscope next to the lock as he turned the dial, so he could hear the tumblers drop and feel them through his fingertips at the same time. In minutes, the safe was open and Dickie was retrieving weapons and ammunition and putting them in a bag.

He took out a large envelope and peered inside and removed two airline tickets. Inspecting them, he nodded. "Looks like Cici Russo and Richard Bradford made it on flight 574 last night out of DC at 10:13pm. Our cover's good." He handed me my round trip ticket; stamped and routed through Tampa International Airport. "Return flight on Monday morning." It was Saturday night.

"We're going to drop you off at ARboc's house and go get my hand taken care of. His girlfriend's there so you'll have someone to hang out with."

"Why can't I go to the hospital with you guys?" *Versus hang out with a total stranger.*

"Because I can't afford it; they have a gift shop there." He gave me a hard stare.

"Shopping's not the only thing I do."

"Nope. You bitch, whine, complain, go clubbing, and smoke weed too."

"Harsh *and* judgmental—nice combination." ARboc was walking out as I spoke; he had a duffle slung over his shoulder. "I am a college graduate, Dick."

"I know; you worked hard to spend Daddy's money."

"Daddy didn't go to class and take my exams for me."

"Shit Cici—you didn't go to class that often yourself."

"Are you two lovebirds ready?" ARboc caught the last part of our conversation. He threw his bag in the back and took a seat on top of the safe. Dickie opened the passenger door and I jumped in. He went to the driver's side, got in and proceeded to drive one-handed.

We drove to Lakeland. ARboc lived with his girlfriend in a large house that had been divided into four apartments, next door to a retirement home owned by his family—theirs was a studio in the back. I was told "Slinky" would be back soon. They had a swimming pool and two pet lions out back—Sheba was the female; Billy often broke his chain and wandered around the neighborhood. They were beautiful animals.

ARboc walked right up to Sheba and patted her chest. She put her paws on him and proceeded to nuzzle his neck and rub her face against his. It was amazing the huge cat didn't knock him over. Billy was the same—appearing to positively adore ARboc. I got close enough to pet them, but was really freaked out because they were so fucking huge. Dickie stood back, smoked a cigarette, and watched. I understood his hand was probably hurting; I just didn't care.

We went back inside. ARboc grabbed a Browning .22 automatic with a gold trigger from his dresser. The two men talked pistols—ARboc argued that a .22 automatic is the only *truly* silence-able hand gun; while Dickie begged to differ. I couldn't have cared less. So, when they decided to take off and leave me to wait for Slinky alone, I was good with that idea. I hadn't been alone with my thoughts in what felt like forever.

I thought about Sal and what I might say. "Hi Daddy. You know when I said I was going out with Tess to celebrate, I was really going out with a guy I met a couple weeks ago smoking marijuana behind Denny's who turned out to be a CIA assassin and now I'm in Florida and won't be back till Monday." There was no way the truth would fly. I decided thinking might not be the best idea after all, so I turned on the television and sat on the edge of the bed. I'd think up a good lie later.

It was a cute apartment. I looked around and imagined myself living in someplace similar when I went off to med school. It would be perfect. With that thought, I noticed half of a joint in an ashtray on the nightstand. It felt like it was an omen and that the roach somehow cosmically had my name on it. Okay, that's total bullshit. I just wanted to get high and it was sitting right there.

I lit that bad boy up and inhaled deeply—easily some of the sweetest weed ever. I still feel high when I think about that pot. I took three or four hits and laid it back down in the ashtray—realizing why someone hadn't finished the joint to begin with. I was staring blankly at the TV when Slinky walked in with a bucket of chicken under one arm and all the sides in a bag in her other hand.

"Hey, you must be the mafia princess. I'm Slinky." She smiled and sat the bucket and bag on the table.

I rolled my eyes. "Friends call me Cici. Remind me to thank Dickie when he gets back for that nickname."

"I'll do that." Slinky had beautiful long, thick, wavy chestnut-colored hair and eyes as dark as coffee. She was curvy and perfectly bronzed without a tan line in sight—wearing denim cut-off shorts, flip-flops and a tie-dyed bikini top. I thought she looked like a mermaid; minus the flippers, of course.

We ate chicken and Slinky talked to me like I knew way more than I did. Bubba and Bruiser (she loved the names I made up) "got their kicks" raping, torturing, and killing young, blonde co-eds. Vladimir's interest in them was purely professional—one could never have too many mindless, sociopathic thugs at their disposal. The CIA had been looking for ways to get closer to the head of the Russian mob and saw this as an opportunity. They sent a young-looking, blonde agent into the field. They thought they were making headway with Bubba and Bruiser until the female agent showed up dead—obviously tortured, raped and beaten just a couple nights earlier. Not knowing what information had been gained by the two evil felons, the agency felt like elimination was the best solution; they didn't want to risk Vladimir finding out they were onto him.

I confessed to taking a couple hits off of Slinky's roach. "I'm really sorry; I don't have a great excuse."

"No worries. I couldn't even smoke the whole thing earlier, but I'm ready to try again now." Slinky smiled. "Let's go for a swim. Did you bring a suit?"

I looked around. "Shit. I left my duffle in the van."

Slinky laid out ten or twelve swimsuits for me to choose from, "Wear one of these." Evidently Florida girls have entire wardrobes of swimsuits. I ended up choosing a somewhat conservative white racer back one-piece.

I wondered what Slinky's real name was, but assumed it'd be rude to ask. So, we smoked and talked and swam. We shared fucked up family stories. I told her about the driving fiasco with my brothers and how the men were treated so differently from the women. She told me about her strict Catholic upbringing and how her mom made her wear a sign around her neck that read "I'm a thief; don't trust me" while doing yard work/penance for stealing a Hershey bar, which she didn't even get to eat. Years later, her mom stole some roadside trees just freshly planted by the county. Those trees are still in her yard today. Nobody ever made *her* wear a sign.

Slinky told me about the retirement home for retired CIA and FBI—though the agency part wasn't something they advertised. ARboc and Dickie had been working together for a couple years; they'd become close friends and visited each other a couple times per year. The CIA had been good to both of them and it was a good thing that I signed the CI agreement because otherwise Dickie and ARboc would be walking away with damned little from the operation.

"What? I signed *what?*"

"A CI agreement—confidential informant." Slinky kept talking, but I didn't hear anything beyond me signing an agreement. I hadn't signed anything other than a room charge. Which I still thought was pretty funny.

"Hey!" It was ARboc with Dickie behind him, "Do you have a joint ready for us?"

"You know I do," Slinky got out of the pool and disappeared inside the house. ARboc followed her.

Dickie sat in a chair beside the pool; his hand casted from knuckle to elbow—a goofy, narcotic-induced smile slapped across his face.

"You look like you're feeling better," I commented.

"I am." On a scale of one to ten, I'd say his pain level was at a negative three.

I got out of the pool and looked around for a towel. Dickie looked me up and down without shame—his eyes boldly and blatantly scanning my every curve with me not realizing exactly how transparent Slinky's white suit became when wet. Without shifting his gaze, he picked up a towel from the side table with his left hand and held it out to me. As I walked closer, he continued to ogle, his stare more intense than what I was comfortable with.

"Thanks," I grabbed the towel, dried off a little and wrapped it around my waist.

Slinky and ARboc returned with a joint and we burned our nightcap by the pool. The agency had gotten us a room at The Terrace Hotel in Lakeland—a beautiful, historic hotel close to Lake Mirror. ARboc handed me the keys to both the room and the van with a raised brow and a nod. I went inside to change and noticed the flower arrangement from the hotel on the table. That was a good idea, I thought. Those flowers could only survive so long in the back of a van.

We said our goodnights and took off for the hotel. ARboc had handed me two passkeys, but they were both for the same room. Dickie agreed to sleep on the sofa, but collapsed on the bed as soon as the room door was open. He was chatting up a storm, sharing secrets I felt pretty sure he shouldn't be sharing. Damn, he was so freaking loaded. And he was cute—more like the guy I held hands with after our dinner at The Wharf in Alexandria.

I jumped on top of him, fully clothed, and straddled his waist; he kept talking. I started to unbutton his shirt. "You're going to have so many regrets in the morning," I whispered—more referring to the secrets he was sharing than the sex I was obviously interested in having.

With his unbroken hand, he seized both my wrists and was on top of me, pinning down my hands over my head before I knew what happened. "Not me. I won't have any regrets in the morning." He stared at me hard. Then, without releasing my hands, he kissed me harder. He helped me out of my clothes—ripping half of them in the process.

I laid on the bed naked, watching Dickie take his shirt off with one hand. He crawled up on the bed, using his knees to push mine apart, watching me from bird's eye view as he finished undressing.

"You have the most beautiful bedroom eyes."

"Is that code for you want to fuck me?" I laughed.

"Yes."

Our priest would've called it fornication; Dickie would say we fucked like rabbits. As for me, it was mind-blowing. I'd always thought "multiple orgasms" were a bit of an urban legend. It was perfectly awesome to discover they were not.

We had room service and more sex for breakfast … and for lunch … and dinner. We ate, slept, and screwed—and, somewhere along the line, I think I fell in love. It was wonderful to be so swept away by pure, physical pleasure—I don't think I thought about home until it was Monday morning and we had a flight to catch back to DC.

I forgot about the wine in my duffle and left it on the dresser with a note to the maid, "Enjoy." I put on the clothes I had worn out on Friday night and shoved the clothes Dickie bought me back into the duffle along with all the personal items—it seemed like a lifetime ago when I was getting ready for my date with a cowboy.

We spoke very little as we gathered gear and considered the trip ahead of us. I had a million questions about Tess and Vladimir and the CI agreement of which Slinky spoke. I felt instant anxiety and impending doom as the plane began its descent. I thought I was going to throw up. I had no clever reason for my disappearance and if this was truly a kidnapping, why didn't I call for help? *What's wrong with me?* I knew I was going to be in deep shit.

Landing ... bags from overhead ... rental car ... then back to Alexandria to get my car. With each step, my heart beat faster and faster and when we arrived at the lot and I found my car gone, I think my heart stopped beating entirely.

"It must've been towed." I wanted to cry.

Dickie said he'd give me a ride home and would make a couple calls and find out where my car was towed.

As we approached the house, I could see too much activity going on—men in uniform and men in darks suits standing, guarding, moving, coming, and going. There was no way this could be good.

"Oh shit." My car was parked out front and it appeared as if all holy hell was breaking loose at *my* house.

Dickie parked on the curb a couple spaces down from the bottomless fiery pit of eternal damnation. He popped the trunk, got out, and came around to open my door.

"Your house looks a lot busier than mine," Dickie smiled and helped me out of the car. He grabbed my bag and then my hand—we walked towards hell together.

We stopped in front of the house, at the bottom of the steps. "I had a great time." I smiled when I wanted to die. One of the dark suits tapped on the door twice. Sal stepped out.

"Cici, get inside."

I started to go and Dickie held onto my hand and pulled me back, "I had a great time too." Then, right in front of Sal, he held my face with both hands and kissed me just passionately enough to make my knees buckle in front of my father. I blushed and turned to go inside—head lowered, no eye contact with Daddy—standard walk-of-shame posture. I was directed into the library by another dark suit. Uniformed police officers were turning the place upside down.

"That's far enough hot shot." It was Sal's voice.

I looked out the window, Dickie was showing Daddy his badge. "On the contrary, Mr. Russo, I'll be joining my friends inside now."

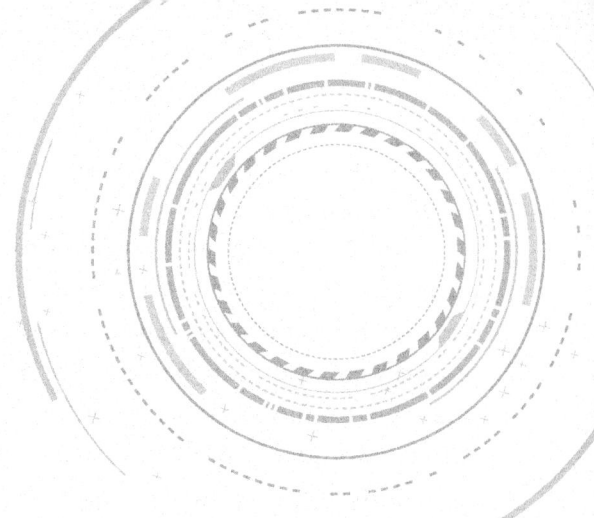

CHAPTER TEN
The World According to Cici

The world sucked. Things aren't always as they seem. People aren't always who they say they are. And no matter how good or bad things get, one can always count on change. These things I knew to be true that morning sitting in the family library—all angry eyes on me; police turning every cushion and going through every closet and crevice.

Dickie Bradford flashed his badge and entered our home as it was being searched and ransacked.

Shit was hitting the fan—gun-running, drug dealing, smuggling, espionage, murder. God only knows what my family was up to back then. As far as all holy hell breaking loose the same day I returned home, now that just seemed like too much of a coincidence—even to me.

As for Sal—there was no such thing as a coincidence or a misunderstanding *ever*; all of life was black and white. He would've been pissed off even without the search. This was just fuel to the fire. Someone would have to pay. Sadly, that someone looked like it was going to be me.

By luck, Antonio and Emilio were both in the garage when the police had arrived; they'd had just enough time to pull the wall partition across the floor, making the garage one-fifth its size before officers were swarming. No one ever tapped on or questioned the wall itself. Emilio had done beautiful work making it appear to be permanent and unmovable—the room looked like a single garage and not the huge chamber of crime that it was. The guy had skill.

The police cleared out and thanked Daddy for his time, apologizing for any inconvenience. They found no evidence of any illegal activity and were probably sorrier for that than anything else. Dickie was behind the last detective and leaned in the library, smiling to me, "Dinner tonight?"

"She's busy." Sal's voice exuded utter contempt.

Both Antonio and Emilio stood up. I was thankful Giovanni was back at school. I could take everyone else's hate, but Gio hating me would've been more than I could handle.

"I'll call you later," I tried to sound calm and casual, but could hear my own voice quiver.

"No Cici, you won't." Daddy's voice had become quieter and more controlled. "Now if you'll excuse us, we have some family matters to attend to."

A look of apprehension shot across Dickie's face. He glanced back to me. "You folks enjoy your day," he said the words slowly as if trying desperately to come up with a reason to stay before he ended the sentence. But, there was really nothing he could do for me at that point. I should've stayed in Podunk, Florida and learned to wrestle alligators or some shit.

The front door closed; the cars all drove away and deathly silence seeped in. I dropped my face into my hands, closed my eyes and bit down hard on my lower lip.

Daddy stood tapping his size thirteen Italian loafer on the hardwood floor; it seemed to echo and vibrate all around me. He breathed in and sighed deeply. I felt like he was winding up for the kill and the longer he tapped, the worse it would be. He walked to his desk and took a cigar from the engraved box Mama had given him one year for Christmas. He sat down in one of the armchairs directly across from me and lit his cigar. I could feel his stare burning through me; his cigar smoke crossed the space between us and enveloped me.

"Oh God!" I ran across the room and puked in Sal's trash can, while he watched in complete disbelief; not a sign of sympathy on his face—more like aggravated and inconvenienced maybe.

Mama handed me a box of tissues and without a word exited the library, closing the door behind her—leaving me alone with the three eldest Russo men. Damn, I started wishing Gio was there.

"Are you done?" Daddy was getting impatient.

"Yes sir." I wiped my face, sat back down, and stared at the floor.

Daddy stood up and made a breathy growling hissing kind of noise, snuffing his cigar out as he did so. He was in my face in two steps, towering over me—lifting my chin between his fist and thumb.

"Look at me you ungrateful little bitch!" He pressed his thumb hard into my chin and roughly heaved me to an upright position—quickly releasing his hold and backhanding me hard with the same hand across the right cheek. I fell backwards into the chair—hitting the arm with my hip and nearly toppling over. I wiped blood from the corner of my mouth. Big black mascara tears streamed uncontrollably down my face—my stinging, throbbing, swelling-to-the-outline-of-Sal's-knuckles *face*.

Daddy lifted me by my chin again and forced my head around, "Do you see what you've done? Do you see the mess you've made—the shit you've brought into *my* home?" He pushed me backwards and I landed square in the chair this time—which, as it turns out, is a wicked position to be in if someone wants to backhand you across the other side of your head. Excruciating, humbling agony overwhelmed and then victoriously took up residence on my entire face. Suddenly, I was not so afraid of my father's *words*.

"You will learn, Cici Russo, what it means to be a member of this family and what it means to disrespect and disgrace us." He paced back and forth.

Oh shit, "disrespect," I'd heard it my whole life. People who disrespected my father often ended up being referred to as "that guy."

He took an envelope from the side table and threw it at me, "Perhaps you'd like to explain this."

I picked up the envelope and looked to both Antonio and Emilio for a clue—they were expressionless observers. I closed my eyes and dislodged a stack of 8 by10 photographs from the tattered envelope. *Dear Lord, please don't let me become "that guy." Amen*, I silently prayed.

It was pictures of Dickie and I. "Fuck," came out of my mouth in an automatic response—a barely audible, frightened whisper.

Daddy grabbed me by the throat, "Watch your mouth young lady." He maintained his hold until I started to gasp.

I'm pretty sure he wanted to kill me right then. But, in his defense, there was some pretty heavy shit going down. 1984 saw more espionage-related arrests than ever before in the history of our country—many arrested that would include many of Sal's "new friends." 1985 would be dubbed "The Year of the Spy" because of the large number of indictments that year as a direct result of the previous two year's investigations and apprehensions—investigations and apprehensions that were taking place while I was busy finishing up my degree, applying to medical schools, and partying my ass off at every opportunity. It probably wasn't a good time to be acting out.

On top of the stack was a picture of Dickie and I on King Street holding hands. Next was a picture of us going into Ireland's Own ... and then Dickie pulling me across the parking lot behind the pool hall—him looking straight ahead, me looking like a deer caught in the headlights ... and then a nice shot of me jumping over the fence into Dickie's arms. The next photo was blurry and striped with the lines of hotel blinds, but there was no doubt—it was me naked on top of Dickie at The Terrace Hotel. I guessed it was taken Saturday night. I slumped lower into my chair—wishing the furniture would swallow me.

"What do you have to say for yourself Cici Russo? Would you like to explain to your brothers and me, why you spent your weekend *fucking the enemy*? Perhaps you thought you could best serve your family with your legs spread."

"Daddy, you don't understand," I started crying—feeling beaten and humiliated.

Sal nodded to Antonio, who removed his handkerchief and a small brown bottle from his coat pocket. He opened and tilted the bottle up, pouring the liquid onto the cloth. He replaced the cap and started towards me.

"No! Wait! You have to listen to me." I jumped up and went around to the other side of the chair; Antonio stepped around as well. My instincts went from flight to fight mode. My eyes darted around the room—hoping to find some kind of a weapon. I backed into the bookcase. "Please." I stumbled behind the desk, knocking over a lamp. I remembered Daddy's .38 that he kept in a side desk drawer. Antonio stepped beside me; Emilio blocked the other side. I looked pleadingly to Emilio; he shrugged his shoulders and maintained his blockade. I reached for the drawer.

Antonio pressed his handkerchief over my mouth and nose, using his other hand on the back of my head to hold me still. I tried to break free and fought hard not to breathe in, but couldn't help it as I attempted to speak, "Vlad ... "

Suddenly, it was dark and the smell of exhaust was making me nauseous; I could hear muffled voices—Russian maybe. My every muscle ached; my face throbbed and my whole head felt as if it would surely explode. I tried to move but found my wrists and ankles duct-taped together. I was being bumped around and noted the sound of car engines whizzing by. I felt drugged and dizzy and slow to process the information. My eyes adjusted to the darkness; shapes started to form. I remembered being in the library; Sal wanted to kill me. And now—I was in the trunk of a car. I panicked.

"Help! Let me out of here!" I kicked and I screamed. The car slowed to a stop. A large man in a navy ski mask opened the trunk, yanked me up by the collar and punched me in the head.

When I came to, I was on a commercial flight with a headache the size of Aunt Bunny's ass—duct tape replaced with shackles. A man in a brown suit and mirrored aviator glasses had the aisle seat next to me; he stared straight ahead. I pressed my forehead against the window, struggling to catch a glimpse of something familiar from the air.

"Where am I?"

I felt a sharp sting in my left shoulder and turned just in time to see the man in the brown suit slide the syringe back into his breast pocket.

I have foggy memories of the man in the brown suit and a security guard dragging me through an airport—passersby appearing melted and blurry ... the back of a driver's head in a car that smelled like old French fries ... chains clanking together as other females aged fifteen to pushing thirty lined up with me to board a bus—some laughing and giddy; others crying. I was too tired and too drugged to do either. I wasn't sure if I was going off to summer camp or being sold into slavery. The shackles reminded me it was more likely the latter. Happy for a window seat, I used the pane as my pillow and tried to sleep—my face bumping and rubbing against the dirty glass.

I heard conversations, but could detect no English—Italian, some French, some Spanish; I really should've learned Italian when my parents were shoving it down my throat. I rebelled against everything I possibly could from the very beginning when I first became a Russo. My life went through my head in a blur along with the landscape. It was as if everything was in slow motion, but it felt like a year had passed since I was with Dickie. When was that? This morning? Yesterday? Maybe the day before.

The decrepit old bus bumped along back roads and mountain edges—occasionally revealing views of beautiful deep blue water far below. We inched through a small town with narrow streets and too many people—produce stands and vendors of all sorts lined our path. And then into Bumfuck we drove for another hour or so. The bus turned down a barren dirt road where we were jerked and jostled along for several more miles. Finally, the exhausted engine squeaked to a stop in front of a large pavilion—screened in on three sides and open in the front, housing a dozen rustic-looking picnic tables.

Off in the distance was an old two-story farmhouse, flanked on either side by rows of much smaller, simpler houses. And, everywhere else, there were gardens and groves. Behind all the housing was an olive grove that stretched over hilly ground as far as I could see. On either side of the pavilion were huge vegetable gardens of tomatoes, beets, potatoes, and soybeans—endless acres that would seem to disappear at a tree line, only to pop up bigger and fiercer on the other side. Beyond all the vegetable gardens to the right, stood citrus groves the size of small villages. And, on the very outskirts of those, an enormous garage had been erected for the men to busy themselves with the huge equipment only they were permitted to operate. Beyond all the vegetable gardens to the left was a large packing shed. I think three or four months passed before I had the chance to figure out the lay of the land. Why you ask? Because everyone there spoke Italian—fluent Italian, broken Italian, Italian in unusual accents, but all Italian, all the time. *Not* because they couldn't speak English, but because part of the game was to force-feed the culture to unwilling recipients.

We were ordered off the bus, marched into the pavilion, and lined up, shackles adorning wrists and ankles. The driver stood in front of us facing the entrance—feet shoulder width apart, hands grasped casually behind his back, shoulders straight, head held high.

Minutes ticked by; all I wanted to do was stretch out on one of the tables and go to sleep. But, the others stood silently, and I followed suit. I heard a car approaching and saw the dark limo pull to a stop in front of us. The driver got out and opened the back door on his side. Two broad-shouldered men exited the vehicle, came around to the other side, and stood waiting for the driver to open the other back door. The man in the car said something in Russian and the first two men went to stand on either side of the front opening of the pavilion, while the driver held the door open. A large man stood up out of the limo, dwarfing the others by his size. My heart sank; it was Vladimir Petrov.

He quickly glanced over the twenty-five or thirty of us and signaled his gophers who handed out white paper "gift" bags and removed the shackles. No one moved to inspect the bags further, but left them sitting on the tables before us until all the bags had been handed out and Vladimir shouted instructions—in Italian, not forsaking his Russian accent.

Immediately, all the girls began taking off their clothes, folding them and putting them beside their white bags. I stared in disbelief; my hesitation was noted by Vladimir, who started to signal one of the gophers. I quickly started taking my clothes off and folding them as well—assuming whatever the goon was going to do to me would be worse.

More shouted instructions in Italian and items were being removed from bags—white t-shirt, white draw-string shorts, 1 towel, 1 wash cloth, toothbrush and toothpaste, shampoo, conditioner, a bar of soap, a pen, and a comb.

The girl next to me used the pen to write her name on the empty bag and then filled the bag with the clothes she had worn there. I noticed others doing the same, so again I did what they did and went to reach for the t-shirt and shorts before me, once my own clothes were in the bag. The girl next to me pushed my hand away and nodded to the front of the pavilion where Vladimir stood—waiting and watching. *Freaktard.* I dropped my hands back to my sides, still naked.

Vladimir snapped more directions and watched as white shirts and shorts were happily and quickly put on. He walked up and down the rows of women—stopping and having some of them spin around in front of him and then directing them back to the bus, while completely ignoring others. Vladimir walked past me without as much as a glance. I felt relief. Before long, half a dozen pretty girls sat happily back on the bus we had arrived on—leaving their old clothes bagged behind and taking only their toiletries with them. Others were singled out and pointed in the direction of the housing, group by group, again leaving their personal clothing behind and taking only what had been given them upon arrival. At the end, six of us remained, were sneered at in Italian, and dismissed.

Vladimir grabbed my arm as I went to leave with the others. "Miss Russo, not so fast." I was actually grateful to hear English.

He tilted my face and examined it closely. "Such a shame for a man to hit a woman in the face, when God gave her this," he slapped my ass hard, "for that very purpose." I gasped; he laughed.

"I have mentioned my little farm of tough love to your father many times. How I do wish I'd gotten you here much earlier—when you were younger." He pushed my hair away and gently ran his fingers across the bruises on my face—shaking his head and looking disappointed. He turned and began to pace in front of me.

"Here, your parents have been promised, you will learn how to be a well-behaved, disciplined, good Italian wife. You're already struggling with the language and are far behind the others. Tonight, while the others are getting acquainted, I will give you your *one and only* lesson in Italian. The rest you will have to figure out on your own. Absolutely no English will be tolerated. If you speak English in front of the others, they will happily report you for the additional conduct points."

Vladimir grabbed my hair and bent me down over the table. "Piegarsi." He slapped my ass again and pulled me up by my hair to a standing position. "Levarsi." He repeated this over and over again, "Piegarsi. Levarsi. Piegarsi. Levarsi. Piegarsi. Levarsi." Bend over and stand up. I got it.

Vladimir then pushed me to sit down on the end of one of the benches. "Sedersi." Then, signaling me to stand, "Levarsi." Again, he repeated the commands and I obeyed—sit and stand. I was learning Italian from a Russian mob kingpin.

There's more to a language than words and accents—there's a rhythm and, in Italian, there's a dash of passion and a dance of mannerisms as well. Without these things, something is definitely lost. I'm sure the little Italian I learned, I learned wrong.

"Inchinarsi." Vladimir pointed to the ground. Confused, I got down on all fours; he used his foot to force my head to the floor. "Inchinarsi!" I bowed before a man I feared and detested.

We did "bend over, stand up, sit down, bow down" drills for the next hour. I couldn't understand what any of it had to do with being a "good wife", Italian or otherwise. But I was exhausted and saw compliance as my only way out.

"Inchinarsi!" I bowed down at Vladimir's feet and prayed he would just leave and let me sleep there. "Trattenersi."

"Good girl." He patted my head like a dog. "And now, the only words you will ever speak to me," he stooped down and pulled my head back with a handful of hair so that our eyes were meeting, "Sì maestro."

"Sì maestro," I repeated.

"This means 'yes master' and no other words out of your mouth will be acceptable. Do you understand puttana?"

"Sì maestro."

"Levarsi."

I stood up.

He pointed to the table, "Piegarsi."

I leaned over the table. Vladimir grabbed my hair from behind and forcefully pushed my face into the table with one hand while using his free hand to beat my barely-clad ass.

When he was done, he pulled me up by my hair and shoved me in the direction of his two goons who'd been standing guard at the entrance. "Muoversi!"

Goon One and Goon Two hooked their arms through mine and half dragged/half walked me to my new accommodations—all the way at the end of the little houses to the far left of the big house. Upon closer inspection, it was the shabbiest of all the little houses. Inside, five young women were already fast asleep. A single toilet, sink and mirror, and open shower area took up the center of the back wall. I stumbled over to the only remaining cot and passed out next to the toilet.

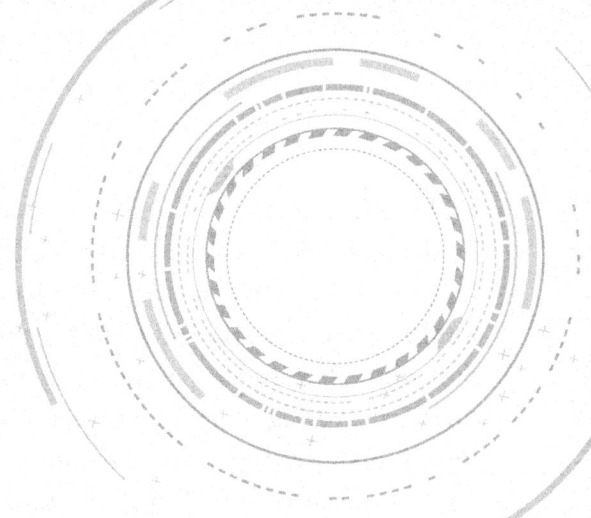

CHAPTER ELEVEN
Tough Love

I woke to the sound of five women fighting for shower time and mirror space. I rolled off my cot and used the toilet and then waited in line to wash my hands and brush my teeth. I was the last one through the shower and wondered if the hot water ran out or if there was never any to begin with.

I stepped outside and saw the first rays of daybreak poking out from behind the olive groves; women were gathering at the pavilion and the smell of fresh bread wafted by. I headed towards the crowd of females all dressed in white, except for a handful that wore pale blue t-shirts and shorts. I later figured out that the pale blue uniforms worked solely in the kitchen and resided in the main house.

Tables were covered with huge baskets of freshly-baked breads, trays of fresh fruit, bowls of hot cereal, and thermoses full of good, strong coffee. Everyone was grabbing food and settling into groups. I saw my bunkmates at one of the tables in the far corner and joined them. I was greeted with condescending smiles, but wasn't there for the company so I filled a plate with food and drank down two cups of coffee and ate until I was full. It was delicious. We stacked our plates up and I followed my bunkmates out to the fields, while the others went their own direction—leaving the pale blue clad women behind to clean up breakfast and begin preparing lunch. My heart went out to them until I discovered how I'd be spending my days.

The six of us lined up at the first of five hundred million rows of tomatoes. We spaced out five or six feet apart armed with burlap sacks and began weeding. When one person caught up to where the person ahead of them had already weeded, they'd jump to the head of the line by another five or six feet until the row was done and the next was started—weeding, jumping, emptying the sacks, and weeding some more. Our backs and shoulders ached; our knees became raw.

Three of my bunkmates were definitely Italian—one very short and petite, one of medium height with an athletic build, and a tall very long-legged young woman. In my mind, I called them "Small" "Medium," and "Tall." Then, there was a redheaded teenager I guessed to be no more than eighteen or nineteen—she looked very Irish and so she became "Leprechaun." The fifth girl was probably about my age and kept a snotty, condescending sneer on her face. She looked Russian to me, but spoke perfect Italian. I called her "Snot," short for snotty bitch. During my time there, I came to know all their real names, but preferred the ones I'd made up—Small, Medium, Tall, Leprechaun, and Snot. The women who lived the high life in pale blue uniforms became "the bitches in blue." And everyone else was just everyone else. I wasn't allowed to speak English; Italian was the only accepted language and, as I didn't know Italian, I opted for conversations and thoughts of my own, in my own mind, in English.

Lunchtime was my favorite time of day. The shade of the pavilion, the antipasto (almost always something with tomatoes which I surprisingly never grew tired of), followed by pasta that was sometimes followed by grilled chicken or steak, the hour-long naps afterwards—eating and then resting during the hottest part of the day was such a welcomed break. Sure, we had to go back to work, but lunchtime signaled you were already halfway through your workday and the regular naps before returning were positively heaven.

By late afternoon, the sun would start to sink lower in the sky and evening breezes would kick up as the scents of dinner cooking would make their way out to the fields.

When the workday was done, we'd mark the spot where we left off, put our bags away, and haul the wheelbarrows of pulled weeds to the burn pile behind the packing shed. Then, it was back to the shack for showers, the clean clothes left for us daily, and to the pavilion for dinner.

Dinner was a social time for most; for me, it was a time to observe and speculate. I could tell if someone was angry or happy or shocked, but without the words I could never know *why* they were angry, happy, or shocked. Things like rules and directions are lost in the non-verbal translations as well. People tended to talk Italian very loud and slow to me. Why does anyone ever think that helps? Hand gestures and pantomimes worked much better. Still, I was the complete idiot in the group and I didn't care and wasn't willing to even try.

After dinner, some would linger around the pavilion or gather outside of one of the little houses. Only the bitches in blue sat outside of the big house. Theirs was a life of cooking and cleaning and laundry and air conditioning and individual bedrooms. I began to envy them.

A week or maybe ten days went by without seeing Vladimir,

or any man for that matter. I wondered why we didn't all just get up and leave. Then, I looked around and realized I wouldn't even know what direction to go much less where I would head to or what I'd do when I got there.

I overheard one of the blue bitches say "Il maestro è andato in Francia." I got "maestro" and "France" from that. It seemed reasonable that he traveled a lot. I wondered if Vladimir would see my family before his return—a quick stopover in the States. It also seemed reasonable that he'd further lie to them as well—finding a way to make me do more time in hell. Still, I assumed it was all temporary—my parents would never let my pricey education to go to waste. Right? This was just another one of Sal's valuable life lessons—the kind that beat you into perfect, unquestioning compliance.

I thought about medical school and wondered how many acceptance letters had already arrived at the house—Sal Russo's house. I wondered if Dickie had tried to call and what Sal would've told him if he had. I wondered if the six of us would ever finish weeding the fucking fields—Small, Medium, Tall, Leprechaun, Snot, and me.

Day after day was much of the same with one day fading and melting into the next in an endless tale of weeds and aching muscles and much-needed rest. All I had were my thoughts to entertain me. If I saw two people talking, I'd make up ridiculous conversations they were having in my head.

"I like the tomatoes."

"Tomatoes are red."

"I told you they were red you stupid idiot."

"I slept with your boyfriend last night."

"I screw yours every Tuesday."

One particularly hot, breezeless morning, Vladimir's limo pulled down a narrow driveway between the pavilion and the field we were busy weeding. Goon One and Goon Two stepped out of the car. Goon One was an exceptionally handsome man—tall and blonde with a square jaw. I hadn't really noticed him before. Goon Two was slightly shorter with dark hair, a dark complexion, and overly-developed muscles. They both wore khaki shorts, white wife-beaters, and tan work boots. Both were fine examples of the male form. I couldn't remember how long it had been since seeing a man. Damn, they looked *good*. I wasn't the only one who thought so either. Work slowed to a near halt—it was as if someone were dangling a steak in front of a group of starving men.

Vladimir stepped from the limo—wearing khaki pants, work boots, and a crisp, white cotton dress shirt with sleeves rolled up to his elbows. His hair was bleached by the sun and pulled back into a ponytail. His body, all six foot five, was beautifully tanned. He leaned into the car and retrieved a safari style hat. At that moment, I remember thinking he was a strikingly good-looking man—for a psychopath.

He looked over the fields immediately before him—the pavilion behind him; the packing shed on the far side of the tomato patch. Vladimir started walking up and down the rows while Goon One and Goon Two unloaded suitcases of equipment and headed towards the shed.

Muffled comments could be heard as the two men passed by; Snot pulled a tube of lip gloss from the waistband of her shorts and generously applied some of the shiny goo. Medium nudged her and, reluctantly, Snot shared the lip gloss. Medium handed it to Leprechaun, who handed it to Tall, who handed it to Small who handed it to me. I put some lip gloss on as well and handed it back to Small and watched as it went back up the line of glossy-lipped weed pickers. Girls were straightening up their hair and tying up their shirts. A surprise inspection or maybe hoping to get lucky? It really did seem like it had been quite a while since we'd seen any men whatsoever.

Vladimir started down the row we were working on; I prayed we hadn't missed any weeds. All seemed to be going well; I kept my head down and my attention on my work. Just as Vladimir stepped behind Snot, she jumped up quickly—spilling her collected weeds and nearly knocking Vladimir down. He was fucking pissed. I didn't need to understand Italian to figure that one out. As he paced and yelled and pointed, his Italian started to sound more like Russian. Snot wasn't my favorite person, but I felt sorry for her—poor clumsy, bitchy Snot.

Vladimir grabbed her by the arm and dragged her over to a table in front of the packing shed; a bushel of tomatoes taking up a third of the table. The maestro pushed Snot over the unoccupied end and proceeded to beat her ass with his bare hand and yell at her. Goon One and Two attached cameras to tripods and took several shots of Snot getting the snot beaten out of her. Goon One caught me watching him and smiled at me. I went back to weeding as if my life depended on it.

Vladimir pulled Snot's shorts down to expose her red ass. He posed her and re-arranged the tomatoes. Her smacked her hard several more times and then arranged her body into a pose with kind, gentle and stroking hands. Snot looked over her shoulder at the camera with a strange pout—a pout that made the corners of her mouth turn upward in almost a smile. I guessed that bad attention was better than no attention for the tragic, broken girl Snot.

Vladimir pushed his goons out of the way and began utilizing both cameras—zooming in and taking shots of Snot from every imaginable angle. The more posing and pictures that were taken, the more Snot smiled and really played up the fake hurt/pouty look. It was super hard not to notice that she was taking a lot of pride in her big photo opportunity and was having fun with it.

Meanwhile, I was scoping the landscape and wondering how far away I could get before anyone noticed I was gone.

Activity started to pick up with more people coming and going over the next couple weeks— more and more workers were moving out to the olive groves; more and more photoshoots with more proud and happy models. Audiences of strangers grew, too. There was definitely more to this game than I was getting—of freaky models and fetish prostitutes. Perhaps, there were monetary gains. But, like all games I cannot win, this was one I didn't plan on playing.

Vladimir seemed to be constantly on the hunt for his next subject. Girls were bumping into him and purposefully dropping their gear—it was taking more and more to get his attention. I couldn't have been more grateful, but wished all the freaking "others" would go away—their staring and pointing and gawking made me uneasy. I just wanted to do my time and get the hell out of there.

Vladimir found me pulling weeds late one afternoon—well after lunch, but not close enough to quitting time for me.

"Miss Russo, levarsi."

I stood up, "Sì maestro."

"Today we go for a field trip. Line up in front of Ivan," he nodded to Goon One who waited off the driveway near the main house.

"Sì maestro."

Vladimir smacked my ass as I walked past him, "Relax, this will be fun for you."

Vladimir's brand of fun wasn't going to be fun for me. I wondered what I had done wrong. Could I have been keeping too low of a profile? I worried what kind of horrible spectacle he would make of me. I thought about running, but knew I could only get so far.

Ivan/Goon One looked me up and down and smiled at me. "With you I would like to have sex sometime." He raised an eyebrow. His Russian accent was thick.

I tried to smile without showing my disgust, and then dropped my gaze quickly to the ground. Seriously? I wondered if that line had ever worked for him.

Ivan laughed. "Yes, perhaps you would like to have rough love with me—fucking like dogs."

Damn, that must've sounded better in his head. It might have been a reference to "doggy style," but I'm not certain. Ivan was categorically better looking with his mouth shut though.

One by one, girls lined up for the big field trip. Ivan began the tour with the main house. He stuttered and the giggles from the others clued me into his obvious butcher job of the Italian language.

"I'm afraid my Italian only serves to make my English sound better, yes?" Ivan smiled; his blue eyes sparkling—a look that could melt hearts around the world. Now, if only I could turn his volume down to zero, he might be doable—on a big drinking night.

The main house was decorated simply, but was perfectly immaculate. The rooms were spacious and bright. The air conditioning was magical; the double beds with fluffy pillows and white, cotton blankets looked dreamy. It made me hate the bitches in blue even more. Geez, I'd totally cook and clean in an air conditioned house to get to sleep in a bed like that every night. They were all definitely doing something right.

We walked single-file back outside and were loaded into the old bus we'd gotten here in. I wondered whatever happened to those girls that first night that got back on the bus and left. We never saw or heard from them again. Fear coursed through my veins, followed by momentary hope—perhaps we were all finally headed home. The whole experience would've been so much easier if I could've done it in English.

The bus rattled down old back roads while Vladimir rambled on in Italian—piss-poor Italian with a heavy Russian accent. Faces looked happy, excited, confused, scared—I couldn't get a good, solid read on the group as a whole.

We pulled over by a huge warehouse-looking building with big, commercial-grade farm equipment parked both inside and out. Men were everywhere—as far as the eye could see. *So, this is where they keep 'em,* I thought. Blonds, brunettes, redheads; tall, short, somewhere in between—but all *super* attractive. I had no idea what Vladimir was saying, but hoped he was telling us to take our pick. Sadly, the bus started back up and bounced onward.

Vladimir smiled and talked nonstop for several more miles of bad road—standing up and gripping one of the vertical support poles, laughing, flirting. There were gasps of excitement and giggles and exchanged glances as he spoke. All I thought was, "Wow, my parents couldn't have put me in a shittier situation." I still had no idea exactly how shitty the situation would become. Sal would've wanted it that way—fucking difficult would not have been challenging enough; he'd want me to face impossible odds and come out on top. Simply to have survived would be the same as failing for the daughter of Sal Russo. As for me, I was good with just surviving.

The landscape changed into rolling green hills and better roads and well-manicured estates. I couldn't think of anywhere our crappy bus would've looked more out of place. The driver turned down a driveway and through an impressive entranceway—complete with fountain, gate, and guard shack. I wondered how many homes were back there. One—just Vladimir's little, thirty-thousand-square-foot country home.

I had never seen anything like it. I was ready to follow Vladimir up the front steps and get the full tour of the mansion. But instead, we were herded around back and pointed in the direction of several outdoor showers, and supplied with some of the best-smelling most luxurious shampoos, soaps, and conditioners ever. We wrapped up in big, soft, fluffy white cotton towels and cushy white slippers and lined up outside of a small building with four hair-cutting stations and four manicure/pedicure stations inside. And so, we spent much of the day getting our hair and nails and facials done. It could've been worse. Still, there is quite the difference between being treated like one in a million and one *of* a million.

We were issued another set of clothes and Vladimir joined us for lunch on the veranda—lobster tails, crab legs, fillet minion, corn muffins and coleslaw. I'd almost forgotten what these things tasted like; I hadn't had a meal without tomatoes or pasta in weeks. It was freaking delicious—no one cared that it was served on plastic picnic plates out back. All but for Vladimir's lunch, which was served on china and crystal. Whatever.

Vladimir talked and it seemed as if a question and answer segment was taking place. More than frustrated, I was bored. It took a lot of energy to fake being remotely interested in something I couldn't understand. I admired my newly painted nails and the way my freshly cut hair felt instead.

When everyone stood up and followed Vladimir inside, I followed them. The tour began in the kitchen. My guess was that it was a "show us our place" kind of thing by using the service entrance through the kitchen—more so than it was a matter of convenience. What an arrogant dick.

The kitchen was spacious with high ceilings and bright, white walls where big 4x6 foot posters hung—unusual posters. Mostly black and white, the first one was unmistakable: it was of Snot at the packing shed on the table bent and looking over her shoulder; her ass and the tomatoes colored red in an otherwise all black and white photograph. Another black and white poster was of a girl with only watermelons colorized beside her—the marks on her ass matching the pattern on the melon. And yet another was of a girl with purplish black olives and round purplish black matching bruises on her backside. I didn't want to know how those marks were made. I knew enough watching Snot and her big photo opportunity. I was seeing a pattern here—fruits, veggies, and bruised butts. Geez, this is what the girls were aiming for—to be a fucking freak poster in Vladimir's house? They'd get no competition from me.

The adjoining room was a big, open gallery with only the artwork decorating the walls and columns. Vladimir continued chatting up a storm in his Russian-accented Italian. The main exhibit was a piece roughly 10x6 feet and covered in naked butts with various markings on a black background. Each round set of ass cheeks were reddened and striped with various instruments—below each ass was the instrument used to make the red, black, and blue marks illustrated over the black and white photography. It looked painful. I saw the instrument that left the round welts on the olive girl in the kitchen—a paddle polka-dotted with round openings that, when struck with, forced flesh through the openings, thus creating the horrendous pattern of quarter-inch circular swollen bruises.

The exhibits on either supporting wall appeared to be twisted, individual case studies of broken women. I found these to be the most troubling.

To the left, centered on the wall, was a 4x6 black and white print of a beautiful Asian girl with long, shiny black hair. Her dress was bright red, sparkly fabric; her lips were red as well and she was smiling. I was starting to appreciate the black and white photography with only bits of color. Back then, this was a newer style. I think it's been done a million times over by now and with software, I'm sure the technique is easier accomplished today. The photo of the Asian girl was perfectly lovely—a glamour shot any girl would be proud of.

It was the photos on either side of her glamour shot that were disturbing. To the left, smaller all black and white posters of the girl hung. Images of her being attacked by men who appeared to be painted with black, shiny paint ripping her clothes off; her face showed the expression of shock and horror. To the right of her portrait were pictures of the same girl—naked, mussed hair, and smeared make-up, huddled against a cinderblock background. Even the lighting looked cold, damp, and miserable.

To the right of the giant butt exhibit was another case study, this time of a blonde in a blue sparkly dress; her blues eyes lit up against grayscale features. It was another glamour shot that couldn't have been any more beautiful. To the left of the portrait there were, again, smaller black and white shots of the subject—this time there was one tall man in a suit and fedora with his back to the camera, appearing at first shot to be just touching the girl casually as he walked past, but with each step and each following shot he ripped off every article of her clothing. To the right of her glamour photo were shots of her, tear-streaked and shivering naked against cold cinderblock.

The fourth big wall was bare. I didn't want to imagine that subject's photo opportunity. We were then led down a hallway that opened into a large entryway and then were shuffled out the front door and back onto the bus. I guessed the field trip was over and we were going back to the farm.

Nope. We made a quick turn down another small driveway into a small village of little, one-room houses. One by one we were dropped off at our individual rooms—just a bed, sink, toilet and shower, but I didn't have to share with anyone. I was pretty sure Vladimir was buttering us up a bit before shipping us home. Damn, I missed home. I curled up on the bed and slept through dinner and the night. I hadn't even realized I was *that* tired. I still felt foggy in the morning.

Our little village was buzzing with excitement. There were racks of clothes in vinyl bags and carts of cosmetics and hair supplies and people running around madly with these things. Yet, I felt most relaxed, spotted what looked like a construction site "roach coach" near some picnic tables, and headed that way. I was hungry and hoping for breakfast, but discovered they only had coffee, tea, and juice when I got there. I grabbed a large coffee and some orange juice and headed back to my room where I found three women waiting for me—hair, make-up, clothes. I was fine with this.

I don't know if it was the change in pace and scenery or one of those weird surreal feelings in life or that I had been drugged, but I kept feeling more and more dreamy—floating easily and happily through the chaos. I drank more coffee and let the world revolve around me.

My hair was 1980's big, make-up was heavy and dramatic; the dress was short and sparkly green—made almost entirely of sequins woven together by stretchy thread with spaghetti straps, a low v-neckline and a back that plunged below my waist, exposing *nearly* every inch of my curved spine. It was totally trampy—even for me. So, I started laughing. When they broke out the emerald stilettos, I thought they looked like 8" spiked heels and fell back on the bed giggling hysterically. Happy, relaxed, uninhibited, mildly hallucinating—yep, I was pretty sure I'd been drugged somehow, somewhere, with something and that made me laugh even more. I could only guess what drugs would have that combined effect. It was pretty euphoric all and all. Looking back, I'm surprised I wasn't pissed off about being dosed up without my knowledge. I guess I was just happy to be somewhere else—if only in my mind.

The three women were shaking their heads as they left me happily in stitches and were quickly replaced by Vladimir, two assistants and a dizzying mass of lighting and photography equipment. Vladimir was funny and charming and entertaining. He took pictures of me from every conceivable angle. I smiled and laughed and posed however he told me to—it seemed like the *only* thing to do. I did look pretty amazing.

As quickly as he waltzed in, Vladimir waltzed out, blowing me a kiss as he did so. Before long, I heard the bus horn honking—I looked out to see several young women in similar shiny green dresses boarding. That definitely looked like my group. I glanced around the room and saw I had no belongings to grab and went and joined the others. I'm fairly certain everyone there was high as a kite based on giggling and glassy eyes—as well as a combination of dilated or constricted pupils. Were there different effects on different people or did everyone receive a different cocktail? I was actually having too much fun to give it much thought. I was liking my buzz *a lot*. What did seem odd was that I didn't recognize any of these women at all. I had no idea where or when my bunkmates and the others who started this field trip with me had disappeared to or who these new women dressed in sparkly green were or where they came from. It was a freaky feeling.

Vladimir's house was hopping—booming music, people painted like marble dancing in the fountain, male servers with trays of drinks and appetizers, and a constant flow of people circling around the house, inside and out.

There was more art on display; I didn't see that anything was way different—just more. More fetish-type artwork, more sculptures, more people. Then, a lamp tapped me on the shoulder, smiled, and winked at me. It appeared to be Leprechaun, my Irish-looking bunkmate, coated in black and silver shiny latex. LSD was the only possible deduction. I had to have been tripping my ass off.

Then, I noticed more shiny black and silver furniture breathing—end tables, chairs, a sofa. Several of the guests seemed most interested in flirting with the gallery furniture. I swore off all hallucinogenics that night, though it wouldn't have done me any good. Reality would be worse than anything I may have imagined.

I walked around a gallery of live shows and interactive fetish artwork—where the giant poster of butts had been, was now real butts with real paddles and real people leaving real marks. I wondered who all those real butts belonged to. In one corner, I spotted Vladimir with one of the other sparkly green girls—she was down on her knees begging for the cracker he held high above her head. Then, there were the freaky zigzagged, thick-walled/narrow-passage hallways set up between the columns—one with dozens of black vinyl-looking hands protruding from its parallel black walls, another covered with various elements of bondage, and yet another with different sized and colored penises. An elderly man was fondling one of the end tables when a green sparkly girl with dark hair leaned in for a closer look at the bondage display hallway. Male servers put their trays down and secured her to the wall—while pulses of light revealed motion-activated cameras in six different locations. Before they could pick their trays back up, another sparkly green girl stopped for too long at the entrance of the exhibit and found herself in bondage as well—apprehension to imprisonment photographed from beginning to end. Onlookers seemed to enjoy the show.

I decided to keep moving and avoided eye contact with anyone. I was thinking about wandering off out of sight somewhere and lying low till the party wore down when I felt a large, rough hand on my bare back. Lucky me, it was Vladimir.

"Anything catch your eye, Miss Russo?" He smiled diabolically; a raised eyebrow accentuating the question.

"Mmhmmm," was the sound that came out of my mouth in a non-answer.

Vladimir laughed and left his hand on my back, using it to guide me back around the room. He stopped in front of the narrow entrance to the shiny latex hand, 30" wide hallway, "Mani Casuali," He smiled brightly, "Random Hands." He motioned for me to go ahead of him. Others were already walking down its length—shaking hands and high-fiving the living latex appendages. The females got more attention from the random hands—as they stroked hair, caressed shoulders, and attempted to fondle butts. My plan was to keep moving and get to the end as fast as possible.

I was barely inside the exhibit boundaries when bright lights began to flash and completely blind me. I tried to block the glare and keep my eyes from watering pointlessly. Latex-covered hands were attacking with every step—grabbing whatever was within reach. I felt a shoulder strap being pulled and then ripped. I frantically swatted hands away and tried to make my way through to the end. An audience was shouting and cheering outside of the exhibit. Then, one hard yank on the back of my dress, while other hands grabbed from all angles, sent all those millions of green sequins flying. I collapsed defeated on the floor—naked, jumbled and matted hair, streaked and smeared make-up; only my shoes left intact. And still the cameras flashed as the random hands groped and grabbed, pinched and pulled for another minute or two. The guests' attention turned to the penis exhibit, which was heating up, and I was escorted off the gallery floor, naked and humiliated, toward the kitchen by two grim reaper-hooded, silent men.

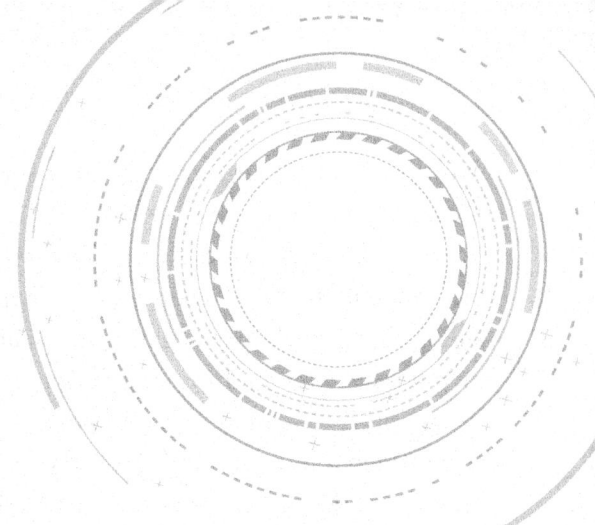

CHAPTER TWELVE
The Trouble I've Seen

While the first grim reaper kept my arm locked behind my back, the second unlocked a pantry door—revealing an old, worn-looking antique elevator cage. I could smell mildew and feel the cold, damp air immediately. I freaked out and kneed the second grim reaper in the groin as he turned from the elevator—trying to twist loose from the first as I did so. It was useless. These guys could've blocked an entire football team. For them, I was like handling a firefly already caught in a mayonnaise jar.

The open cage creaked down the musty cinderblock walls. The first floor was a mere opening in the wall with a twin size bed, sink, and toilet. I was grateful and terrified that wasn't my floor as we continued downward. The second floor was the same—a jagged opening in a wall exposing a bare bones, cinderblock room. It was becoming more difficult for me to breathe. The cage squeaked to a halt on the third floor. The dank air was choking me. A single light bulb flickered dim light; illusive shadows danced spastically around the small space. Claustrophobia was pressuring my heart to stop beating.

The two men escorted me off the ancient contraption and into my cubby in one giant step. They pushed me into a corner and the camera flashes began from all angles. As if on cue, both men removed large, shiny daggers from their sheaths—using the sharp points to scratch lines and poke at my bare skin. I screamed and begged and cried, and the cameras rolled. I have no way of knowing if the cameras were motion-activated or if Vladimir had simply gotten the shot he wanted, but the flashes stopped, the men left, and the cage ascended back to the main floor.

There was no blood spilled and no permanent physical harm, but the emotional scarring from being brutally terrified was designed to linger.

Two more people were dropped off in the units above me and maybe two or three more below me over the course of the night. I heard sobs and screams and saw reflections of sudden outbursts of light. I remembered the case studies of broken women and the empty wall in Vladimir's gallery. I couldn't remember if it had remained empty or had been covered in art for the party that night. Based on the elevator traffic, my guess was that Vladimir wanted plenty of photography to choose from for his personal collection and perhaps was looking for another case study to fill that space. For the first time in my life, I hoped I photographed poorly.

I woke to the stop and go screech of the outdated elevator. When it stopped at my section, no one was there—only a stack of covered breakfast trays. I assumed they were all the same and grabbed one off the top. It was probably two or three minutes before the cage continued its descent—stopping at each space in the wall for a few minutes and allowing the occupant time to get a tray.

I can say a lot of negative things about how I was treated that summer and of the people who put me there; but, in all fairness, the food was consistently delicious. I would've paid top dollar for a second cup of coffee that first morning though—jailed inside the opening of a cinderblock elevator shaft.

I leaned over the entranceway and looked down. Shit, it looked like one hell of a drop.

The silence felt lonely and I decided to fill the space with noise. I sang every song I knew the words to or even *some* of the words to. I didn't know what else to do and I felt like I was saying "You're not going to beat me down motherfuckers." I was starting to get into it and it was killing some time. Time, I appeared to be destined to do.

"Silenzio!" The angry, deep voice seemed to permeate the walls and close in around me. I froze.

No television, radio, telephone, pen, or paper and now no singing. I guessed dancing was out of the question as well. I did sit-ups on the bed and push-ups off the wall. I paced and walked straight lines—one foot directly in front of the other. I combed through my rat's nest of hair with my fingers. I braided and re-braided my hair. At one point, I had a dozen or so braids sticking out of my head. I stared at the ceiling. I thought about home. I washed my face with cold water. I brushed my teeth. I counted the holes in the ceiling. And, after 30 minutes, I had nothing left to do.

I could hear the elevator moving again below. When it stopped at my hole in the wall, I thought about jumping on and going for a ride, but opted to just leave my finished breakfast tray on it instead. A few hours later, the elevator came back down with lunch trays, hung out at the bottom for a while, and then returned with the empties. It was like being held captive by robots—no human interaction whatsoever.

After lunch, elevator traffic picked up and it looked like we were all being turned loose. One by one, the girls below me were being retrieved and taken back upstairs. I waited anxiously. I heard the ones above me leaving, and then everything went dead silent and the lights were turned off.

"Hey! I'm still here!" I yelled and screamed and banged the bed against the wall trying to get anyone's attention. But the house was completely quiet. Hours passed as I strained to hear even a hint of human activity. Nothing. I crawled to the opening and tried to look up and down. It was pitch black and my eyes couldn't seem to adjust. I thought about trying to make my way to the top of the elevator shaft, but knew if I fell—it'd be all over for me.

Depression took up residence as the dark, dank, disturbing, and totally miserable bitch it can be. I had been left for dead. They'd smell my rotting corpse when they all returned next summer. Or, maybe the rats would find me before then. I stretched out on the bed and folded my hands across my chest. Darkness seeped in all around me and claimed my soul and any shred of hope I might've had. I slept like this and woke with barely enough energy to stretch. I wished I had a rose or a lily—that would've made the whole dismal, woebegone picture complete as I lay in my cinderblock coffin with my will to live all but gone.

Time played tricks on my mind with no daylight to clue me in on its passage; no voices, no meals, no movement. It was as if time was standing still and marching on without me at the same moment. I'm not sure exactly how long I lay there—maybe twenty four or thirty six hours, but I grew weary of waiting on death and decided to scale the cinderblock wall to the top. Even if the damned elevator blocked my getting to the exit, I figured I'd still be closer to daylight.

I gripped a rough cavity in one of the cinderblocks and attempted to hoist myself around and up the wall—because I was a fucking ninja in real life. I'm lucky I didn't fall to my death. I ended up scraping the hell out of the left shin—leaving a flap of flesh dangling and plenty of blood spilling. "Damn, this should hurry up the process," I said to death. Then, I collapsed on the floor bawling. I ripped my sheet into a few strips and used them to bandage my shin.

I stayed on the floor and kept my leg raised on the bed. I could feel my skin tightening as the tissues swelled around the injury site. It would need to be cleaned or infection would be inevitable. I grabbed my pillow and fell asleep on the cold floor with my leg propped up.

I thought I heard keys and a door opening, but assumed I was hallucinating when I strained to hear more through the desolate silence and could only make out Death laughing and mocking me in the corner. What an asshole—only Death would find this shit funny.

But then I did hear footsteps—maybe thirty minutes later. I wanted to call out, but was suddenly afraid of whoever or whatever was walking around up there.

The door to the shaft was unlocked. Light filtered down the elevator shaft—sweet, bright white light. The ancient elevator shrieked with the transferring weight of its passenger. It moaned and whimpered as if a lifetime had passed since it was asked to move. I knew the feeling—if I laid still for much longer, I was certain rigor mortis would have set in.

As the cage creaked closer, greater reflections of light became more noticeable and the cage appeared to glow. I could see a man's shiny Italian loafers ... then the crease in his slacks ... the cut of his jacket and the crisp lines of his shirt ... his square jaw ... and the sparkle in his eyes. Light seemed to pour in from all around him.

"Cici, you've hurt yourself," Vladimir rushed over to me. "I was hoping for some time alone with you and didn't expect business would have me gone quite so long. What have you done to yourself?"

He gently examined my injured leg and helped me up and onto the elevator. "I will have to punish you for making this horrible mess, but first we will take care of you."

Vladimir escorted me to the third floor of his mansion—his personal suite. His bedroom had to be 1500 square feet alone. The maestro's bath was probably another 500 square feet; it was really beautiful, if not somewhat stark—white walls with black trim and black curtains over white sheers, really unusual black rod iron furniture, white cotton bedding and white bear skin rugs on cold black marble floors. Empty, ornate frames hung on the walls—void of any artwork. A floor to ceiling, white marble fireplace divided the bedroom from the bath—glass panels on both sides allowed the person in bed to see the bather easily. The bathroom floor was black and white marble; the fixtures—black porcelain with silver accents. Fluffy white, Egyptian towels were rolled and stacked neatly in a silver basket by the tub.

Vladimir drew me a bath, removed my shredded-sheet bandages, and gently cleaned the wound with peroxide and gauze. It didn't look nearly as bad as it felt earlier. I slipped into the bath tub as Vladimir sat on the bed—watching me while dialing the phone. At first, the hot water stung, but in no time I was dreamily relaxed and only somewhat aware of Vladimir's conversation in Russian.

"Take your time, Miss Russo. The doctor won't be here for another hour." And with that, Vladimir disappeared. I was so grateful to him for rescuing me—not really thinking he was the one who put me in solitary, cinderblock confinement to begin with. I thought I had been left for dead and now felt safe, warm, and cared for.

I drifted off for a little while and decided to get out and dry off as the water was getting cool. I barely had a towel wrapped around me when I heard voices coming down the corridor. I looked around for clothes and remembered I didn't have any.

Vladimir walked in, followed by a short, fat, elderly man with bushy gray hair. "Good, you're out of the bath. Come sit and let the doctor examine you."

The doctor examined me all right and then he actually took a look at my injured leg. He muttered in a gruff voice; his accent was Russian and he spoke under his breath as he reported his findings solely to Vladimir. The doctor cleaned my wound, applied an antiseptic cream and bandaged my leg.

Vladimir shook his hand and opened the door. "Ivan, show the doctor out." Damn, I didn't even know Ivan was in the building.

Vladimir closed the door and pointed towards the bed. "Piegarsi." He smiled diabolically. "Is time for your punishment."

My heart sank and I leaned over the bed as Vladimir retrieved an ornate silver hairbrush from the dresser. Without warning he hit my ass brutally with the patterned side of the brush—smack, smack, smack, smack. Then, he ran his fingers across his handiwork and continued until my entire butt was covered in an elaborate and unusual design of rising welts and bruises. I thought he stopped because of a certain number he reached or maybe even because of my muffled sobs. I thought that right up until I heard the camera cl-clicking. It was a particular look he was going for. My personal level of discomfort or a certain number didn't even figure into the equation.

Vladimir adjusted lights and positioned me and took the next hour or so spanking and shooting pictures. I assumed the worst was over when he began to put equipment away. I flopped on the bed—hurt and exhausted.

"I am not done with you." Vladimir pulled me up by the waist. "I will tell you when you can rest." He slapped my ass callously with his hand and went to the dresser to choose his next implement of punishment.

Vladimir turned around holding a large wooden paddle. Much to my surprise, it was nowhere near as painful as the silver apparatus had been. He paddled and stroked and fucked me until the early morning hours. Pain was followed by pleasure over and over in a pattern of expectation until pleasure and pain became one. I don't know how that happened and it didn't occur to me that it was strange until right before falling asleep. Vladimir whispered in my ear, "Thank you. I have wanted to fuck Sal Russo's daughter for a long time." The six foot five Russian man then kissed me, rolled over, and went to sleep.

The comment should've been a turn off and maybe it was—but the house and the cushy bed and luxurious sheets were most definitely a turn on. I'm not proud; I'm just trying to explain. It had been a harsh freaking summer and taking a few ass-beatings and less-than-kind words in exchange for being the pampered sole recipient of Vladimir's kinder attention felt like a good deal. I didn't know any better.

I spent the next few days upstairs in Vladimir's personal quarters. He came and went and kept me humble and busy in between doing my nails and reading some of Vladimir's English smut on the balcony off of the master suite. It was easier than how I had been spending my time.

Of all the women he could have, he chose me. Somehow, I found that flattering. I think I spent close to a week without clothes and completely controlled. Vladimir dressed every day; I didn't at all. It became my normal surprisingly quickly; I didn't question any of it. I had done manual labor all summer and stayed in a crappy shack; it felt wonderful to be someplace so lovely and to feel so cared for.

Vladimir trusted me more and more and I was just happy to be able to have conversation in English. He told me all about his little camp scam; it was a drinking night. Vladimir poured vodka and talked; I listened. He owned several pieces of "summer property" that he converted into his own work camps. Vladimir spotted parents with difficult children and approached the ones he knew would be able to pay—$10,000.00/kid (generally between ages fifteen and twenty-five, but sometimes much older when angry husbands paid double to send their wives to one of Vladimir's camps.) So, now his labor was cheaper than free because parents paid him to work the kids and the cost of housing and feeding a kid for three months was nowhere near $10,000.

Then, there were the profits from the farms, orchards, groves, and vineyards—fairly substantial amounts and with Vladimir's profit-sharing program, this became of interest to me as well. Yes, he had profit sharing. Because I worked the tomatoes, my share of the profits would come from the tomatoes I weeded. Regrettably, the planters, pickers and processors made more than the average weeder. "But do not worry Cici. There is always next year."

Next year? I wasn't coming back to farm next year. I was actually thinking Vladimir and I were kind of working on something together. Yet, he was drinking and talking and I knew better than to interrupt.

"To attend the living gallery exhibition is $25,000 per person or $35,000 per couple for the one evening. For the entire three-day/two-night event, that price doubles. Of course participation is extra, as are copies of artwork and the rights to re-print, ummmm … " Vladimir had to think for a moment as he added the dollar signs up in his head. "Sex of course is much more, but depending on contract and generosity of our guests with tips, many of the prostitutes make more than we do when they turn a trick as you Americans say. Your girlfriend, Sarah, did very well this year. I will not understand sex with inanimate objects or thrill in screwing a lamp or end table, but people will pay for their perversities," Vladimir smiled, "and I will take their money each time." He was starting to slur his words and stagger some as he rose, sat, paced, and rose again. His Russian accent was getting thicker. Drunk *and* wound for sound—it was the '80s; hard to tell what he might've been into.

"You would've done well with sex contract. I was disappointed for you not to raise hand. Perhaps next year you will make more. There are many that would pay high dollar to fuck the daughter of Sal Russo. I will tell you the prostitutes are to make more money here than they will back home for the whole fucking year."

Vladimir went to his desk and came back with a calculator; he tapped away. "Not including whatever artwork proceeds may still come in … in American dollars … minus $7,500 for Tess's $5,000 finder's fee and $2,500 for use of contingency plan … you made roughly $27,350 this summer. Not bad for being stupid farm bitch, yes?" He smiled brighter than I'd ever witnessed before—as if he'd just said something beautiful and kind. Then, he kissed me. "When you are fucking for me full time, you will make $100,000 easily."

Parents signed waivers giving the camp permission to use corporal punishment as deemed necessary. They were reassured this was only done in the most extreme of circumstances. What kept the campers from telling Mom and Dad what was really going on? Big bucks in a bank account of which Mom and Dad were unaware. Daddy checked the box to give permission for necessary corporal punishment. Vladimir showed me the agreement. My parents spent $10,000 (which was freaking substantial back then) to have my ass beat into shape. Geez. There's no way they could've known everything else.

Campers who agreed to the extracurricular activities received an additional $5,000 sign on bonus plus a percentage of their "sales" and all of their tips. Leprechaun was a full time hooker in real life and made a mint every summer. I thought she looked so very young, but we were the same age, as it turned out.

The bitches in blue were minimum wage employees. They probably didn't make a tenth of what I made that summer. I guess they deserved the better quarters.

Vladimir would be selling rights to his photography. I would receive a portion of the profits for my photo shoots. The thought made me die a little inside. But my looks would be changing soon enough and no one would ever recognize me—so for that, I suppose I am grateful. I just didn't know it then.

Vladimir's big inspiration for the camp idea had come from a zero tolerance for rowdy kids—girls in particular; the boys he left up to someone else. He'd grown up on a farm and thought that kids needed to work hard to appreciate what they had. So, he bought a farm and got better-than-expected responses from parents of bratty children. Between camp fees and selling produce, Vladimir was doing well. Then, one summer, there was a terrible drought. Irrigating equipment was brought in and Vladimir took a couple pictures of the female workers enjoying the manmade rain—like children running through a sprinkler on a scorching day, but curvier and with bigger boobs. It wasn't long before he recognized the potential for profit; having blackmail material on other high-ranking leaders in organized crime was initially just icing on the cake. It wasn't long before the work camps became his sideline and espionage became his number one game of choice and biggest money-maker. His connections to major gun runners led him to Sal. His interest in controlling young women led him to me.

Vladimir Petrov was proud of his accomplishments and if he could reform a few brats along the way, that was okay too. He enjoyed spanking, paddling, caning, and the general bruising of butts overall, and he'd figured out a way to make big profits doing so. He was a legend in his own mind. We had some pretty hot, steamy sex that night—as his ego wasn't the only thing excited by stories of himself.

The next morning, Vladimir was already dressed when I opened my eyes. "I have business in the city. Ivan will give you a ride." Vladimir spoke quickly and kissed my forehead. "Tell *Daddy* I said hello." He was out the door and down the hall before I could say "What?"

Daddy. I wondered what Daddy would have to say if he knew his $10,000.00 ended up netting me more than $27,000.00 and Vladimir a *great* deal more. Vladimir was brilliant and no one could pit child against parent in a single sentence better than him.

For the teens and young adults he legitimately scared and who never wanted to return regardless of the money—happy parents provided endless references. For those who still had animosity towards their parental figures, many took the money and ran; others created reasons to have their parents send them back year after year. I don't know that anyone ever told their parents or if it would've done any good if they had. Troubled kids lie. Would anyone have believed them?

I wasn't going to tell Sal. Screw him; he's the one who put me here to begin with. I felt like he was solely to blame; Vladimir merely took advantage of the situation. Plus, I *earned* that money. If Sal Russo didn't fully know what was going on, then he should've made it his business to know.

Ivan opened the door and leaned in; I covered up with the sheet. He threw a standard white t-shirt and shorts at me. "Get dressed. I do not have all day."

Freaking thug—I could only imagine what things might be taking up his time these days. I showered quickly and got dressed. Ivan was banging on the door as I pulled the t-shirt over my head.

"Coming!" *Jerk face.*

The good part in all of this was that I felt pretty positive no one wanted to kill me— it just would've happened long before now. So, there was that.

Ivan sneered at me and growled the entire ride back to the farm, "What is your issue?" I finally asked. *Camp* was over and all the *only Italian* rules seemed to have left with summer.

"You! You are my issue!" Evidently he wanted to talk. "*You* make me sick. If my mother knew of you, she would cut your throat—much as I would enjoy doing so myself if I thought my father would not kill me in retaliation." His English was definitely improving.

"I don't even know your mother."

"You fucking bitch! You do not even take the time to know the woman whose husband you are fucking?"

Whoa. What? "I...uhh ... " I stammered. "Your mother is married to Vladimir? You're his *son*?" It was not so much a question as me trying to process the information.

"Yes, you are fucking brilliant you stupid whore. I should make you walk the rest of the way!" *I take back what I said about his English improving.*

"I'm okay with that." We were about a hundred yards away from the pavilion and by the time he screeched to a halt—maybe fifty yards. *Dumbass.*

"Get out!"

"Not a problem."

Ivan was spinning tires as I closed the door. He skidded around in a quick U-turn, kicking up dust, and flipping me off as he drove back in the direction we had come.

So, I was a home wrecker and the promise Vladimir made to his wife was broken because of me? Who the fuck even knew he was married? I refuse to accept sole responsibility here. I'm not even completely sure that saying "no" would've been an option.

I walked back to my old house. The farm was abandoned; it looked like everyone had gone home already. I pushed open the door and was surprised to see Leprechaun there. She was wearing her regular clothes and was throwing stuff into a bag.

"Hey."

"Oh, hello. I thought I was the last to leave," her accent was British; not remotely Irish—as her looks suggested. "It's been a fabulous summer. I made enough that I might just take the rest of the year off. How did you do? I bet bloody great. Vladimir had his eye on you and I'm certain his photography will capture the moment perfectly. You should make plenty of beer tokens for that *and* banging the boss as well. Was he quite the rattle everyone says? I've not given him a go at it yet. Will you be back next summer? Maybe we'll make it up to pickers, although that's mere peanuts comparatively, eh?" A horn honked outside of the main house. "Oh dear, I'm afraid that's for me. So, glad we got to speak. All that Italian was boring me to tears. Best of luck." And with that, Sarah the British Leprechaun grabbed her gear and headed toward her waiting cab.

I fell back on my cot and closed my eyes—recent information and too many questions pounding through my brain. The whole thing with Tess was heart-breaking. She had somehow sold me out to Vladimir and had financially benefited from doing so. I wondered if she was the one who took the pictures of me and Dickie. No one else knew about him. Or maybe she tipped Vladimir off and he got the pictures himself. Either way, she wasn't to be trusted; it was disappointing to say the least.

Just as I was fully diving into blissful melancholy, the door swung open and a large woman in a tight-fitting blue t-shirt and shorts burst in. "Here are your things. Be ready to go in fifteen minutes." She threw the white paper bag I'd written my name on months ago with my clothes in it on the bed beside me.

"Go where?" I asked, but the large lady in blue left without answering.

My clothes were clean and folded; my strappy black sandals in a shoe bag lay nicely on top. I threw on the black jeans and sandals, the green camisole and black mesh tank—leaving the chains, bangles and fishbone earrings in the bottom of the bag. The outfit was a little looser than I remembered, but it was fine.

I folded my white paper bag of accessories and carried it like a clutch outside. Up by the main house, the stupid, old, decrepit bus waited. "Great. I don't even get a cab."

The ride to the airport was horrific; I kind of wished I could've been drugged up for the return trip like I had been for the trip out to the farm. There was some beautiful countryside, but my body was in no shape for the bumpy ride. Really, where were the drugs then?

The bus was met curbside by the man in the brown suit, who smiled when he boarded. He handed me my passport and driver's license and then offered me his arm, which I took. We walked into the airport and checked in—the man in the brown suit handled our tickets and I simply showed my ID.

We boarded before everyone else and rode first class; it wasn't a private jet, but it was still much nicer than the passengers in the back had it. I had a glass of champagne in my hand as the handicapped and elderly boarded.

After we ate, the man in the brown suit ordered another glass of champagne and broke out a comic book. I broke out one of the pillows, curled up in the cushy leather seat and fell asleep next to the man in the brown suit laughing into his comic book.

Before I knew it, we were landing in DC; I must've slept hard. The man in the brown suit pocketed his comic book and disappeared into the crowd. I grabbed my folded white paper bag of accessories, passport and ID and followed the crowd off the plane. I had no money and no game plan to get home. I figured I'd have to call Daddy, but saw Mikey towering over the others waiting for me. I ran to him and threw my arms around his neck. "Boy, are you a sight for sore eyes."

Mikey laughed and swung me around. "I'm supposed to keep you occupied for a few hours," he whipped out Daddy's credit card, "and make sure you're taken care of."

"Hell yes," I laughed back.

Mikey had a friend who managed a close-by hotel known for its fabulous restaurant. We ate and drank and laughed and then got a room and screwed like rabbits—which Mikey's friend charged to Daddy's card as a somewhat pricey bottle of wine. Then, when Mikey called Sal to check in, Sal told him we should get a room and get ready for the "surprise party" there; so, we went ahead and ordered that pricey bottle of wine and the manager charged it as the room.

Mikey confessed that he was supposed to say that since all the kids would be back from summer activities, Luciana wanted to have a party and they'd be sending clothes over. But, the truth was that Luciana missed me and thought I'd want to celebrate as much as she did and she planned this big-ass surprise. Yay.

The good news was that we didn't have to be there until much later. We drank wine and smoked a quarter ounce of some fine hydroponics weed gearing up for the monumental event. Mikey never asked about my summer and I never offered any information.

Mikey's tux and my garment and cosmetic bags arrived to red eyes and a room full of smoke. We couldn't stop laughing. I unzipped the vinyl dress bag. There hung a green, sparkly, sequined dress—much like the one I wore at Vladimir's freak farm. I bit my lip and looked closer. Thankfully, it was fully lined and didn't appear to be quite as fragile as the first one. I'm sure it was a gift from Vladimir. The dark green shoes were there too—those I was entirely grateful for. Screw the memories; these were amazing shoes. My ability to compartmentalize sure came in handy once again.

While I was given no wardrobe options, my cosmetic bag was packed full of great make-up, soaps, shampoos and perfume. We laughed till we cried when I saw the Visine and two pairs of tinted designer glasses. Mama Luciana knew me well.

We got dressed, made use of the eye drops, and thought we looked like celebrities in the designer glasses. Mikey wore his tux with his shirt collar open and the tie left in the bag. He wrapped the cummerbund around his head like a headband. I raised an eyebrow, smiled and just shook my head no. Mikey shrugged and threw the cummerbund in the bag with his tie.

We pulled up in front of a dark house with low lights glowing in the back yard—the sound of distant traffic barely covering the murmur of our three hundred guests.

Mikey parked on the curb and got out to open my door. I took a deep breath and attempted a smile. "Home again, home again. Jiggedy jig."

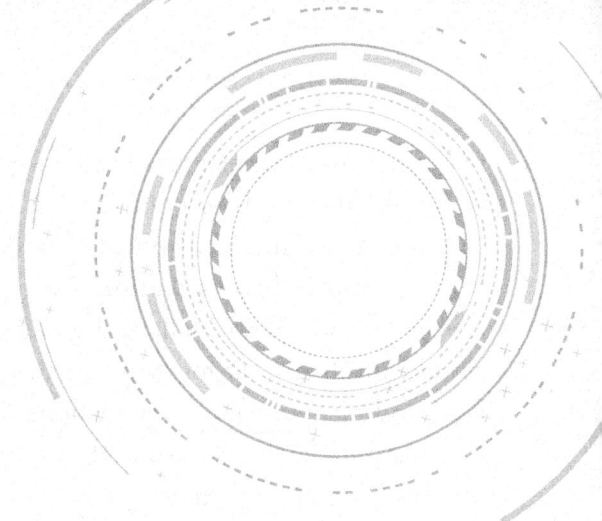

CHAPTER THIRTEEN
There's No Place like Home

"SURPRISE!" Now, multiply that times three hundred already inebriated guests. I'm glad Mikey gave me a heads-up; otherwise the first words out of my mouth might've been, "Oh shit."

Instead I opted for, "Oh wow. This is so great." I half smiled, hating being the focus of attention and grateful when the crowd went back to doing whatever it was they were doing before I walked in.

My parents hugged and kissed me and smiled like I wasn't returning from the hell they sentenced me to three months earlier. Pretending is so much fun; it means never having to say you're sorry. So, I pretended and didn't apologize for my actions either.

Say what you will about Mama Luciana, but that woman could throw a party. It never crossed my mind how much money and time must've been spent to host such lavish events. Food, booze, servers, entertainment—it had to have cost a small fortune. I got to meet a lot of celebrities and party with roadies and shake the hands of politicians. It was a lifestyle that I had very much become accustomed to and, despite my discomfort from too much direct attention, I really liked the ability to get lost in a crowd of cocktails and good food and famous people along with those that followed them. People are so attracted to fame and success; aside from the politicians, I found the famous to be no different from anyone else—with the possible exception of the whole "talent" aspect.

Mikey and I wandered around the party for a while, drinking champagne and eating hors d'oeuvres. I wondered where my brothers might be hiding when I spotted three men on the back deck who looked as if they had just walked off an episode of Miami Vice. Talk about a site for sore eyes. Giovanni wore an ivory suit, coral Henley, and bone-colored loafers without socks. He hugged me warmly.

"Damn Cici, you look beautiful."

"Thanks. It's good to be home."

"Fit to sell," Antonio joked as he hugged me and smiled. He wore a black tux with a snow white t-shirt, black shiny Italian oxfords, and a gold medallion around his neck.

"I love you too, Antonio."

"Hey stranger," Emilio smiled and then whispered as he gave me a hug, "I know you're ready to burn one." Emilio wore his tux jacket (sleeves rolled up) over blue jeans and a red rock-n-roll t-shirt; his white high-top sneakers completing the look.

I hugged Emilio back, "More than ready."

"Meet me in five," Emilio gave us all a raised eyebrow and a nod in the direction of the narrow strip of trees we called, "the woods."

It was ridiculous—we'd all wander off in different directions to meet up at the same out-of-site location inconspicuously.

Then, we'd get stoned and relaxed and all walk back out of the shadows together—not so inconspicuously. Seriously—different groups of people, different times in my life, I bet I've seen this phenomenon a million times. We preformed the same ritual that night.

It was fun being back home with Mikey and my brothers; it was like old times—our greatest challenge to get away from the parents and smoke a joint; our biggest concern: getting caught by the parents smoking a joint. For all of my whining and complaining, life could've been worse.

We never discussed how we spent our summer "vacations" or the night I felt so ultimately betrayed by my family. I knew my brothers and Mama were only doing what was expected of them—unwavering loyalty to Sal. It was okay—business isn't personal; it's just business. Even when it's *family* business.

We were all laughing and stumbling when we exited the shadows and stepped back into the light of the party. I saw Joey Marconi, the asshole rapist, headed in our direction; I ducked under Mikey's arm and together we headed for the shelter of the crowd. I could hear Joey's voice behind us, "Tony, what the hell? Why didn't you guys come find me?"

I didn't care what Antonio told him or why he hadn't invited Joey The Torch to burn one with us; I was grateful Joey had not been included and thoroughly enjoyed his being snubbed.

Mikey and I danced and laughed and flirted with the band members. I was thrilled to see Gio joining us on the dance floor and completely surprised to see he was leading Bailey by the hand onto the designated area. Bailey, the woman who made my father and brothers shamefully drool—whether she was murdering a shared adversary with a pipe wrench or kicking up her heels on the dance floor. That woman really needed to get over her fixation with my family.

Bailey was a fine little dancer and had some moves that would put a pole-dancer to shame; she even had my brother blushing. Gio took it as an opportunity to do his classic bump-n-grind maneuvers on her and I took the opportunity to excuse myself. There were some things I just didn't need to witness.

I figured I'd go touch up my lip gloss and wander around long enough to say hi briefly to as many people as I could before bolting and maybe talking Mikey into hitting a club or something.

Just as I was approaching the back steps, I saw Tess talking with Vladimir. My buzz was shot to hell and the taste of bitter betrayal took its place. I started to turn away but, before I could, Tess nudged Vladimir.

"Cici, there you are!" Vladimir approached quickly and placed his hand on my exposed back, digging his fingers in just hard enough to guide me into the house. "I have a surprise for you."

I entered the library ahead of him and spotted Mama and a couple of her friends examining a picture—the easel turned so I could only see the back of the canvas. I stopped dead in my tracks. Mama's face looked critical, but she had that look a lot. Her friends tilted their heads as she spoke. Suddenly, I was back in Italy and all I could hear was a multitude of cl-clicks as visions of pictures taken over the summer crossed my brain in a humbling slideshow of horror. Oh shit—what had he done?

Vladimir dug his fingers in deeper and pushed me forward; I forced a smile as the three women looked up at me and the six foot five Russian to my side.

"Excuse us ladies, but Miss Cici hasn't seen her portrait yet."

"But of course," Luciana stepped aside and gestured for me to join her.

"Wow," was all that came out of my mouth. The portrait was beautiful—in Vladimir's style of black and white with bits of colorization. My hair looked fabulous, make-up was flawless (probably re-touched) and I genuinely looked happy in black and white with bright green eyes, a sparkling green dress, and laughing smile. It was easily one of the best pictures I ever had ever seen of myself, but the memories of all the other pictures taken that same night continued to flood my mind.

I thanked the women for their compliments and listened for as long as I could with Vladimir's hand still firmly on my back—fingers embedded in my spine. "This is really lovely Mr. Petrov. Thank you so much. Now if you'll excuse me …" I removed Vladimir's hand and gently pushed away with a reluctant smile.

So, now the name of the game was to avoid any further interaction with Vladimir and dodge Tess at every turn. I went to the bathroom, powdered my face and re-applied some lip gloss—staring into the mirror, I wished I could hide there until all the guests were gone. With a deep breath, I put on a fake smile, opened the door and went back out into the chaos. I found Mikey right away; he was a wonderful friend and a willing dodger of people I wanted to avoid. When he saw Tess approaching, he spun me around, dipped me, and led me off the dance floor with the exaggerated flair of a tango. Mikey made even the most challenging of times fun. We ducked, dodged, dipped and kept moving all night—every now and then making a break for the woods to smoke and watch the party from the shadows. It felt good to laugh again; it felt good to sleep in my own bed and wear my own clothes and drive my own car. I loved that car. But most of all, it felt really good to have Mikey as a friend. Because of Mikey, men with glasses always get a second look from me and if they can make me laugh—well then, they have my undying gratitude and admiration as well.

Over the next several days, the men seemed to be running in different directions and so Luciana and I spent time running to different shopping malls. It was a time of bonding for which I will always be grateful. I'd spent so much of my life wanting to be treated like one of the boys; I hadn't really enjoyed being one of the girls. Mama Luciana was fun to shop with—giggly and light-hearted. We'd go into dressing rooms with armloads of clothes and occasionally throw on an outrageous or hugely poor-fitting ensemble to make the other laugh.

On one such trip, I put on a too-short, snug-fitting bright orange polyester pant suit. I came out of the dressing room hunched over mocking Steve Martin's "wild and crazy guy" moves. Mama nearly died laughing.

"No, I'm serious. Can't you just see me out clubbing in this?" I winked at her and shimmied. "I am too sexy, yes?" I raised an eyebrow and did my best smarmy salesman smile.

This inspired Luciana to model some baggy purple long underwear. We greeted other shoppers as they came in the dressing room in our own wild and crazy way and then we took our act into the showroom. It was the only time we were escorted *out* of Macy's. This, of course, made us laugh even more. The security guard even laughed a little as he shook his head. The snotty salespeople and uptight manager saw no humor in it whatsoever. Snobs.

We caught an early happy hour and enjoyed margaritas at a sidewalk café. We ended up too smashed to drive and called Mikey to the rescue, who brought Emilio with him to drive back Luciana's car. Mikey laughed and made fun of us while Emilio maintained a look of disapproval. Mama and I both opted to ride home with Mikey.

I'd missed the fall start for every single medical school out there and asked Sal about it one night. He said we'd talk about it later. I said, "Yes, sir." I wasn't going to push the issue. Sal Russo would let me know where I was going to school or what

I was going to do for a living when he damned well felt like it. I figured my best bet was to keep my mouth shut lest I be back pulling weeds in Italy for another summer.

Some days I would drive out to George Washington Memorial Parkway, hoping to run into Dickie Bradford or some equally as charming stranger that would sweep me off my feet and take me far, far away. I wanted all the perks of being a Russo with maybe just a little say in my own life. I dreamed of marriage and children and Sal and Luciana as adoring and generous grandparents from afar. I didn't want to raise my own children under the same dark current I had been raised, but the financial security remained attractive. I'd changed that summer; I was colder and less emotional—more business and more realistic. No one saw this more clearly than my father.

I came home from people-watching on the parkway late one afternoon to find Bailey and Luciana in the dining room oohing and ahh-ing over pictures—Bailey's wedding.

"*You're* married?" I blurted out.

Bailey laughed. "A year ago this past August. And now we're expecting our first child in the spring."

"Congratulations." Was she not just bumping and grinding on the dance floor with my brother a couple of weeks ago?

As it turned out, Bailey's relationship with my family had been purely business and dancing with the boss's son was simply that – business. *Whore.* Bailey had married Damien St. Claire in 1983. They had a lovely ceremony somewhere in the mountains of West Virginia. I tried to remember how many times I had seen her since then. I feel certain I would've remembered any mention of marriage. Whatever—nice to know Gio had no problem screwing around with a married woman.

Bailey had dinner with us that night explaining that "Damien is working late" and she wouldn't be missed.

Dinner was uneventful. I don't remember the small talk or what we ate or if anything of any significance was discussed. What I do remember is the glimmer in my father's eyes as he got up to move into the library with Bailey and the boys, "Cici join us, won't you?"

"Wha … yes, yes sir," I stammered.

There was nothing terribly amazing about that first meeting, other than the fact I'd been included. There was no grand announcement; I was apparently the only one surprised in the group. But I was part of the group; the one thing I'd wished for and never saw happening *was* happening. But, as the wise saying goes: be careful what you wish for.

Over the next few days, work started off slow—I did some driving and some cleaning up; I heard stories and witnessed things I wish I never had. It was everything they had tried to protect me from. It was a loss of innocence and a harsh lesson in reality—one that would desensitize me towards violence and crime and make me forever harder; one that would feed a darker side of me.

Meetings took place all the time—daily, nightly, over lunch. To tell the truth, I was getting pretty bored and turned off by the family business in general—guns, drugs, secrets, stupid code, respect, control, icky people, blah, blah, blah. I ached for a day off to go shopping and get my nails done without knowing where the money came from to pay for it all. But there was no turning back; no unknowing the knowledge I now knew.

I walked into Sal's office one day—bored out of my mind from spending a morning shredding documents I had no interest in reading and daydreaming about shopping malls—just as some kind of hell was breaking loose and Sal was announcing, "Bailey, I'll need you to take the lead on this." He handed her a piece of paper and she took out a small leather-bound notebook from her back pocket and began to scribble notes down.

"Cici, it's time to earn your keep," Sal continued.

"Yes sir, absolutely."

"Bailey will fill you in. Emilio, bring my car around. Gio, Antonio—you know your jobs."

With that Bailey and I were left in the library alone. It would be her last job before retiring into what she hoped would be a "normal" family life. And, isn't that what we all want? Normal.

The job involved taking out a vile, despicable, low-life degenerate. The target was involved in a great deal of criminal activity, but his kidnapping of young women and forcing them into a life of prostitution had crossed some personal lines with Sal. The dirt bag had abducted our family mechanic's seventeen year old daughter, promising her a career in modeling, and then pressuring and threatening her into turning tricks for him.

"It won't be that bad. We know where he hangs out and what alley he parks his car in. No name, but we'll have spotters that will beep us when he's in range." Bailey tossed me a beeper.

"I have a phone in my car," I offered.

"Too easy to trace; we better just stick with the beepers."

So much of this crap would've been easier with modern day texting and disposable phones. Back then, it wouldn't have occurred to us that there'd ever be such a thing. We had high dollar, hard-wired phones for cars that were expensive to buy and to operate; and we had beepers. Besides walkie-talkies, that was as mobile as the average guy got. And, disposable? Not even a little bit. We bought our shit to last.

In the days that preceded the event, Bailey and I spent time reviewing notes, scoping the target area and hanging out at the shooting range. I was a damned good shot; Bailey could draw smiley faces on the targets and completely obliterate certain other regions if provoked—which I did provoke because I thought it was funny.

The night arrived when all that needed to be in place was. Bailey and I dressed up to look like two girls out partying in DC—she wore a short black denim skirt with a snug-fitting sweater, black stockings, and black knee-high boots, along with a short, black, spiky wig. I went platinum blonde and wore an acid-washed denim skirt, off-the-shoulder gray sweater, fishnets, and platform shoes that were made for dancing—or in this case, running. Both of us had enough make-up on to rival Tammy Faye Baker herself.

Our bags were packed with cold cream, hats, weapons, ammo and a change of clothes. We went in and out of surrounding clubs pretending to be drinking and partying—waiting for our signal; we'd have minutes to get to our location. My heart was beating fast and hard; my hands were shaking. The signal came. The vibration of the device in my pocket made me jump—as if something had just bitten me.

It was time to "earn my keep." The kill shot was up to me; it would officially make me one of the guys—like Bailey. Adrenaline kicked Fear's ass and I was pumped and eager to put my skills to the test. I knew what had to be done and was ready to do it. Part of me wished I had a face to go with my target, but another part was happy that I didn't—just an anonymous scum bag that the world would be rid of courtesy of my .38 and the hollow-point bullet that he'd never see coming. I'd never killed a man before though I'd witnessed men shot, men beaten to near death, and others tortured. I thought I was bad-ass. It all still haunts me today.

Bailey and I locked arms and stumbled down the sidewalk like drunken girlfriends—chatting and giggling softly and blending in nicely with all the other drunks. We rounded a corner and walked behind a building—coming up on the backside of our target alley. The car sat as described; a man's back was turned as he stood watching the street just outside of the vehicle—impatiently tapping his foot and glancing at his watch. He looked huge, even from a distance.

The bigger they are, the harder they fall. I thought.

A young girl in shiny, revealing hooker apparel timidly walked up to the man. He pushed her against the car and was yelling at her. I went for my gun—holding it low and waiting for a clear shot. I took one step back and knocked a beer bottle off of a stoop; the shattering sound echoed in the alley. The man turned to look over his shoulder; our eyes met and exchanged mutual contempt. It was Ivan Petrov—Vladimir's son. He started to laugh as he reached inside his wool trench coat. *Is it possible that Ivan is really the man I'm supposed to kill?* I raised my gun to fire and the automatic bitch locked up. I wish I'd insisted on a revolver. I panicked and smacked the weapon against my palm. Ivan retrieved his gun and had a bead on me, but before he could get a round off, Bailey quickly took aim and shot.

Bang. Bang.

Ivan's right shoulder was thrown back and then his head went back and he was dead on the ground—blood pooling around him. The young girl took one look at Ivan's body, took off running, and didn't stop. I stood frozen. Bailey nudged me, "Time to go."

We threw our weapons in our bags, locked arms and scurried off together the way we had come. We stopped at a run-down gas station and used the outside entrance restroom. Wigs came off, make-up removed, casual clothes out of the bag and party girl clothes back into the bag along with weapons, ammo, and beepers. We pulled our hair back and scrubbed our faces quickly. I changed into blue jeans, a Washington Redskins sweatshirt, and a ball cap with white sneakers. Bailey wore a University of Maryland sweatshirt, blue jeans, pigtails under a knit hat, and brown hiking boots. We exchanged looks, but never spoke a single word.

After walking for several blocks, we checked into a sleazy motel and paid with cash. We used the payphone outside to "beep" our contact and alert them to our safe arrival. Our room was a dive; we dropped our bags and peeled the bedspreads off immediately. I sat on the bed staring blankly. Holy cow, what was I going to tell Sal? I fucked up? The gun fucked up? Sal hated excuses—unless they were his.

Bailey turned on the TV and sat down facing me on the second bed. "I was worried for a minute there, but you nailed the bastard. You don't need to tell Sal I shot the target in the shoulder first; that was just to stop him and give you enough time to recompose. I didn't know it was going to be that Russian guy that hangs around your house either. Everybody freezes every now and again. Really—don't worry about it. You got the shot that counts."

"No, I didn't." I handed Bailey my gun.

She took the weapon, popped out the magazine and examined it; not a single bullet was missing. "How can this be? I *know* I hit his shoulder. Someone else must've killed him," Bailey spoke slowly, trying to contemplate what had happened.

Bailey handed me her weapon. Only one bullet was missing. I know I heard two shots, beyond a shadow of a doubt. *Bang. Bang.* It was one right after the other. Bailey and I stared hard at each other. There was no getting around it; the kill shot was fired by a third shooter. It wasn't hard to believe others might want Ivan dead; he was a psychopath and a perfect asshole. But the timing and coincidence was too much. I wondered if Bailey wasn't my only back-up; maybe one of my brothers was standing close by. Geez—it just seemed like we would've *seen* something.

Bailey was pregnant and wanted to move on with her life, but Sal Russo owing you a favor could be a really handy thing to leave town with. I understood; it was a rare opportunity and a job she thought would be relatively easy. We both questioned exactly how much more we wanted to complicate things. Lying seemed like the best thing to do at the time: we spotted our target, Ivan turned around, I froze, Bailey hit his shoulder and I took him out. We felt like an element of truth lent credibility to our story. I earned my keep; Bailey earned her favor. Win-win.

We pocketed the ammo and broke the guns down—they'd go in the bag with all the party attire to be incinerated. I tried so hard to force myself to believe everything was okay and it was no big deal, but I was fucking rattled and knew it was a big deal. How could it not be?

A loud knock came to the door; we both jumped a little. It was Joey "The Torch" Marconi—our ride and eliminator of evidence. He slid in the door, glanced towards me and then looked Bailey up and down. "Hey sexy." He smiled and put his hands on her waist.

Joey worked days for a local funeral home and did side-work for Sal whenever possible. I think he liked the money and being connected to my family, but it was aging him even then. His hairline had started to recede and the circles under his eyes were becoming more pronounced. I wasn't sure what I ever saw in Joey The Torch.

Bailey grabbed his wrists firmly and removed his hands from her, "Not even on your birthday." She took his empty duffle from him and began to throw our bags of things to be torched at the funeral home into it.

We left the key to the room on the dresser and Joey drove us to Greenville Farms Campground in Haymarket, Virginia. It was a bit of a cruise with all three of us piled in the front seat of his crappy pick up; I was grateful Bailey volunteered to sit in the middle. I'm sure sleazy Joey was grateful too.

Joey left us at the campsite before daybreak with a pup tent, sleeping bags, a couple bags of clothing and supplies, as well as his apologies for not having time to stay and help set up camp. With flashlights and without nancy-boy's help, we set about pitching a tent in the dark. My guess is Bailey had done it before. Had it been up to me alone, I would've slept in my sleeping bag on top of the spread out tent.

We should've been there for a day or two max, but Joey brought word, cash, and additional supplies on the third day. Shit had hit the fan and we needed to lay low for a bit longer. Joey couldn't or *wouldn't* say anymore, except that Bailey's husband Damien was notified of her having to work late. Damien hated the Russo's and detested the idea of Bailey working at all outside of taking care of him and their home. She was certain this information wasn't going to go over well with him.

We spent the next week at the campsite—cooking on an open flame, hiking, hanging out by the pool, occasionally getting bold enough to brave the chilly water. Naturally, we assumed there was a reason for the delay, but with nothing to do but wait, we made the most of our time.

We talked about family—Bailey knew mine already, but I'd never heard a word about hers. She had an older sister named Briana, a fraternal twin Brooke, a younger sister Brigid, and younger brother Ian. Five kids in all.

"Wow, you have a twin? What's that like?"

"Brooke and I have always been close. It's been weird lately—with me getting married and moving to the Shenandoah Valley and now having a baby in the spring. And, since Brooke started selling new homes, she's not around on weekends like she used to be."

"What I meant was do you guys look alike at all? I get that you're not identical, but do you look like sisters or polar opposites or what?"

Bailey looked at me like I was the single shallowest person she'd ever encountered. I shrugged and waited for her response. I wanted to know what her twin looked like and Bailey wanted to tell me what she was like as a person—as if looks didn't matter at all. She answered my question nonetheless as she pulled a photograph from her wallet.

Brooke stood nearly five-feet nine-inches tall and weighed 145 pounds—four inches taller and forty pounds more than Bailey. They shared similar coloring and freckles, Brooke's eyes were hazel, Bailey's eyes were greener. Bailey's hair was a deep mahogany, while Brooke's was a paler shade of the same color and not as straight as Bailey's, though nowhere near as curly as mine was minus blow-drying.

"She's taller and heavier than you, but you have similar coloring. I can tell you're sisters; would've never guessed twins." I flipped through Bailey's pocket-size photo album—her brother was a redhead, older sister totally blonde, younger sister strawberry blonde. Her mother had dark brown hair and her father (who had already passed away) was a sandy blonde. "Based on your pictures, we'd pass as sisters." I handed the book back to her, "What's your bet that the mailman was a redhead?"

"I know! That's what everyone says." Bailey had heard that one before too, but we both still laughed.

My copper-colored hair would've blended right in with the Hutchenson clan—just another shade of red. My freckles looked like they belonged more in their family photos then my own Italian clan. I definitely thought I looked more like my biological mother than any Russo.

I thought of Clare McPherson for the first time in a long time. I thought about telling Bailey the story of my pirate parents. I thought about what Sal would think about me sharing a story with Bailey that he and Luciana wouldn't even discuss with me. I'd been hit in the face by his anger before; it wasn't worth the gamble.

Bailey and I had lots of time to talk and plenty to talk about other than family—men, sex, firearms, explosives, driving adventures, hair, make-up, fitness, art, music, careers, life, love, pursuit of happiness. I began to see why Gio thought so highly of Bailey; she was fun and easy to be with.

It was probably best we were oblivious to the holy hell that was breaking loose back in DC. We would've never enjoyed Greenville Farm Campgrounds quite so much. After a week of wholesomeness and shopping at the campground country store, hiking and lounging by the pool, we were much more relaxed and decided to tell Sal the whole truth about the shooting. What the heck. Lying to Sal would be an unforgiveable level of disrespect; I already knew the forgivable version and was certain I didn't want to risk taking his anger up a notch.

Mikey brought the old, non-descript white panel van to pick us up. The three of us smoked a joint and Mikey told us shit hit the fan when Ivan was killed. Supposedly, someone had spotted us and the entire Russian mob was out for blood—specifically, mine. *A child's life for a child's life.* To kill Sal Russo's only daughter, who Sal had searched for, found and "rescued" so many years ago, would serve as the ultimate justice for the death of Vladimir's only son. Mikey assured us that Sal was an intelligent man and all would work out fine. This probably would've been a good time for me to ask what Mikey's definition of "fine" was.

Home sweet *holy hell* home. Seems the good times never lasted too long. Looking back now, the details are blurred; the images and words blaze through my mind in an unstoppable instant. I can't help but want to go back in time and do things differently. Though, I'm not sure exactly what instant or action I would change. I suppose I'd like to have had a healthier, happier childhood overall. I'd like to have *not* caused so much pain myself. There must've been more options but, on this night, in Sal Russo's mind no other options existed and that was the only place that counted.

Sal ushered Bailey and me into the library. He nodded to Mikey who closed the door and stood watch on the other side. "Cici, have a seat. Bailey, I'm afraid I have bad news for you." He opened the door that led to the deck out back and motioned for Bailey to step outside. I watched her head drop and then she slumped into one of the patio chairs as Sal spoke; it looked as if she might be crying. I tried not to stare. I wondered if he was asking her to take the fall for me or something. Whatever it was, it didn't look good.

Giovanni burst through the library door. "Gio," I jumped up and exclaimed, but he made a b-line straight to the deck. He stepped outside and immediately pulled Bailey up to a hug. He held her for a moment before sitting her back down and pulling up another chair so close their knees were touching. He leaned in and held both her hands in his.

Sal and Gio and Bailey talked for a good thirty or forty minutes. I was feeling left out and wondering if I could casually join in on their conversation somehow. Gio lit Bailey's cigarette. I remember feeling a little jealous of her then. Sometimes, it's just embarrassing to remember what a dumbass I was.

Sal had just broken the news to Bailey that her twin sister, Brooke, had died tragically in what appeared to be a cover-up for a drug deal gone awry two nights earlier. No family or law enforcement had been contacted; Russo family adversaries were involved. Sal would be out for blood, but revenge would be a long time coming.

Meanwhile, according to Sal, the hit on Ivan had been the result of worthless intelligence. Sal denied any advance knowledge and blamed the mechanic whose daughter we were "saving" and who now had suddenly vanished after several years of faithful service. Holy cow—it appeared Sal Russo had been played. The family mechanic obviously wanted Ivan dead, but knew Sal wouldn't take out a business partner's son. So, he lied about knowing Ivan's identity; it was enough to know what the monster had done. I didn't think the story could get any worse, but it did.

The three of them came back inside just as I was thinking I couldn't sit still any longer. Sal brought me up to speed.

"So, you see Cici, this is a very difficult situation. Originally, we had discussed getting you out of the country and hiding you someplace safe. But there is no place we could hide you that the Russians wouldn't find you," Sal re-lit his cigar and inhaled slowly. "And now, with Bailey's sister's death, we have other matters to attend to."

"Daddy, I didn't kill Ivan." I told him about the *bang bang* I heard and Bailey and I inspecting weapons in the hotel room and how I wondered if Sal himself had sent backup for me—just in case.

"A third shooter on the grassy knoll? This is what you're going with? Even if it was true Cici, it wouldn't matter. The Russians want you dead and they won't rest until they get what they want."

Sal snuffed out his cigar and moved around to the other side of his desk. He sat down with his elbows on the desk and hands folded. He stared blankly into space, occasionally leaning back in his chair and rubbing his fist thoughtfully across his mouth. "I've got an idea."

It was the one, short sentence that would change my life for the remainder of time. It was an idea that would affect not only those in the room, but whole families and generations to come.

It was the idea I'm here to apologize for now.

Sal's plan involved using Brooke's body (which the Russo's were in possession of, as well as her car—holy cow) to essentially fake *my* death. A plastic surgeon was called in, measurements of my and Brooke's skulls and features were taken and compared. My eyes could be left alone—the space between my eyes and Brooke's eyes were amazingly close, as were the same size and shape. Brooke had a small nose; I had my mother's sloped and slightly upturned nose. The doc drew on my face to show cut lines. I had full lips that men commented on endlessly and that I thought were my best feature; Brooke's lips were thinner. I cried when those lines were drawn. As for her slightly crooked front tooth, an orthodontic surgeon would be called in. Gaining weight, as it turned out, would be the easiest part.

After the surgeries were complete at a private facility, I would be moved to a trauma unit at a public hospital. Brooke's family would be notified that she was in a car accident, but was in a stable condition. My face would be bandaged, and doctors would tell them the damage was severe, but that I (Brooke) should be fine. They'd also be told that there was a significant head injury sustained and only time would tell how much was lost in the accident. Of course, that gave me a future excuse for "memory loss" and an obvious out when cornered by any questions of Brooke's personal history. I would *be* Brooke Hutchenson; Bailey's fraternal twin sister.

Brooke's body would pose as Cici Russo's corpse in an unfortunate auto accident that started with a severed brake line and ended in flames. My beautiful, little corvette would die with me. This would even the score with the Russians—hopefully. Sal would line up some patsy to take credit for the kill and then wax him for the money he'd collected in doing so. Cici Russo would be dead. Her family would mourn her loss and her mother would set up a shrine in her daughter's memory.

Brooke would be in a car accident, but live to tell about it. I'd study hard to become Brooke and assume her identity. Her family (outside of Bailey) would blame physical and personality changes on the accident. They wouldn't know *their* Brooke was dead. They wouldn't have the opportunity to mourn her death or celebrate her life. Her murderer would be free to move on without question. It was business as usual.

We went over every possible detail; there'd be no loose ends. We went over every second of the night Ivan was killed—every club, every bathroom visit, the alley, the exit. We speculated about the third shooter—someone who wanted to set me up or maybe someone else that wanted the psychopath dead? A professional? A ninja? A random shot?

Sal got his hands on the police reports and we read them word for word hoping a witness saw something other than Bailey and me, of course. But, in all of the excitement, no one ever noticed us or the long-legged, blue-eyed, red-headed girl climbing down the fire escape—weapon safely tucked away in the duffle she slung casually over her shoulder. She started up her green 1969 Volkswagen Bug and headed home. We never saw her on that night or later in the police reports. She never looked back and we looked no further.

We didn't hang around long enough to see the ambulance that picked up Ivan's body and left the DC police with a crime scene and no victim either. But that happened too. The whole mess just happened so fast.

I was flown to New York and stayed with trusted friends during the days that immediately preceded surgery. Cici's funeral came and went. I was told Luciana couldn't stop sobbing. My father, brothers, Uncle Guido and my cousin Dante were pallbearers—though it was Brooke's *cremated* remains that were concealed in the closed-casket ceremony.

Brooke was to be staying with Bailey while Damien was away on business—so that was an easy enough cover. Brooke's "accident" would be said to have happened on the way back home from there.

Everything was sucking so bad. I couldn't fully comprehend my immediate future, much less the lives and futures of all those affected. While in New York, I studied notes on my *new* family, and friends Bailey knew of and looked at pictures. I had a map and directions to Brooke's apartment in Alexandria, Virginia. Brooke was a real estate agent and sold new homes. I guessed I'd have recovery time to sort through that mess. How hard could it be, right?

D-day arrived; I was heavily sedated and remember feeling somewhat giddy and excited—really good drugs evidently. There was nothing unusual about the hospital room itself, but I can't remember hearing or seeing anyone outside of my family—the Russo family.

I had an IV in my arm and Daddy, Mama, Antonio, Emilio and Giovanni were all saying good-bye. I don't think Mikey was there. At first, I thought it was more of a "see you later" kind of good-bye, but their teary eyes and serious expressions conveyed something else.

My head was getting light. I began to think about the Russo's, the McPhersons, my life, and Brooke's life. Geez, it was just so overwhelming; I tried hard to think of a different plan that didn't involve my face being cut or altered to look like someone else's. I looked at Daddy Sal and stared, my heart breaking, "I don't want to do this."

I wanted him to say it was a bad dream and we'd think of something else. I wanted him to smile, pick me up, and take me home. I wanted to go back in time and change everything that led up to that moment.

But instead, Sal leaned in closer and breathed out, "You'll be fine. Look for a gremlin in the Washington Post should there be an emergency." He spoke the words as if they had some special cryptic meaning; or maybe I heard him wrong. Either way, that's the last I remember of that particular day. It was the last time I'd see Sal Russo as his daughter Cici. It was the last of Cici Russo altogether.

PART TWO

Who I Am

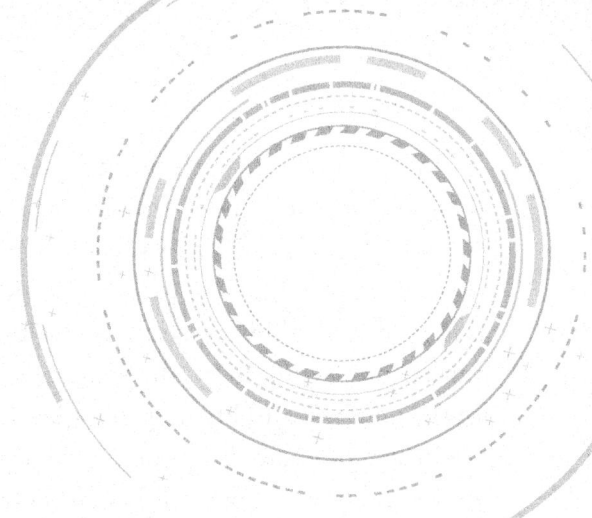

CHAPTER FOURTEEN
Thursday's Child

"I'm Brooke Hutchenson. I was born October 25, 1962, along with my twin sister Bailey, to proud parents Liam and Elsie Hutchenson."

I sat in Brooke's studio apartment in Southern Towers (a village of apartment buildings overlooking I-395 in Alexandria, Virginia), memorizing the new facts of my life. I turned twenty-two twice that year—once as Cici Russo in March, and then again on Brooke's birthday in October.

I spent hours staring out over 395 and watching the cars in the parking lot—hoping for a glimpse of the old Jeep or the Gremlin or maybe Sal or one of my brothers making a drive-by to check up on me. I looked, but I never saw anyone. I cried over Cici's death and found it impossible to accept this new existence as a permanent role. In the back of my mind, I knew I would be reconnected to my family again one day.

In addition to the emotional pain, there was the physical pain—my face felt like it was on fire and someone was trying to put out the flames with a 2x4. I couldn't smile or cry or sneeze or attempt eating a Big Mac without considerable pain. So, I stayed as looped as I could on narcotics—which worked well on pain, but left me feeling itchy and nauseous. Benadryl was awesome for the itchiness and Phenergan took care of the nausea, but then I slept for too many hours and woke up in a terrible fog. Sadly, there was no one magic pill I could take to cure all my ills. And when the bandages came off, I cried for days at what was left of my face—still bruised and swollen.

And then, after the swelling went down and the bruises disappeared, I cried even more—knowing what I was left to live with. I worried people would see the perfectly straight faint scars on my now small nose or the symmetrical lines around my mouth and jaw line. But as it turned out—most people simply tried to adjust to Brooke's car accident-altered looks. They didn't question the lines. The deeper scars were the arbitrary work of a surgeon told to "give her a couple random 'glass' cuts."

With my hair lightened a bit and blow dried and make-up copied from an old photo, I suppose I kind of looked like Brooke Hutchenson—after a car wreck. I bawled and bawled.

Brooke's apartment was small. Her job as a "new homes sales consultant" in Manassas was awful. Her music was way more on the "easy listening" side than mine and, when I looked in her closet, I cried for two solid days. It was mother-fucking tragic: one single solitary Liz Claiborne blouse amongst *all* off-the-rack suits, dresses, slacks, and everything denim. She owned *five* pairs of shoes—black pumps, brown pumps, sneakers, worn black Beatle boots, and new-looking drugstore flip-flops in bright orange. Her look was somewhere between "Dress for Success" and dressing on a dime. I think I died a little inside when I realized this was, in fact, *my* wardrobe. Surely, Luciana would be sending me care packages. No one could possibly survive like this. I *needed* more wardrobe choices. Holy cow—I had a sucky job to go to for crying out loud.

And then there were all the people that went along with Brooke's life. Bailey's family was a lot to take in; I mean my *new* family. Between the Hutchensons and the overwhelming non-stop flow of Brooke's friends, it's no wonder I didn't have time to be depressed for too long, I was in a constant state of overwhelming, mind-blowing anxiety. I missed my old pal, Valium.

The Hutchenson family was the polar opposite of the Russo's. They were casual, laughed easily, and seemed to genuinely *like* each other. Ian was the baby (thirteen at the time) and the only one still living at home. His four older sisters had all moved out the millisecond they turned eighteen—Briana the oldest, Bailey and Brooke the twins, and Brigid the baby girl.

The whole family visited me, and my bandaged from head-to-toe body, in the hospital. I was really lit on narcotics and, if it weren't for Bailey, I'd never have survived. Thankfully, any screw up I made could easily be blamed on the drugs or the head injury. Sober or not, it was a lot of people and personalities to take in. I went from having three older brothers to having three sisters—an older, a younger, and a twin, plus a little brother. I had been an only child for a brief five years and the baby of the family up until this point. The middle was very different.

Briana, the eldest, was two years older than Brooke and Bailey. She was all of twenty-four then—long, thick blonde hair, big blue eyes, pouty lips, and curves that made the men go crazy. Briana was outrageous and outspoken, sexy, funny and confident. The limelight was her constant companion. I liked her instantly.

Briana was married to Lou Johnson—a man she'd met from West Virginia and someone Bailey and Brooke had partied with back in the day. I liked hanging out with Briana and Lou—they were fun and easy to be with and lived in nearby Annandale, where the Hutchenson kids all grew up. With Bailey in the Shenandoah Valley (a couple hours away) with her husband Damien and daughter Simone on the way, I just didn't get to see or even talk to Bailey as much as I would've liked to or could've afforded to. Briana filled that void and would soon occupy a special place in my heart for the remainder of time.

Next, in order of descending age, were Bailey and Brooke, the twins. When Bailey married Damien, she had begun to distance herself, both physically and emotionally, from her family. Bailey had once shared with me that Damien entertained immense contempt for the Russo family and I feared him somehow discovering who I *was*. So, I kind of kept some distance as well.

Brigid was the baby girl—three years younger than "the twins." She had long strawberry-blonde hair, sparkling teal-blue eyes, an angled nose, high cheekbones, and a perfectly dazzling smile. With her narrow waist, long limbs and killer bone structure, she was a natural born model and the kind of girl it was hard *not* to hate. And, as if being a nineteen year old model wasn't enough reason for envy, her sharp intellect, witty personality, and general appeal to the opposite sex was.

If Brigid could've been ditzy or maybe not quite so beautiful or not have had the unwavering attention of *every* man in the room or if she could've *not* been my sister, I may have realized what an amazing friend and confidant she was much earlier in the game. But as it was, I was mesmerized and somewhat jealous. Quite sadly, years would pass before I would see beyond her physical beauty to the person that lay within. That's life—sometimes it's good to discover you were wrong. I'm glad I was wrong about Brigid. There was much more to her than what met the eyes.

Ian was the youngest and only male child in the family. At the age of thirteen, he was slender and lanky with red hair and soft blue eyes. Evidently, someone had given him a joke book sometime before then and Ian had managed to memorize all 150,000 jokes. Holy cow, he could get an entire room full of people laughing as he'd rattle off a seemingly endless stream of jokes, none of which anyone could later recall.

He was a cute kid with a sharp wit and loveable persona. And he was probably Elsie's favorite, though Brigid was definitely close. Briana, Bailey, and Brooke often referred to their two younger siblings as "the royalty" as Elsie's favoritism hadn't escaped their observation.

Elsie and Liam Hutchenson were the biological parents of all five children. They'd gotten married when Liam was getting out of the Army and while Elsie was still working for the FBI in the late '50s. They were each other's first and only spouse. And they were together until death did they part. Theirs was a true, yet short-lived love story.

Liam passed away at the age of forty-three from an acute cerebral hemorrhage in 1980—leaving his wife, four teenage girls, and nine year old son behind. They were by no means wealthy, but Elsie was a strong woman and somehow managed to raise her children and make ends meet on her own. She remains a hero in her children's hearts to this day.

I should've been lost in the shuffle of this interesting family, but alas, I was not. I was somehow inexplicably valued as a member of the group. No one seemed to resent my presence. Incredibly, they all seemed to simply accept me. But I wasn't me; I was Brooke. It still felt like an acting job back then. I just got to play a more likeable role.

And then of course there were the family friends, and friends of friends, and work friends, and neighborhood and public school friends and their families, and aunts, uncles, cousins, and grandparents, spouses, and boyfriends, and girlfriends, and store clerks, and front desk personnel. It was maddening to keep up with.

I'd been directed to be familiar with Brooke's friends, but to use this as an opportunity for Brooke to make new friends and to end as many of those old friendships as possible—thus lessening my odds of getting busted. But there were several of Brooke's friends I wanted to hold onto—mostly easy-going pot-heads I found entertaining and interesting. Most of them had enough insanity in their own lives to fill a book. It may have been a "misery loves company" kind of thing. Or, it may have been destiny.

Either way, Annie Lane was one of those friends. She had long blonde straight hair, an athletic build, thick glasses, the spirit of a warrior, hearing of a tawny owl, and memory of an elephant—all of which served her well as a bartender.

Brooke and Annie both grew up on Medford Drive and attended Annandale High School. But, it was after high school that the two had become close friends. Annie's impeccable memory was an awesome asset. She not only had stories of her own to tell of Brooke, but she easily recalled and retold stories Brooke had told her of childhood and such. I got a ton of history and a lot of free drinks at the bar from Annie Lane. Still, I'd end up with more than I bargained for.

I liked Brooke's boyfriends—Roger (rock-n-roller), Steve (mailman), Patrick (model), Biff (a guy she met at 7-Eleven), Chuck (high-school track coach) and David (a married but totally hot co-worker). To be perfectly honest, it was difficult to differentiate between the platonic and the romantic relationships. Perhaps it was difficult for Brooke herself to distinguish the difference. I don't want to call Brooke a whore, but it did appear she discovered variety to be the spice of her sex life. It's a shame she couldn't have applied that same principle to her shoe wardrobe.

At first, I accepted everything anyone told me as gospel, but in time I'd learn that there are three sides to every story—mine, yours, and the truth. I repeatedly said "no" to Brooke's boyfriends and simply said "I feel differently now." I didn't care who Brooke was doing or why—I felt no obligation to any of them. It wasn't like any of them were going to step up and pay my bills for me. They just wanted to screw me—the new Brooke. I couldn't have been less flattered. Not that they weren't cute or fun or interesting or that I was above picking up a stranger, it was more because they weren't *my* choice. And I didn't want to have sex with the strange men Brooke had chosen. I didn't even know *her*, much less them.

Having to work a crappy job and pay bills with the very damned little I made sucked beyond all reason. I had to *save up* to buy a bag of weed. I couldn't afford the payments on a new pair of boots, even if I had the credit to finance them. And sales in general just sucked; I hated being nice to people I didn't like. I simply had no idea this was how the other half lived. I finally understood the "princess" part of Dickie's nickname for me, "Mafia Princess." I suppose that's what it must've looked like.

Reality was harsh. The face, the lies, the abandonment, the lack of money, the shitty job, the crappy wardrobe, and the absolute hopelessness—I'm so grateful to every single person out there who stopped by to smoke a joint with me back then. Heaven knows I couldn't afford it myself. So, just a big *shout out* to you guys. (You know who you are).

On top of everything else, I had to give up my degree—which my ego had become very attached to as well. I traded an MBBS from Georgetown for an AA from a community college. It might be reasonable to assume this was because I was smarter and worked harder than Brooke, but it cannot be ignored that the wealthy simply have more opportunities afforded them. I'd learn to row the boat I'd been given in time. I sure did miss my old cruise ship though.

So, I hid from the world whenever I could get away with it and cried swimming pools of tears. Then, I'd dry my eyes, put on my best fake smile and go on with Brooke's shitty life.

I'd just finished doing the cry-cry-cry-get-over-it routine and had taken a shower and put on some make-up when I got a knock on my apartment door one spring afternoon in April 1985. I grabbed the doorknob thinking it was probably a random pal looking for a place to sit still and smoke some weed, for which I was prepared to be grateful.

I swung the door open without a second thought. My mouth dropped open and no words could form. I knew the face, the smile, and the man. He stared back, analyzing my face and rubbing his chin, "Nice work. I don't think I would've recognized you if I didn't know better. Are you going to invite me in?"

"But of course." I stepped aside and allowed Agent Dick Bradford to enter, closing the door behind him. I had no idea why he was there—to arrest me, to kill me, just stopping by, in the neighborhood? In my mind I wasn't guilty of any crime. The whole freaking ordeal was done *to me*. I suppose a good argument could be made for identity fraud—still not my idea and it's not like I killed anyone. Although, being part of a conspiracy to cover up a murder to save our own hides in a completely unrelated incident probably wasn't going to help me either.

I let Big Dickie Bradford talk. I needed to know how much he knew and how screwed I really was. Shit, what would Sal have to say about this? The thought made me shudder.

Dickie smiled and continued to analyze my features as he talked. I'd watched others doing it—trying to figure out exactly what was so different. "I knew you weren't dead. There was too much coincidence going on with the death of Cici Russo and an FBI person of interest ending up in a *near* deadly drug-related car accident within days of each other—and that person of interest was related to Bailey Hutchenson no less. I knew there was a connection, but I just didn't get it, so I watched the Russo house for weeks and, when not so much as a bottle of nail polish or a can of hairspray was delivered, I assumed they moved you."

Dickie took a cigarette from his shirt pocket, lit it, and inhaled deeply. "Then I started watching Bailey and her husband Damien St. Claire. What a piece of work that guy is. Anyway, I noticed a Toyota Tercel backing out of their driveway one day and, with no other leads and nothing else to do, I followed the Toyota. Do you have an ashtray?" He held up his cigarette.

I handed him an ashtray off the table without speaking. Dickie continued his story.

"I ran the tags and discovered it was Bailey's sister's car—*Brooke Hutchenson*. I followed her all the way back to Fairfax. There was something familiar about her—the way she kept one hand on the wheel with one hand on the gearshift; the way she seemed to notice me two cars back, slump in her seat, and take a last minute exit off of I-66 before losing me entirely." Dickie locked eyes with me and sighed, shaking his head. "You should try to drive sitting up straight more—maybe with both hands on the wheel. Anyone who's ever followed you is likely to have the same sense of familiarity I did, if not immediate recognition." Dickie began to pace slowly. "I did some research on the evasive Brooke Hutchenson. Her whole car accident sounded shaky. The police reports were a joke and a six month investigation had been ended without resolve. Do you have something to drink?" Dickie snuffed out his cigarette.

"How long have you been spying on me, you creepy fucker?"

"I dunno—a couple weeks maybe. You kiss your mama with that mouth?"

"Fuck you."

"No thanks princess, but a cold beer would be nice."

"Why are you here? I'm guessing this isn't purely a social call."

"Oh, but this is a social call." He held out his hand. "Hi, I'm Tad Bronson." He paused and dropped his hand back down to his side; I kept my hands on my hips.

"So now you have an alias? *Tad Bronson*?" My tone, expression, and body language joined forces to depict my utter contempt.

"Not exactly." He sat down on the edge of my bed (which, in a studio apartment, is the middle of your living room), forearms on knees, hands clasped. "I am Tad Bronson; my alias was Dick Bradford."

"You *chose* to be called *Dick*? What the hell is wrong with you?" I stared at him for a moment and then answered my own question, "Something."

Tad Bronson had served as a Navy Seal and was recruited by the CIA from there—where he was soon to become Agent Richard Bradford. Guessing whoever gave him the alias knew him well and the last name Cranium was already taken. Tad found work in construction and began seeking out government contracts—which became routine for many of the agents "Dick" was to work with. The CIA referred to them as "The Cabinetmakers." They were all construction personnel by day, almost always on a military base or some equally impressive government contract, and CIA agents by night or on days off, sick days, vacation days and sometimes during the work day.

After several years of working that pace, Tad Bronson discovered he'd built two very different resumes—one he'd never be able to use under an alias, the other intended only for cover.

CIA work slowed down the first part of 1985 and by that April it was more reconnaissance work than anything else for Big Dickie Bradford. Indictments, as a direct result of the previous year's arrests, were coming to the forefront and those responsible for assisting these efforts "off the books" were being phased out. The Cold War was entering its final years and the need for information diminished, leaving a surplus of spies entering into their cover jobs as full-time careers.

"See that building over there?" Dickie pointed across the parking lot.

"Yeah. So what?"

"Count six windows up and four over from the right." Dickie smiled at me. "That's the last of the Cabinetmakers' apartments. You really should close your blinds at night."

My mouth dropped open as I thought about how many times I'd walked through my apartment naked, gotten dressed (and undressed) in the living room and worst of all—how many times I'd sat and cried and stared out over I-395 missing my family and my old life and feeling sorry for myself for the fucked up situation in which I was. I hated the idea of anyone seeing me so tragic and broken and snot-slinging weak. My assumption had been "if I can't see them, they can't see me." I was too busy looking out for the creepy people I knew to even think about the ones I didn't know. I dropped my head. "Fuck."

"Three dollars socks on, five dollars socks off, and I'll need a note from your parent or legal guardian." Dickie held his arms open. I mean Tad. *Tad* held his arms open. It would take me forever to start calling him by his real name. Dick just seemed more fitting.

Tad Bronson was 32 then—nine years older than me; nine and a half years older than Brooke. (That's how I thought back then—me and Brooke as separate people). Tad confessed his interest in finding and dating me. He said he'd never met anyone like me, blah, blah, blah. We ended up with a twelve pack and talking well into the wee hours of the night that odd spring evening. There was something about him that made it easy to be around him when he wasn't being a dick. He seemed to let his guard down and spoke openly. It was a side I hadn't seen of him before—kinder, more genuine.

At some point, we were both sitting on the combination queen size bed/make-shift couch in the middle of the combination living room/bedroom. Tad lifted my chin and examined my face closely. I pushed his hand away. "Please don't."

"Don't what?"

"Don't look at me like that." I turned away from him.

He put his hand on my shoulder and slid it down my arm. "I was just thinking about how you looked the night I got back to ARboc and Slinky's and saw you coming out of the pool." He turned me around, "I never thought you could be even more beautiful."

"You are so full of..." Tad kissed me before I could finish. I tried to remember the last time I'd been kissed properly. I suppose it must've been Mikey when I first got back from Italy. Tad kissed me again. Suddenly, there was "here" and there was "now" and there was nothing in between.

I got up and closed all the blinds. I'm not sure why there are those that insist on invading others' privacy; I think it's a bad habit that never ends well. Nonetheless, it was a quick turn of my wrist and the world and its entire creepy population disappeared.

Tad rocked my world and, like Billy Ocean, I woke up suddenly in love. Little did I know that no man would ever grab my heart and my attention like he did. There was a passion between us that couldn't be logically explained. I could hate him one minute and not want to know what life was like without him the next. And we had a connection.

Tad was a connection to my past—a past I was warned to avoid, but a connection that somehow comforted me. And Tad Bronson (much like his alias Big Dickie) was an awesome roll in the hay.

Comfort and joy—I suppose that's why I married him only a few short weeks later in May of 1985. I felt protected with Tad. He knew my past and there wasn't a need to lie—to each other anyway. That, and I just didn't want to do any of it alone anymore. The idea of someone having my back and being a committed partner made me feel warm and fuzzy inside. And Tad was crazy in love with me; that seemed good enough. I'm not sure what he saw or why he tolerated my moodiness, but there are things in this life that only love can explain. I didn't know what love was or why people wound up with their spouses; I simply longed for normalcy. Not that I knew what that was either. It all just sounded like a good idea.

I was asked to leave my job at the Manassas project when my back-stabbing, two-faced, narcissistic assistant, Bernadette, went behind my back at every opportunity bad-mouthing me to the builder in an effort to make herself look better and steal my project as the full-time agent—which she did, all the while pretending to be my friend and confidant. I was never less than good, kind, and decent to Bernadette. Such shameful disrespect and disregard warranted my every ounce of contempt—what a low-down, cheap-shooting, dirty dog of a fucking bitch.

Regardless, Brooke Hutchenson eloped with Tad Bronson on Thursday, May 16th after having met him only three weeks earlier when he came into her new homes project in Waldorf, Maryland, off of Mattawoman Beantown Road—shopping for a new house. It was love at first sight—or that's how the story would go. Best of all—no one questioned Brooke's decision at all. I'd done something for me and broken all the rules. As it turned out, it was something Brooke would've done herself. Story sold—hook, line, and sinker. Maybe this lying thing wouldn't be so tough after all.

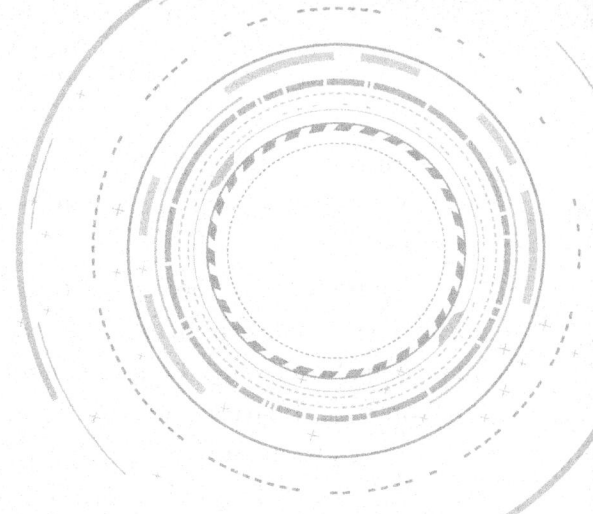

CHAPTER FIFTEEN
Latour Court

I talked to Elsie, my new mom, on a pretty regular basis; she always seemed to know where to go and who to see about getting things such as insurance and car inspections and all the weird required-by-Virginia law stuff done. If we had to do these things in DC, I'm perfectly unaware of it. I jumped in a car and I drove. If I knew I had plans in advance, I'd ask Mikey or one of the boys to gas up my car. If I was already out and about and running low, I thought I was super independent because I could pull up to a pump and hand an attendant Daddy's credit card. Reality was bound to be a bitch.

Tad and I had contracted on a townhouse being built by one of my real estate company's clients. I'd told Elsie about meeting Tad and about the townhouse. We'd just gotten married the previous week, the weekend had been crazy, and I hadn't made time to share the good news with my family; as such, her phone call to my office the following Monday caught me a little off guard.

"Are you planning on marrying Tad? I'd just feel better if you two were married before you moved into the townhouse together."

"Would you feel better if I told you we got married last Thursday?" I asked hopefully. At that moment, a prospective new home buyer walked into my model home office. "I have to call you back. I have a customer."

Seconds later, after just barely having time to greet the customer, Elsie called back, "What's your new last name?"

I laughed and told her "Bronson." And that was it. No tears. No grief. No guilt. No big family meeting wrought with emotional abuse and physical pain—ending in the trunk of a car. It was probably my first inkling of what freedom really meant. It wasn't just about making one's own choices; it was about having those choices accepted. It was like taking fear out of the equation entirely. And it sparked a new kind of rebellion in me—one I hadn't been free to express when I should have the first time through puberty.

So Tad, the thirty-two year old assassin turned carpenter foreman, and Brooke, the *pubescent* twenty-two year old mafia princess, moved into a brand new townhouse on Latour Court in Tartan Village with a big, fat mortgage payment. Nobody could've seen this train wreck coming.

I continued to manage the new homes project in Waldorf, Maryland. It wasn't an especially busy project, and, during the slower weekdays, I'd often put a sign on the door and go shopping for an hour or so. Even though I couldn't afford to buy anything, I still liked to go and look. Weekends, of course, were much busier, and the days went by faster.

Briana and Lou moved out of the big city, closer to Bailey and Damien in the valley. Sometimes, on one of my rare days off, Bailey and Briana would carpool and meet me halfway in Front

Royal for lunch. A lot of the time, it was just Briana and me. It was roughly an hour for each of us. And nine times out of ten, we'd stop at the Apple House for cider and cinnamon donuts afterwards. Every time I stepped foot in there, I was transported back in time and reminded of my childhood days as a Russo.

Tad's income got down to practically nothing in construction. The CIA was undergoing some scrutiny and ongoing checks to the agents previously involved in covert operations had ceased for the time being. Tad had a nice chunk of change coming his way, but there was no telling when this would happen. It became the secret treasure we'd dream of in tough times; as it so happened, those times were just getting started.

"Jesus, I don't know how we'll manage to keep the electricity on this month," Tad mumbled as he sorted through bills.

"It's a bummer," I said with no solution in mind.

"I'm going to check on some side work. I know there's a project downtown that's looking to hire a nighttime crew." Tad smiled and put the checkbook down. "Don't worry. I'll take care of this."

How I loved those words, "Don't worry," and a man who promised to take care of everything. Despite financial uncertainty, I felt safe and cared for. Whether Tad would actually take care of everything remained to be seen. The words, however, still sounded good.

Tad and I both wanted children and we kind of assumed I'd eventually end up pregnant within the next year or two. Three months into our marriage, I was pregnant with our son Michael. I had a difficult pregnancy from the beginning and was plagued with tension headaches from the job. At four months pregnant, I left the real estate agency I'd been working for and took a job working at a toy store in Springfield Mall. My headaches disappeared, as did my ankles and dollar signs in my checking account. I was pregnant and on my feet all day, making nowhere near enough money.

Remembering Sal's last cryptic words to me, I placed an ad in *The Washington Post*:

WANTED TO BUY: 1972 AMC Gremlin V8 w/ Grem Bin.

I added my number and ran the ad and got one reply from a guy who didn't own a '72 Gremlin, but whose best friend did back in the day. He thought it was funny anyone would ever go looking for this car. I decided to run the ad for ten weeks and go back to my crappy paying mall job in the meantime.

It was a big year for Pound Puppies and Teddy Ruxpin. I bought a couple of Pound Puppies and a Teddy Ruxpin for my unborn child's only Christmas in utero—with my employee discount of course.

As Christmas got closer, a black market for these toys emerged. The profit margins were nice. I worked truck days—not physically unloading trucks, just running register so the non-pregnant employees could hump merchandise off the back of the truck. However, I still had the opportunity to purchase every single available Pound Puppy, as well as a couple of pricey Teddy Ruxpins. My apologies to Springfield Mall customers of Christmas 1985. I had a mortgage payment and new baby on the way. "I've heard people are selling them in the newspaper."

And so I ran more ads in *The Washington Post*: one for Pound Puppies and one for the occasional Teddy Ruxpin. My mark was a little over 300%. I had one credit card with a very small line of credit that I'd max out and pay off over and over again, pocketing enough cash to make a difference.

One man who came to our townhouse to purchase a stuffed puppy for his three year old daughter just stared at me while handing me his cash. "How do you sleep at night?"

I stared right back. "How will you sleep tonight knowing your little girl is going to get a Pound Puppy on Christmas morning?"

If people weren't willing to sell their souls for the year's most sought-after toys every Christmas, there'd be no underground market for them. And I can tell you beyond a shadow of a doubt, I wasn't the only one capitalizing on hard-to-find Christmas toys. The black market was already in full swing by the time I jumped in. I knew it was opportunistic, but I didn't care. I made minimum wage, had bills to pay, and a baby on the way.

Tad seemed to be drinking more and more and every single night. He was still basically nice to me, but he had a lot of anger and financial stress because of "unavoidable processing delays" of CIA funds. Our budget was getting super tight. On a good week, we had $12 left over for groceries *and* our baby would be arriving that spring. I felt certain Daddy Sal and Mama Luciana would want to do everything in their power for their grandchild.

The ad for the Gremlin ran with no response. I knew my father read several papers every freaking day. He read classified ads religiously. He told me to post an ad for a Gremlin in case of an emergency. I had done that for several weeks in a row and all I got were tons of calls for Pound Puppies. NOTHING from Sal.

Then one night, after work, Tad stormed in and slammed a stack of newspapers down. "What the fuck Brooke? Did this somehow seem like a good idea for a woman who's trying to run from her past and keep a low profile?"

"What's the big deal? Cici never worked in a fucking toy store. I'm pretty sure no one will make the connection. Besides, it's decent money. You're being ridiculous."

"You think that I'm talking about your stupid Pound Puppy ads? No Brooke." He slapped the stack of newspapers. "I'm talking about your ongoing ad that's gotten the attention of every fucking agency out there. A 1972 Gremlin? Really? Are you thinking it's not any one person's job to scan the ads looking for cryptic messages? And how about the 1972 Gremlin? Any guess whose name might show up on a DMV search of past Gremlin owners? Do you think your father's name might stand out like a sore thumb? And what is the connection between Sal Russo and the person who placed the ad? Thoughts?"

I had nothing to say. If Sal could've just responded the first fucking time, I wouldn't have run the ad for so many weeks.

"I didn't think so. Thinking wasn't really a part of your process, was it?" Tad slammed the door on his way out and screeched out of the parking lot. What a dick.

Michael was born that spring—May 12, 1986. He had red hair and dark blue eyes, which almost looked black. By the time he was six months old, Michael's eyes were the same rich, chocolate brown I remembered Daddy Sal having. But Michael was pure joy. I never knew I was even capable of such profound love before Michael was born. Nothing could ever compare to how I felt about my son.

He was a really good baby too. I walked the floors with him maybe two nights; he was sleeping through the night by the time he was six weeks old and taking his first steps at seven and a half months. By the time he was a year old, his dimples reminded me of a young Giovanni. I imagined his red hair must've come from my biological mother's side of the family.

Elsie went from zero to four grandchildren in no time. First, Bailey and Damien's daughter Simone, then, one year later, Michael, then, six months later, Lou and Briana had Dylan, then, six months after that, Bailey's son Syler was born. It was great being part of a close-knit, fast-growing family. It was great raising our children together.

Tad was a wonderful father. When he was home, he and Michael spent lots of time together—when he was home, that is. He traveled a lot doing freelance type work while keeping up with a full time construction job. When in town, he got home by 3:30 in the afternoon. If I called him crying over finances or whatever, he wouldn't make it home till 6:00 or 7:00 and was usually pretty faced by then. I knew he loved me, but he was overwhelmed and doing everything in his power to provide financially. He couldn't handle my emotional crap.

One night, I went out with Annie while Tad babysat. Annie knew all the great local clubs and was a blast to go out with. We heard a rock-a-billy performer named Lorelei Hooker that night—she played "You Might Be a Hound Dog, But I'm Not You're Bitch" in honor of all the women present. Annie and I hooted and hollered and danced with reckless abandon. We made quite the team back in the day.

We met a cute guy in a wheelchair named Van and partied with him in the parking lot of a local spot. He told us he had a great weed connection and invited us over to his house in a wooded neighborhood in Annandale.

We'd been drinking all night and weren't ready to call it a night, so Annie and I loaded up Van's chair and gave him a ride home. Van called his pal Dougie the weed man and the four of us smoked some of the sweetest herb ever and had great conversation well into the early morning hours.

Dougie Herman was an awesome guy. Tall and fit with reddish-blonde hair, shady blue eyes, and an angled nose that looked like it took more than its share of punches. He laughed easily and I felt like I'd known him my whole life over the course of a few hours.

It wasn't long before Dougie became my weed man, friend, and confidant. He stopped by the townhouse one day and found me teary-eyed over bills and looking for evening and weekend work so I wouldn't have to leave Michael with a babysitter or in daycare every day.

Dougie asked about my friends that I sometimes scored weed for and the quantities they generally consumed weekly. He then proposed a business plan where he fronted me a quarter pound of weed at a substantially discounted price every week. I'd turn around, cut it up, and sell the weed to friends at market prices. I ended up making a $100 per week or so and maybe a quarter ounce for myself. Back then, $100 per week was grocery, gas, and pizza money. And I got to stay home and raise my son—waiting till nap time or bedtime to celebrate 4:20.

That was Dougie. If there was a problem and there was something he could do to help, he did it. He knew I needed money, a way to work without added childcare expenses, and he knew I liked weed. Most of all, Dougie knew that I loved my son. His solution let me be a mom.

Michael and I had a regular schedule on a piece of poster board I hung in the kitchen with tons of daily activities—from educational to craft projects to playing with shaving cream, going to the neighborhood parks and bigger parks in surrounding areas (we discovered Candy Cane City in Maryland when Michael was just a tot; we returned there often). We laughed, sang, danced, played, swam, and went walking and running together—well, more like me running after him. In a lot of ways, we grew up together. And in all fairness, he probably grew up a little faster than I did.

Michael went everywhere with me. I'd meet Dougie by the lake or at a park; we'd watch Michael play and we'd talk and then swap backpacks before going our separate ways. Sometimes, we'd go out to eat, Dougie would come by the house, or I'd go by his place. We became close friends—not lovers, more like brother and sister. Although rumors circulated among our family and friends and Dougie and I had some fun, flirty friendship going on, that was all it was. He once told me, "If you ever leave Tad, it had better be for me." Regardless of the context, I always found the thought comforting and flattering.

Honestly, I wish I had *half* the sex everyone seems to think I had. But, in real life, Tad and Dougie became pals and we all hung out together. Tad knew what I was doing—selling marijuana to friends who were happy to have a new source in an old friend; I just think he really didn't have time or energy to worry about it. He took a couple hits of weed every now and again, but was by no means a regular *shmoker*. All in all, I think it was a non-issue to him.

Life was starting to look up a little. Tad still worked and traveled, but I now had a regular group of pals to hang out with, a jingle in my pocket, weed in my bowl, a son to raise, and a husband who was happy to see me when he got home and, for the first time in a long while, I was okay.

Then, one day, Annie Lane called me, "Hey, are you going to be around today? I was hoping to stop by and pick something up."

"Sure. I'll be here. What time were you thinking?"

"Within the hour—Tess is coming with me."

Annie said goodbye and hung up before I could formulate a response; I froze. Tess was coming with Annie to my house. Damn, it couldn't be the same "Tess." Tess Marconi went to Annandale High School, as did Annie and all the Hutchenson kids. I suppose it was possible, but holy cow, there was bound to be more than one Tess in the DC Metropolitan area. I paced, thought, and worried, but decided it would just be too much of a coincidence right up until I opened my front door to Annie Lane and Tess Marconi.

Gratefully, Tess was fucked up and kept nodding out during the visit. I sold Annie an ounce of weed and felt certain Tess made no connection between me and Cici Russo. I'm not sure she even knew where she was. Still, when I told Tad, he went the fuck off.

"First your fucking classified ads and now Tess Marconi shows up. Do you honestly think this is a coincidence?" He paced and smacked the walls and countertops as he ranted. "Holy shit Brooke. What the fuck is wrong with you? The whole damned world doesn't revolve around your sole existence. We have a son and a house and a life to think about. Get your head out of your ass. There are other people besides *you* to consider." Tad put a cold beer in his back pocket, grabbed his keys, and headed for the door, "Just another fucking mess for me to clean up." The door slammed and, once again, he was gone.

The call came shortly after 3 am. "I'm sorry to wake you up, but Tess died tonight!" Annie's sobs jolted me into an upright position.

"What? Tess died? How?" I reached beside me and felt Tad's shoulder. Good, he was there. I'd gone to bed much earlier and had no clue he'd made it back home, much less was already in bed and asleep.

Evidently, Tess had been out with Josh Shnotschlinger (an old drug-shooting pal) and there was some kind of altercation between Josh and Tess that led him to pull off the shoulder of I-395 and that led Tess to get out of the vehicle and attempt to cross eight lanes of traffic. She was hit by a car and then was said to have sat upright before a truck plowed her down to her untimely death.

The image of her horrible accident rattled me. I replayed the visual over and over again in my head. It felt like I had been there and witnessed it myself. Tess had been a shitty friend and had sold me out, but I still wouldn't have wished this death on anyone.

Tad rolled over when my sobs woke him. "What's wrong?"

"Tess was killed tonight."

"Fuck her and anyone that looks like her," Tad mumbled as he rolled back over. "Go back to sleep. Michael will be up in a couple hours."

I understood Tad's dislike and mistrust of Tess; he had good reasons. However, to be so unaffected and so callus about another human being's demise was troubling. My guess was that he had a lot going on in his mind and had no room to worry about Tess. Still, it bothered me.

I didn't attend Tess Marconi's funeral, though I was extremely curious about who'd show up. I knew her brother Joey would be there, but wondered about Sal and Luciana and my brothers. And I feared Vladimir Petrov being there. So, I mourned my old friend's death alone. We'd been so close as kids and as teens, and then she'd ratted me out to my father and sold me out to Vladimir. It all felt desperately sad to me. I wanted her story to end differently.

The weed biz continued to be very good to me, which came in handy as Tad was drinking more and relying solely on construction money to keep us afloat. Without money made from selling weed (to friends all over the age of twenty-one), I'm not sure how we would've survived so long financially.

I was even helping Briana and Lou make ends meet. Bri had lots of friends over twenty one that *shmoked* too. The Johnson's second child Dakota had just been born and business was an excuse to meet at the Apple House or spend a night or two at each other's house.

So, when I packed Michael and all of our gear to stay with Aunt Briana and Uncle Lou shortly after Tess died, it wasn't anything we hadn't done before. We'd just never done it for quite so long before.

Michael and I had already been there for four or five weeks—spending every sunny day, which was just about every day, on the north fork of the Shenandoah River. Bri was easy to be around. We laughed a lot and I stayed stoned and relaxed. I suppose that's why I didn't see her suspicion coming.

"Your hair is really curly. Do you have a perm?"

Not thinking much about my wet hair from swimming in the river, I said, "Nope. It's just my hair."

"Brooke, I've known you your whole life. We grew up together and spent every summer day at the public pool. Your hair might've been wavy, but it was never curly."

"I know. Weird, right?"

There'd been other comments made I hadn't given much thought to. For instance, one time, Briana mentioned she'd been talking to her old friend Shelly and how Shelly was surprised the two of us were spending so much time together. "Isn't this the sister you never got along with?"

"Right? Life is so strange. I'm glad we get along now." I pretty much thought my over-simplified answers were working for me, but Briana was much more intuitive than I gave her credit for.

There was one night that this became painfully clear. Michael was sleeping in Dylan's room with him and Dakota was sleeping in his crib. Lou had already gone to bed as well; he's always been an early to bed, early to rise kind of guy. Briana and I slipped outside to sit on the trampoline and smoke a fatty under the stars. It was a beautiful, clear, breezy night. Briana brought two blankets in case it got chilly and she handed one to me to use as a pillow.

We leaned back from opposite sides of the trampoline with our heads in the middle and our feet near the edge, we stared into the stars, smoking while we talked. Bri was rambling on about random childhood stuff. I made comments like "Yeah, that kind of sounds familiar." Out of nowhere, Briana rolls over on her stomach, grabbing a .38 she had stashed in her blanket, and had that bitch pointed at the top of my head before I could exhale my last hit.

"What the fuck?!" I coughed out.

"Who are you? I *know* you're not Brooke."

I lay still on my back, trying to stop shaking. "If you could please just put the gun down, I'll tell you everything." She pressed the gun into my scalp. "Please! Briana, my son's inside!"

She pulled back the hammer of her trusty revolver. "Then it's a good thing he has another parent. Talk fast."

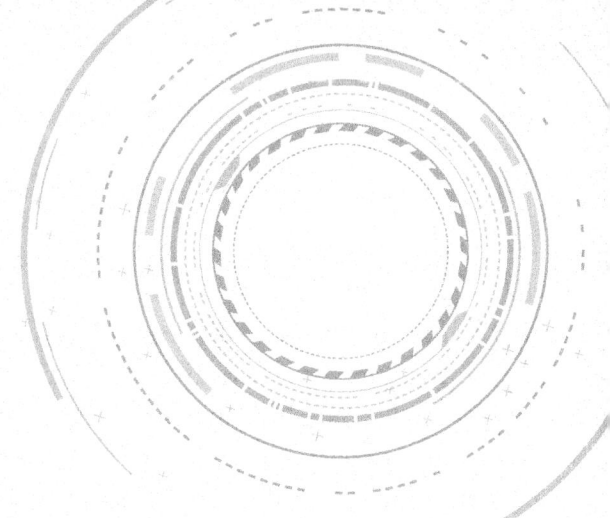

CHAPTER SIXTEEN
As Fast As You Can

It's amazing how fast I can talk with a gun held to my head. Although, growing up in Washington, DC (the city of fast-talkers) definitely gave me an edge. I begged for my life and told Briana my entire life story in a matter of minutes—the Readers' Digest version anyway.

She dropped the gun from the top of my head and sat up. "Damn, it's no wonder you're such a fucked up person."

I sat up slowly. "Thanks."

Briana took a small pipe from her pouch and filled it with some fine hydroponics, lime green bud. We smoked until daybreak. I told her absolutely everything, including things I simply couldn't put into writing—things I'm not at liberty to discuss. However, Briana knew it all. She knew things I couldn't even tell Bailey about back then. It was a chatty night for me. Adrenaline can do that—adrenaline and a weight that ached to be off my chest. And Briana never told a single soul—not even her husband Lou.

We theorized and played out different scenarios and talked about a lot of "what ifs," but in the end, we decided no good could come from exposing the ugly truth, as it was.

I stayed in the valley for another couple of weeks. Dougie met us in Front Royal for an exchange and it wasn't long before he became a friend of the family. Bri and I became very close during the rest of my stay as well. And something else happened; I learned to relax a little. I had absolutely no reason to be on guard when I was with Bri; she already knew all there was to know and I got to share some of my celebrity encounters with her—stories I hadn't been able to brag about before. It was one of those shitty situations that turned out to be a perfectly awesome thing.

Bri and I went out dancing a couple of times—she was always that crazy, curvaceous, outrageous blonde on the dance floor. We made quite a few memories and partied with a lot of the local talent. One band even thanked us for coming and getting the crowd up and dancing. They were a group of young guys, but they invited us up to their room to smoke a joint with them nonetheless; I guess they thought we were fun. Regardless, I've always been treated like a goddess in the Shenandoah Valley—it's probably why it remains one of my all-time favorite places. *I love you guys!*

I'd return to the valley often and take turns staying with Bri and Bailey. Bailey's husband Damien drove a truck at the time and I really preferred staying with her when he was away. An apology to friends and family, but Damien was an *asshole* to me, my husband, and our son. I never felt comfortable around him and, overall, I found him to be mean-spirited, unwelcoming, unkind, and rude. And we all had no choice but to accept his assholery; he was Bailey's husband and father of her children—well, at least father of her first born, Simone.

I'd always had my doubts about Syler; he looks and acts like a Russo. Damien traveled a lot back then. Bailey always had the hots for Giovanni. Giovanni was a whore. It just wasn't that far-fetched of a theory. And it would in fact explain why Damien kept Bailey on such a short chain; perhaps he had his suspicions as well. Or, it could've been Curse of the Cheater, a phenomenon that occurs when one person is cheating and then begins to believe that the other person is doing the same thing, when more often than not—they aren't.

One time, when Michael and I were spending a few days with Bailey, Simone, and little Syler, Damien left the house around 4:00 p.m. to go cat fishing with a friend and his friend's girlfriend. He was out all night and didn't get back home until after 10 a.m. the next morning.

Bailey was livid. We'd put the kids to bed and stayed up late the night before worrying if Damien was okay. We'd gotten up early with the children, made coffee and breakfast, and were collecting pictures and taking notes for the missing person report we knew we'd have to make—just when the cheating bastard staggered in.

"Holy shit Bailey, I was fucking cat-fishing! That's done at night! You should've known I wouldn't be in until now." Damien was a lying, cheating asshole mother-fucking son-of-a-bitch. I hated him. Bailey deserved better.

That night, we got the kids in bed, put on our best blue jeans, and went to meet Briana for dinner at the Edinburg Mill. We'd gotten a late start and, by the time we were finishing up dinner, a local band was just getting set up. Bailey was more than ready to cut loose, so we ordered shots and all three of us were on the dance floor when the band opened with their first song. We were crazily uninhibited. I blame Briana; that girl loved the limelight and didn't know the meaning of "holding back."

Sadly Briana had to take off early. She was working the graveyard shift at a convenience store not too far away and we promised to come by and check on her later. Bailey and I stayed and drank and danced our asses off and laughed more than either of us had in a very long time. It was easily one of the most fun nights ever.

We stopped by the convenience store and hung out with Briana for a while—snacking on convenience store delicacies and sharing dance floor adventures. Bailey still remembers some of the guys we danced with and men who bought us drinks that night. I can't remember any of them at all. I just remember dancing and laughing, feeling invincible and never wanting the feeling to end.

Bailey and I got in late. Damien probably passed out an hour after we left, but he was well-rested when he got up early with the kids the next morning, pouring three bowls of cereal, and yelling at Bailey about having to leave and do some fucking stupid shit somewhere else.

It would've been nice to get a couple more hours of sleep, but Damien had already spent fifteen minutes caring for his own children that weekend and I suppose not a lot more could've been expected.

We staggered out of bed, finished the coffee Damien left behind, and made another pot. It was a beautiful, sunny day, so we opened the sliding doors to the deck, filled the baby pool with water, and let the kids splash around—Simone, Michael, and little Syler played well together. Bailey and I laughed and relived our antics from the previous night.

We'd been at it for a couple of hours and, at one point, we were laughing so hard it hurt. That's when we heard Damien's voice from below the deck. "It's not that fucking funny!"

Holy shit. We had no idea how long he'd been eavesdropping on our conversation. Bailey and I looked at each other and simultaneously started cracking up again. We covered our mouths to muffle the laughter down to snickers and snorts. I could feel Damien's hate seeping up through the decking. He hated that Bailey had fun with anyone other than him.

I told Tad all about our weekend when we returned home and he launched into a full-scale investigation. "What were you and Bailey talking about on the deck? Did either of you make any reference to your past or any of the Russo's or drop any names that might link you to your past?"

"I don't think so. We were just laughing about being out dancing and going by Briana's store shit-faced."

Tad could be so reactive and overly analytical. He watched everyone's every move and questioned their every possible motive. I suppose it was his training and background. And then Tad could be such a goofball, telling stupid jokes and beer-drinking stories, as he'd stagger to grab another cold one. I don't think anyone ever suspected he was collecting information and taking notes—handling background checks in his spare time. It seemed excessive to me.

Tad Bronson was a nice guy. I can't believe y'all bought that one hook, line, and sinker the entire time you were under his microscope. It maddened me; I thought it seemed an awful lot like pretending to respect someone's privacy after you'd gone through their underwear drawer.

Anyway, after the cat-fishing/Edinburg Mill weekend, things seemed to improve between Damien and Bailey. He quit his truck-driving job and found local construction work. She seemed to be enjoying life in the valley and kept herself busy with children, pets, and a garden.

None of us saw or heard from Bailey a whole lot back then, but she'd pack up Simone and Syler and bring them into town to see Grandma Hutchenson every now and again. Elsie adored her grandchildren and spoiled them all positively rotten.

Grandma's house on Medford Drive was maybe fifteen or twenty minutes from our townhouse on Latour Court. My life as a marijuana broker allowed me the flexibility to take off with Michael so he could spend the day with his cousins and me with my sister on her rare visits without Damien.

On one such visit, Bailey had barely gotten the kids out of the car and bags unloaded when the phone rang. I wasn't rattled that someone was calling her before we could so much as have a cup of coffee and a cigarette—people were always cutting into my time with Bailey. I was rattled, however, when I saw Bailey's expression—shock, horror, fear, and grief.

Ian was there, Brigid had just walked in the door, and the kids were gathered around Elsie in the living room. We all froze with racing hearts waiting to hear what looked like bad news.

"It's Damien. There's been an accident." For the first time ever, Bailey looked pale and frightened.

Faulty welding was blamed for the crane that snapped and dropped 2700 pounds of sheeting on Damien's body that day. Bailey grabbed her own suitcase, leaving the kids with us, and headed back out 66 West and down 81 South for the two-hour drive back to the valley.

She arrived at the emergency room two hours later to find Damien with his back and legs broken and his body crushed. Something told me the only thing accidental about the whole ordeal was that Damien was still alive.

Before long, Damien was home with Bailey by his side, nursing him faithfully back to health. In a matter of months, he was out of his wheel chair and up on crutches. By the time they put their house on the market and took off seeking seclusion on the Hutchenson family farm in Danese, West Virginia, well, Damien was perfectly capable of pointing to Bailey with his cane and instructing her how to physically move the entire family while he indulged in the humble beginnings of a horrible addiction to alcohol and pain medication.

Liam and Elsie Hutchenson purchased the 98-acre property in remote Danese, West Virginia in the late '60s as a get-together and vacation spot for the whole family. The big house had sat vacant, save several teenage parties hosted by local trespassers, for many long winters.

The first time Tad and I visited the property, I wasn't sure we could even make it up the rocky road in my Toyota Corolla. And we thought simply *finding* "the road" would be the hard part.

Beside the five-bedroom early 1900's farmhouse on top of that mountain was the "milk house," an old milking parlor once used as a playhouse for the Hutchenson kids and later converted into a two-bedroom/one-bath apartment by Grandma Ziegenfuss (Elsie's mother)—her gift of gratitude to Elsie and Liam for years of gracious hospitality. I imagined the milk house was easier to heat in the winter than its barely-insulated neighboring house, with two full floors and a big, hugely creepy basement. I'm pretty sure the whole damned place was haunted. Gratefully, my five-year old son was a ghostbuster with mad skills and a new proton pack.

Tad, Michael, and I enjoyed visiting Damien and Bailey and Simone and Syler. Damien seemed happier hidden safely away in the mountains growing some of the finest weed I'd ever known anyone to grow themselves. He had it down to an art form. Later, I'd discover that this is just one of those things that West Virginians in general do really well. My guess is that he did some research and got some pointers from someone local—truly a scientific art form.

My life continued on, caring for Michael and brokering pot deals. Dougie had a new girlfriend, Terry Lynn, and often we'd hang out at her place in Fredericksburg—barbequing, boozing, and burning on the weekends.

Terry was a tall and slender brunette who was outrageous and outspoken and just a shit-ton of fun. We became friends and sometimes Jazzercised in Alexandria together—Terry worked for a law firm in DC and lived in Fredericksburg; Alexandria was on her way home. She was a hot, successful lawyer by day, but she partied like a rock star by night. I suppose Jazzercise is what kept her up to the ongoing challenge.

It was Terry who called and told me about Dougie. "Are you sitting down?"

I hate conversations that start off that way. "Yeah," I lied.

"Doug was in an accident last night. He was flown to Georgetown University Hospital early this morning."

My heart sank, knocking the air from my lungs, and dropping me into a kitchen chair—another car accident. His six-two frame had gone through the back window of the Nissan Stanza he was driving down Route 1. He wasn't wearing a seatbelt and no one was surprised there—we'd all known him to cut seatbelts out of vehicles.

I don't remember what I drove, who watched Michael, or how I got there. I do however remember the eerily familiar landscape of Georgetown University Hospital and how I had to mentally push past it to get to Dougie's room in ICU. Even driving through the city, I felt like there were eyes on me; on university grounds, the feeling was more suffocating.

Dougie lay comatose in a body cast with a halo holding his head together. Lots of friends and family came and went. I brought a boom box and played Roxy Music "More Than This." Anyone that knew Doug Herman would've said that Gregg Allman's "I'm No Angel" might've been a more fitting choice, but they didn't know Dougie like I did. I saw his kinder, more loving, and more spiritual side. He was my friend.

His parents flew in from Florida and kept watch by his bed. When they had to fly home for doctor appointments of their own, his mom worried no one would be with her son during the day; after work visiting hours seemed to bring the crowds in though. I promised Mrs. Herman I'd be there during the day. Dougie wouldn't be alone.

I got up early and got Michael off to school. I cried on his first day of kindergarten and checked his schedule constantly, trying to imagine what he was doing and how his day was going. But by now, we'd settled nicely into a routine and his half-days at school gave me a little time to run errands and such.

I thought about waterproof mascara. "No. I am not going to cry today." I boldly applied my non-waterproof mascara and grabbed a book full of positive, healing affirmations I planned to read to Dougie while listening to some Roxy Music.

I strode into the hospital full of hope and looking forward to hanging out with Dougie. I didn't care what the nurses said; he knew I was there. Call it "muscle spasms," but he reacted and responded to the sound of my voice. And even if *he* didn't know I was there, *I* knew I was there.

I rounded the corner to the ICU and saw a group of people at the end of the corridor. They were all in jeans and tees and were roughly my age. *They look like they could be Dougie's friends*, I smiled to myself.

No sooner had the thought crossed my mind, Dougie's brother Gavin stepped out of a doorway. "Brooke, what are you doing here?"

"I told your mom Dougie wouldn't be alone during the day. She was worried no one could be here till after work."

The group from the end of the corridor began moving our direction. I could make out Terry Lynn and some others I'd met in passing over the years.

"Oh my God, you don't know. I'm sorry I didn't call you. I couldn't even think who to call this morning. I thought maybe Terry called you."

Dougie's condition had deteriorated severely over the course of the night and the damage to his brain was beyond repair. His parents were en route back from Florida as we spoke. Dougie was being kept alive with the aid of a respirator; his heart was hardly beating on its own. We'd be allowed to go in groups of three to say goodbye.

Before I could process the words, I found myself walking into Dougie's room behind his sister, Jenna, and another female friend. He lay flat on his bed—his chest rising and falling to the rhythm of the machine that forced his respirations. All of my medical training and experience along with every ounce of self-restraint flew out the window—leaving me with nothing but raw emotion. I cried big, black, streaming mascara tears as I barely choked out my goodbye, not understanding why it was all happening as I held onto that stupid book of positive affirmations.

I joined the group at the end of the corridor and hugged Terry Lynn. Her eyes were red, but she remained composed. "I wanted him out of my life, but not this way."

Dougie had never mentioned them having troubles, nor had she that I remembered. I thought she was a cold-hearted bitch. Years and years and years would pass before Terry Lynn would have her chance to share her side of the story. Despite all outward appearances, Dougie and Terry's relationship had been on a downhill slide for some time. She was a professional, as well as a big-time, after-hours partier. He was a working man that should've never consumed alcohol, as it seemed to bring out his angrier, more violent side. I'm so sorry I ever remotely thought ill of Terry for that one comment spoken in a time of grief.

I always felt very safe and protected around Dougie. I'd heard stories and knew no one would fuck with me and thus tempt the wrath of Doug Herman. But I'd never seen him completely lose his temper, punch through someone's truck window to get to their face, break, bruise, maim, or otherwise harm a single human being. But he did those things. Just never around me.

Despite his anger issues when drinking, Dougie was loved by many—not just for his weed services, but because he'd helped out all of his customers with personal issues at one time or another. For me, he gave me a deal on a quarter pound every week, knowing I needed to make money and wanted to find a way to be at home with my child as well.

As we all stood teary-eyed that day in the hospital corridor, one friend recalled the story of Dougie building a wheelchair ramp for him when he was injured. Another woman told about Dougie watching her dogs while she was out of town with her dying mother for three months. And yet another of him repairing her car so she could get to work. Stories poured out as we all stood around not knowing how to walk away.

Tad and I both mourned the unspeakable loss of our dear and trusted friend for all the days that preceded the funeral. We cried and drank and relived every moment we'd forever cherish. I thought I'd have no tears left for the funeral.

The morning of Dougie's funeral, we met a group of maybe seventy-five or a hundred people at Fuddruckers's in Annandale. Gavin's plan was to connect, carpool, and follow each other to Dougie's funeral in classic pothead style. Mary Jane blew through all the windows of our convoy, traveling out 66W and South on 81 in an unplanned, ongoing toast of smoke to Dougie Herman all the way to a small town in southern Virginia where the private services were held.

It was the viewing and services of a rock star in the quietest most remote part of the state. The people flowed through the small funeral parlor into the parking lot and onto the lawn and surrounding property. Dougie's parents were good, decent, working-class people. His mother was sweet and kind and maybe a little overwhelmed, but still happy to see that her son had so many friends that cared for him so deeply. I cried as I watched her kiss Dougie's forehead. Nothing in life could've have prepared her for this.

The family limousines led the funeral procession to Dougie's burial site. By the time we got parked and walked way too far for heels on a rainy day, the family was already seated and the preacher was speaking. I couldn't hear a single word he said standing in the crowd of people carpeting the hillside shoulder-to-shoulder around Dougie's grave site—umbrellas sporadically popping open to greet the scattered drops of rain. Heads bowed and prayers echoed. Above it all, I could hear Jenna's sobs turn to wails turn to heart-wrenching pain. If Tad hadn't been there to hold me up, my shaking and sobs would've dropped me to my knees. Jenna's big brother had been her hero. It was the end of an era, the loss of a hero, and the death of a friend.

The crowd parted so that family members could exit. Heads remained bowed and the crowd slowly thinned—some moving in closer, some headed home. I moved in closer with Tad—a sea of black raincoats and umbrellas circled in. Influential people stepped forward, and words regarding business were spoken. Tad and I exchanged glances. Then, the seven or eight people who seemed to be leading this gathering held up oversized joints. "To Dougie." These were the movers and the shakers of the east coast marijuana market. These were the people who'd indirectly taken care of my need for weed for more than a decade and Terry Lynn was smack dab in the middle. Holy cow. Was *Terry* Dougie's contact? I'd assumed it was the other way around. Perhaps my part-time business would continue after all.

"DOUGIE!" The crowd cheered back. And in the misty rain on that tiny mountain top, more than a hundred and fifty people torched up as smoke gathered and hung like steam above us in tribute to our friend taken altogether too soon.

It was late when we rolled back into Annandale. Grandma Elsie had been watching Michael (who she absolutely adored) and gave me a ration of shit for being gone so long. I suppose I had it coming. I didn't mind so much, as it made me feel like part of the family. I apologized.

I was numb for a long time, but life carried on regardless. Tad worked daytime construction and nighttime whatever. I learned that asking too many questions got me nowhere real fast. Sometimes, he'd have to take off for the weekend and I'd just do my best to make it a time for Michael and me to hang out. He was sweet and funny and easy to be with, though not so easy to keep up with sometimes and Elsie said he was a "bull in a china shop who could tear up a steel ball," but always sweet-natured.

Tad kissed me goodbye and off he ran for another weekend away—the third one in a row. Michael broke out his ghostbuster gear and we set up my 35 mm to take some auto-timed action shots of us busting ghosts. We were total bad-asses. Good thing too, as that ghost-busting skill was bound to come in handy.

That night, Michael and I read several books including "Where the Wild Things Are" by Maurice Sendak. It was one of my favorite books as a kid and I found and bought a copy so Michael and I could share the experience of "the night Max wore his wolf suit." We took turns reading, though I'm pretty sure Michael simply had the words memorized. He rolled over and was out-for-the-count in less than a minute. He was and remains one of the best sleepers of all time.

I double-checked the locks and placed the metal bar so that it snuggly secured the sliding glass door in the basement. The sliding door directly above it was off the living room and blocked off with wooden railings, though we always had plans to build a deck eventually. And, on the third floor, directly above the living room slider on the backside of the house, was my bedroom window. The front of the townhouse only showed two windows from the parking lot—Michael's bedroom and, below it, the kitchen window.

I took a hot bath, watched whatever dumb crap was on television, and turned off the lights. I prayed I'd sleep well, but didn't remotely bank on it, as insomnia had been my constant companion for so long; a night without waking probably would've freaked me out. So, when I woke up a couple hours later, I instinctively checked on Michael across the hall, went to the bathroom, and got a drink of water. I froze when I heard a scraping/scratching noise outside. I peeked out my bedroom window and thought I caught a shadow, but after scanning the area for several minutes and allowing my nerves to settle, I decided I was being paranoid and went back to bed, curling up with my .38 Smith & Wesson revolver. "Happiness is a warm gun."

I awoke suddenly for the second time that night. This time I was certain I heard breaking glass. I let the safety off my revolver and reached for the phone, only to find an empty charging station. Why the fuck couldn't I remember to put the cordless back on the base at night?

I remembered the corded phone in Michael's room and crept quietly out of bed. I peeked around the staircase and heard a step creak from the staircase directly below leading up from the basement. I was torn between holding my higher ground and backing up towards Michael's room to get to his red Ghostbuster logo phone.

I pulled the hammer back as I took a step closer to Michael—still sleeping soundly. I heard another two steps creek from below and tried to choke back my panic. Then, something snapped within me. I'm not sure if it was maternal instinct, self-preservation, shock, fear, or the Holy Spirit itself that moved me down those steps, but I crept downward with the stealth of a professional. I eased around the corner to find my assailant turning the corner of the basement stairs and facing me—light reflecting off the knife he held in his right hand.

Bang! I fired my first shot. The shadowy male figure stepped backwards and dropped the knife. He was reaching behind his back as I stepped in and shot again—over and over again. Cock, step, shoot. Cock, step, shoot.

I wasn't sure how many times I should shoot or when I should stop, so I kept on going. "Run, run as fast as you can!"

I'd shot him six times before I realized I was quoting a fairy tale and not Dirty Harry. I breathed hard and collapsed against the wall, shaking my head in disbelief. Out loud, I heard myself say, "I killed the Gingerbread Man."

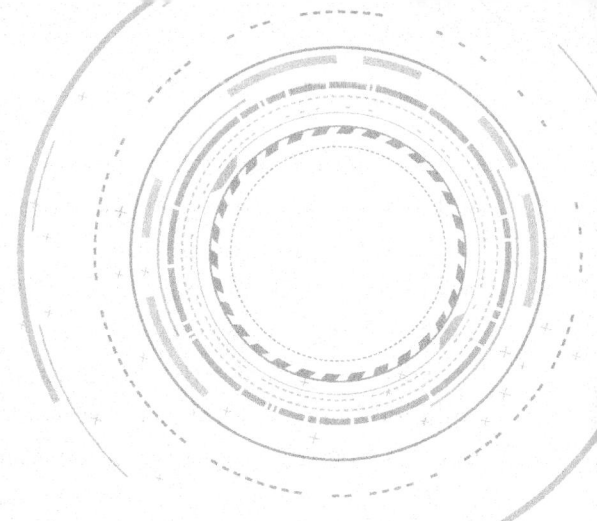

CHAPTER SEVENTEEN
Hide-and-Seek

Looking down on this man whom I didn't recognize, I wondered who he was and why he wanted to kill me. I needed to call the police and check on Michael and maybe call Terry Lynn. "But this is self-defense," I told myself. "I don't need a lawyer, right?"

I'd killed a man and protected my child. I should've felt like a bad-ass, but in that moment of truth, I recited a nursery rhyme. I didn't feel tough. I felt like a woman with a child who just freaked the fuck out and, by the very grace of God, lived to tell about it. "The Gingerbread Man." I'll never be able to read that book again without thinking of this horrible night. A night that wasn't over. I started crying. There was so much shit I had to do. Alone.

At that moment, I heard rustling in the basement. Fuck. The killer had a partner and I'd emptied my gun on the Gingerbread Man. I spotted my cordless phone on the coffee table, picked it up, and quickly dialed 911 as I scrambled upstairs, slamming and locking the door to Michael's room behind me.

I'd left my additional ammo in my bedroom—not that there was room to tuck anything into my night clothes consisting of a tee shirt and underwear.

I'd killed the Gingerbread Man and forever tainted a favorite childhood story. Even the dessert would never be the same. And now his partner, (maybe the Baker Man?) was in my basement. Holy crap. Someone really wanted me dead to send back-up.

The 911 operator's voice echoed from the handset I still held by my side. "911. What's your emergency? Hello? Do you need help? 911. Please state your emergency."

I could hear the operator dispatching units from another line in the background. "Someone broke into my house."

"Yes ma'am." The operator was back on the line with me. "Is the intruder still there?"

"Yes, but he's dead. I shot him."

"Police are on their way. Try to remain calm."

"*Remain* calm? I'd have to actually *be* calm in order to remain there! Fucking hurry! I think there's another *intruder* in my basement!"

I stayed on the line as directed, but sat the phone down so I could listen more closely—for a creek of a step or the cock of a gun. Nothing. I sat curled up in front of Michael's bed—my arms wrapped around my knees, shaking.

After what seemed like an eternity, I could hear sirens in the distance, coming closer. Praise God. The cavalry was on its way.

The police arrived, asked a bitchload of questions, and before long, my house was swarming with uniforms. And still, Michael slept. I heard the term "overkill" used more than once and received my share of sideways glances.

"I panicked and he just kept coming and I kept shooting."

"Ma'am, where is your husband tonight?"

"He's out of town like mother-fucking always when I need him!" It went on like that for a while. I was a perfect wreck.

Finally, the uniforms left one by one. They taped plastic over the busted up sliding door in the basement and left me with the name of a "good glass man."

The police and the body were gone, but the blood and guts remained. Sadly, there was no magic clean-up police and, at 5 a.m., with Michael due to be up at 7:00, I had no time to seek help. So, I grabbed rubber gloves and a gallon of bleach and put on a pot of coffee. I scrubbed and cleaned and puked right up until it was time to get my son up and ready for school.

Michael got up, dressed, had breakfast, and was off to school without incident. I dialed the glass man, hoping the shop might be open early. I was in luck. Eddie informed me, "We'll have someone out there before lunch." Thank goodness. My heart stopped every time I heard the wind rattle the plastic in the basement.

"Before lunch" ended up meaning a quarter after two that afternoon. It was close, but the glass was replaced and the glass man gone by the time Michael's bus dropped him off. Michael had such a sweet disposition and was so young; I was happy that he wouldn't have the images and memories I'd have to carry around with me for the remainder of time. My job included protecting my child and I felt like I had done that part perfectly well. As far as Michael was concerned, it was just another day in his life.

Tad came home later that afternoon, wearing his construction clothes and looking like he'd put in an 18-hour day by 4:30 p.m. We had dinner and bath time and bedtime. Michael was out-for-the-count ten seconds after his head hit the pillow.

I was anxious to talk to Tad about someone breaking into our home and me shooting the son-of-a-bitch. "It was a hell of a weekend. Where the fuck were you?"

"I had some side-work on the Eastern Shore. I told you before I left for work on Friday. Are you okay? I see you got the glass fixed. You must be kind of fucked up over killing the *Gingerbread Man*." He looked at me and raised an eyebrow. "You really need to get out more often."

Before I could say "What the fuck," Tad continued, "I was here last night. I parked my car and heard glass breaking before I could get my key out of the ignition. I went around back to investigate and had my worst suspicions confirmed when I saw the busted glass to our basement and some guy poking around down there with a small flashlight. I was just about to nail the guy when I heard the gunfire. Geez, I had no idea you could shoot like that. Anyway, the noise jerked the guy around and there I am standing right in front of him. We scuffled for a minute and finally I managed to knock him out."

"I *knew* I heard something."

"The *Gingerbread Man*?" Tad laughed his weird laugh and shook his head. "I gotta say, I was damned happy to hear your voice though."

Tad dragged the unconscious man into the woods behind our house and handcuffed him there—just in case. Then, he scooted back into the basement and kicked the glass around some to cover up the drag marks before exiting the scene of the crime.

"We have to get out of here Brooke."

"What do you mean? Now?"

"No not now, but soon."

Tad knew what I didn't want to admit. Vladimir had found me. The local police later determined the whole incident to be a "random home invasion" and since the perpetrator was dead, the case was eventually closed. But, the issue of Vladimir wanting me dead remained very much alive.

With damned little money and even less time, our options were few. We put our townhouse on the market and began to pack. But where would we go?

Damien and Bailey had built a house above where the main house and the "milk house" sat on the Hutchenson family property in West Virginia, leaving the big old, uninsulated farmhouse and its smaller counterpart vacant. It would be nearly impossible to heat the big house affordably over the course of Danese's eight months of winter. So, the plan was to *temporarily* live in the milk house where Damien and Bailey had lived while building their new home.

Ninety-eight percent of our house was packed and then wrapped up in garbage bags (even the boxes were wrapped up). We then marked each bag with a single square of duct tape and left them on the curb. Later, in the middle of the night, some of Tad's friends with trucks picked up the marked bags and drove them nearly six hours away. Once at the farmhouse, they'd drop the crap off in a side room Bailey had cleared out in the farmhouse for that specific purpose. It took several trips and I worried about my stuff looking like garbage on the curb, but everything made it to West Virginia ahead of us just fine.

The furniture was trickier as it took the whole crew from late night to just before dawn to load it up from the back of the townhouse in a U-Haul and hit the long, lonesome trail before the neighbors rose. When the three of us walked out of the townhouse for the last time, we carried the luggage of a family going on vacation for a week—leaving a listing agreement with a local Realtor to begin thirty days after our departure.

I spent three very long years saying "This is my last winter in West Virginia." But *all things for a reason*, right? At first, it was pretty much perfect; we were hidden in a remote part of West Virginia and "roughing it" for a while, just the three of us as a family. We hiked the mountainous property and lived on beans and rice, as well as the hospitality and generosity of others and *eventually* the proceeds from our fine-ass, hidden, hydroponics grow room, which was built inside an old cinderblock silo behind the milk house.

It was pretty badass. You had to move two cinderblocks to climb through a 3' x 3' hole to get to the shabby-looking structure inside and under a roof covered with broken branches from fallen trees (so from the air, it looked like an old, unused silo). Once inside the room inside the silo, you were greeted with warm, super-bright lights and the smell of sweet sensimilla (seedless female marijuana plants that produce the sweetest, most kick-ass pot ever). Tad and Damien ran a water line to the building and had underground electricity powering it. They worked on a lot of projects like that together. Michael played well with both Simone and Syler, and I got to spend more time with Bailey. At first.

Then, things got weird. For instance, Damien made plans with Tad to work on a fence on Wednesday and then Tad showed up at 6:00 a.m. only to discover Damien had gone ahead and done the necessary work on Tuesday. More and more often these things would happen, as if Damien didn't want Tad's help. Tad just said "fuck it" and set off to find a real job with a paycheck, which of course he did. He found work with the county school board—more quality-control related construction stuff.

Then, Damien started getting weird about Bailey spending time with me. She got to the point that she couldn't tell him we were going to get our hair cut together. So, I'd tell Tad "I'm going with Bailey … " and before I could finish he'd interrupt and say, "I know. Don't tell Damien." Bailey would leave her home up on the hill and have no choice but to pass the farmhouse and the milk house on her way out. She'd slow down at my driveway and I'd run along the side of the truck till I could yank the door open and jump in—Bailey knew Damien would hear her stop and God forbid she do something so extreme as cutting the engine off. Damien was a controlling asshole and he definitely didn't want her spending *any* time with her sister alone. What good could come from that?

But, still we managed. And there were still parties and get-togethers and stuff where he could keep an eye on Bailey that allowed us some time together. Or, if it was an event involving the kids and school, Damien had no problem letting Bailey off the chain for a couple of hours. It was work, but we got our time in.

Bailey was elected president of the PTA and I landed the role of PTA vice president. This alone gave us numerous excuses to be together. In the summertime, we helped create and run a summer reading program at the Meadow Bridge Public Library. We enjoyed working with the kids and made an impressive team together—like opposite sides of the same coin.

Tad and I learned to handle Damien's assholery to us, but when Damien's evil plan to box his family in and control their every move started to affect our son, I wanted to take Damien out in his sleep and make it look like he died from natural causes. Which, by the way, I could do, as I had taken and passed the EMT test, knew some basic chemistry, and would eventually become a National Registry Paramedic while "roughing it" in Danese, West Virginia. Sal warned me to stay away from the medical industry and anything that might link Brooke back to Cici Russo, but I felt safe in Danese and I love medical people.

There are certain things that medical people know and never advertise, such as "how to kill someone and not get caught." It's messed up, but probably fair to say it'd be a good idea to be good to the medical staff that cares for you. It's generally a good idea to be good to the people around you, period. But, that wasn't Damien's rule.

The first party Michael got to attend after a very long winter on the farm was little Simone's seventh birthday party. There were several little girls there in frilly dresses; Syler, five years old at the time, and Michael, then six, lay down on the floor under the coffee table on their backs in order to see the girls' frilly panties as they walked by. All I can do is shake my head and shrug on that one. I've since been told that it was Syler's idea, but honestly, these two have always had invincible energy together. Even today, if you're in the same room with Michael and Syler, you're either laughing or shaking your head or sometimes both.

Anyway, both boys were corrected and sent outside to play, but Damien blamed Michael and used it as an excuse to exclude Michael from Simone's future parties. It was heartbreaking to watch Michael alone in the yard, staring at car after car with pretty little girls on board go by his house and up to his cousin's eighth birthday party.

At one point, Michael yelled happily, "Someone's here to see me!" But when I went to the door to see who it was, Michael was already returning with his head hung low and tears streaking his face. "It was Bobby. I thought he was here to see me, but he's going to Simone's party too!" I held Michael and thought about what fucking great fertilizer Damien would make. I think I have a little bit of my daddy in me sometimes; or, maybe just some fierce maternal instincts. Either way, God be with the bastard that makes my child cry.

Back then, I didn't really understand why Bailey walked on eggshells; but that was long before I'd make the same choice. Sometimes, fighting the good fight means not fighting at all, but rather biding one's time until the opportunity is ripe.

I was but a mere EMT when Tad and I took off with Michael to spend some time with his family on the Eastern Shore of Maryland. We needed to get off the farm for a while and Tad's brother needed help building his log cabin. The "kit" he'd purchased turned out to be more of a challenge than he bargained for and because Tad had built huge government projects as a cover job, the cabin was the equivalent of Lincoln Logs to him.

Tad's family was perfectly awesome to me. In fact, I believed they all loved me. I was wrong. As it would turn out, it was his parents who loved me. After Pop and Squeeze passed away, I was all but accused of being a gold-digger who wasn't very good at math. It was the "not good at math" part that hurt. I'd done clinical hours at retirement facilities and intensive care units; if I were a gold-digger, I *know* where I'd do my shopping.

Still, I had enjoyed my time on Tad's family's farm. It was a real farm with commercial equipment and hundreds and hundreds of acres. Tad's older brothers ran the farm, while Pop oversaw and managed daily operations. There was several times that Squeeze kept an open ear for Michael as he napped and I rode around the farm with Pop in his Mercedes, listening to classical music and drinking white wine. I wish we could've kept both of them for longer. It was a welcomed break and a time of story-telling and bonding with his parents we'd never have the opportunity to experience again.

Once we got back to the milk house, it felt familiar and good to be home. Tad and I had done some bonding as well—traveling together and sneaking off whenever we could. It was an adventure, but it was also nice to be home, where Tad wasn't so worried about his parents hearing the bed squeak. We were there for six weeks! I'd argue that they'd be more suspicious if they didn't hear the bed squeak.

Those were my "Rhythm Method" days, a fine means of birth control involving the counting of days. I was brilliant at it for a solid eighteen months. I woke up our first morning back in West Virginia counting, "Thirteen, fourteen, fifteen ... what is today's date?!"

One day late and I was in the doctor's office. I can still remember the RN's condescending tone. "Hmmm. You're *only* one day late."

"Trust me on this one," I assured her.

I was eight months pregnant with Marie when I took the paramedic entrance exam with my pal Becky. I only went with her because everyone else backed out the last minute. I was as big as a house and had no clue I'd be going back to school by the time my baby was three months old.

Happily, I didn't go into labor while testing more than an hour from home and two hours from my hospital, though I had a room full of paramedic-wannabes offering to lend a hand if I did. But, I was home when I went into labor. I called Tad at work and tried to wait patiently. I did a better job than Bailey. "We can't wait any longer. He'll have to meet us at the hospital." She drove me all the way to the end of our dirt road, where we ran into Tad. Mid-contraction, I switched vehicles and let Tad take over driving.

An hour later, we were at the hospital. I opened my mouth to say "Hi. I'm Brooke Bronson," but what came out to the receptionist was "GIVE ME DRUGS!"

"We'll have to check you first ... "

"TRUST ME!!!!" I'm pretty sure the staff expected my head to start spinning and for me to start spewing pea soup.

Eight hours later, Marie was born—the most perfect and beautiful little girl ever. She had a head of dark hair (that would be golden blonde by the time she was one) and big, clear blue eyes. I held her for hours, staring into her eyes and making the nurses wait to do whatever was on their list of things to do with a newborn. I didn't care. No one was going to rob me of this bonding time with my child. Their tests and paperwork could wait.

Tad ran all over Danese telling anyone who'd listen about his newborn baby girl and how she was as beautiful as his wife; everyone thought he was a wonderful, proud father. Meanwhile, Marie and I were an hour away in the Lewisburg Hospital, completely on our own and unaware of the celebration. Elsie was watching Michael and I thought Tad's place was with me and our newborn daughter. But what the fuck, it was a good excuse for him to party.

Tad was working for both Fayette and Raleigh County Schools Boards at the time—construction quality control work with odd titles that didn't seem to fit the job.

Tad enjoyed driving from county to county and job site to job site, meeting new people and running into many local neighbors. It was beautiful countryside. We may have lived in poverty, but we woke up to majestic landscapes. Babcock State Park was maybe three or four miles down the road. Even if you've never set foot inside the state lines, chances are you've seen photography from Babcock State Park—their Grist Mill, a working mill, is one of the single most photographed mills of all time. I've seen artwork of the Grist Mill from every season—the mill snow-covered with icy water on Christmas cards, looking green and lush in the springtime, surrounded by rhododendrons in full bloom in the summer, and, perhaps the most typical, framed by the rich foliage of the fall – from yellow to gold to orange to bright red and dark maroon. There are cabins and hiking trails, swimming and horseback riding, a swinging bridge, playgrounds, picnic areas, and lots and lots of scenic views. Sadly, most of us that lived in that area couldn't afford the stuff that cost money, but we all damned sure enjoyed the park nonetheless.

We went to Babcock often, had family dinners together, talked about Michael's day at school, and enjoyed opening the many gifts that arrived for newborn Marie and her older brother. We were dirt poor, but it somehow felt more normal than any other family life I'd known.

One day, shortly after Marie's birth, I received a huge bouquet of a dozen pink and a dozen white roses with white baby's breath arranged in a lovely crystal vase. It was delivered by a young man with dark hair and eyes and an olive complexion. He seemed out of place in Danese. He smiled and left quickly. It was one of the most beautiful arrangements I'd ever seen. The card simply read "Fayette County." Tad had been working for both Raleigh and Fayette County School Boards, but when he asked around, no one ever took credit for the beautiful flowers. And who signs a card "Fayette County?" Unlikely the whole county pitched in for flowers. An image of Vladimir with me in his crosshairs flashed through my mind. *If that was the case, he'd pull the trigger, not send flowers.* I dismissed the thought. Maybe it was Sal.

Still, it was odd; most gifts we received were picked up at the post office, which, in Danese, is a three-room building with one postal employee at *the* intersection. Even if a person had directions to the farm itself, it'd be tough to find. It's the old Orville Allen Farm, past where the little country store used to be, and a left on a dirt road just before a white, cinderblock bus house and after old man Glass's place (if you make it to Hell's Half Acre, you've gone too far). You'll need to go down that first hill before you begin your very rocky ascent to the property. There's a pretty big rock you'll want to get around; it eats oil pans. The neighbors don't take kindly to a lot of traffic and tend to be heavily armed, so keep moving. A four-wheel drive vehicle is probably your best bet; a low-riding sports car will never make it. Don't rely solely on your GPS, as you'll need to have some survivor skills. Good luck. Call when you can get a signal or find a pay phone. And don't even bother trying if no one is expecting you, as the gate will probably be locked and turning around means backing your vehicle onto someone else's property. No one really wants to see an entire family armed with shotguns facing them head-on, or in their rearview for that matter.

Think no one is paying attention? Wrong. We could hear a vehicle's wheels hit the dirt road from way up on the mountain. The neighbors actually heard you slow down before you turned.

I'd think about the flower delivery guy every now and again, but I had a new baby, damned little sleep, and paramedic training starting in the fall. Months would pass before my brain would have the time and energy to process the event more analytically.

In order for a flower shop to get to our place, *someone* would have had to give them directions and no one Tad had ever worked with had been to the farm. Then, there were the delivery boy's looks—Greek? *Italian* maybe? There was something eerily familiar about him, at least in my mind's recollection. I was in remote Danese, West Virginia; if I couldn't hide there, where could I hide?

Paramedic training started in late August in Charleston. The air was already getting cooler and the tips of the leaves were just beginning to turn. Fall would be in full swing in a matter of weeks. Summer seemed to last longer and winters weren't so harsh in Virginia. I don't think it occurred to me that the seasons would be so different in neighboring states.

The next year of school included driving two hours to class twice a week and a third day into Charleston for clinical hours. Every spare minute I had between being a mom and a wife was spent reading and studying. I tape-recorded notes to listen to while I drove. My medical training from what seemed like a lifetime ago was definitely an asset, but being a doctor is not nearly the same as being a medic; not that I was a doctor, but I was at least on that path.

A doctor is well educated and trained and is often in a controlled environment surrounded by other skilled professionals. Even when a patient is brought into the ER by family, the doctor is generally not alone. Shoot. It's probably an RN that triages the patient first. But, as a doctor, you're the highest ranking person in a medical facility and thus have the highest level of responsibility.

In the field, on the other hand, a paramedic is the highest ranking officer. We even outrank law enforcement. A medic's assessment skills must be sharp, as the call for "load and go" or "stay and play" is made in seconds. Of the "Golden Hour" (named as such because if a patient receives definitive care within one hour, their survival chances drastically increase), a paramedic is allotted five minutes. The environment is inconsistent and often unstable because of the medical condition, the trauma suffered, the weather, the circumstances, or the act of starting an IV on a hysterical patient in the back of a truck racing around sharp curves and over a bumpy road to get to the hospital. An EMT is generally driving and you might have one to assist you, but you might be alone.

It's the same kind of adrenalin rush that firefighters experience. I went to school with a few guys like that or guys that were first responders, then firefighters, then EMTs, and then paramedics. They were tough competition, as they'd literally grown up in the industry.

Classes were sponsored by West Virginia Tech and taught by some of Kanawha County's finest. I not only learned paramedic skills, but also that just because someone has a country accent, it most definitely doesn't make them stupid. I think it's a misconception of city dwellers. I met and had the opportunity to be trained and work with some of the greatest heroes and fastest thinkers ever. They were well-educated and well-exercised and nearly every one of them had what many of us considered a country accent. *A big shout out to the heroes of Kanawha County.*

Twenty eight men and five women were accepted into that class of 1994. Not all my classmates made the long trek to my bonfire and beer graduation celebration, but a lot of friends from Northern Virginia did, the same ones that would roll in for annual hippy reunions in Hell's Half Acre.

Of course, Annie Lane and Terri Lynne were there and we partied our asses off. I loved the big field parties and bonfires and pig roasts, but I also enjoyed many of the quieter times I had with close friends and family. Some of my favorite memories are of intimate gatherings and impromptu parties and random opportunities that led to closer relationships with members of Brooke's family, which was rapidly becoming more and more *mine*.

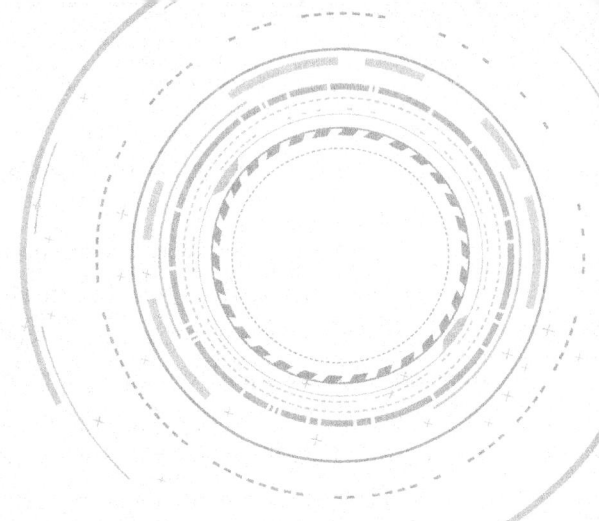

CHAPTER EIGHTEEN
Almost Heaven

Brigid came into town the weekend after the big bonfire and beer graduation celebration, just to get out of the big city. She'd divorced Dickhead (her first husband and short-lived mistake) by then and was single, successful and perfectly radiant. I hated her a little bit. Or, perhaps more accurately, I hated myself for not being like her. It's hard not to envy the woman who seems to have everything. God, even if I could *look* like her and still be me, life would be easier. I was certain of that.

Brigid ached for the mountains and some time at Twenty Foot—a favorite spot on Meadow River known only to the locals and marked only by a foot-trafficked trail and, occasionally, a pair of sneakers hung over the power line. I don't know if I could find the spot on my own, even though I actually lived close by. Brigid could, probably even in her sleep.

Tad stayed home with the kids and Brigid and I packed a couple of cans of Mountain Dew, a bag of Cheetos, and a bottle of tequila and set off for Twenty Foot. I have to admit, the spot is magical.

Once making your way down the narrow path, it's a small opening to a huge, flat rock, which is often referred to as the "Party Rock," hanging roughly ten feet above the river. Just to the right of it, its smaller, not quite as smooth cousin is a couple of feet closer to the water. On the opposite side of the river is a small sandy beach, complete with a rope swing. And, to the left of that, a large rock formation stands, which roughly rises twenty feet above the river, depending on the season and weather conditions—The Jumping Rock and Twenty Foot's namesake. It's a steep climb and a dangerous jump under the best of conditions. Unless you're a daredevil or an adrenalin junkie, don't let the locals talk you into this one; it's definitely not for the adventurously timid or those who place great value on their future mobility, as well as mental stability.

Brigid and I spread our towels on Cousin Rock and looked out over the river. The sun threw diamonds of light off the water and warmed the rock we lay on to therapeutic temps, together providing the renewing energy of the glistening river and the grounding energy of Cousin Rock. It was part of the Twenty Foot experience—mix three parts nature with two parts tequila, add laughter, and serve with a big fatty.

Brigid looked over and up at Jumping Rock. "I'll never forget when you jumped off Twenty Foot. Do you remember?"

"It would be a hard thing to forget." *Holy shit. Brooke jumped off that freaking rock? I really didn't know her as well as I thought I did.*

Brigid continued, "Damn, I knew you were scared and there really is no turning back once you get started up. When you jumped, I just knew you were going to hit that one sharp ledge that juts out." Brigid pointed to the dagger-like rock formation adorning the face of Twenty Foot's epithet.

"Hard to believe it was even me," I uttered without thinking.

"I know, right?" Brigid laughed.

We did shots of tequila and ate Cheetos and stared out over Meadow River. "I killed a man once." Brigid seemed to say out loud to no one in particular.

"What?"

"He was a dirt bag that took advantage of young girls, mostly runaways, promising them modeling careers and then turning them into prostitutes. I ran into him on a big photo shoot one time. The girls he seemed interested in were young and very hungry-looking. He was a pig. And then one night the whole scene got to me and I knew where he'd be and I climbed up a fire escape overlooking his pimp parking space; I took aim and fired. I thought I heard another shot that night and it occurred to me I wasn't the only one that wanted him dead, but after I saw him go down, I packed my gear and never looked back. Weird that I never got caught, right?"

"Weird." I had a million questions, but I had no clue where to begin. But just then we heard car doors slamming up on the main road. We watched the path to see who was coming down to join us.

"Hey y'all! You don't mind if we come join ya, do ya?" It was a young girl with chubby cheeks and blonde pigtails. I guessed her to be twenty two or twenty three. She carried a bundle of towels and blankets and was followed by her tall, lanky boyfriend whose hair looked like a frayed brunette mop, which, I was convinced, made him look at least three inches taller. He carried two coolers and was followed close behind by a younger male, maybe by two or three years, and who was almost an exact replica of his older brother.

"Hell no, we don't mind. C'mon down!" Brigid jumped up and waved the newcomers on down the path as she introduced us. The party of three spread out their blankets and set up camp on the adjoining Party Rock. In no time, we were sharing a joint, passing around the tequila, and chasing with icy cold beers provided by the newcomers. That was Twenty Foot.

"Hey, y'all want to hear a joke?" Brigid took a big swig of her beer and jumped up.

"Hell yeah!"

"Sure."

"Go for it."

"Tell it to us."

Laughter is fun, contagious, and uplifting, second only to love. The Russo's didn't value it quite like the Hutchensons did. The Hutchensons were the entertainers and the audience; the writers and the performers. They were the yin and yang of laughter. So, it really shouldn't have been that much of a surprise to see that side of Brigid, but it was. She took her last drink of beer and shook the last couple of drops from her can, holding onto the empty can.

"A West Virginia man goes to his doctor. He says, 'Doc, I got me ten kids and I love my kids; I just don't want anymore. I believe I'd like to get me one of them there vi-sect-o-mees.' The doctor says, 'That's no problem. All you need to do is go home, light a cherry bomb, put it in a glass, hold it up to your head, and count to ten.' Brigid animated the act of putting a cheery bomb into a glass and holding it up to her head, using her empty can as a prop as she spoke. "The man went home scratching his head. Somehow it didn't seem quite right to him, so he told his wife 'I believe I'll get me a second opinion from one of them big city doctors in Charleston.' So the man drove to Charleston and went into the doctor's office and said, 'Doc, I got me ten kids and I love my kids; I just don't want anymore. I believe I'd like to get me one of them there vi-sect-o-mees.' The doctor says, 'That's no problem. All you need to do is go home, light a cherry bomb, put it in a glass, hold it up to your head, and count to ten.'

"Again, the man went home scratching his head. It still didn't seem quite right to him, so he told his wife 'I believe I'll get me another opinion from one of them high-dollar doctors in New York City.' So the man drove all the way to New York City and, when he got there, he told the doctor, 'Doc, I got me ten kids and I love my kids; I just don't want anymore. I believe I'd like to get me one of them there vi-sect-o-mees.' The doctor says 'That's no problem at all. The procedure takes minutes and we can send you home with an ice pack.' The man is completely relieved and tells the doctor, 'I knew them West Virginia doctors didn't know what they was talking about …' The doctor interrupts and says, 'Wait a minute. You're from West Virginia? There's an easier way. All you need to do is go home, light a cherry bomb, put it in a glass, hold it up to your head, and count to ten.'

"The man went home thinking to himself, 'Dang, my doctor in town told me 'bout the cherry bomb and that there big city doctor in Charleston told me the same thing. Even the high-dollar doctor in New York City … they can't all be wrong.' So the man went home, lit a cherry bomb, put it in a glass, held it up to his head and began to count." Brigid went through the motions, holding the can up with her right hand and using her left to count off one finger at a time. "One, two, three, four, five." Running out of fingers and still holding her five on the left up, she quickly put the can between her legs and continued counting off fingers with her right. "Six, seven, eight, nine …"

And that first joke triggered another and another as one person's joke would remind someone else of another joke until nothing but laughter could be heard echoing off the rocks and traveling down the river. A twist of fate made us sisters; a day of laughter made us friends. I decided to let her little confession go, though the thought would cross my mind from time to time. But the could-be-possibly-maybe would always lose out to the real life memory of that day on Twenty Foot with Brigid. It was real and it's what I will forever choose to remember and celebrate.

It was the summer of 1994. Michael was eight, and Marie turned one that summer. We'd spent three very long winters on that mountain, but our friends and neighbors were exceptionally good to us and I never felt judged for our poverty or the clothes we wore or where and how we lived. We had been the poorest amongst the poor and no one looked down on us for it. Whenever there was a need to be met, the people around us ran to meet it. Some of Brooke and Bailey's closest friends from back in the day remain some of my dearest friends today from our three-year camping experience in Danese.

And, even more amazingly, Tad and I and Michael and Marie had become a family. We were a real family with hopes and dreams, challenges, goals, and frustrations—all working, dreaming, living, and planning together. World events took a backseat to community events. Time spent was better than money saved. Friendship trumped fashion. And these things just happened naturally.

The winters we survived had been brutal by our estimation, with record-breaking low temps and titles such as "Worst Ice Storm in the History of the State," "Coldest Winter," and "Most Snow Fall in a Single Season." So, when Tad said "We should move to Florida," while we were watching national weather and noting temps of 75 degrees in Tampa, while ice was coming through the locks in our doors and snow continued to dump mountains of white on top of us—I was totally up for the idea.

I had completed paramedic training and was geared for change. Our local fire and rescue department did nothing to support my training—financially, morally, or otherwise—and

I felt no loyalty to them whatsoever. I sensed Tad had other reasons to bolt, but I didn't care; sunshine and palm trees sounded fabulous to me. I boldly proclaimed, "I've done my last winter in West Virginia" to absolutely anyone that would listen. Looking back, I definitely could've been stealthier and left that trail a little colder.

In the midst of mountains and mass solitude, Vladimir had only flashed through my mind for that one moment a year earlier when the mystery flowers were delivered. But, if Sal could find me, Vladimir could too.

It was late August 1994 before the kids were packed and the truck was loaded and we were ready to head south. If we hurried, we could still get to Florida and get a tan before Christmas.

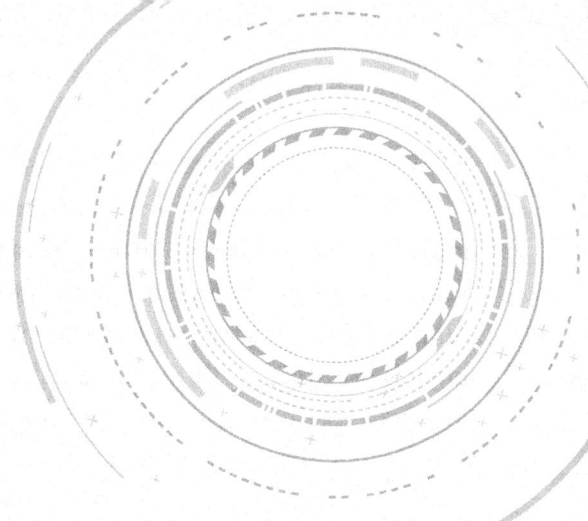

CHAPTER NINETEEN
Scattered Sunshine

With my natural "run and hide" reflex and Tad's ability to bolt quickly, we were a pretty good team. Adversity had a way of bringing us close in one moment and miles apart the next. It was good to be close. We used our VDL saved funds (that's *very damned little*) to rent an apartment at Hunter's Ridge in Plant City, Florida. Why Plant City you ask? Well, I knew someone who lived in Tampa and Tad's brother lived in Sarasota, so when the coin toss didn't work out, we threw darts until we agreed on the location. Plant City wasn't the beach and it wasn't Disney; it was something entirely different—less tan, less Mickey Mouse, and more red necked than I'd imagined. But, Plant City was the Winter Strawberry Capital of the World, and we both liked strawberries.

My "friend" in Tampa bailed on helping unload the truck, so Tad and I worked alone, all the while keeping an eye on our eight and one year olds. After Tad dragged our dresser through the breezeway and up the stairs, we took a break for lunch. When we finished our sandwiches and headed back out to continue unloading the truck on our own, we found a note on our door from the downstairs neighbors. "Can you be more quiet?" Never mind the poor grammar. It was the middle of the day. We were moving furniture and unloading a huge U-Haul after driving a top speed of thirty-five miles per hour through the mountains of West Virginia and another million miles after that due south. We were already exhausted and still anxious to get moved in. Tad took the note and wrote back, "No," and stuck it on their door. We both laughed.

But, they got the last laugh when on hot, muggy days they'd open all their windows and turn on their ceiling fans, letting the heat rise to our apartment above, all while enjoying the benefits of our air conditioner running non-stop, providing naturally falling cool air. When monthly utility bills came out, they'd happily skip back to their apartment as I held my chest and staggered backwards. To this very day, I'm still not sold on this thing they call "Southern Hospitality." People in West Virginia were *way* more hospitable. I'm convinced the terminology is an insider's joke.

Regardless, the apartment was lovely. It had three bedrooms, a nice master bedroom and bath, a Jack-n-Jill bathroom dividing Michael's and Marie's rooms, and a swimming pool and hot tub only a short walk away. It took me a while to get used to people living stacked on top of people. For the first couple months, I'd peek through the blinds every time I heard a car in the parking lot. Three years on a mountaintop in near perfect seclusion will do that to you.

Tad found work in construction pretty fast, making less than he did in West Virginia while spending more to live in Florida. Money was tight, so while studying for the State of Florida

Paramedic exam (my National Registry status wasn't enough), I took a job at Taco Bell. I worked around Tad's schedule and did the graveyard shift. It was piss money, but the experience gave me the opportunity to meet a lot of pot heads, so it was all good.

While living at the apartment, I got to meet all the people who had spouses working during the day—moms, dads, and kids of all ages. I'd often run into the same parents at the playground or in the swimming pool. It was good to have casual friends.

Briana came to visit us for a week and she met a lot of these pals. We had a blast. I took a lot of pictures swimming and in the hot tub late one night relaxing—steam filling the air around us. They were snapshots of a time I wish I could jump back into, if only for an hour.

Briana was working on her degree at the time and had to write one of those dreadful "how-to" papers. She'd had a terrible flight into Tampa—the combination of turbulence and pain meds making her quite queasy. When her nausea was no longer containable, Briana made a mad dash towards the bathroom. Her timing sucked, however, as two flight attendants had already started from opposite ends of the aisle with their metal snack carts—one blocking the bathrooms at the front of the plane and the other blocking the bathrooms at the rear of the plane. Briana became a puking version of Monkey-in-the-Middle. I'm pretty sure the flight attendants and other passengers were never the same again. I told her, "You should write about how to be an airline passenger from hell—you know how to do that," I teased. And thus Briana's "How to be an Airline Passenger from Hell" paper began. We talked and wrote and laughed so hard that we cried. The paper was a pretty big hit back home in her class in that small Shenandoah Valley town. But, that was Bri—she was always outrageous, always front and center stage. And I was forever entertained.

ILLUSIONS OF PRIVACY

We stayed at Hunter's Ridge, scraping by for the entire seven-month lease. I'm not sure what it is about this area, but everyone does seven-month leases. Regardless, we'd shopped around and eventually found a house on Knights-Griffin Road in Plant City that March of '94. It was a barn red house and easily a step up from the milk house in West Virginia, but not much more. However, the price was right and we liked being out in a farming district with a bit more space. There was even a horse on the property and cows grazing beside us.

Hilda was the owner of the property. She was probably in her 70s and was shacked up with her boyfriend Hal who was about the same age. Her husband had passed away years earlier and rumor had it he was the biggest tightwad in the county. We shared a driveway as Hilda and Hal lived in the house behind ours, a brick rambler.

Hal was awesome; he brought me flowers from the yard and always had something lovely, kind, or uplifting to say. Hilda was a crazy bitch who closed her eyes while talking to you and asked questions such as, "Is that one colored teacher still at the middle school?"

Hilda was as cheap as her late husband was rumored to have been. Our septic was backing up one Christmas and instead of calling the septic tank guys, she left for the holidays and assumed we'd be okay. I wanted to punch her in the face; I hated that she looked at us like underclass subhuman beings. But, instead, we chose to take the kids and go stay at the Holiday Inn until the septic dude could make it out and the disgusting situation was resolved. That month, Hilda got a receipt from the Holiday Inn and a bill from the septic dude instead of rent. She closed her eyes and opened her mouth, but no words came out. It was a first.

Hilda and Hal traveled a lot and relied on us to pick up the mail and care for the horse. It was no big deal. The farm was quieter when Hilda was gone. It would be sad when Hal died though. He was sweet.

I hate that the screwed up choices in my life have had a negative impact on my children in any way. But, holy cow, they've both turned out beyond awesome. I'm not certain why the guilt lingers, but it does. I only wanted the best for Michael and Marie. Alas, one's best is a variable and not a constant. Demons, on the other hand, can maintain a constant attack on your spirit without wavering and live forever. They can beat you down.

Tad had battled his share of evil and I had run from my share, or so we thought. But, the demons that still existed in our minds were the most difficult to battle and were damned near impossible to run away from. Meanwhile, the physical aspects of our lives began to crumble around us.

Knights-Griffin Road was a shit storm. The house offered some solitude and was in our price range, but we had no central air conditioning (only a window unit), no dishwasher, no clothes washer, no clothes dryer, threadbare and buckled carpeting, dated jalousie windows that the simplest of criminals could jimmy, cracks you could see daylight through, and doors that could be opened with a butter knife. But, the house wasn't the real problem.

Tad and I fought constantly, mostly over money and sex. One was a lack of quantity, the other quality. We were both so angry. Or, maybe it was just me.

Tad continued to work construction, but was drinking more and more and coming home later and later. Men just seem to connect their self-esteem with their jobs and I think he secretly missed the Cold War and his glory days.

I ended up landing a job at a hospital in Zephyrhills as a critical care technician—it wasn't ER, but ICU would do. Besides, I was overqualified and the job would allow me time to balance my checkbook, paint my nails, write letters, and read trashy romance novels. Everyone would want my job. Sadly, no one would want the pay that went along with it. So, I did my best to have fun and I ended up meeting some great people and making a lot of friends.

I worked from 7:00 p.m. till 7:00 a.m. every Friday and Saturday night. Tad was working out of town as construction work was hard to come by in Florida and he was only home on the weekends. Construction would continue to see ups and downs and travel for work would become an ongoing necessity. To get around the cost of childcare, I worked weekends when Tad could be with the kids. But, sometimes, those logical financial choices end up being bad marital choices. We only saw each other in passing and our exchanges were icy at best.

Krystal Von Kline worked opposite me during the day shift. She was tall with legs that went on forever and had layered blonde hair when I first met her. Then, one morning, she showed up with British rocker, short blonde hair. She was born Krystal Morris and married Wilhelm Von Kline in her twenties; they had a daughter, Mackenzie. Krystal's new look was the beginning of the end of her marriage. There'd be plenty of little changes she'd make on her path back to her authentic self. Wilhelm wouldn't like any of them. We supposed he'd get over it.

Krystal and I followed each other on the weekends and thus had the chance to get to know each other over "report time"—an overlap of shifts where the night shift reports to the day shift who will later report to the night shift again.

Our job was super clerical and, over time, I developed the following report dialog, "All of these people are our patients and they are very sick," pointing to the dry erase board with patients' names and room numbers in ICU. "It'll be your job to keep up with them. If anyone comes or goes, write it in the book. If the phone rings, answer it. There will be doctors' orders—it's your job to process them. Keep an eye on the monitors. You'll need to notify the nurse if there's a problem." And then, we would go on to spend the rest of "report time" catching up on gossip. The job was a bit more involved than that, but Krystal had been doing it for years and didn't require any direction from me. Often, my feet would be up on the desk after my twelve hour shift, while gossiping with Krystal. "What is it they mean by 'passive overtime' again?" I'd smile.

We enjoyed ourselves in ICU. I met some of the coolest people ever and many that I still call friends today. Krystal was one of those people. And, as it would turn out, she'd be the link to my old world crashing into my current world.

Krystal Von Kline and I had quickly become friends and as pot heads often do, we'd recognized and confessed our mutual fondness for weed early on (it's like beer drinkers being able to spot one another). Krystal's sister Lydia sold PartyLite candles back in the day and Krystal invited me to her candle party, much like a Tupperware or lingerie party, but with lovely scented candles, lavish candle holders, and beautiful accessories. I fell in love with Krystal's PartyLite candle parties. Her family and friends were a hoot. We catalog-shopped and ate and placed orders and told cheesy jokes. "Hang out for a little while. After my mom takes off, we're going to burn one," Krystal whispered to me.

One of the friends that stayed behind was Mary Giquinto. There was something very familiar about her laugh, her long dark curly hair, and the way she spoke. I felt like I'd met her before, but couldn't quite put my finger on it till much later that night when I was back home with Tad.

It was that first trip to Florida with "Dickie Bradford." Mary reminded me of the girl in Lakeland with the safe-breaking, magic shop-owning husband and agency pal of Dickie's with the lions in the backyard. Slinky and ARboc. "What were Slinky and ARboc's real names?"

"Why do you want to know?" Tad didn't bother looking up from his newspaper.

"I met someone at Krystal's candle party tonight that kind of reminded me of Slinky and, well, I was in Lakeland. Wasn't that where we ended up on our first date?"

"Brooke, you and I were never in the state of Florida prior to ten months ago. You probably should get your story straight." He gave me the straight-faced, one eye brow raised look.

"Mary said her husband's name was Don. Was that one of ARboc's names?" This got Tad's attention.

"ARboc was code for Cobra; it's just spelled backwards. You need to leave this one alone, Brooke. Don was my pal, but he was a dangerous man who played both sides of every game; he made a lot of enemies."

"What do you mean?"

"I mean he used his skills to help out whoever he thought worthy of his help, regardless of where lines were drawn. Leave it alone Brooke."

I thought about what Tad said, but I couldn't leave it alone. "What did you and Don do the night you left Mary and me at their house?" Don and Mary; ARboc and Slinky; it was a small fucking world indeed.

"If you must know, there was some psycho killing prostitutes in Tampa at the time and Don had scored a few hundred .38 automatics wholesale and was packaging them with ammo and selling the kits to the working girls for $35 a pop. It was one of his many causes. I helped him with deliveries that night while we talked about what the fuck we should do with you." Tad turned his attention back to the paper he still held, signaling the conversation was over.

It wasn't long after that the one project ended and Tad accepted a position on another project in Panama City—400 miles north of us. He stayed there all week and made it home on Friday in time for me to take off for work—all Friday and Saturday night. Then, on Sunday, he'd head back on up to the panhandle. I'd always be amazed at how badly he and two children could turn my house upside down so quickly; it'd take me till the following Friday to get it back in order. The iciness between us continued.

I'm not sure what form of evil lived and worked with Tad in Panama City, and I generally like the construction guys, but these guys were assholes. It's fine that they were cokeheads, but the fact that they found so much joy sharing the addiction with others so that they had more people to get them high fucked up my life and the lives of many innocent spouses. I would've never dreamed that Tad, the *one or two toke occasionally* man, would become addicted to cocaine. I get that Tad is responsible for his own actions, as are we all. Still, a big "FUCK YOU" goes out to those who know what they did in Panama City. No names. No glory. You're probably all dead by now anyway.

So, while my work and social life were on the rise, my home life was starting to suck. There was one entire month that Tad sent no money home whatsoever. Our fights were no longer verbal debates geared towards resolve, but rather hateful, mean-spirited attacks with the only goal to be right or to hurt or to maim or otherwise diminish the other.

Tad was a dick. He was angry and insulting when he wasn't simply dismissing or ignoring me altogether. I suppose he could've simply been reacting to my negative energy or maybe just dealing with his own issues. I blamed him for my bad decisions and the idea of divorce was central in my thinking, although I had no earthly idea how I would ever manage on my own. I felt abandoned by love—poor, weak, broken, tragic me. If it weren't for sex back then, we'd have had nothing besides children and a roof over our heads in common.

Meanwhile, some lives went on and some lives ended. Knights-Griffin Road remains a horribly tragic time in my life to revisit. Pop died in October of 1995, two days before my thirty-third birthday. There was no way we could afford airfare times four, so Tad flew into D.C. with his brother from Sarasota and met the rest of his family for his father's funeral to be held at Arlington Memorial Cemetery. It was the end of an era.

Pop had always been good to us. He was kind, loving, and generous. He treated me like a daughter and gave me good advice and loving encouragement. We shared stories and laughed together. If I needed $500 to buy yet another P.O.S. car, he sent it to me. I loved that man and I believe he loved me. Not knowing me as an adolescent probably made it easier to do so.

Tad and his brother got reprimanded on the flight out for throwing peanuts at another passenger. I'm going to go out on a limb here and guess that was a drinking episode. They later met the younger of their two sisters at a local pub and continued with their goal of getting perfectly shit-faced. Tad managed to talk his way out of a "drunk in public" charge when a police officer on a bicycle discovered him trying to enter various vehicles in the parking lot. He was looking for his sister's car to pass out in.

In the interim, I'd driven the guys to the airport in Tad's brother's car only to discover when I got home that Tad had left town with our house, gate, and car keys. I parked in front of the gate knowing that Hal and Hilda would honk when they got home and I helped the kids over the gate. There were probably a dozen different fast and easy ways to break into this house, but I opted for the credit card method on the back door. It's not like the card could've been used for anything else.

Michael took off with his friends for game night at the church. I decided to throw a load of laundry in only to find we had no water. It turned out to be a pump issue that would be fixed the next day, but I had no way of knowing that. So, Marie and I went outside to get the clothes we did manage to get washed off the line. I was grateful for that load of whites that made it through the washer before the pump died.

Stepping through the back door, I looked up and saw a black racer snake on my kitchen window sill. I tried to see it on the outside, but alas it was inside. Tad was out of town and Michael was at church—doggone it, I had no choice but to kill it myself. The process involved a butcher knife and some screaming on my part as I chased the little bastard down over the countertop and onto the floor. I hacked it up into a million pieces, cried hysterically, and tried to pull myself together.

I cleaned Marie up for bed with some baby wipes (no water, remember?) and went to her room for clean pajamas. I opened her dresser and there, on top of her favorite blue bunny jammies, was a big, fat, black widow spider. Instinctively, I grabbed whatever was heavy and close and smashed the spider until it looked like part of the flannel it laid on. I remember feeling so alone and yet so under attack at the same time. Poor, tragic me; I cried and cried.

My reality seemed gloomy, and I began to create a village in my mind and fill it with everything and everyone I considered to be happy, fun, and joyful. I'd find myself at the ever-evolving village of my mind more and more often as I ignored thoughts of certainty and opted for fantasy. It was a good place to be.

Genetically linked ovarian cancer was discovered and diagnosed in the Ziegenfuss family. Elsie's identical twin Eliza died in April of 1996 at 59 years of age. Five months later, the same disease claimed the life of Elsie, the woman who had been my mother and grandmother to my children.

The Ziegenfuss family may have had their issues, but those that I met I found to be good and decent people. I'll understand if you all disown and deny ever knowing me. I meant no harm, but I apologize for not taking enough time to consider anything other than my own self-preservation. I was wrong.

As for Elsie, she told us all on more than one occasion, "Don't say anything. Keep your mouths shut. You can say anything you want when I'm dead." I'm pretty sure she had no idea that we'd all take that one quite so seriously.

When Elsie died, a part of each of us died. It was heart-wrenching and bewildering and so, so terribly sad. She deserved to know the truth. I was just too weak to tell her. I'm so sorry.

Elsie was good to me and Tad; more importantly, Elsie was good to our children. She was the best grandma ever. I loved her with all my heart and I wanted to keep her forever. I hate that she died and would do anything to go back in time and make it so she was alive and healthy and with us today. Just to hear her laugh one more time or see her hold a great grandchild—even now I want to change her story.

Meanwhile, the medical industry was wearing me down and I was ready for change—again. I can't even remember all the shit entry level jobs I took. I was grateful for all the friends I'd made at the hospital, but even in the toughest of times, I never really wanted to go back. I suppose that was mostly the case because of the business itself. Or, more accurately, that healthcare was a business and not just a thing we did to heal others. There simply had to be something better, something more joyful.

A combination of despondency, daydreaming, and crappy jobs led me to the International Academy of Design in Tampa. I thought I could be a web designer or something; it was trendy then. Not too far into getting my degree, I found myself in the middle of the great World Wide Web crash—it went from everybody needing a website to an over-saturated market almost overnight. It'd work out okay because, eventually (and periodically thereafter), all those websites would need to be redesigned and updated to stay on top. But, with a big student loan hanging over my head, I worried I jumped into the game too late. And with no real love for web design to begin with, I changed my major to graphic design, focusing more on print work and logos and whole corporate images. Fun stuff.

Was it the smartest move financially? Probably not. But I found a lot of joy in print work and vector drawing and basically playing with creative software. And after a couple of rough years, I'd end up making a decent living freelancing from home, which suited both the mom and the introvert in me just fine.

I gained a lot from my experience at the International Academy of Design & Technology. I'm just hoping they don't take my degree away from me for the whole "fraud" thing. I did pay for it and it was me that took and passed all the classes, even though I did use someone else's name to do it.

After all these years, I do feel like "Brooke" *is* my name. If I couldn't use the name Brooke, what would I use? Going back to being Cici Russo damned sure isn't an option. And Camilla Colleen McPherson, I don't even know who that is anymore. I'm not completely convinced about the details of my early life. Finn and Clare McPherson, the people were real. The names? Probably not. I do wonder about you guys. Did Sal send you pictures and keep you updated to comfort you? Or torment you. Were you forced to let go altogether? And, at my age, I wonder if you're even still alive. Maybe I have brothers or sisters I don't know about. I spit in a test tube and shipped it off to ancestry.com in search of answers there recently. If nothing else, I have been blessed with "family," even if not entirely my own.

The year 2000 came and went without planes dropping from the sky or a major communications crash. There were some small, non-life threatening outages, but in the end, the doomsdayers would have to hold onto their canned goods until the next predicted end of civilization.

The beginning of the new millennium witnessed Bill Gates retiring as chief executive of Microsoft, Charles M. Shultz dying, the last original "Peanuts" comic appearing in newspapers the very next day, and an announcement by Bill Clinton that super-duper accurate GPS information formerly restricted for the military would be available to the general public. It would be a few more years before I'd own one of these clever little devices myself, so I have no real idea what changes were made. Al Gore won the popular vote that same year, yet lost the electoral vote, thus losing the election to George W. Bush. It was bullshit and everyone knew it, but George W. Bush took office anyway.

Skinny jeans, UGG boots, leggings, layered clothing, and plenty of animal prints emerged in fashion. Red Hot Chili Peppers were popular, along with Santana and Manic Street Preachers. I listened to a lot of R.E.M., while my young daughter loved Britney Spears and was just discovering Pink.

Cell phones grew in popularity and were no longer for just the elite and privileged. Hillary Clinton was elected to the U.S. Senate. Thousands of dot-com businesses went under in the big dot-com crash. A new home averaged $134,150. The average income was just over $40,000. A gallon of gas costed $1.26, and a first class U.S. Postage Stamp was 33 cents.

Brigid met and fell in love with Frank O'Sullivan in 2000 and, later that same year, their son Ethan was born—a beautiful child with a kind heart and a super sharp intellect. At two months, he displayed a gift for language, as the infant attempted to mimic my words, nailing the rhythm and syllables, if not the actual sounds. It was impressive.

I don't remember what day or month or even the year it was when Briana called. I do remember it was pre-unlimited long distance days. We both kept ongoing, horrendous long distance bills, just because we were talking to each other. Bri sobbed into the phone; she was calling from her office job. The biopsy had come back on the lump in her breast; she tested positive for cancer. It was after Elsie died and maybe just before I starting back at school. I don't remember partly because my life was crazy, yet mostly because I chose not to acknowledge the disease. Even when the doctor told me Bri had a twenty-percent chance of living for five more years (that's an 80% chance she wouldn't), I ignored it. Repression works until it doesn't.

Bri and I talked every day. She came to Florida and I went to Virginia. We swam, danced, sang, cried, and shot an obscure 3:00 a.m. video on my couch on Knights-Griffin Road—Bri said we might not have the chance to do it later. She was my sister and friend—someone who knew my darkest secrets and my most unattractive flaws. And she loved me and celebrated me nonetheless. She was my biggest fan while I was at the academy, and an inspiration and uplifting and encouraging force in my life. When her energy and her voice began to fade, I was pretty sure I'd never make it through.

I cried out to God, *Please let me keep her.*

I was told it was four years between Briana Jo's diagnosis and her death. In my mind, it had been closer to four minutes when she died in early December of 2000. People tell you that it gets easier. People lie. It was less than five months after that when Tad's mother died. Squeeze and I had become close during a long summer stay on the farm. She had told lots of great stories about falling in love and marriage and kids. Squeeze had shared her wisdom and insight, her heart and soul. She had laughed easily and was a joy to hang out with. I wish I'd taken notes or recorded her stories.

Of course, we were still completely broke with no sign of CIA back pay in sight. So, we scraped enough money together to get Tad back home for his mother's funeral. It's what we did—he went home for his family and I went home for mine. It's what we could only barely afford.

With Tad's parents deceased and mine either deceased or disappeared or otherwise unavailable or unknown, all we had was each other to lean on. It wasn't such a great place to be as I don't think we even liked each other back then. I felt desperately alone—once again focusing on prayers of gratitude for beautiful, healthy children, good friends, kind family, palm trees, bright blue skies and sunshine. *Beaming, beautiful, desperately lonely sunshine.* It all felt forced.

I kept up with my friends from the hospital and attended not just Krystal's occasional candle parties and such, but her friends' parties as well. I saw Mary Giquinto at a lot of the get-togethers; we became pals and got to know each other over many a shared joint. But, I wouldn't have the opportunity to run into her husband Don (the illusive ARboc) for some time. Never would I have guessed we'd turn out to be good friends. I couldn't have guessed much of Don Giquinto's story at all. I wish I could've gotten to know him earlier in the game.

Our seven-year sentence on Knights-Griffin Road was finally coming to an end. Hilda had always said she'd sell the property to us one day for a really good price when she was ready to go to a retirement home. That "really good price" turned out to be roughly $7000 above the appraised value; Hilda didn't want to pay the realtor fees and thought we should do that. We told Hilda to piss off and she gave us thirty days to move out.

"My kids are in school and only have two months till summer break. We won't be moving before then," I informed her. I knew I'd need some time to find something affordable and come up with deposits and such. What a hoser—we'd picked up her mail and taken care of her horse and the property for seven years. She ended up selling the two houses for less than she'd offered to us and donating all the acreage to her alma mater in some grand gesture. Whatever. It was good to leave Hilda and that part of our lives behind.

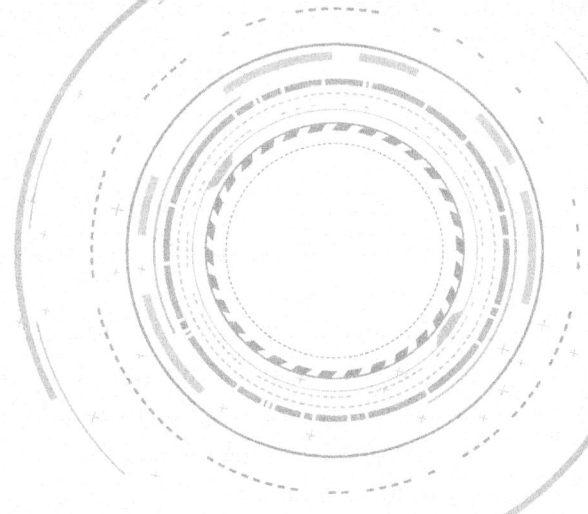

CHAPTER TWENTY
Home Again, Home Again. Jiggedy Jig

We moved into a three bedroom apartment on Park Road in the summer of 2002; it was lovely. Our rent doubled and we weren't sure exactly how we'd make it, but we really liked the change of scenery.

We had a family vacation planned with my Hutchenson siblings in Destin. However, two weeks after moving in—Tad was laid off. So, I took the kids to the beach while the old man job-shopped.

Of course, my lovely new apartment looked like shit when we got back. Job hunting is messy and evidently left no time for tidiness. Tad had irons in the fire, but no solid offers. I loved our new, little place, so all my spare energy went to worrying about losing it. Such an unnecessary waste of energy worry truly is.

Tad ended up finding work—in Texas. It sucked pretty hard for both of us. He was just more of a dick about it. We signed a second 7-month lease. I saw my husband roughly once every six months. I continued to do freelance graphics work and enjoy the swimming pool across the parking lot every sunny afternoon.

I don't remember if it was one of the many vehicles Michael totaled or some other fubar situation, but I do remember bumming rides to the grocery store and often carrying groceries on the bus and from the bus stop to our apartment, a half of a mile away, for some time.

Bailey ended up driving her old T-bird to Florida, staying with me for a week and then flying home, leaving her car with me. She'd become an angel in my life and a huge help with *everything* when she was in town. I cried and cried when she had to go back home to Tennessee and I was left alone to raise my own children.

Puberty sucks for everyone concerned. I never worried so much about my kids—I knew they'd be fine. Me, on the other hand—I didn't feel so certain about my survival. I'd hoped over time my own life would settle into something somewhat "normal." I just didn't have the foresight to realize this time would be just out of reach at about the same time my children would be beginning puberty and soon entering their "turbulent twenties."

Michael believed he was going to high school to play sports, meet girls, and have lunch. He went through public school with Ds and Fs in the first three quarters of every year, and kicking butt in the fourth quarter with As and barely passing. He ended up taking pottery to get through high school—important life skill that it is.

Meanwhile, Marie was really struggling academically. Everything was like pulling teeth. It was frustrating. I could tell she was bright. I didn't get what the problem was.

Here's what you need to do to get through school:

1. Show up for class
2. Do the homework

If you're not passing, it's because you are failing to do one of these two things. Doing your homework is like taking a mini test to see if you understand the material and can apply it. Showing up for class is seeing how you did on the test, learning from mistakes and moving on to the next assignment. IF you do these two things, the big exams will take care of themselves. Period.

Marie was tested and re-tested with every test the school had in their arsenal. Her IQ was 110—a high average. Her hearing was fine. Her corrected eyesight was good. She was given opportunities to hear or speak test questions out loud—as they were convinced *via testing* that she was an audio learner. Still, there was no real change.

I became so frustrated that I decided to pull Marie out of school and do it myself. Every parent should home-school their own child for two weeks. You'd never send them to school tired or unprepared or, heaven forbid, sick. This parenting thing is work. But home-school your own child—you'll have new-found respect and appreciation for your child's teachers.

By November of that first school year, I was calling an expert in. I worried I was doing more damage than good, though I read all the lessons and taught the material to the best of my ability.

Marie was an eager student—enjoying history and trips to the library and research and art and writing and even some math. But, holy cow, when it came to reading, I wanted to punch myself in the face.

The homeschooling expert came in and spent an entire day with Marie and what she discovered would make all the homeschooling hair-pulling worthwhile. She believed Marie had a vision issue—eyesight being one's 20/20 and vision being how your brain interprets that information. It appeared that Marie was seeing the first and last part of a word, but not the middle. She recommended a specialist in Palm Harbor.

The diagnosis was binocular dysfunction. Our doctor prescribed therapy—an at-home computer program that tracked and recorded progress that was saved to a *floppy disk* and upgraded by the doctor upon monthly exams. It was nothing shy of miraculous.

Marie would go back to public school a year later—better prepared. She missed the social part of school and I never reached out to homeschooling support groups as I had (and still have) issues with other people in general.

So, my days were freed up for graphics and afternoons devoted to the kids. Sometimes I'd sit and smoke on my balcony in the evening. I had a side view of the pool and clubhouse; I could see people swimming or socializing around the pool. The clubhouse and parking lot were to my right. I had a good view of the workout room side entrance and maybe half of the front parking lot.

One night I spotted a shiny, dark Lincoln pulling into the clubhouse parking lot—its headlights in my general direction. It cut the engine and sat motionless in the dark. I thought about grabbing my binoculars, but took another hit and walked over and leaned on the railing instead. I stared directly into the windshield, seeing nothing but black. I tried to imagine a logical reason why someone would park there and then stay in the car. Maybe they were waiting to pick someone up and it was easier for the resident to tell their ride to go to the clubhouse? I was stoned and continued to stare at the motionless vehicle when the shiny Lincoln started its engine and left as quickly as it had come. I thought it was odd, but then sat back down, took another hit, and watched two people play a drunken version of swimming pool volleyball with a 4-foot, inflated plastic SpongeBob SquarePants. If someone was watching me, that's the only unusual episode I can remember.

Overall, we were enjoying our time on Park Road. The apartment was lovely and the swimming pool and weight room were close-by. Money was tight, but that had always been the case for us. I came to terms as best I could with Tad being so far away for such long periods of time. I missed having another adult to defer to or to lend a helping hand or to simply share life with. Still, I kept busy with graphics work and was able to throw some web work Brigid's way from time to time.

The best part was getting to work with and talk to Brigid on a near-daily basis. We laughed a lot, both on the phone and online. If a client was rude, we'd Photoshop his or her head on other bodies in crazy situations, with each email one would try to out-do the other. We created a logo of sorts that was our "Asshole Rate: Charge Accordingly" graphic. That one came in handy every now and again. It was our way of blowing off steam.

So, Brigid and I talked and laughed and did graphics and web work. And we worried about Bailey. It was getting harder and harder to track Bailey down—she was working full time and raising teenagers, active in her church and community, and was in the middle of divorcing Damien St. Claire.

Damien was a weak man who slept with and lied to his therapist, his wife, women he met at bars, and female sub-contractors that crossed his path while building custom homes. If one person was capable of making a marriage work, it would've been Bailey. But these things really do take two people.

Damien continued to whore around while Bailey waited until their divorce was final to even go out on a date. And, even then, she was hesitant. They put their big house with its wrap-around porch on the market. Bailey moved into a townhouse rental with the kids and Damien built a two bedroom loft cabin, just below the big house.

Syler and Simone lived with Bailey, but visited their dad often on the weekends. Damien had really hit a downward spiral with pain medications and some homemade recreational chemistry—trying to heal more than just his physical pain would be my guess. Somehow the kids became a part of this. Until then, Syler had been such a straight-and-narrow kind of kid; I supposed it was his way of connecting with his dad. And Simone was such an adventuresome social butterfly; I presumed it was more a case of what can happen when youthful curiosity meets opportunity. Either way, it was dreadful; the little bits and pieces of information Bailey was collecting were driving her insane.

Further, Damien was becoming more and more outspoken about the Russo family—going off on tirades in bars and public places. Evidently, the Russo's were to blame for all of his ills and misfortunes. It seemed like a slippery slope to me, but I'd felt the backside of Sal's hand across my face. I wouldn't risk pissing him off again. And Sal Russo *loves* me. At least the only way he knows how.

I hadn't heard from Bailey in weeks and was surprised to get her call on that late Friday afternoon in February—Friday, February 13th. It was the day before Valentine's and my assumption was she had no big plans—just like me. However, big traveling plans were about to be made; Damien had been shot and killed. Police had ruled his death suicide, but our shared silence revealed its suspicions.

I called Tad, who flew in from Texas to drive us to Tennessee. All my bitching and whining over the years didn't matter; I needed him and he came. I wondered if there might be some truth to the old saying "Absence makes the heart grow fonder." Regardless, I was a wreck and it was good to have Tad to lean on.

Bailey arranged a lovely service and carried herself with the air of a senator's wife. The Hutchenson family dropped what they were doing and began packing the moment they heard their sibling was in need. The St. Claire family seemed to appreciate Bailey's efforts and was quick to make travel arrangements. Nothing in Rosemary St. Claire's life had prepared her for this moment; mothers don't imagine burying their sons.

While the occasion was sad and tragic, there was something more going on, something magical. It was people coming together to care for and cheer up and pray for each other. It was family. And I would see this particular phenomenon at other family events—but mostly funerals: highs and lows and damned little in between.

Life in Tennessee had transformed drastically for Bailey and her kids. There's a stigma attached to suicide they all struggled to rise above but, in a small town, these things are not soon forgotten. And so the St. Claire's of Tennessee sought change; Bailey was considering locations closer to her siblings—Ian and Brigid in Northern Virginia (at the time) or me in Florida. (Yes, I made the list.) I really, really wanted Bailey close by and I knew she wanted change for the kids. I also knew she sometimes operated out of parental guilt as we all do. I'm not proud, but this *does* illustrate exactly how selfish I can be: I pulled out all stops and went for the kids angle—the benefit of Michael and Syler being closer and having each other, Disney World less than an hour away, beautiful beaches about the same distance away, sunshine, swimming pools, movie stars … okay, not movie stars, but everything else.

Bailey was sold. By summertime, she was my neighbor. Both of us had the same three-bedroom floor plan on the front side of our separate buildings, but a quick trot down the back steps found us in a shared playground/picnic area where we shared many a cigarette and good conversation. We set up and organized her kitchen exactly as mine was set up, so we could always find stuff in each other's kitchen easily; we had twin kitchens. We had keys to each other's apartment and would routinely bum coffee creamer or cigarettes and Bic lighters from each other.

Sometimes, Bailey and I would be sitting at her apartment with all the kids running around and I'd look at her. "If all the kids are here, that means no one is at my apartment." I'd grab my keys, cigarettes and lighter and look back to her. Bailey would nod, I would exit, and then she would follow. When the kids caught up to us, as they often did, we'd reverse the process. We got it down to the point where all I had to do was grab my cigarettes and lighter and glance at Bailey or she would grab hers and give me a nod. Hide-n-seek with the teenagers, I think it was big fun for all of us. The kids just didn't know they were playing.

We did it once while on a camping trip with all the kids in a three level cabin—I nodded toward the upper balcony, grabbed my smokes and received Bailey's return nod and Brigid caught it, "Who whoa whoa—what just happened? I don't know this signal." She knows it now. We also have a signal for "I don't care how much fun it looks like I'm having, get me out of this conversation!" I have a low tolerance for boredom and it's a survival maneuver I use often and whenever necessary. The signal's still active today, so I won't be sharing that particular nugget of information. But I'm sure you can all see valuable application and will be motivated to create your own.

Ian Hutchenson met Susan Spar, the great love of his life, a beautiful blonde with sparkling blue eyes and a cover girl smile. Susan was well-educated, ambitious, and successful. They married in the fall of 2004 and had a big rocking reception with an open bar and a live band. Ian made sure his sisters were seated on the dance floor as he knew that's where we'd want to be.

Before long, Bailey landed a good job with Hillsborough County. It was a heck of a drive in traffic, but it paid the bills and gave her the means to purchase a house. Then, Frank and Brigid moved to Chesapeake, Virginia and bought a mansion of a house.

I saw Bailey at Jazzercise two and three times per week and we spent many a weekend at her house grilling out, but I missed her being my neighbor. And I really liked the idea of having a house to call our own too. I couldn't see homeownership for Tad and I coming anytime soon, but both Brigid and Bailey said it would be. Crazy Hutchenson women with their fortune-telling instincts—if nothing else, they are entertaining.

Tad was home in May 2005 and answered the call. It was rare that he was home and even rarer that he'd actually answer the phone—either we all dive for it at once or no one wants to touch it. He stood up and became very serious for a moment as he paced the apartment. I watched and caught parts of sentences. "Right." "I understand." "I hear that." Tad laughed happily. "Absolutely." He wandered off to the bedroom and closed the door.

Whatever, I thought. *Have your little private conversation.* I went back to doing whatever it was that I was doing.

Moments later, Tad strode into the living room with a smile on his face and kissed me. "Happy anniversary! Go pick yourself out a house. The CIA is finally cutting those back-pay checks."

"Really?" I smiled. "You know I'm going to want a nice one, right?"

And a "nice one" I did choose—in one of Plant City's nicest neighborhoods, Walden Lake: complete with golf courses and a country club. The Realtor called it a "nice, little house," but with

2100 square feet, four bedrooms, two bathrooms, an office for me with French doors off the foyer and a sliding glass door on the opposite wall that led to the screened-in pool—it was more than little or just nice.

I had prayed for a good neighborhood so Marie could play outside again. The last six months hadn't been kind to her at the apartment; other girls in the neighborhood seemed to have gotten meaner—or perhaps God's grace was no longer needed and now, was simply gone. I veered away from Walden Lake at first—I thought it was too pretentious. But Bailey insisted I at least take a look. I'm glad we did.

We were homeowners again! And guess what else? Our legal names just showed up on public record together purchasing real estate—not quite so "off the grid" anymore.

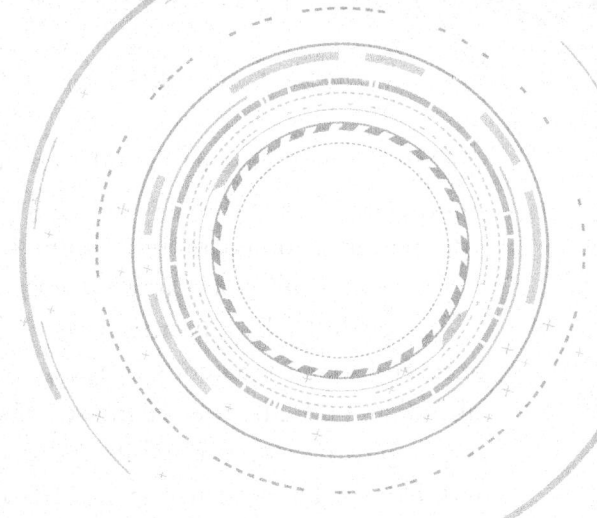

CHAPTER TWENTY ONE
Goat-Roping Russo Style

I'm not sure if I'd become terribly complacent or unbelievably lazy, but I just didn't want to think about any of my past at all anymore. Tad and I were *starting* to get along better and we had a lovely swimming pool home in a quiet and safe neighborhood where Marie could play outside without worry and Michael could get anywhere he needed to be in less than ten minutes. This was a good thing as gas prices were on the rise—up to a national average of $1.86 by early 2005 and hitting over $3.00 per gallon that same year.

Business picked up substantially (so I could afford gasoline). Before long, checks starting rolling in more frequently. Again, I wasn't rich, but we were making ends meet and I had cleaning people come in once a week and had my nails and hair done regularly. I was working ten to twelve hours a day, but I spent hour-long lunches in the pool and was home when my kids got home (or got out of bed as the case may be).

Michael had graduated and was working part time fixing computers. He would've liked me to be gone more often; it was a decent house for a party or to impress a girlfriend. But, there's very little possibility of that when your mom works from home.

Bailey and I had another year of Jazzercise three times a week and many weekends in the pool before she decided to take off and head back to Tennessee. She'd escaped and had fun and even earned a degree while she was here, but she was done with Florida. For years to come, she'd say I was the only interest she'd had in Florida—me and the women at Jazzercise. That class had some of the most fun and entertaining people in it ever. It was an interesting and extraordinary group of women. *Big shout out to Donna, Heidi, Shirley, Maribeth, Nancy, Cheryl, Martine, Gloria, Cecilia and all the other fabulous Jazzercisers we met in Plant City—whoop-whoop! LOVE you guys.* ☺

I know Bailey was only listening to her spirit and I only wanted the best for her, but I was a perfect wreck when she left. I must've cried for a week; my heart felt broken. With Bailey and Brigid, it's always been the same—we love being together, but feel physical pain as the physical miles become greater between us. Therapists might say we all have *abandonment issues*.

I felt on my own in a lot of ways—Tad traveled often and I pretty much did my own thing: graphics business, swimming, sunning, reading, shopping, working out, and watching movies and whole seasons of TV shows on DVD. There were the near-constant interruptions of kids after school until finally in bed and clients from nine-to-five, but I did okay.

Still, I should've been on guard more. I should've paid more attention to my surroundings. Sal would've smacked me in the back of the head had he been close enough. "Cici! Pay attention! You cannot survive this world in an idiot's clothing; you must put on the armor of awareness and carry a sword of sharp instincts."

He must've said it a million times as he threw his shoulders back and puffed out his chest. He had a lot of crazy sayings. As a kid, I thought he was being over-protective and wouldn't have been surprised had he insisted I wear a bulletproof vest and carry riot gear at all times.

But, I had no armor of awareness or bulletproof vest that fateful day I went shopping at Walmart, and there was nothing *sharp* about me. Getting stoned and going shopping was a teeny, tiny, little bit of a regular, daily habit of mine; it made tolerating all the "other people" possible. Judge if you must; obviously, I don't care.

I loaded up some groceries, felt like I had to cross town to find toilet paper, and stopped to look at every shiny piece of plastic that caught my eye along the way. Eventually, I made my way to one of the three long-lined, open check-outs. The hairs on the back of my neck stood up and I could feel someone watching me. I tried to fight the sensation and focused on reading the tabloids.

Anyway, when I couldn't fight the feeling any longer, I casually turned and looked around the store—pretending to merely be gazing up from my tabloid entertainment. As my eyes met those of the man that stood behind me with two carts full of groceries, I froze. The words "short and squatty; all butt and no body" went through my mind.

Older, fatter, and with fewer teeth—still, there was no doubt, behind me stood Uncle Guido. He said something to me about fixing dinner. I smiled, turned around, and focused on loading my groceries onto the slow-moving conveyer belt. Uncle Guido continued to try and make small talk, but my run and hide instinct had already kicked into overdrive. I started to bag while the cashier busied herself ringing everything up.

I'm not certain if it was his intent to more fully establish his identity or simply to embarrass the crap out of me—either way, he succeeded. Out of nowhere, he broke into song, "YOU ARE SO BEAU-TI-FUL TO MEEEEEEEE. CAN'T YOU SEEEEEE?"

The cashier looked to me for an explanation. I shook my head, held out my hands and mouthed the words "I don't know."

"YOU'RE EVERYTHING I HOPED FOR. YOU'RE EVERYTHING I NEED … YOU ARE SO BEAUTIFUL TO MEEEE!!"

I wanted to die. Customers in other lines and passing by with paid-for goods, and cashiers and other employees were staring; I pretended the old Italian guy wasn't singing to me—I felt my face flushing red as I hurried for the exit.

It had been like twenty-five years and trust me when I say the years had not been kind, but it was Uncle Guido singing the same song he'd sung to me on my sweet sixteenth. It made me puke then and now I was overcome with that same nauseous feeling.

With groceries in cart and debit card swiped, I smiled, thanked the cashier, and bolted out the closest exit, through the parking lot to my Jeep, swung open the back, threw the bags in, and took off like a bat out of hell.

I went home and went to The Washington Post Classified Ads online. A quick search for a Gremlin found this ad, not listed with cars, but in with general merchandise: "NO GUTS. NO GLORY. Just the shell of an old 1972 AMC Gremlin Voyager in desperate need of muscle." The ad had evidently been running nonstop for weeks.

There was no phone number or contact information; other than a "Contact Seller" link. Oh and how I did want to reply; the ad had the stench of Antonio all over it. I could've been wrong, but couldn't resist taking the chance.

I wrote to seller: "My 1972 AMC Gremlin Voyager is in fine running condition—but I do have a little rust around the edges. Is your gutless body in good shape? Please send pics."

The seller wrote back: "Nice. Get your head out of your ass. Your neighbors can't be trusted. Awesome response time BTW. 6 months + ads + direct mail + singing telegram."

It definitely was Uncle Guido in the Plant City Walmart and, as much as I hated to admit it, their little ploy did work. I wondered how long they'd been keeping tabs on me—the whole time? I'd never noticed any ads or direct mail pieces. They can blame me, but maybe their marketing skills sucked, or maybe a *phone call* would've been faster. But leave it to my family to make things as difficult as is humanly possible. I'm not sure why all of life must be a test or a lesson or have some ridiculously cryptic message—but I'm not going to be that person who's constantly watching for someone to be watching me. It seems too much like a job.

As for my neighbors, I really didn't know them that well. But my assumption was that there must be an immediate danger that was somehow linked to Vladimir. I was freaking out and wanted to ask *which neighbor,* but knew the order to get my head out of my ass was a direct order from Sal and it was probably best not to ask questions. I'd have to figure it out on my own and hope they meant a neighbor in our little corner of Walden Lake and not someone who happened to live in one of the *many* neighborhoods here.

Matt and Marianne Woodard lived on one side of us. They were a few years younger than us. Whenever I saw them outside, they were super-nice and once offered a small, sharp shovel when I was trying to plant bulbs with a useless bulb-digger tool. Another time, my lawnmower conked out and they overheard the engine's demise and loaned me their mower to finish the job.

When they noticed a tree was growing too close to our house and could cause damage, they mentioned having some work done themselves that week and offered to send their guy over for a tree-removal quote. They smiled and were kind and helpful and seemed entirely genuine to me. I felt certain Matt and Marianne weren't the neighbors Sal was referring to.

On the other side of us was the Drapiere family. Tom and Eve were in their late thirties/early forties with three children. Eve always did that plastic, fake smile thing with micro-expressions revealing her true contempt—typical of passive-aggressive personalities. I caught her eavesdropping one time; I attributed it to a low, easily-entertained IQ, and lack of anything better to do. The poor little thing probably didn't understand half the vocabulary we used anyway. It was rude and disrespectful though.

Eve drained her pool in my yard for months and months before I realized she was killing my shrubs around our pool. We'd never had a pool before and I had no idea that the chemicals would kill grass and shrubs and such. Tom and Eve Drapiere were original owners and had been there since 1993; I'm pretty sure Eve knew what she was doing. She hadn't been draining her pool in her neighbor's yard for the past twelve years or there'd be no shrubs at all; obviously she'd begun this practice when we moved in. All the better to see into our backyard. Creepy fuckers.

My sociopath family would definitely regard this disrespect of one's privacy and property as a *huge* issue. I wondered how her husband, who seemed so quiet and laid back, tolerated her crazy ass. Eve Drapiere was on my list of possibilities, though I couldn't imagine a link to Vladimir. I just thought she was a rude, nosey neighbor who really needed a hobby. I supposed I could eavesdrop on her personal, private conversations, but I have that low tolerance for boredom thing going on and I just didn't find her that interesting.

Sometime later, Bailey and I would catch her husband, Tom, peeping while we were out back swimming. Well actually, my grand dog Copper (a trusty beagle) would catch him while I was dog sitting and Bailey was in town.

It was the middle of June and it was just after dark sometime. Out of nowhere, Copper started barking and then baying, keeping his nose toward the far corner of our screened-in pool. While a puppy in many ways, Copper was still a lazy hound dog at heart and rarely barked for any reason; I'd never heard him bay like that at all before.

I went inside and got his leash; I opened the back screen door and Copper took off—nearly jerking my arm from its socket. The dog stopped short at the corner of the yard, sniffing a Coke can. I picked the ¾ full can up, noticing it was still icy cold. Our peeper had brought refreshments.

Copper yanked hard against my grasp—going around the house toward the front. I had no idea where the dog was taking me. Bailey was grabbing gear and fast behind me. Suddenly, the dog stopped dead in his tracks at my neighbor's truck; Tom was inside the vehicle with the front door opened; He looked embarrassed and flustered as the dog sat down at his door and continued to bay.

I remember being shocked and saying something lame about my grand dog. Bailey and I went back in the house. The thought of all the soda cans and snack-size chip bags I'd found in my backyard over the last five years and how many times I'd had the feeling someone was watching me as well crossed my mind; I felt sick. Though the immediate danger had passed, I called the local police the next day just so there'd be a record of my call. Then, I started documenting everything.

The house across the street had a revolving door once the original owners sold and moved north—new owners, new renters, new renters, new renters, and more new renters. There were plenty of interesting and colorful people—but no one who seemed to last for too long. I supposed I should have paid more attention; it was just hard for me to care, much less keep up.

Mack and his wife Agnes had also been original owners and lived catty-corner from us. They were an elderly couple. She became ill and was bedridden, while he kept watch over her and still managed to be social with all the other neighbors while out in his yard fighting weeds and fire ants.

When Agnes passed away, Mack seemed lost. Even though I was busy, I'd take a few minutes to talk and give him a granddaughter-like hug. He'd occasionally mow my yard—way too short and kicking up dust all over the place. He created more work than what it was worth, but I figured he was just looking for something to do.

He asked me to watch his house and move the car from time to time while he was away visiting family. These types of anti-burglary efforts don't work as well as one might think for a number of reasons—but it was no big deal, so I did it. When Mack returned home, he offered to buy me dinner to say thank you. Tad was out of town; Michael had recently gotten an apartment with friends, so it was just Marie and I. I did think it was odd or maybe just cheap he didn't invite Marie, but she already had other plans for dinner and I said, "Sure."

I walked across the street and met Mack in his driveway. The little sixty-five year old man with small feet and hands seemed oddly nervous. Pulling out of his driveway, he spotted a neighbor walking with her baby in a stroller down the sidewalk. He rolled down his window and shouted an exaggerated, "Shhhhhhhh … Don't tell anyone!" He smiled and held a finger up to his lips, nodding, and winking. Gross, right?

The evening went downhill from there; I should've gotten out of the car and said "never mind" when I had the chance, but I guess I was a little stunned. Mack knew Tad—the man I'd been married to for better than twenty-five years, with whom I'd had two children, who paid for the roof over my head as well as my utilities, perfume, scented candles, wardrobe, groceries and home décor, to name but a few—and Mack thought he stood a chance with me. So, not only did he think I was a whore, he thought I was a stupid whore. *Dream big little man; small dreams have no magic.*

He stared at me while driving and nearly had a head-on in the restaurant parking lot, making a left while looking at me; the driver and passenger of that little sports car will never be the same. They honked and yelled and made rude hand gestures as they stomped on the brakes and swerved to avoid a collision. Mack never noticed. Idiot.

We had dinner. He rambled on about himself while I focused on random conversation in my own head, which was way more entertaining. He drove us back to the neighborhood; I prayed for safe travel. Mack pulled into his driveway and parked. I got out immediately said, "Thanks for dinner," and walked across the street to my house—pretending not to hear whatever he was mumbling as I unlocked my door and went inside.

I wanted to punch him in the face, but those dentures would probably be $5,000 and a broken jaw could mean a week or ten days in the hospital for the old guy and then we'd be talking tens of thousands. He just wasn't worth it. I could completely redecorate my house for that kind of money. I opted for avoidance whenever possible and ignoring him as a second resort. Oh, but Mack was persistent with his sniper comments:

"You need to teach Marie how to mow the lawn."

"I'm not worried about the lawn. There are other things I want her to concentrate on right now."

ILLUSIONS OF PRIVACY

By this time, Tad and I had already done a bunch of interior upgrades and maintenance on the house in addition to a $5,000 air conditioning unit and a $10,000 roof. I'm not sure why the neighbors spent the time they did analyzing my yard. Really—you do you.

"If she were my teenager, she wouldn't eat until the yard was mowed."

I spat back, "She's *not* your teenager, Mack! And withholding basic nourishment as a means of punishment is considered child abuse these days."

Then it was:

"Send Marie over—I'll teach her how to run the push mower."

"Send Marie over—I'll teach her how to run the riding mower."

"Send Marie over—I'll teach her how to use the edger."

"Send Marie over—I'll teach her how to use the blower."

I snapped one day, "I don't want you to teach my daughter *anything*!! She has two parents. Back off, Mack!"

Mack was a sleazy old man; he had that much in common with Vladimir, but nothing more. Vladimir could've knocked him down with his little finger. I imagined Sal would consider Mack a potential threat if he'd ever seen him remotely give Marie a second glance. I was being watched; it stood to reason Marie was as well. Mack would remain on my list until out of the blue one day, he packed up most of his worldly possessions and moved into a retirement village with old pals—leaving his house and upside down mortgage for the bank to deal with. That's according to a neighborhood rumor anyway. I never saw a thing.

Neighbors said he came back for a carload once or twice, but it was no time before the bank took possession, changed the locks and had a "For Sale" sign in the front yard. After watching the house directly across the street sit for so long—the last owners having given it up in bankruptcy, yet continuing to rent it for two years before the bank took action—I was surprised to see Mack locked out inside of two weeks. I didn't give it much thought beyond "Hey maybe the market is starting to pick back up."

It was somewhere around that same time that I needed some minor repair and maintenance done to my 1994 Jeep. I called Bill, my trusted mechanic for years, only to discover Bill had sold the business and someone else had taken over. Ed was happy to pick up my Jeep and take it back to the shop—the same curbside service Bill had always provided. Ed's daughter worked for him and he'd have her drop him off within the hour.

I met them outside with my Jeep key in hand. The older man wore blue coveralls and his long gray hair was pulled back into a ponytail; his long, windblown beard, mustache, and eyebrows giving him the air of a crazy scientist who just invented something. I was pretty sure that "something familiar" about him was based on a childhood memory of a cartoon. His daughter was blonde and lovely—she waved, smiled, and drove off.

I talked to Ed briefly about the Jeep. He asked what I did for a living; I told him "graphic art."

"Do you think poetry is a form of art?"

"Sure." I went to hand him my Jeep key and as he took it, he grasp my hand in both of his.

"The eagle leaves his post for flight—flying, flying into the night. Guided by heavenly light—knowing, knowing wrong from right." His grasp remained tight over my hand as he stared into my eyes, "Thank you," he smiled sheepishly and released my hand, "we really appreciate your business."

I had hoped none of the neighbors were out in the yard and looked around nervously. Holy cow, what would they think? That was super weird, but I kind of attract weird people. I considered the possibility of some cryptic message, but didn't make the connection till much later.

Ed took off with my Jeep and when he called to say repairs were made, I paid the bill over the phone with a credit card and had him leave the Jeep in the driveway with the key in the ashtray. If his poem was some sort of cryptic message, it evaded me and I wasn't up for another awkward poetry reading in front of my house. I assumed he was a lonely old guy and had probably watched one too many episodes of *Desperate Housewives*.

The next time I needed the Jeep serviced, it wouldn't start and Ed sent a tow truck driver to pick it up. The driver asked me if I was single and when I said "no," he asked what time my husband got home. Tad was out of town and not due back for a couple more weeks. "Any second," I smiled and lied.

It's no wonder women in the south aren't as hospitable as one might imagine—holy cow, be a little polite to a southern man and they think you want to sleep with them. I would need to learn to be more snotty and aloof. I made a mental note to talk to Brigid about this. She had "snotty and aloof" down to an art form.

Tad thought these instances were because of my heart-stopping beauty. *God bless his bad eyesight.* He'd laugh and before long was advising me "Don't talk to strangers," every time he'd take off on business. But he'd also do firearm and ammo checks while he was in town, just in case. We both enjoyed blowing random things up and shooting stuff to shreds—it was something we often did while visiting our Lakeland pals, Don and Mary Giquinto.

The four of us had become good friends—Don and Mary included us in their big, rocking, friends and family gatherings and smaller, quieter Sunday dinners and weekend get-togethers as well.

Some days, I'd take off for Lakeland after Marie had left for high school. Mary worked days and Don always had a long list of things to do, but never seemed to mind re-arranging his schedule to hang out—Don's place became the spot for those of us without regular, daytime jobs to retreat to on a regular basis. Sometimes it'd just be Don and me—smoking cigarettes, drinking coffee, and burning a big fatty. Other times there'd be three or four other people.

I pulled into Don's yard on one such occasion, Laurie was already there. She had long, thick blonde hair and wore denim shorts and a white, cotton, sleeveless button-up top with flip-flops. Laurie was Mary's best friend and I loved her instantly; I was happy to see she was hanging out that day too.

Laurie was sweet and kind and a down-to-earth/no bullshit kind of person. She laughed easily and was always fun to hang out with. Her husband was twenty years her senior and apparently she'd left him at home. "Don, what will your wife say when she hears you've been with *her* girlfriends all day?" Laurie teased. We all knew exactly how devoted Don was to Mary and Mary to him. They didn't do jealousy; there was never a need to.

Before long, Jimmy joined us. As I knew the history, Jimmy had been Don's long-standing, loyal pal forever. He wore jeans, a t-shirt, and a ball cap that concealed most of his strawberry blond hair. Jimmy was tall and slender with boyish good looks camouflaging his fifty-something years. His smile was genuine as he jumped out of his pick-up truck. "Hey, I didn't know Don was throwing a party today!"

We smoked a couple joints and drank some coffee and out of nowhere Laurie suggested, "We ought to play a round of Ten Shot Sally!"

"Ten Shot Sally" was one of our favorite target-shooting games involving printed human-silhouette targets we called

"Sally" and ten shots in ten seconds from a holstered weapon of one's choice—always played in rounds of ten. The last time the four of us had played we split into two teams: boys and girls—each person taking five of the ten shots for their team. Laurie and I kicked their asses—over and over again. *Eight out of ten rounds.*

"Hell yeah!" I chimed in. "Boys versus girls?"

Don pulled out a chest of his favorite handguns and I selected a Ruger P95 9mm. I'd fired just about every gun in that box, but always had great luck with the Ruger whenever we'd play Ten Shot Sally.

It was the bottom of the tenth round and we were tied with the guys—Laurie nailed her five shots within the center of the target, as close as we could tell from a distance, and I'd have to do at least that good to win. As Laurie stepped to the side and dropped her gun, I stepped up to take the last five shots. Bang-bang-bang—I knew my first three shots were somewhere in the center, though I didn't know exactly which ring I was inside of. Then, my hand started cramping. I pulled the trigger as I pulled the barrel up and to the right, nailing a shoulder shot. Anything outside the marked center torso rings are worth zero points. "Fuck you Sally!" I fired again—this time hitting the target square in the forehead. I killed Sally and signaled the end of the game. "Dang."

It was still a good day. I jumped in my red 1994 Jeep Cherokee and took the back roads home—Rockridge Road, crossing over Route 98, through Kathleen, and winding around to Knights-Griffin Road and into Plant City. I'd make it back home and have an hour to myself before Marie would be out of school.

I drove through Walden Lake and into our neighborhood. I could see a black SUV parked in front of my house. My neighbors, the Drapiere's, routinely parked their vehicles and had their visitors park in front of my house even when there was room in their driveway *and* in front of *their* house. I'm not sure why—maybe they didn't like the view from their front yard blocked by their own car or the potential oil stains from the vehicles on the street in front of them. Overstepping boundaries was their thing; I continued to document it all—noting they were more likely to overstep when Tad was out of town. I considered it rude and often wondered if I should park my old Jeep in front of their house for a few days.

But I was in a really good mood and the dumb-head neighbors were *not* going to rob my joy. I pulled into my driveway and popped open the back to grab my gear. As I did so, the driver of the SUV opened his door and stepped out. I glanced over my shoulder, expecting to see some kid heading over to the neighbor's house. But it was no kid. He was older. He was fatter. His chauffer's cap sat square atop his now bald head. His suit was Armani. Joey "The Torch" Marconi smiled briefly at me and proceeded to walk around the vehicle to open the back passenger door. It looked like I wouldn't be spending the next hour alone after all.

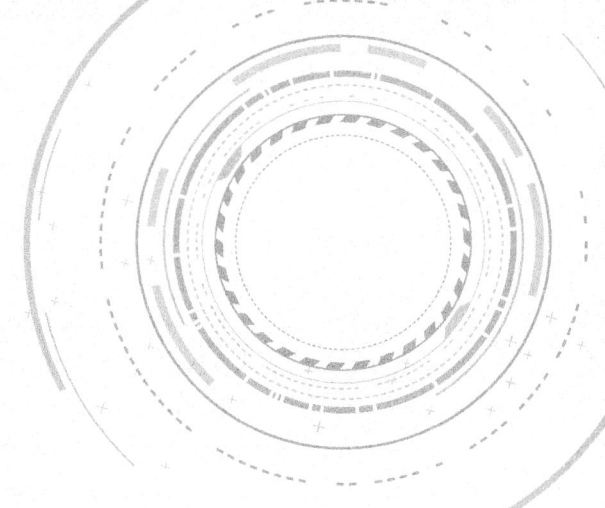

CHAPTER TWENTY-TWO
Game On

Joey held the back door open and motioned for me to get in. "No thanks. Maybe some other time." I grabbed my duffle, knowing my shotgun wasn't shot that day and was still loaded, but not remembering if I left one in the chamber or not. I threw the duffle over my shoulder and slammed the back of the Jeep—sorting through my keys as I headed towards the front door.

"Cici." Hearing the name startled me; hearing Antonio's voice mortified me. I turned around slowly. Antonio looked amazing; which made it all the more difficult to face him. *Why couldn't he have aged more liked Joey?* Antonio wore a slim-fitted black Armani suit with a single front button closure over a black cotton t-shirt. He smiled and put his hands in his pants pockets—leaning against the SUV and crossing his no-socks-with-shiny-Italian-shoes, sun-tanned ankles. Antonio could still rock that *Miami Vice* look.

I felt awkward and underdressed in my denim capris, gladiator sandals, green tank, and gray cardigan sweater—my pony tail and rectangular glasses completing the librarian-gone-grandma look.

He motioned towards the door of the SUV and smiled broadly, "What do you say? For old time's sake?"

I considered my options—decline the invite for a family reunion ride and risk Marie getting home and having to explain the two Italian guys hanging out in front of our house; or take my chances with my estranged, older half-brother and his little bitch friend, Joey The Torch. And if they meant me any harm, did I really want my daughter walking into a bad episode of "wrong place; wrong time"? I had no choice. On the upside, maybe I'd have the opportunity to bitch-slap Joey Marconi.

"Fine, but I don't have a lot of time." I jumped in the back seat, keeping my duffle close and sliding over to the other side.

Antonio followed as Joey waited for him to get situated before closing the rear door and trotting around front to the driver's side.

We pulled out of Walden Lake, down Alexander to Park Road and some unfamiliar back roads off Knights-Griffin. Antonio relaxed in his seat and pulled a neatly-rolled joint from his inside pocket. Before he could speak I cut him off. "Let me guess—for old time's sake? What's the game plan here big brother—get me stoned and off my game so I won't see your attack coming? Are the *two* of you so intimidated by a middle-aged mother of two that you think she needs to be high for you to stand a chance against her? I'm not surprised by your punk-ass, bitch girlfriend," I smacked the back of Joey's seat, "but I am a little disappointed in you, Antonio."

"Sal always said you were 'piss and vinegar.' Actually, I thought Joey and I showing up out-of-the-blue might be a helluva buzz-kill and you'd appreciate the midday bump." He lit the joint and inhaled like a pro—exhaling the skunky-sweet scent high-end marijuana aficionados know and love.

"A 'buzz-kill?' There's the understatement of the year. Holy shit—y'all threw me out of the whole fucking family. I've done the best I could with what I had. When I needed help paying rent or with a car or buying diapers—none of you were anywhere to be found. But *now* that I finally have some semblance of a decent life, you want to come around? What the fuck?" Antonio handed me the joint and I took my first deep breath and inhaled like it was pure oxygen. I needed to slow down and calm down—being a hysterical female never played out well with any of the Russo men.

Antonio leaned over and examined my face. "*Middle*-aged mother of two?"

Joey snickered at Antonio's comment. "She said 'y'all'."

"Fuck you Antonio." I shook my head and then added, "I do plan on living well into my nineties."

"Damn girl—maybe you should focus on just getting through today." His expression became serious.

"This is fun—good, wholesome sibling rivalry with a side of kidnapping that your attorney will no doubt get reduced to involuntary imprisonment. What's this all about Antonio?"

We drove and smoked. Joey rolled down his window and coughed pathetically—objecting not-quite-silently-enough like the passive-aggressive, whiny, little, snot-nosed girl he is.

Antonio told me all about how the family had kept tabs on me for years and how if I'd just paid attention, I would've known they were there all along. "Unfortunate circumstances led to your leaving, but you never looked back; perhaps it was just easier to forget all of us."

"I wasn't aware I had a bitchload of choice. What possible good could've come from looking for and wondering about a past I was *told* to forget anyway? The name of this story isn't exactly

'Cici's Choice.' I made the best of what I was handed while trying diligently to do what I was told to do. Don't try to spin it."

"You've got problems, kid." The big brother in Antonio was surfacing. And dang—I did have problems. Vladimir Petrov was rumored to be somewhere within the state of Florida—age only serving to solidify his position and power. It was Vladimir's presence that prompted my family to move closer, though there were no indications his visit had anything to do with me. But, while my family was here, they might as well pay attention to my surroundings since I obviously had no inclination to do it myself.

So. there were the neighbors. I figured out the mystery of Peeping Tom and Eve Drapiere. My family considered this to be extremely disrespectful (the greatest crime of all time), but I reminded Antonio that if my neighbors were waxed, my property value would most likely go down and I didn't think extreme measures would be cost-effective.

The truth was that as angry as I was about the Drapiere's disrespecting me, my property, and my privacy, I couldn't justify yet another senseless "accident."

"No matter what—they're still human beings and parents and the disrespect thing doesn't seem worth dying over. Plus, is this attention you need right now?" I didn't want to go to bat for them and I wasn't willing to start calling in favors, but I hoped my logic would pacify the family. Besides my concerns and fears were well-documented and if anyone's actions escalated, I was more than capable of shooting and playing hysterical, frightened female in self-defense. I argued my point to the best of my ability.

Antonio nodded his agreement and we exchanged cell numbers and initiated some single-purpose alert codes. We laughed about the stupid codes we used as kids and then talked about initiating an outdoor lighting protocol that was so complicated, I was sure I'd screw it up. In the end, we modified our old "please interrupt this date" light set up from our teenage years to mean "something suspicious/drive by/be on alert." We used to do this when daddy and mama were out for the night and we brought members of the opposite sex into Sal Russo's house.

If the outside lights were on and the inside lights off, this was Antonio's sign to stay out and keep watch for the parents; he was busy. If the opposite was true—outside lights off and inside lights on, we were free to come in. The grand idea was that we'd all play lookout for each other; the reality was that Gio, Emilio, and I played lookout for Antonio nine times out of ten.

We had all grown up and now my brothers had additional skills. Just because I didn't keep up with my family, didn't mean they hadn't kept up with me. Everyone had been on high-alert and I had been oblivious.

Uncle Guido tried to bump into me at Walmart, then got in line behind me and tried to strike up a conversation. Then, with no other option, he chose to burst into song—a little *somethin' somethin'* he'd come up with on his own. Antonio and Joey both laughed and laughed about Uncle Guido embarrassing the crap out of me. Big fun.

As for the poetry-reciting mechanic—he came out of the woodwork when the high-alert circulated. No one had heard from him in years and no one knew exactly how he came by his information. It was the old mechanic's belief that I killed Ivan Petrov in the alley that night and saved his daughter from a brutal existence, if not death. He knew nothing of the third shooter and as quickly as he appeared, he disappeared. The shop was resold and no one has heard from him since.

I wasn't surprised I hadn't recognized the old guy—I was a child who didn't hang out in the garage; I couldn't even remember having a single conversation with him in my life. He'd shown up in coveralls with long gray hair, beard, and mustache.

We figured he was a clean cut, close-shaven brunette wearing designer smoking jackets and living in the south of France or some crap by then.

As for the creepy tow truck driver—he was just another creepy guy who routinely hit on married woman. He's still driving a tow truck and remains single to this very day. *Watch out Walden Lake women.*

I wasn't sure what to do with all of this information. The biggest threat seemed to be the whole Russian mob thing. What if Vladimir did know who I was? What if Vladimir or one of his goonies approached Marie or Michael? How could I tell my kids to beware of creepy Russian men in expensive suits and think for one minute they wouldn't want some kind of an explanation? How could I ever tell them my deepest, darkest secrets? My life, in retrospect, was shameful. I wouldn't know where to begin; I thought my head was going to explode.

"The next thing is *you* kiddo," Antonio's voice got softer as he grabbed my hand and looked directly into my eyes, "I love you sis, but God Almighty, you have gotten *soft*!" Joey and Antonio bust into a fit of girly giggles.

"I hate you both."

"Then, you're going to love this idea." Antonio smiled broadly.

I hated the idea, but it was coming from Sal, which meant "the top" and, like it or not, I would have to go along with it. The consensus was that I was "weak and unprepared," so the only solution was to prepare me and make me stronger. How? Well, that which doesn't kill you makes you stronger, right? Preparedness training was the only answer. The next several weeks would be full of surprises designed to make me stronger if they didn't kill me first—with the help of Antonio and Joey. "Consider this your 'heads up' kid."

It was around this time that Michael had met Olivia, the great love of his life and together they were planning their wedding for the following October. He was twenty-one. Olivia was nineteen and a natural beauty with chestnut hair and deep, rich blue eyes that positively lit up when she looked at my son.

All I had to do was be mother of the groom. Having eloped more than twenty years earlier, I didn't have a clue about weddings—other than the showing up, drinking, and dancing parts. I was amazed at all the little details, choices, planning, and organizing required—not to mention the money. Whoa. But Olivia was amazing with her charts and graphs and time schedules and flower and color and cake and menu choices.

I just had to smile, be supportive, and plan the rehearsal dinner. Olivia's parents had a lovely home on the outskirts of town and neighbors they'd been friends with for years. The ceremony would be held in the neighbors' beautifully landscaped garden under a trellis of tropical plants, with the reception being held at Olivia's parent's house next door, with tents set up around their spacious and manicured-to-perfection lawn, along with an interesting fountain spraying up and splashing down bubbles in the swimming pool.

Olivia came from a family of master chefs; the menu would include a choice of Beef Wellington or Chicken Brian prepared by her family and served by a fleet of volunteering friends. I had considered reserving the Walden Lake Country Club House for the rehearsal dinner, but because the kids were doing an "open house" format for the wedding and reception, they asked if we'd do the rehearsal dinner at our house instead. That's *all* I had to do—dinner for fifty at my house and show up for the ceremony the next day. Easy-peasy, right?

Meanwhile, I was constantly looking over my shoulder—waiting for Joey or Antonio to jump out and say "boo!" But several days went by without a peep. Were they making plans for a grand attack? Did they just drop by to freak me out and have me on my toes with no intention to follow up on the "heads up" warning? There was no telling. Sal would never make a threat without seeing it through, but Antonio and Joey could've been bored and thought terrorizing me would be fun. If they'd done that using Sal Russo's name, there'd be hell to pay. Still—better safe than sorry.

Bailey flew in on the guise of home renovations to check up on me every couple of weeks. In the process, my entire house was painted and new bathroom faucets, ceiling fans, new carpeting, and lighting fixtures were installed. Closets were cleaned out and the garage was organized. And then in Bailey's downtime, between projects and dishes and laundry, she found a couple great appliance deals and my kitchen had upgraded stainless steel in no time. Lucky for me, Bailey had been a girl scout and that motto to leave every place nicer than you found it stuck with her into adulthood. There never was nor will there ever be a houseguest as completely helpful and considerate as Bailey.

Tad was traveling for work (pretty much like always) and we weren't sure exactly what insanity to expect from my family, but something changed in Tad—he stopped drinking altogether and beefed up our security—cameras, privacy screen, and outdoor curtains around the pool, a couple small changes to the security system already in place, a few additions to our firearms collection, and a bitchload of ammo. We started spending more time on the firing range and hanging out together in general when he was home. It was crazy times, but we were having fun and it was a lot like falling in love all over again.

The cameras provided a lot of entertainment: four large, hugely visible cameras—one on each side of the house. Above each of those were pinhole-sized wide-angle cameras. Below each of the four conspicuous cameras (low and to the left and right looking up) were eight more pinhole cameras, for those camera-shy guys with ball caps that look down and away from the visible security cameras. We had a seven-inch monitor in the living room showing the four cameras rotating from one to another. The pinhole cameras had a live wireless feed to my computer only. So, kids and visitors could see the obvious shots, but not have a clue about the hidden cameras.

Overall, I got more footage of teenage boys looking down into the teeny pinhole lenses than anything else. There's nothing like a guilty look on the face of the kid that's there to pick up your daughter. Before they'd leave, I'd take pictures of Marie's dates, their vehicles and tags and copied their driver's licenses—just in case the security cameras they thought they'd dodged had given them too much confidence.

Tad generally did the interrogations and laying down of the law—nobody could beat a dead horse like Tad. It would embarrass Marie to no end, but we were entertained and felt like the boys were sufficiently intimidated and fair warned—so it was all good.

I kept my alarm system armed every night. I paid attention to the vehicles behind and in front of me when I was out and about. I listened to my instincts and watched out for danger. I questioned everything and everyone. And still—I didn't see it coming.

It was after Jazzercise. Shirley, Donna, and I were the last ones to leave. Donna locked up and the three of us made the trek down two flights of stairs and then two ramps, across the sidewalk and to the parking lot. Donna pulled out first, then Shirley, then I. They both made a right as I waited for traffic to clear to make my left. I studied traffic to my right and then left. When I turned back, Antonio was standing in front of my

Jeep smiling with his hands on his hips. I revved the engine. He didn't flinch, but instead gave me a sideways nod—still smiling and as he did, my passenger door yanked open and in jumped Joey Marconi. Before I could react, Joey shoved a gun into my ribcage, bruising my right side, and snarled, "Drive bitch." That was round one.

Proceeding rounds would result in increasing injuries. I gave Joey a knee to his groin when he tried to grab my new Anuschka bag that I saved for months to buy. He returned the favor by knocking me down and throwing random punches at my head until Antonio dragged the crazy bitch off of me.

Then, I slapped Antonio across the face when he walked up to me outside of the library at closing time and said, "Hi, I'm a rapist and am I glad I ran into you." He saw my slap and raised me one sharp kick to the knee—knocking me down and leaving me to crawl back to my vehicle while nursing my left knee. That incident kept me on crutches for eight weeks.

They planned their attacks when I was alone and often when Tad and Bailey were both out of town. I was just starting to walk without crutches as my latest hip injury had healed to the point where I could put weight on my left leg. I was damned tired of getting my ass kicked and making up excuses for all of my injuries. I had bruises, breaks and cuts, twists and sprains on damned near every joint and muscle. I lived on crutches and dreamed of owning a really nice walker one day. The more I tried to defend myself, the worse it got. I started carrying my trusty .38 Smith & Wesson revolver with me everywhere I went. I had no intention of shooting Antonio or Joey, but thought it might spare me another ass-kicking.

I had weapons stashed throughout the house and pool area during Michael and Olivia's rehearsal dinner at our house—which went on without incident. I was surrounded by heavily-armed

Hutchensons and a husband with an itchy trigger finger—relaxing and enjoying several glasses of wine came easily to me that night. I felt certain my two-bullies-on-a-mission would never strike when I had so much backup.

I had my .38 revolver in my bag for Michael and Olivia's wedding. During the reception, I noticed a mysterious limo parked across the street. I saw shadowy figures leaning over the hood and on the roof, peering through what appeared to be binoculars. I imagined whoever it was taking night-vision pictures with high-end surveillance cameras.

Don't ask me how, but I could feel Sal Russo's presence—watching, judging, and directing the photo shoot for Mama Luciana's later viewing. And so I drank and I danced. A lot. Somewhere around 10:00 p.m. I snuck out front and smoked a big, fat joint with those that followed me—inhaling deeply and blowing smoke in the direction of the limo. Toke after toke, I toasted the Russo family that once was my family.

Less than a week later, I was coming home from the grocery store just after dark. Marie was out with friends and Tad was back on the road. I backed into my driveway and hit the garage opener, then backed the rest of the way into the garage. I grabbed my .38 from under the seat and tucked it in the back of my waistband before unlatching the back of the Jeep. I opened the door to the kitchen and stopped short of entering. There was no door chime and no 60-second warning beeps from the alarm system. It had quite obviously been disarmed. I closed the door and exited the garage to see if I could see anything from the windows. I hoped it was stupid Joey and Antonio, but had no way to tell for sure.

I attempted to peek through the blinds to no avail. As I edged my way along the side of the house towards the back, I instinctively grabbed my gun and froze at what sounded like voices. With breath held, I slowly leaned around the corner and darted back quickly before being spotted by Joey—who was humming and dancing, his .32 caliber, sissy-girl handgun firmly in his palm. I had to cover my mouth to keep from snickering. I doubted he could even shoot it.

I tucked my .38 back into the waistband of my jeans and proceeded to sneak up on Joey with the intent of goosing him—knowing he'd jump and scream like a girl and Antonio, who was no doubt close by, would come running.

That was the plan. But, as it turned out, I stubbed my toe on one of our stepping stones, startling Joey who let out a high-pitched squeal as he fumbled with his .32 and inadvertently pulled the trigger in a lame attempt to maintain control of his weapon.

Horrific pain tore through my leg—burning, searing, throbbing pain. I fell to the ground—grabbing my outside thigh in a weak attempt to ease the misery and stop the bleeding. I felt dizzy and nauseous; my head was spinning. I cried out in excruciating agony.

"Cici, shut the fuck up." It was Antonio. "You're barely bleeding. It's a flesh wound," he angrily spat out the words in a hushed tone.

"He could've have killed me!" I argued. My leg still throbbing, blood oozing out from under my hand.

"Not likely. Get up. Got any Band-Aids inside?"

"Oh my God! Maybe we should just rub some dirt on it! Think I can walk it off?" Antonio and Joey lifted me to my feet. I pushed Joey away. He stumbled back. Assisted by big brother, I staggered into my room and collapsed on the bed.

I tried to go somewhere else in my mind to escape the pain. I could hear Antonio on the phone. "Yeah, I guess we need a doctor."

A beach. A beach would be great right now. With margaritas and palm trees and a perfect breeze. Much as I tried to create a mental diversion, no cabana boy on the beach could help me escape the pain. I curled up in a ball, keeping pressure on my wound and waited.

"Idiots!" The voice was warmly familiar as was the sound of Antonio and Joey being Sal-slapped in the back of the head—like two ripe melons.

"Daddy! Joey shot me!" I was again the broken, injured girl of my childhood and he was the same man who stole me back from my pirate parents a lifetime ago.

"Shhhh ... it'll be okay," he whispered as he quickly tied material around my leg and helped me up and into the back of a white, panel van backed into my driveway that had appeared magically out of thin air next to my Jeep.

I remember looking up at Sal at some point and thinking that he'd aged, but was still a very handsome and fit man. He was my dad and he was there to rescue me.

"I hate Joey Marconi! Why did he have to shoot me Daddy?"

"He's an idiot. If I thought it would make you feel any better, I'd shoot him myself."

"That," I thought about it for a second, "that *would* make me feel better, Daddy."

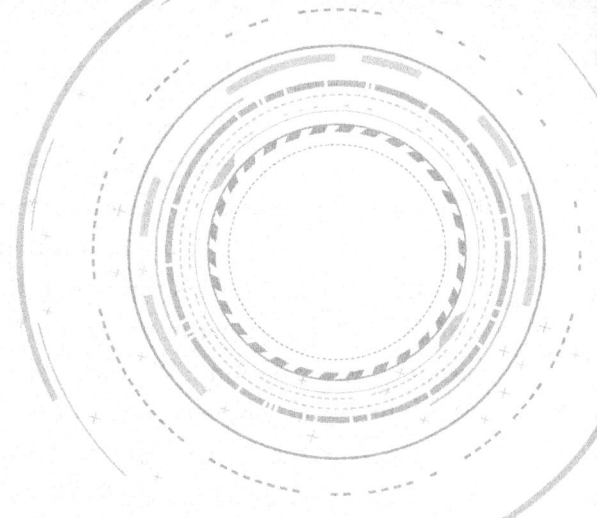

CHAPTER TWENTY-THREE
To Tell the Truth

I remember hearing murmured voices—coming from another room. There was boisterous laughter—Michael? No, Sal. It occurred to me for the first time how they had the same unruly, tumultuous laugh—a laugh that could always be heard above and traveled farther than, all other laughs.

I awoke in my own bed, my own bedroom, my own home—I took inventory. I reached for my left thigh and found it bandaged and aching. Bummer, that wasn't a dream. I found prescription drugs on my nightstand—not in amber-colored, plastic containers with labels from a real pharmacy like normal people have, but in small plastic, zip-lock bags with things like "PAIN (1) 4-6 HRS" handwritten on the outside with a black Sharpie.

I heard the front door open and close. Seconds later, Bailey peeked in my room, "Hey, are you awake?"

"I think so."

"How are you feeling? Do you want something to eat or drink?"

"I'm good," holding up a bag of pills, "I just took two of these PAIN (1) pills. They're not just for breakfast anymore." I smiled lamely. "Was I hallucinating or was that Sal's voice I heard?"

"Oh, it was Sal. He's sending a doctor by to check up on you. You seem a lot better today. You've been pretty out of it—yesterday you called me 'Briana' and said we should hang out with John Candy more often. How much do you remember?"

"We *should* hang out with John Candy more often! I'm pretty sure narcotics are the answer." We *both* laughed like idiots. I do feel like I had a little more of an excuse than Bailey did; she must've had a Russo-charm high going on—how those Russo men adored her so.

"I remember Joey the sissy-britches/girly-man shooting me in my own back yard with his teeny, tiny baby girl-sized gun. I remember a white van and looking up and seeing Sal for the first time since I'd said good-bye and underwent surgery back in the day," I rubbed my eyes and tried to shake some of the cobwebs from my brain, "I remember telling Sal shooting Joey *would* make me feel better."

"He told me that; we both laughed our asses off. I told him I thought I'd feel better too."

Bailey and I laughed a lot that day; I suppose it was that or cry. I felt completely overwhelmed—and now I had a gunshot wound to lie about and cover up. Later, it would cleverly be called my "knee injury." *Klutzy me.* A clunky knee brace and ace bandages, along with a set of crutches, would help further cover the gunshot wound and sell the lie.

As it so happened, that bullet that ripped through my skin, with burning, searing intensity leaving me in raw, throbbing torment, with a permanent scar was, after all a "flesh wound."

Bailey sat down on the edge of my bed.

"Where's Tad?" I asked. *Surely someone had contacted Tad.*

"He took off after you were home and settled. He said he loved you and you told him he was a dick and he should've let you keep the alligator," Bailey paused. "Was that some kind of code? An alligator?—I don't think so; a *cat* maybe." Bailey laughed.

"It's a long story." Bailey and I had become as close as sisters and shared so much, I wondered why I'd never told her about Big Dickie Bradford. I suppose it was just easier to say things like "Tad is working out of town—doing his stupid shit," rather than telling the whole long story and how when Tad was working out of town, there always seemed to be some "side work" of some description completely unrelated to construction going on *and* because of his history—that side work could be damned near anything. *Open the door to Tad's history.* It was just too much. Real life, right now was more than enough for me to handle.

"Is Joey still alive?" I asked.

"Afraid so. But when I ran into him outside of the," Bailey thought for a moment, "*temporary surgical unit*, he looked beaten up. Not way bad, but he had a black eye, busted lip and a bruised and swollen ring imprint on his cheek. Antonio's knuckles looked a little banged up—Joey's face may have had a run in with them."

"Tad stayed with you in surgery the whole time," Bailey continued. "He looked like hell when he walked out of there and then freaking snapped when he saw Joey—it took both Sal and Antonio to pull him off, although Antonio seemed super reluctant to interrupt Joey's second beating that day."

"Bummer Joey's not dead—not sure what I really expected though. How'd I get here?"

"Sal's Secret Ambulance Service." Bailey smiled.

"White panel van backed into the garage?"

"Yep."

"Pretty classy. Guessing Sal was in standard Armani attire?"

"No. He was wearing jeans."

"What? Did you just say my *father* was wearing *jeans*—as in blue, denim jeans?" I was pretty sure I misheard Bailey. Sal Russo *never* wore denim; I seemed to remember him having a genuine hate of the material.

"Yep—blue jeans, blue-striped, button-up shirt, and white sneakers."

"Sal Russo had sneakers on?!" I was sitting straight up now and had all but forgotten about my injury.

I had a million questions, but before I could even begin my interrogation, there was a sharp knock at the door. Bailey jumped up and I reached between my mattress and box springs for my .38 without thinking. A little shocked to find it so easily, I wrapped my hand around the grip and pulled it out slowly—listening for any indication from Bailey who might be there. *Did Tad slip my gun back into its normal resting spot? Damn, I wish I could remember more.*

"Brooke—Dr. Draco is here." I quietly tucked my gun under my cotton quilt—keeping it handy. The old man walked in ahead of Bailey smiling momentarily and mumbling something as he dropped his bag on my bed and started sifting through it. Sal sent a doctor who looked like the Monopoly man and walked like Tim Conway from the Carol Burnett Show. I wasn't sure if he could even speak English.

Dr. Draco pushed the quilt back, exposing my bandaged thigh. Picking up a pair of stainless steel scissors, he held the layers of gauze in place with his left hand, as his right slowly cut through the wide bands of white, surgical tape. With every snip, Dr. Draco slid his left hand further up the inside of my thigh.

I couldn't handle yet another creepy man and had my gun pressing against his forehead before I knew it. "One more inappropriate inch and I'll be cleaning your brains off the wall. Stick to the injury doc." I blame the narcotics. That, and knowing Bailey wasn't far away, I felt like Superwoman.

My gesture encouraged the doctor to focus on the injury. He finished changing my bandages as fast as any eighty-year-old man could with a gun held to his head and left mumbling—the same way he came in.

I knew I'd hear about my rude and disrespectful behavior and wasn't surprised when I answered the phone later that evening.

"Brooke—you must be feeling better." Daddy Sal's voice sounded as stern and as threatening as ever.

"I sure am, Sal, and no real thanks to Dr. Feel-Me-Up either. Why, pray tell, can I never, ever, ever have a real freaking doctor who's not a crusty old, creepy man? Why not my rock-n-roll doctor here in Plant City with the country singer's name? He's kind and competent and prescribes *real* medicines from *real* pharmacies for patients whose names he knows because he has a real-life medical chart in front of him with real-life history and allergies and other freaking pertinent information! After getting shot by Joey the dirt bag Marconi, is it just too much to ask for?" I was surprised all those words came out of my mouth so quickly and without thought.

There was a long hesitation and a deep, audible breath. "I see you've found your pain medications."

Sure, blame it on the drugs if it spares me the responsibility. Regardless, I was able to continue to find my pain medication fairly easily for the next several weeks. One day faded into another and then into the next. I was grateful for Bailey's frequent flights into town and Tad actually using his sick and vacation leave to come home often. Tad was sharper and more attentive without alcohol. He was also kinder and more prone to random acts of kindness—like setting up a lounge chair and table by the pool for me, so I could watch him do some screen repair comfortably while listening to my favorite mp3s through outdoor speakers he set up for me. Then he'd take a break and run inside to cut up some fresh fruit to bring to me. He didn't peel any grapes, but he was still super-sweet nonetheless. We started laughing more, playing more, liking each other more. He became so nice and "nice" really worked for me.

I was grateful for all the company. We'd become close friends with Don and Mary Giquinto and they stopped by often—despite the long drive from Lakeland, we'd see them every couple of weeks.

Don was from a huge Italian, Catholic family and it seemed like some cousin's neighbor's aunt's nephew was flying in from New York or New Jersey on a regular basis. Sometimes Don and Mary would stop by on their way to Tampa International for a quick shmoke and bathroom break.

Don stopped by on one such occasion on his way to the airport to pick up his mother's sister's cousin's brother. He grabbed a cup of coffee and checked the flight arrival status; since leaving his house an hour earlier, it changed—delayed two and a half hours. He had enough time to drive all the way back home, turn around and head back and get to the airport in time. Don took me up on my offer to hang out instead.

I was busy writing up a big, black, dark, sinking black hole of pure nothingness, some lamely call "writer's block," and welcomed the distraction as part of my ongoing dance with procrastination. I thought of the old saying, "Procrastination is like masturbation; you're only fucking yourself." And still, I was okay with that.

Don told me a lot about his family heritage that day—they were related to Charles Lindbergh and more recent research revealed a possible family link to Frances Scott Key. But, it was the more infamous family ties I found most interesting.

"Do you mind if I take notes?" Don knew I was a wannabe writer.

"No, go ahead."

I grabbed my notebook and scribbled madly as Don Giquinto spoke. My heart was racing—these were freaking great stories. Finally, something worth writing about! I felt elated and excited and motivated to get writing again. It was glorious—for about a minute.

"You know you can't write about all this, right?" Don's words stopped my note-taking and were met with a blank stare.

"Why not? I thought that's *why* I was taking notes?"

"Brooke—there are too many people out there to consider that could be hurt by this information." Don went on to explain the potential negative effects that could *possibly* result from me writing these stories even if I changed the names.

"Why did you think I wanted to write the dates and places and people's names down if I wasn't going to use them for something, Don?"

"I just thought you were trying to keep it all straight in your head."

I wanted to punch him in the face, but instead I went through my notebook and ripped out all the super-interesting/would've-been-fun-to-write-about stuff and torched the pages in my fireplace. Time has since passed and I don't remember any specific dates or places and the names were burnt from my memory the day I set fire to my notes.

"I better take off. If there's traffic, I don't want to be late." Don was saying as I left my daydream, rejoined the conversation, and he finished his black coffee.

Don and I said our goodbyes. Part of me wishes I'd saved those madly scribbled pages, but people like Don Giquinto don't want all of their stories told. I realized then I might have overstepped some boundaries in the compiling of stories for this text. Image that, right? I thought about every secret I had told and found the thought of going back over all of my material thus far and questioning every detail overwhelming. I wasn't even sure *who* I was writing for anymore. I didn't want to make any more decisions. I decided to let my trusty editor make those calls and just move forward.

I remember a paramedic training officer in West Virginia named Dewey once saying "In choosing not to decide, you've still made a decision." Dewey was young and knowledgeable and competent and super-hot—he was the perfect instructor. How we all love a man in uniform.

I sank back into my black hole of despair. I struggled with so much self-doubt writing my life story and confession. Down deep inside I knew I was a poser. And, holy cow—is this even the kind of stuff anyone should actually write down? I wondered how much of my past I really wanted to share. Would it just end up pissing people off? Was there any way Tad and I could maintain the lie a little bit longer—say long enough to get the heck out of Dodge and start all over once again? We really could've used a few weeks in the mountains—just to unwind, relax, and think things through.

But we had social obligations—hands to shake and smiles to fake. One such event was Tad's company party in St. Petersburg, Florida—a weekend event at a lovely tropical resort and golf club located on a Tampa Bay waterfront property, complete with its own private marina and less than an hour from our home. For those that traveled, I'm sure the novelty of bright blue skies and balmy temps in January contributed greatly to their experience. As for me, I was pretty entertained by the idea of wearing formalwear in Tampa Bay, one of the single-most casual places ever. Still, the resort was amazing.

Built in the 1920s, the Mediterranean Revival style architecture made it look like a castle or maybe an opulent waterfront villa. Every detail was truly stunning and beautifully executed. There were individual check-in stations with slightly-over-the-top service personnel and a huge lobby that was decorated to create many sitting areas on either side of the main passageway—each lavishly decorated with extravagant art and ostentatious furnishings. I suppose it was designed in an effort to transport their visitors back to another time and place while providing room to socialize or sit alone. I thought it was magical; Tad thought it was pretentious and found the entire event to be "much ado about nothing."

It was *Tad's* company party; he'd have to suck it up. After an hour or so of fashion debate with the white t-shirt and denim cowboy (still my favorite most-of-the-time look for any man), Tad finally agreed to wear a tux. I planned on wearing a beautiful, deep green sequined dress, cut just above the knee with fitted sleeves and open shoulders and lovely black pearled details on the back. I bought the dress to go with a square-toed pair of black suede *Oh!* heels I'd been aching to wear, along with a silver and gold metallic clutch and big, dangling silver fishbone earrings. That was the plan.

We ran around St. Pete that day in shorts and sandals. Tad took me for a pedicure and a historical tour of the area and, later, we found the GPS location of where his mom grew up. We laughed and played and had fun and almost forgot who we were. The sun was just beginning to set as we headed back to the resort and it felt like it was going to be a chilly evening—low 50s maybe. I remember wishing I'd worn warmer shoes instead of the strappy sandals I'd opted for. It would've been nice to have had the rest of the day and that evening to take a hot bath and lounge around the resort without obligation, but we had a dinner party to attend and strolled through the lobby holding hands and headed back to our room to shower and change.

A man stood at one of the check-in counters with his back to us wearing a dark charcoal-colored suit; he was tall and broad-shouldered, "Yes, thank you," he was saying to the bellhop, as the employee loaded the expensive-looking luggage onto the cart, "I'm looking forward to a much needed vacation."

I froze for a moment and then quickly pulled Tad into one of the little, lavishly-decorated sitting areas, picking up a trifold some other guest left behind featuring local attractions, then sinking back in one of the wing-backed chairs, hanging my head enough so my hair fell in front of my face, completely horrified while I pretended to read.

Tad bent over, quickly untied and slowly began to re-tie his first shoe and then his second. "What are we ... "

"Shhhh," I stopped him. I was still shaking—it was the man's voice. His very presence still rattled me. Tad and I sat quietly until I regained composure, felt certain the lobby was clear and nodded to Tad.

We held hands and walked directly to the elevator. After the doors closed, I held up my hand up and shook my head to stop him before he even started asking questions.

After we got in our room and the door was closed and locked and I turned the TV on, and closed the drapes, I spoke, "That man in the lobby was Vladimir. *Vladimir Petrov*." My voice quivered as I spoke the name.

"Are you sure?"

"Are you fucking kidding me?"

"Damn," Tad said thoughtfully, "we need a game plan."

He started throwing stuff in his suitcase. "We need to make a quick appearance for dinner or it'll look suspicious. Start getting dressed and pack what you don't need for tonight."

I grabbed the beautiful, sequined dress from my garment bag.

"Not that. Too flashy; we need to blend in more." Tad turned away, and then quickly turned back. "Wear shoes you can run in."

I pulled my black, suede *Oh!* heels out of the bag; Tad raised an eyebrow and frowned at me with a sigh.

"What? I can run in these. They're super-comfortable."

"Whatever."

Tad wore a gray sports jacket and slacks with a white shirt and a navy and silver striped tie, along with a pair of black, leather oxfords—the outfit he planned on wearing to Sunday brunch, which we now wouldn't be attending. I wore a lightweight charcoal jacket with black pants, black *Oh!* shoes, an ivory embossed blouse, my big fishbone earrings and a deep green paisley scarf. We were a vest, a hue, and maybe an accessory away from looking like the wait staff. Not only was I looking forward to getting dressed up and doing something pretentious, I hadn't seen Tad in a tux since Michael was married and was excited about that as well. My life could be in danger and I was bumming about having to dress down; I shook my head.

Tad took our luggage out to his truck while I smoked a joint in the bathroom with the fan on, brushed my teeth, put lip gloss on and thought about my predicament. The second the word "coincidence" crossed my mind, Sal's voice was right behind it, *There is no such thing as coincidence!*

I felt like it was a big leap for anyone to recognize me from back in the day, much less be able to connect the new me to someone the old me had once had a weekend fling with. *There is no such thing as coincidence!*

"Fine!" I yelled back to my subconscious that spoke in Sal's voice. "Vladimir's here to take revenge for the death of his son thirty years ago." When I said it like that, it did sound more ridiculous than a coincidence, yes? But I was willing to roll with it. I thought and thought—our children, families, jobs, friends, house, and swimming pool. I couldn't get past. "It's time to cut and run. Again."

Dinner was good; the company was nice. Tad told a couple of his pals he just wanted to get home and sleep in his own bed and would be taking off after dinner. He didn't mention our bags were packed and loaded and all that was left was dropping off the room key.

Somewhere between dinner and dessert, I started to feel nervous, then paranoid. I watched the party guests and the wait staff and never saw anything out of the ordinary, but the feeling chilled me. I could *feel* Vladimir Petrov watching me—like his own personal prey.

Tad made his necessary goodbyes (that took entirely too long from my perspective) and we strolled hand-in-hand out the front doors—laughing and playing and stumbling until we were out of sight and then we ran like hell through the parking garage, jumped into the truck and took off for home.

Highways, byways, back roads and circling back, watching the rearview—no one was following us. We left Marie with her girlfriend Marlo to hold down the fort for the weekend and knew we might be interrupting a party, but got home to an empty house with a set alarm. I called Marie frantically to check up on them; she and Marlo had gone over to another friend's house and *probably* wouldn't be out late.

Tad threw our bags in our room. We knew we had to make some serious plans, but we also knew we had a couple hours to ourselves. We put a pot of coffee on and sat out back by the pool talking and laughing about stupid mistakes made and favorite childhood memories and early days when we first met and everything except Vladimir Petrov until we were too tired to talk anymore. I dozed off in a lounge chair and vaguely remember Tad taking my hand. "Hey, we should probably go to bed." It was easy to relax with Tad; it was easy to feel safe—even under the most stressful situations.

As the days passed, my family was no doubt calling in their back-ups and it didn't hurt for us to do the same. Our friendship will Don and Mary Giquinto continued; we loved and trusted them. We drank coffee and shot weapons, smoked weed, and occasionally blew stuff up; they were natural allies. We told them everything they didn't already know, which wasn't much, and it felt good to have highly-skilled individuals on my team. But, over time, Don seemed to become more paranoid and perhaps rightfully so. It was hard not to notice parked vehicles along a highway in the middle of nowhere or the buzzing of flying vermin louder, larger, and faster than the average mosquito. Don said they were drones; I hoped for any other possible explanation.

Don's behavior became more erratic and less predictable; he was nervous, but he had a plan. I didn't like Don's plan, especially since it involved me keeping a secret. As a matter of fact—I hated Don's plan. He needed a spot to lay low and appear to be less of a threat. Hospitals were relatively secure and patients are rarely viewed as threatening, but a mental facility's security and surveillance couldn't be beat and nobody really listens to the crazy guy after a while. He simply needed to convince everyone around him that he was losing his ever-loving mind. Mary couldn't know; it was the gift of plausible deniability. He needed a friend to know what was going on in case he went too far.

"Too far? What the hell, Don?"

"It'll be fine. Just go along with it."

Don's craziness started off slow with random laughter and occasional comments about fishing with Jimmy Buffett earlier that week. No one was really taking him seriously and thought he was just stoned and being a goofball. He felt the need to take his game up a notch.

Mary and Don had come over to our place for a poolside cookout. Tad was in great spirits and we were all busy buzzing around talking and preparing food and drink and smoke and such. Don caught me outside alone for a moment and showed me a small, purple, barrel-shaped pill in his hand.

"What is that?"

"It's acid, LSD. Nothing makes you look and feel crazier than when you're tripping." He tossed the pill into his mouth.

"Wait! Don, this isn't a good idea."

He laughed at me and walked away. "Just have fun; roll with it Brooke."

Don was a certifiable, yet entertaining and completely loveable, idiot that night. Mary had him institutionalized within a week. I think we all were on edge and a little jumpy for lots of reasons and both Mary and I were excited and happy to accept Krystal Von Kline's invitation for a candle party—a girls' night out drinking, snacking, partying and shopping the new PartyLite catalog at Krystal's house. Good times.

The presentation was over and I stepped outside to smoke a cigarette and wandered over to the mowed edge of the lawn—when rainy season came, the area I stood on would be swamp. The property further back was dark and damp and somehow seemed haunted by the Spanish moss-covered trees and creepy shadows. I instinctively reached for my stiletto—a family knife choice more than my own. Had I not been raised how I had been, it could've just as easily been a switchblade. I took a couple more steps in, trying to see through the very dankness as my eyes adjusted to the dark; I could almost hear the impending doom music playing in my head, warning me. But, like the stupid girl in the movies, I continued forward.

Suddenly, I felt a hand on my shoulder and spun around—slashing out with my stiletto without thinking. Mary's reflexes were pretty good—making the difference between a minor wound and a slashed throat. We were able to control the bleeding and get her to the ER for a few stitches without further incident; it could've been worse. Mary's still a little butt-hurt over the whole accident, but the scar is barely visible and the story is kind of funny. You know—now that everyone lived to tell about it and all. *I really am sorry Mary.*

When I got Sal's call the following week, I assumed he'd heard about the stiletto incident—he misses nothing—and was calling to give me grief. Mary was a friend and I injured her while overreacting. It was a fail. Had Mary been an enemy and I merely injured her with a flesh wound, fail as well. It was a no win situation, but I answered the call anyway—better over the phone than at my doorstep.

"Hi, Daddy."

"Get ready for dinner—nothing fancy, a casual steak and seafood place we discovered. Your mother wants to see you. The car will be there in an hour." *Your mother wants to see you.*

He hung up without giving me a chance to reply—classic Sal. Tad had just flown out the previous morning and Marie was already at work, so I was on my own and had no lame excuses to make to my daughter. I flat-ironed my hair and applied some make-up. I went through my closet and wished I'd been selected to go shopping with Stacy and Clinton from TLC's *What Not to Wear* any time prior to that moment. I was going to see Luciana for the first time in a lifetime; I was beyond nervous. *Damn, why didn't I get my hair cut?*

I hair-sprayed my hair and went with dark denim jeans, a pair of open-heel, open-toe black suede bootie wedges, and a dark brown, tan and gray print silk blouse with long sleeves and cut-out shoulders. I tossed my Anuschka hobo bag over my shoulder. More than enough room for all my essentials—including my trusty .38 revolver.

The big, fat, hugely embarrassing, shiny black limo pulled up in front of my house right on time. I set the alarm and hurried out, jumping in the door Joey Marconi held open—hoping none of the neighbors were out watering their lawn and saw the spectacle of an automobile. Joey slammed the door shut and I breathed out—looking up into the faces of Sal, Luciana, Antonio and Giovanni Russo.

"Hello Ci, I mean Brooke." Mama Luciana was the first to speak. I could feel decades of emotion welling up inside of me. She smiled broadly and leaned forward to hug me.

"Hello Luciana. You look amazing." She wore white jeans and a teal and blue and white flowered, short-sleeved blouse, and silver and gold strappy sandals. Her dark hair was pulled back, showing off her obviously expensive gold earrings and locket. She looked stunning.

I turned my attention to Giovanni Russo. He looked as gorgeous as ever in blue jeans and a white cotton button-up with sleeves rolled to the elbow and brown leather shoes. I swear he could make a paper bag look good. "Holy shit, how long has it been Gio?"

"Since you've seen me or since I've seen you?" Gio laughed and we hugged.

"Hey Antonio," I nodded and then turned my attention to Sal. "Daddy, this came as such a surprise. What's the occasion?"

"Just dinner. Your mother wants to see you."

That was twice he referred to Luciana as "your mother." Maybe she just needed some closure.

I leaned over to Luciana and held her hands and smiled, "It's really great to see you *all* again. Where's Emilio?"

"That's a story for another time. He is still alive and in good health," Sal stated matter-of-factly. "I think you will enjoy this restaurant," he changed the subject.

"Of course Daddy—I'm looking forward to it."

We arrived at Blackstone's Reef and Grill in Zephyrhills in perfect silence. The Russo rules are the same as the rules of negotiation —whoever talks first loses, unless it's Sal. The restaurant was lovely and busy for a weeknight. Joey stayed with the car. "We'll bring you back a doggy bag, buddy!" Antonio yelled as we headed inside. He wasn't an entirely bad big brother.

The hostess was going to seat the five of us at a six-top, but Sal whispered in her ear and a four-top was added—giving us ten seats in all. I wondered if we were expecting other people, but apparently the extra space was for food.

Sal ordered for everyone: starting with drunken clams, remoulade shrimp, escargot en coquilles au beurre d'ail and four bottles of white wine, followed by grilled salmon spinach salad, shrimp and scallop linguine, more wine, stuffed grouper, Alaskan snow crab legs, Florida lobster tails, I think we switched to red wine here, filet mignon, and chocolate overload cake (more than appropriately named) with coffee for dessert. Nobody in the entire world can eat like the Russo men, except maybe Michael and Syler—who both seem to come by it honestly. Nonetheless, if their plans were to wax me afterwards and this was going to be my last meal, I was okay with that; I couldn't have come up with anything better had I tried, which I was entirely too full to do. I could barely take one bite of everything and everything was so freaking delicious; it was almost painful.

People came and went and we sat and ate and drank for hours—reminiscing and laughing and appearing to the outside world like a normal family. I hoped Sal would be a generous tipper; being cheap is so unattractive.

Luciana seemed to be paying particular attention to the door and when an older couple entered in casual walking shorts, sneakers and cotton tops, I saw a look of contempt cross her face. They walked by our table and I smiled at them—feeling both confused and apologetic for Luciana's harsh judgmental glare. The couple smiled back briefly as they passed; there was something oddly familiar about them. Perhaps it was his stature and the angle of his jaw or maybe her sloped and slightly upturned nose as well as her somewhat pouty lips. My mind was occupied and my belly was full and I suppose it was all a good deal to digest. Later, I'd remember Sal's words, "Your mother wants to see you." The McPherson's had walked past me and were gone before I realized who they were.

We finished our coffee and had the leftovers wrapped up for the dog driving our limo—which probably would've fed my whole family for a week, but which gave me a certain amount of gratification knowing Joey "The Torch" Marconi would be eating our cold picked-over leftovers for dinner that night.

We pulled into Walden Lake just after dark. Turning the corner into our little neighborhood, Sal calmly stated, "I think it's time we meet your children."

"*Whaaaaat?* My children, *your grandchildren* don't even know you exist. Golly, Sal, it seems a little late in the game for a round of blatant, hardcore honesty."

"Make it happen, Brooke. We are getting older and want the children to know their real family."

"What should I tell them?" I thought about the McPhersons for the first time in a long time, my early childhood abduction by my biological father from by biological mother, my three half-brothers and their mother who raised me as her own through puberty, New Jersey, New York, Washington, D.C., Italy, Vladimir, Northern Virginia, West Virginia, Florida, the people, the lies, the plastic surgery, Big Dickie Bradford, the Hutchenson family, Brooke, Cici, Camilla, the medic, the artist, the writer, the spoiled brat, the sociopathic mob family; I was shaking, "I don't even know where I'd start."

"There's no place like the beginning," Gio smiled hopefully.

I imagined how the conversation with Michael and Marie might play out; I started crying and then quickly dried my eyes before losing it completely. I looked at Sal and Luciana and Antonio and Giovanni. I ignored Joey the rat-bastard Marconi. I wondered about Emilio and made a mental note to search for him on the Internet. In some ways, the idea of letting go of the charade and coming clean was a liberating one. In others ways, it was perfectly overwhelming.

"On the upside, it would give our kids some insight they may never have had," I thought out loud. I looked back to Sal; I thought about Michael and Marie. I thought about the whole bloody mess. Sal was waiting for an answer and I needed to buy some time, shake the wine from my brain and talk it all through with Tad before committing to a date and time. "Maybe it would be better if I just wrote it all down first."

PART THREE

Who I Want to Be

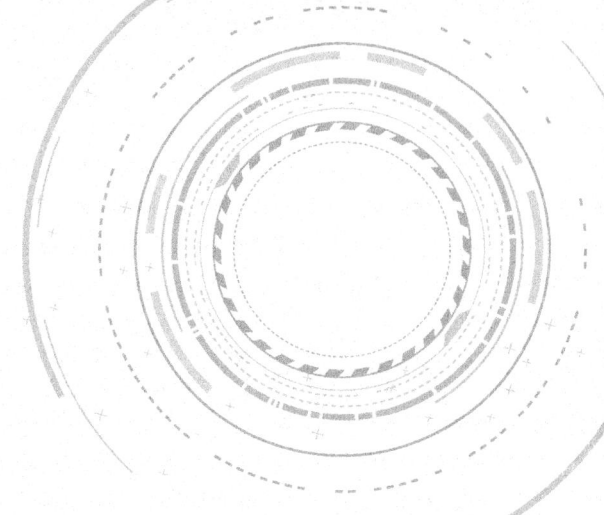

CHAPTER TWENTY-FOUR
Cut & Run

I'm not sure I'm ready to jump back on the Russo rollercoaster just yet. I agreed to let Sal look over my text and make edits; I didn't agree to use any of them. Yesterday, I sent him chapter ten with apologies for taking so long.

As my editor reads my final copy, Sal will be receiving what I like to call "The Vladimir Chapters." And when this book is published and available for sale under a different title than the "agreed upon" *A Mother's Apology,* Sal will just be receiving the beginning of Part Two. I've bought whatever time necessary with excuses of "writer's block" or being "super-busy."

By the time you read this, Daddy, Tad and I will have long since been gone and relocated to a more remote location. Right now, you're watching Marie's friend Marlo live in our Plant City house and move my old, red Jeep around to keep up performances *as me* as best someone less than half my age can, but you haven't looked that close.

Know that the children are well-informed, heavily-armed, and highly skilled. They've known our story for over a year now. Did you honestly believe I needed to write a novel in order to explain this mess to my own adult children? It gave me all the time I needed and more. And our time has been well-spent.

While you were busy having Joey and Antonio harass me and watching the neighbors like hawks, everyone else was at the firing range and on the farm learning tactical maneuvers. Don leaving the farm was brilliant; no one thought to even look there once he was institutionalized.

It seems as if certain skill sets were completely overlooked. Did you for a moment consider Michael's passion for martial arts and years of training or his expert level IT career? Or, did you wonder about Syler's similar ninja skills, and expertise in weapons and security? You watched Tad and Don and never thought about the kids. You know they're all in their twenties and some pushing thirty now, yes?

Many thanks to all the girls; I knew my family would ignore you as a possible threat altogether—little, blue-eyed, blonde Marie and her sassy brunette sidekick Marlo, lovely Simone, stunning Brigid, savvy Terry Lynn, fierce Annie Lane, talented Lorelei, resourceful Mary, gracious Krystal, bad-ass Laurie and my army of exercise buddies who helped with our move—they ignored you all. We relocated our entire family and all of our possessions to more than one location under your noses. Somedays, it's good to be underestimated. Bailey, of course, they've always loved and respected and watched altogether too closely. But y'all must've been watching her ass and not her actions, because she fooled you too.

I don't know what the future holds, but as for today—I'd like the sun to shine, to live my quiet life, enjoy those I love, and celebrate my privacy. And, maybe in the course of doing all these things, I will find the time and energy to write or paint or garden or some shit.

For those who seek us and refuse to respect our privacy—I feel certain our paths will cross again. Know that if you scare me, I will shoot you. But for now: *Adiós mother-fuckers.*

...